FAITHFUL

FAITHFUL

a novel by Janet Fox

speak

An Imprint of Penguin Group (USA) Inc.

SPEAK

Published by the Penguin Group

Penguin Group (USA) Inc., 345 Hudson Street, New York, New York 10014, U.S.A.

Penguin Group (Canada), 90 Eglinton Avenue East, Suite 700, Toronto, Ontario, Canada M4P 2Y3
(a division of Pearson Penguin Canada Inc.)

Penguin Books Ltd, 80 Strand, London WC2R 0RL, England

Penguin Ireland, 25 St Stephen's Green, Dublin 2, Ireland (a division of Penguin Books Ltd)

Penguin Group (Australia), 250 Camberwell Road, Camberwell, Victoria 3124, Australia
(a division of Pearson Australia Group Pty Ltd)

Penguin Books India Pvt Ltd, 11 Community Centre,
Panchsheel Park, New Delhi - 110 017, India

Penguin Group (NZ), 67 Apollo Drive, Rosedale, North Shore 0632, New Zealand
(a division of Pearson New Zealand Ltd)

Penguin Books (South Africa) (Pty) Ltd, 24 Sturdee Avenue,
Rosebank, Johannesburg 2196, South Africa

Registered Offices: Penguin Books Ltd, 80 Strand, London WC2R 0RL, England

Published by Speak, an imprint of Penguin Group (USA) Inc., 2010

1 3 5 7 9 10 8 6 4 2

LIBRARY OF CONGRESS CATALOGING-IN-PUBLICATION DATA IS AVAILABLE

Speak ISBN 978-0-14-241413-2

Printed in the United States of America

Designed by Jeanine Henderson
Set in Venetian 301 BT

To Jeff and Kevin,
for their unwavering faith in me.

FAITHFUL

PROLOGUE

I KNOW A PLACE ON THIS EARTH THAT CONTAINS wonders enough to stop the breath. A place where the very rocks whisper and whine, where the rivers boil and the snow-studded peaks thrust into a bowl of blue; where great shaggy beasts press the earth with cloven hooves or threaten with claw and fang; where new life and lurking death coexist in the shallows of varicolored pools.

I went to this place to search for what I had lost, but instead found a life unexpected.

Chapter ONE

To lose one's faith surpasses
The loss of an estate,
Because estates can be
Replenished,—faith cannot.

—"Lost Faith"; *Poems*, Emily Dickinson, 1890

THE TRAIL WAS TOO CROWDED FOR A HARD RIDE. Too groomed, too manicured. I wished I could fly, could gallop away from my raging confusion, but I couldn't give Ghost my crop and set him off at a canter. I urged him into a fast trot instead and even then I saw it in the faces we passed: the raised eyebrows, the surprise, the disapproval. Disapproval draped over me like a funeral crepe.

I pressed my lips together. I imagined the glares I'd receive if I rode astride instead of sidesaddle. Mama had worn a split skirt when we rode. When I was little I'd thought it fun—they all watched her, my mama! But when I reached my teens I saw the attention for what it was. The eyes had skimmed from Mama to me. I was guilty by association.

I sighed as I slowed Ghost to a walk, then bent forward and caressed his silky neck with my gloved fingers and stuffed my warring thoughts all the way down.

Ghost twisted his ear toward me. "You're always ready to listen, aren't you? I wish you could come with me. That would be such a comfort. But I have to go, and you have to stay. It's not forever, old friend. Only a little trip. I promise I'll be back." Promise. Like Mama had promised me. I squelched that thought, the misery of broken promises. My lips drew tight. "I promise."

Ghost tossed his head; he understood. I sat up in the saddle and thought it all through again.

Papa's plans, having come from out of the blue two days ago, had thrown me into conflict. First, I'd felt excitement.

"There is some suggestion—only a possibility, mind you," Papa had said. I tensed, waiting. "Your mother was there before. We took a trip out west, right after you were born. You stayed in Newport with your grandparents, but we went west. Did I ever mention it? No? Well. Your mother and I were there, years ago."

Papa's eyes had grown bright; he leaned toward me with a smile. "Your uncle John's been investigating. He's made some discoveries. There may be a chance, only a chance . . ."

"What?" A chance she was alive? My breath quickened. I reached out my hand, tugged his shirtsleeve. This was the thing I'd prayed for these many months. "Papa, are you saying she's alive and we can find her?"

But Papa looked away; he didn't answer. He bent and picked up the train schedule, flipped it open, and pointed. "If we leave within the week, we'd be there by the middle of June."

"Wait. So soon?" My mind twisted in another direction, my feelings in conflict. Elation turned to shock.

Leave within the week. This week. Be somewhere out west in the middle of June. And back—when? To find Mama was my greatest hope. But to leave Newport at this very moment, even to find her, was . . . I pressed the heel of my palm against my forehead to quell the ache. We'd be gone well into the start of Newport's season.

"Papa, wait. How long will we be away? You know I have so much to do! Kitty and I have so many plans!" It was my season, and it should have been Mama planning with me. The conflict in me began to boil and my voice rose with it. "There are the clothes, and the orchestra, and the flowers, and the invitations . . . all the little details to manage."

It was my sixteenth spring, the eve of my debut. This was the summer I'd dreamed about for as long as I could remember, the summer in which my future would finally be sealed. A debut required hundreds of preparations. The ball alone would take weeks to plan. Most girls planned theirs with their mothers, but my mama was gone. I was on my own, with only Kitty to help me. Yet now, here suddenly was the possibility of Mama . . .

Mama. I wanted to know what my uncle John had learned, out there in the wilds of Wyoming. For the past year I'd stubbornly insisted that Mama was alive; now Papa had given me fresh hope.

I felt dizzy. My hand clutched at Papa's shirt, twisting the cotton. My stomach twisted, too.

It was unfair that this was happening now. That Uncle John and Papa would make this unnamed discovery now—it was unfair! I didn't expect Papa to understand how much my debut meant to me. If Mama had been here she would have understood. I like to think she would have understood.

Ghost whinnied and brought me back to the moment. I caught the eye of Mrs. Wolcott as we passed on the trail. I smiled; her return was faint, not quite a sneer yet not a smile. I stiffened. A glittering debut with all the right trappings was one of the few things that might make the Mrs. Wolcotts look at me new. Since Mama had left, I'd tossed and turned at night, alone with my wretched thoughts. And now, when I'd finally begun to make some peace with my life, to let go of my desperate insistence that she'd be back, now everything was about to change.

I'd asked Papa two days ago (two days! A lifetime!), "Can we be back in time? If we're back by July, that would be all right. Maybe Kitty can manage till then. But Papa, we have to be back by then." I remembered tightening my hold on his sleeve.

"Yes, yes," Papa said, waving his hand, the train schedule flapping, brushing off my questions. He paused and looked at the floor, tugging his mustache with two fingers. "There's something else, Mags. Listen. You must promise not to tell anyone that this is anything but a pleasure trip. You must promise especially not to tell your grandparents." He looked up at me with a piercing gaze.

I was taken aback. "Not tell? But . . ."

"It's important, Margaret." Papa took my free hand. "You must promise. I don't want to give them false hope." He searched my face, his eyes unusually bright. "Lord knows your grandfather is angry enough with me."

His grip tightened around my hand, so I put my other hand on his and lied. "I understand." Why wouldn't he want my grandparents to know that he may have found their daughter?

"Good girl. Now, I have some things to do, eh?"

"But, Papa. I want to hear what Uncle John . . ."

"Margaret, please." And he ushered me out of his studio and shut the door. I stood in the dark hall, alone, my lips pursed in frustration.

Ghost snorted and I stroked his neck again. He knew me better than anyone, my Ghost. "I have to go." I sighed. "I'll miss you, my friend." I would miss the pleasure I took in our daily rides. I'd miss our unspoken connection.

There were many things I'd miss. Like Kitty. And the first round of parties that Mama should have been here to help me prepare for. Sad, gray, boring winter had yielded at last to spring—my spring. In only a few weeks the wealthy from all over the East Coast would descend on Newport to hunt, sail, mingle, and play the complicated social game.

Which seemed simple in comparison with the tangle of feelings weaving through me now.

I adjusted my seat, restless, and fidgeted, the wool riding habit chafing my thigh even through the silk of my petticoats. Most people said Mama was dead. Now I'd be proved right. When we found her, out in that terrible Wyoming wilderness, we'd bring her home. We'd make her well. Then the matrons of Newport would forget her eccentricities. I'd have everything—Mama, my season, my future, everything.

But there was the other possibility. We might go west and not find Mama. Mama might return to Newport and find us gone. I picked unhappily at a loose thread on my velvet cuff. I wanted to find Mama and have her back home with me. But even if we did find her and bring her back, there was still the chance that she could drag me down with her unsocial behavior . . . or with her madness . . .

That unspeakable thing. I reached my hand to Ghost's neck and smoothed the stiff braids lacing his mane. I ticked the riding crop against my knee, *tick-tick, tick-tick,* tapped the pace of Ghost's footfalls. The breeze, carrying the faint scent of salt water, lifted the veil on my hat. Ghost's ears twitched.

I wanted a normal life. But I also wanted Mama.

Normal had not defined Mama; *bohemian* had. Other mothers served tea, my mother painted landscapes. Other mothers wore hats, while mine wore ostrich feathers. My mother laughed, openmouthed with joy; thin-lipped sedate smiles were all the others could muster. Even as a child, I'd watched Papa gaze at her, awestruck; I'd seen how other men stared at her, too. She was compelling, magnetic. Her silky black hair always ended up falling loose, the buttons open at her throat, her cameo pinned low.

Bohemian was a likable word once—a flamboyant word, like ripe grapes on the tongue, conjuring something naughty but fun—but now it fell harsh on my ears. I now understood the flinty looks of Newport matrons and felt the slights from their daughters for myself. Her cameo hadn't only been pinned low; it had been eye-gathering low.

And the whispers—I'd heard them, too, about her lonely walks on the Cliff Walk. Whispers that she was mad.

But I pretended not to hear for as long as I could.

Last June, they grew so loud I couldn't ignore them any longer. And on a morning when I stood in the doorway to her room and witnessed a dreadful thing, I feared they were right.

"Mama?"

It was a glorious summer day and I wanted a new shirtwaist, something cool for the coming heat. I went to Mama's room to persuade her to take me to town, where we could shop and have tea and sweet cakes. My mood was so gay, I was unprepared for what I saw.

Perched on Mama's splay-foot easel was not her usual dreamy landscape, but something ugly. A nightmare vision of hideous vapors and smokes. It was unfinished, a painting of frightening landforms—spires and terraces in the reds, ochres, and oranges of hell. Other new paintings like it leaned against the walls, against her dressing table. Fire . . . bubbling, steaming pits . . . it was grotesque, the product of a sick mind. While I knew Mama had been distracted of late, here I saw that she had drifted into something dark and horrific. And I hadn't noticed until that moment.

She'd left her oils to pace before the brilliant window, her form a dark silhouette framed against unearthly light. Her watered-silk dressing gown gaped open. I froze, staring from the hall at her and at those hellish landscapes, misery flooding my body. She did not see me. I suspected that she could not see me.

"Mama?" I repeated, louder.

She stopped pacing, her face tilted away, her hair cascading in unkempt waves loose to her waist. "I don't know where she is. I can't find her." She resumed pacing, never looking my way.

She was talking nonsense. I bit my lip. I balled my hands into fists in frustration. I whispered, "I wish, I wish . . ." I wished Mama would turn and look at me.

"Mama?" Nothing. I turned away into the empty hall.

My chest formed tight knot. She wasn't normal. If she loved me, she wouldn't act this way. Whispers snarled in my brain: "she's mad," "she's shocking." I leaned against the wall and swallowed the hot tears that rose into my throat. I wanted a mother who played by Newport's rules, not a mama who was peculiar.

Not a mama who frightened me with her odd behavior. With the thought that I was too like her.

I pulled up on the reins. Lost in memories, I didn't realize that Ghost and I had reached the far end of the trail. I was surprised to feel the fresh sting in my throat, as if I'd stood in Mama's doorway only moments ago. Across the rolling granite outcrops I spied the gray ocean, the ocean that I hated, the thieving sea. Light danced on the water, scattering sparks that made me blink. A gull keened; how lonely a sound that was, and how deeply I felt it, sadness like a weight pulling me down. My hands tightened on the reins.

I turned back to my season and the preparations. Kitty would have to do it all.

Kitty. Dear Kit. We both lived in Newport year-round. We went to the same schools, moved in the same circles. But I knew what a closer look revealed. Kitty's parlor never wanted for callers. Her tray was filled with calling cards by the end of each Sunday afternoon. Our parlor had been empty for a long time, long before Mama's accident.

Or disappearance. Or departure. Or . . . I'd heard so many euphemisms for it this past year.

I squeezed my eyes shut and opened them again, as if that might bring Mama back. I missed her even though I was tarred by her behavior. Even though I feared we were alike.

I clicked my tongue at Ghost and we set off for home.

Uncle John had made some "discoveries." Papa's words: "only a chance, mind you." But it was a chance to find her. A chance was all we needed.

My shoulders grew stiff despite Ghost's easy gait. Newport society was unforgiving. By going west with Papa I could miss my chance to make Newport see me differently, to see me for me, and not as my mother's daughter. I'd miss friends who hadn't seen me since Mama disappeared and who thought I was tainted by her scandal.

Friends like Edward, who I hoped was more than a friend. He

wasn't due back from New York before mid-June. Edward's dark hair and soft eyes floated in my daydreams. Last summer, at one of the first cotillions of the season, he asked me to dance. After that short waltz, I was smitten. My cheeks burned now, and my heart beat faster as I remembered Edward choosing me over all the other girls.

He could be a perfect beau. But we made no lasting promises. No promises could have been made before now, anyway, before my season and my introduction into proper society. And now . . . Now everything was uncertain.

I inhaled deeply, pulling the faintly briny air into my lungs.

Maybe I'd driven Mama away. I was ashamed of Mama, and so angry at her. Those paintings frightened me. After that day, I'd hardened against her. Maybe it was my fault that she'd gone; here was my chance to make it all right.

Ghost, sensing my emotions again, picked up his pace to a trot. Finding Mama, bringing her home, and making her well could solve everything. I would be absolved. We could plan the season together, and I could have my debut. And Edward. Society would forgive her, and I could forgive myself. Going west with Papa and bringing Mama home could make everything right.

The sun was low in the west as Ghost and I approached the end of our ride. I turned him in at the gate that led back to the stable. As he trotted through the narrow file and I leaned to avoid an overhanging branch, a sudden kick of sea breeze flicked the branch at Ghost and he bolted.

I hung on, caught unprepared, my chest tight with fear.

Chapter TWO ❧❧❧❧❧❧❧❧❧❧❧❧

May 31, 1904

To-morrow will also be a gala day for weddings.
There will be three in town, each of which
will occupy the attention of fashionable society,
and two of which will be in the Newport set.

—"What Is Doing in Society,"
New York Times, April 20, 1900

GHOST FLEW. I FELL BACK AGAINST THE CANTLE. HE barreled across the grassy field and I leaned forward, desperate to regain control. Sweat beaded on my forehead; my hands gripped the pommel; I tried to keep my seat.

Fear begets fear. Mama had left me and my life was in turmoil because of it. My body shook with effort and with emotion. I let escape a terrified cry.

But the release of sound released my fear; terror turned to exhilaration. Ghost was at a full, reckless gallop, but finally I gathered his rhythm, felt the rush of throwing off restraint. This I'd longed for, this freedom. I let myself go, let Ghost have his head, even if I hit the ground all broken bones. Charging away from the tight trail, we were one. We approached the hedge, and I let out a different cry. Ghost slowed. I reined him in and we stopped, both of us heaving with joy and exertion.

I turned him and we galloped back across the field, and then back yet again. Ghost relished it as much as I did. I lost my hat, ribbons flying, and I didn't care.

By this time the stable hands were out and several other riders were watching, hovering near the stable. I drew Ghost up and knew that my cheeks were flushed and my hair was in disarray.

"Missie! Miss Margaret!" Joshua yelled as he ran. "You all right?"

"Fine. Never better!" And it was true. I felt exhilarated, and free, for once, of the weight of my memories. Joshua grabbed Ghost's bridle and helped me dismount. I stood on shaky legs, leaning in against Ghost as he snorted and I panted, and I gave his damp neck an affectionate hug. "Be sure to give him a good rub and extra oats."

Timmy ran up with my hat. Behind him I saw Mrs. Proctor, sidesaddle on her ancient, fat gelding. She regarded me with contempt, then turned to her companion.

"If you ask me," she said in a voice just loud enough for me to hear, "she's exactly like her mother. Utter disregard for propriety. Lack of self-control. That's what got her mother into trouble. I've heard it all, you know, the whole story. And right there is living proof that the apple doesn't fall far from the tree."

"Shame," agreed her companion. "What did you hear?" They both eyed me, then Mrs. Proctor leaned over, and as the two moved away I strained for their words but heard only murmurs.

I drew myself up. I thought of my grandparents, who would no doubt hear of my unseemly behavior from Mrs. Proctor. I turned my back to her as I fed Ghost a treat dug from the small pocket buttoned at my waist.

She's exactly like her mother. My cheeks flushed. I was angry at Mrs. Proctor, but I was also angry at myself. I didn't need to go about compounding my situation with wild rides for all to see. Mrs. Proctor echoed the troublesome voice in my head—exactly like Mama. I burned with shame now, recalling how I'd confronted Mama after I watched her for weeks as she retreated into silence and painted those dreadful landscapes.

Last July was sticky and damp, and all the doors and windows were open to the wash of the ocean and the hum of bees. Maybe it was the heat that had turned my mood. Again, I'd stood in the doorway of Mama's room, full of pent-up feeling.

"What are you doing to me?" I surprised myself with the sound of my own voice—like a crow's caw, harsh.

She was painting again, but unlike before, she was not so lost in herself that she could not see me. This time she turned at the sound of my voice, with a smile on her face. "Maggie?" But her smile evaporated as she read my expression. "Maggie."

I could not control myself. "Stop it! I want you to stop!" I moved fast, snatching the paintbrush from her hand. Paint splattered the canvas and dashed a black line across the white linen of my dress. "I hate what you're doing! I hate it!"

Mama sagged and crossed the room, collapsing on the narrow end of the chaise.

My lip trembled as I faced her. "Why are you punishing me?" I burned with bitterness. For many weeks she'd been like this. My cruelty, built over time through my frustration, knew no bounds.

"Oh, Maggie." She lifted her face, distorted with misery. "You've done nothing. It's my fault. You were so little. You have to understand. Back then I was torn in two. I didn't know what to do."

I didn't understand what she was saying. She made no sense. I shook my head to clear the confusion. "Mama. When you act like this, they snub me, too." I choked on the words. "They look at me like I'm smudged. Stained. I'm beneath them. They leave me out." My voice dropped, and my chin shook. "I wasn't invited to Isabel's party last week."

She said it so soft I could hardly hear. "That wasn't my intention."

"But that's what happened. That's what you did." I spit the words out as great tears rolled down my cheeks. "You've made my life miserable."

Mama looked up then, her own eyes red and full. "I'm so sorry."

"Really?" My voice caught. "Good! If you are, good!" I wanted her to hurt. "So do something. Make me believe you're sorry. Act normal. Like everyone else. Be a mother." Fury rose in me again, thinking of what I'd missed, what she'd missed. I lashed out, wanted to hurt her out of spite. "And you can start by getting rid of that." I raised the dripping paintbrush that was still gripped tight in my fist and pointed it at the easel, at her current painting, at the drifting forms from the pits of hell.

Mama looked from me to the paintbrush to the painting, horror dawning on her as her eyes moved. She stood and went to the painting, and when she turned to face me again, she was lost. Possessed. "Oh. But . . ."

"Mama! Get rid of it!" My voice pitched to a shout as she stood frozen, staring at me. "You can't, can you? That painting means more to you than I do. If you love me, really and truly, you'll get rid of it. You'll get rid of all of them, and never paint another." I swept my hand, the brush splattering the room with slashing strokes. "But you don't really love me, do you." My tongue was a whip. "Fine." I threw the paintbrush across the room, heard it clatter against the wall, turned my tear-blinded eyes away, and ran.

I ran to my tower room and sobbed on my bed until my face was raw and swollen. I heard Mina, dear Mina, my nurse, come into the room. She touched my shoulder softly, *tsking* and muttering in German. On most days Mina was my comfort, my soft shoulder, but not that day. I pulled roughly into myself and spoke into my pillow. "Go away," I muttered, and she did.

I lay on my bed until the sun cast long red rays against the far wall and bathed my room in flaming streaks of dusky light. My door opened again. I thought it was Mina coming to ready my room for the evening. I clenched my pillow tighter to my body.

But it was Mama. She sat next to me as I lay sprawled, the bed creaking softly. "Maggie? Maggie? It's done. I did as you asked. I got rid of them. I threw them all away."

I turned and looked at her. She'd pinned up her hair, and was dressed in a simple white shirtwaist and blue serge skirt, her cameo fixed at her throat. She looked like Kitty's mother, like so many mothers in Newport, like the mother I wished her to be.

"I'm so sorry." She stroked my hair, separating the strands with her fingers.

I twisted away from her and spoke into the spread, my voice muffled. "I just want you to be normal. Please." I shook, my stomach heaving with agony, and my heart welled with my selfish need for her.

"All right." Her voice trembled, but she said it.

I lay still while she stroked my hair, her hand so soft it might have been a bird. I wanted everything to turn out right. I wanted to believe that my mama wouldn't disappoint me again.

I turned back to her. My eyes were swollen; tears still welled and slid down my cheeks and into my hair. I reached up to touch her cameo, as I had when I was little, running my fingers blindly over and over the carved face on its surface. My voice came out in a whisper. "Will you be here for me, Mama? Please, Mama?"

She sat silent, looking at the great window of my tower room, looking at the red sunset, the purple and blood-threaded sky, her face in profile to me. "Yes."

"Promise?" I touched her fine, porcelain cheek.

"Yes. I promise." She bent down to hold me.

I hugged her and didn't looked at her face again. I was afraid of what I might see there.

I should have looked.

I rested my forehead against Ghost's neck and forced myself not to think further into the past. I heard the mindless chatter of the stable hands, the *clap-clop* of hooves on brick, the soft, fluttered exhale of a passing horse. I pressed into Ghost, felt the cameo push against my throat. If I'd looked into Mama's eyes that evening last July, I might have seen the promise broken. I might have seen why, only two months later, Mama was gone.

After Mama disappeared, Papa insisted on a massive search. Bored officers carried out a job they believed to be fruitless. They found her robe, tangled in the rocks. "The waves, sir. You must understand. The riptides, sir. Surely you understand . . ." Papa was shocked to silence and retreated; he was like the rabbit in the mouth of the fox—not yet dead, but no longer able to struggle. For weeks, I'd watched them all—Papa, the police, my neighbors, my friends— relinquish themselves to thinking Mama had been lost to the waves. Not me. I refused to believe she was dead. I wouldn't believe she could break her promise and abandon me.

Papa would do nothing, lost as he was in his own grief. And so finally, I did the only thing I could. I threw myself into planning my season and my future. With or without her, my life would go on—it had to. I refused to let my prospects die while I waited for her to return.

Until two days ago. Two days ago Papa had surfaced from his self-imposed imprisonment with tales sent by his brother and with maps in his hands. Maps of far-off places, of Montana and Wyoming, of the wilderness; maps of rivers and mountain ranges and plains that were unknown to me. Papa emerged from his study with bright eyes and plans and hope.

I gave Ghost another treat and pressed a few coins into Joshua's palm. "Take good care of him while I'm gone. Make sure he gets daily exercise."

"Yes, miss." I watched as Joshua led Ghost away, his white coat shining until he vanished into the gloom of the stables. I found Papa's man, Jonas, polishing the brass on the lanterns of the phaeton, waiting to take me home.

When I joined Papa at dinner, he rambled on about his plans for our trip. Yet I was distracted. I kept returning to Mrs. Wolcott's sneer and Mrs. Proctor's snide gossip. I picked at the linen tablecloth, having lost my appetite.

"We'll have a grand tour along the way, Maggie." Papa carved into his beef with intensity.

I watched Papa's knife saw back and forth. "Papa, why west? Why do you and Uncle John think we will find her there, and not somewhere else?"

Papa concentrated on the piece of beef on his fork. "It's complicated, Margaret." He took a bite, then looked at me, wiping his mustache with his napkin while he finished chewing. "We can discuss this later. It'll all be a surprise! An exciting surprise." He flashed a smile at me and returned to his meal.

My stomach knotted. I lifted the glass to wet my dry mouth. I didn't want to lose Mama, not again. Nor did I want to lose my season and my only chance to make a good match and secure my future. I picked up my fork and twisted the tines against the plate. "I hope we can find her. Bring her home. I hope we can make her well."

Papa said nothing. The click of metal on china filled the room, bouncing off the oakwood floor and plaster walls.

"Things are hard, Papa. Hard for me," I said in a low voice. "It's all so hard without her."

Papa sawed his meat, his eyes cast down.

"People—Newport people—they aren't sure about me. They say things . . ." I searched for Mrs. Proctor's words, "They say I lack propriety. That I'm shameful. Like Mama. But I'm not. And if I am to find a husband, I need to prove to them that I'm respectable." I picked at the tablecloth, making tight little fabric hills. "It's important to me, Papa. It's my future." I looked up at him. "This is all I have, right here in Newport. This is where I belong. And right now, they don't want me."

His hands stopped moving.

"I need my debut, a really fine debut, with everything done exactly right, to make them want me. I want to prove to them that . . ." I didn't finish the sentence, but what came to my mind was, "that I'm not like Mama."

I reached down the table and took Papa's right hand, forcing him away from his food, willing him to look at me. He leaned back, wiping his mustache with his napkin again, regarding me with dark eyes. I needed to make him see how important my debut was, that it was as important as finding Mama. I needed to have my debut as much as I needed her back. Without a proper debut, I had nothing. If I was not introduced into society, I would not be able to find a husband—not one of good standing. I didn't know what would happen to me if I did not marry. I would have nothing—not Mama, not a future, nothing.

"We'll be back in time, won't we? We have to be back by the middle of July. And then we can make Mama well, here at home, and then she can help me plan. All right, Papa?"

He hesitated only a second before looking away. "Of course, Mags. Of course."

Chapter THREE

When the guests at the ball, who numbered about 200, arrived, they drove to the house from the massive gates through an avenue bordered with bay trees set in tubs. These trees were outlined with vari-colored electric lights . . . There were two orchestras. Dancing did not conclude until almost dawn.

—"Mrs. Ogden Goelet's Ball: First Important Function Given at Ochre Court, Newport," *New York Times*, August 29, 1900

FOR FRIENDSHIP, I HAD NONE BETTER THAN KITTY.

Dear Kitty! We'd been inseparable since we'd babbled at one another over the edges of our prams. We shared tea parties and doll clothes, school gossip and hair ribbons. Now we were to share our future. At least, that was my wish.

The morning after my ride, I finally worked up the nerve to tell Kitty about Papa's decision to go west. I found her lolling on the divan with Bear, her spaniel, curled beneath her arm. My voice trembled a little as I started in, and I gave a delicate cough. I needed Kitty's support to make everything work. I paced around the room, exaggerating, trying to make this "tour" sound fun and romantic, glancing at Kitty from time to time and watching her great blue eyes grow round.

"But this is dreadful, Maggie! You can't leave now!" She leapt from the divan, tumbling Bear to the floor, and rushed to my side, clutching my hands in her tiny fingers. "We have dresses to

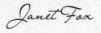

order and decorations and—goodness! Thousands of details!"

When we were little, only able to watch the preparations for a ball—the ordering of gowns, the fuss of coaches, the top hats and silk gloves of departure—Kitty and I had pledged that one day we would share our debuts. "It will be the talk of Newport!" We'd giggled. "Two balls in one!"

Now Kitty's eyes sharpened with annoyance and she returned to the divan and flounced down in a spray of silk and bouncing blonde curls. "Once again your mother is ruining things."

My breath caught. "Kitty!" The sting went deep, all the more because I feared it was true.

"Well?" She pursed her lips. "I'm sorry, Maggie, but you know I'm right. Your father hasn't been the same since she fell into the ocean." The image that her hurtful words conjured was terrible, and I bit my lip to stop myself from saying something rash in response. "It's been almost a year, for pity's sake, and he's still making bad decisions. Dragging you off to some godforsaken place at the start of your season. What is he thinking? How are you going to find a husband now? Clearly, this is the influence of your mother's irresponsible behavior." I could see that her eyes registered my balled fists and rigid posture. She sighed. She came to me, oozing sympathy. "I'm worried about you, Mags. It's your year now. I can have my own debut. Why, the Danforth boys have been fighting over me ever since last summer. It's time for you to catch an eye or two!" She reached up and tugged at a curl on my forehead, adjusting it as if she were designing a table setting.

Kitty's quick turns of mood tempered my frustration. I could never stay mad at her for long, and I didn't try to admonish her for her thoughtlessness. I watched her eyes fixed in concentration on my errant curl. When she finished playing with my hair, she flounced back to the divan and I slipped to her dressing table. I fingered the silver-backed hairbrush that lay there and let out my breath in a sigh. "I think boys will never be fighting over me."

Kitty giggled. "Margaret Bennet, you'll have boys eating out of your hands. Those long legs of yours will keep them on their toes. Literally! Of course, they'll fall in love with me first. Boys like to dominate. But I can only love one at a time, so surely there will be someone left for you." She batted her eyes.

Was she joking? I couldn't tell. I didn't know whether to laugh or be angry with her. "What do you think of Edward Tyson?" I examined the hairbrush as if I'd never seen it before, looking at every tiny badger bristle.

Kitty sat straight up. "Why, Margaret Katherine Bennet. I do believe you have a secret crush."

My face went hot. "Maybe."

Kitty came and took my cheeks between her palms and turned my face to hers. I looked down into her perfect blue eyes. "Liar," she said smoothly, then smiled. "I guess I'll let you have him."

I pulled back. She had to be joking. Yes, she was teasing me, she just had to be. I smiled back at her, uncertain of her motives, but needing to trust her.

I still hadn't told Kitty that at Mary's ball, the last of the summer before, Edward had kissed me, his full, soft lips pressed to mine. The memory of that moment was so sweet. But the memory of what happened only moments after that dear kiss . . . I moved away from Kitty toward the window.

I tapped my fingers on the wood window frame and inhaled the calming lilac scent that drifted in from the garden. "I don't know what I'll do, Kitty. I won't be here when Edward comes back from New York. Isabel, you know, she thinks he's for her." A little buzzing fear crept into my brain. A breeze lifted the sheer curtains so that they billowed around me like sails.

"Pooh on what Isabel thinks!" Kitty said. "But that's beside the point, Maggie. You need to stay right here. You need to tell your father you won't go. Besides, who wants to go west when you can go to Paris? Really, Mags."

"Do you think Edward would wait?" I turned back toward Kitty. "Do you think he might be the right one? You know, for me?"

"What do you mean, does he have money?" Kitty sank onto the divan and reached down and tussled with Bear. "We know that already." She touched Bear's nose with her fingertip, and spoke to him, baby-voiced. "Don't we, Bear-Bear?"

"No, Kitty, that's not what I'm talking about. I mean, I'm looking for someone special."

"As in . . ."

"As in, I don't know. Someone who can take care of me. But not take over me. Someone who'll let me be who I am."

"And who are you, Miss Margaret, O Emancipated One?" Kitty laughed out loud, her sarcasm ringing through the room.

"I don't know. That's just it." I bit my lip. Was I my mother, bohemian and lost? Was I my father, crippled by loneliness and propriety? I'd been brought up to marry someone of the right social status, bear his children, run his household. This should be my future. I still wanted this future. I wanted all the lovely things a doting husband could provide; and, with any luck, I could sit at the top of the social tier and command respect and admiration, like Kitty's mother did now. Like Kitty surely would. Like Mama

24

never had. Mama had rejected all of that, and had been rejected right back.

I wanted to be more like Kitty than like Mama, but there was still one deep-dwelling dream inside me. Now I dared speak it out loud for the first time, and I felt a passion rise up in me as I spoke. "I do want to fall in love. I want a true love. I want to fall in love with a boy who would stand next to me on a mountaintop. And with him next to me I wouldn't be afraid. Not because he was rescuing me. I wouldn't be afraid simply because he was there. That's what I want. That's what I think true love is."

"Well!" Kitty stood, her hands on her hips, eyeing me. "A mountaintop? You? Miss Margaret Bennet, paralyzed by heights, at the top of a mountain with a handsome man?" She laughed. "Aren't you ever the romantic!"

I blushed, my passion fading. "I guess."

"And dear Edward?"

Would Edward be the boy standing beside me? I so wanted to believe it would be him. "I think so. Yes. Perhaps."

"Well, there's no time for romance now, Mags. There's hardly even time to pack for this silly trip of your father's."

I sagged. Kitty's words brought me crashing back to earth, landing with a hard thump. "Yes. I should go. Mina will pack only the most boring, sensible clothing if I'm not there."

Kitty pressed forward, taking my hands in hers again. "Maggie. I wish you wouldn't go on this silly vacation with your father. Stay—your grandparents will take you in."

She was right, they would. I knew they would. But I couldn't stand suffering Grandpapa's reproving looks and unspoken criticisms while I waited for Papa's news as he went alone to find

Mama. Despite my conflicted feelings, I was resolved. I had to go with him, find Mama, and bring her home. I searched for the words to explain this to Kitty. I clutched Kitty's hands tight and drew her to the divan. "I have a secret. Can you keep it? Promise me."

Kitty nodded solemnly.

"Papa says that Mama may be out west somewhere. He heard from my uncle John that there may be some . . . news. That's why we're going."

Kitty's eyes were saucers.

"You must not tell a soul, Kitty. Especially not my grandparents. Do you promise?"

Kitty nodded again, silent. Then she drew her hands out of mine. "But think, Maggie. Maybe what your father says is true. What if it isn't?"

I shook my head, denying the thought. Denying my own doubts.

Kitty pressed forward. "And if it isn't, how long will you search?" She leaned back and looked up at the coffered ceiling. "We've planned our debut ball for late August, Mags. That's a deadline."

My throat swelled, and I swallowed hard and nodded, then stood. "I need to go pack."

Kitty's blue eyes met mine. "I'll do what I can to get things ready while you're gone. But I won't give up my own debut, Maggie. You have to be back by the end of July. After that . . ."

Kitty's warning rang in my ears all the way home.

※ ※ ※

The house was alive with preparations. Trunks were strewn about, half full, mostly with Papa's books and papers, blueprints, and drafting tools. Papa called orders out to Jonas. Men hired for the purpose covered the furniture with sheets. The house already looked empty and haunted.

Mina was busy in my room, tossing gowns on the bed, draping skirts over chairs. One gown hung from the door of my wardrobe. Black and white, with lace at the throat, and tight through the waist, where a crushed satin belt was a slash of scarlet. It was a dress that made my cheeks go dark with memories.

"Not that one, Mina," I said.

"Good. Good." She waved her hand in the air as if making a sign, then gathered the gown into her arms and laid it on the bed. "That red sash, like blood. Bad luck. I will put it away." She left it on the bed and bustled out of the room to fetch more packing materials and tissue paper.

I went to the bed and fingered the red sash. The silk shimmered in my hand, flowed through my fingers. I knew why Mina thought it looked like blood. Why she had called it "bad luck." I'd worn it to that ball last August that had promised so much and delivered such misery.

Promise and misery.

Mary's ball had been the last debut of the season, held on an August night that began so hot and still, even the flies seemed drunk with stupor. Through the open windows of Mary's grand mansion I heard the sea, the huge foaming breakers that crashed in the still air, overwhelming the delicate efforts of the small orchestra. Lightning flickered on the far horizon, echoing the tiny lights strung from branch to branch in the gardens outside. In the small parlor where the women gathered to primp, I found Kitty, and we admired one another's dress. She was done up in blue silk that spilled in ten yards of rustling train. Her hair glittered with

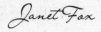

diamonds that matched her necklace. My black-and-white gown was daring in the company of the other girls' sweeping pastels.

Black and white with a bloodred sash. I'd wanted something bold and romantic. I hadn't thought about the other implications.

"Well, it's not truly bohemian," Kitty said, twisting me around, and that word hit me like a shock of cold water. "Not really. Although . . . ." She paused as she ran her fingers along the red sash. Her voice dropped to a hush. "That's a bit dangerous."

"Radical," said Isabel with a sniff. "I think it's over-the-top."

Isabel moved away. I narrowed my eyes and flashed open my red oriental fan, feeling both nervous and annoyed. Had I pushed it too far with this daring dress? But Kitty leaned in close. "Isabel's miserable," she whispered. "She's had a thing for Edward and he no longer gives her the time of day."

My heart took a little jump and my nervousness vanished.

"In fact, I think I saw him arrive," Kitty said. "Shall we go in?"

Mina returned to my room with tissue paper and I dropped the sash, sighing as the memory of that evening heaved and swelled like the sea. Mina folded the offending gown in the paper and removed it from my room. Maybe Mina was right. That dress with its dripping sash may have been cursed, one of my only rebellions paid for in blood.

I looked at the other gowns and day dresses that lay piled on my bed waiting for my selection. From deep within I saw a glimpse of seafoam green. I tugged it out from under the rest and laid it on top of the pile. That one I would take west. That gown conjured a sweet memory of the time when Mama was still keeping the promise she'd made to me. I picked up the gown and pressed it to my cheek, feeling the cool silk. I would take this gown west and carry a charm that would bring back Mama as she was that day last July, when we'd chosen it for me together.

Madame Bouchard could tailor the latest French fashions. It was a late July day, not too warm, soft and breezy. Mama and I had huddled side by side over the great table in Madame Bouchard's shop, choosing fabrics and examining patterns. Sometimes Mama seemed to forget the task at hand, but I gently tugged her back to the moment with a careful word or a touch of my hand. We'd chosen three light-wool street costumes and two tea gowns when the small bell rang merrily and the door opened behind us.

Kitty swept in. I gazed at her, jealous of her beige silk gown and jacket; her waist was rapier thin. Her sleeves belled fashionably and her hat dipped to the right, dripping silk tuberoses. Her eyes, as they took in Mama's staid outfit, dripped curiosity.

"You look wonderfully healthy, Mrs. Bennet." Kitty smiled, soft ringlets framing her angelic face. "Have you put on some weight?"

Mama blushed and spoke carefully. "Maggie and I have returned to evening exercise together. Along the Cliff Walk."

"Maggie on the Cliff Walk?" Kitty's eyebrows arched in surprise.

"Mama takes the outside when it's steep. I try not to look." The path was terrifyingly steep in places, and merely a glance at the sheer drop could paralyze me.

"How sweet!" Kitty giggled, and leaned toward Mama. "Why, a few weeks ago Mags couldn't even climb the ladder to help our teacher pin up the confetti streamers for our last-day party!"

I blushed, but it was true. I only walked with Mama because I could cling to her hand. When the sea thundered close and the rocks became steep, I shrank, weak-kneed against her. Ghost's back was the highest I could climb from the ground.

Kitty skirted the table, lifting bolt after bolt of cloth. "My mama hopes you'll call soon."

Mama glanced at me. "I shall." She looked pleased at the unexpected offer. I was thrilled.

"Oh, look at that lovely green!" Kitty fingered the silk fabric the seamstress had thrown on the table. "That would suit Maggie so, don't you think?"

I took the silk and held it up to my throat. Mama nodded, and I saw an almost imperceptible flash of sadness in her eyes that vanished as quickly as it had appeared. "We can have that made up into a dinner gown," she said to the seamstress.

"This wool tartan is suitable for a morning dress," I chimed in. "Oh! But I'd also like sleeves like Miss Gardner's." Kitty smiled and dipped her head. I fingered the green silk and smiled back.

Now the precious green gown lay quiet on my bed. When Mina came back into the room, I held it up to her. "This one. It has to come with me." For its magic powers. Because I wanted Mama back as she was that day, when she was normal, happy even. Still keeping her promise to me.

I tried not to think about what would happen if we found her and she couldn't keep her promises again. Maybe we would only find Mama as miserable as she had been late in the evening of Mary's ball. Maybe, as Kitty had insinuated, we wouldn't find her at all.

Mina interrupted my thoughts. "*Ach!* Three trunks already!" Her voice dropped. "Your grandparents are here."

I stiffened. My mother's parents. I would have to go down.

Chapter FOUR

The most prominent object was a long table with a tablecloth spread on it, as if a feast had been in preparation when the house and the clocks all stopped together.

—*Great Expectations*, Charles Dickens, 1861

THE VOICES RANG UP TO GREET ME AS I STARTED DOWN THE stairs. I stood on the hallway landing and listened.

My grandfather's voice thundered through the house. "What? What did that cad of a father tell her?"

"I don't know, I don't know." My grandmother's voice drifted up to me. "I can't stand this. History is repeating itself. He's doing it all over again. She'll never find a suitable husband. They'll never accept her."

My heart slowed. Never. That's what Grandmama said. They'd never accept me. I'd never find a suitable husband. I pressed my back against the wall and slipped down a step or two to hear more clearly.

"Where is the man?" Grandpapa stormed. "Why, I'll break his neck!" A metallic taste rose in my mouth. Grandpapa stomped out of the room, on his way to Papa's studio.

I slid down the stairs into the hallway and tiptoed through the gloom until I stood just outside Papa's studio door, at the far end

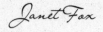

of the house, hiding behind the open door, where I could hear everything.

Grandpapa was angry. More than angry; livid. I'd heard his rage directed at Papa ever since Mama had disappeared. Papa's silence in the face of these tirades was even more frightening than Grandpapa's shouts.

Now I heard Grandpapa's fist hammering the table in Papa's studio.

". . . will not support this! If you can't make it back, man, you're finished! And now you leave in the high season when you should be here lining up new work? I did not take you into our firm for you to destroy it! Intolerable!"

Papa said something I could not hear; I pressed closer to the doorway, straining to catch the snippets of his conversation.

"I don't care about your foolish dreams! Nincompoop dreams! I'm hearing other things, from every quarter of Newport. Jobs not complete, work that's shabby. If you leave now, you will lose everything!" He was quiet for a moment. "I'll cut Margaret out of her inheritance. You are condemning yourselves to a life of shame."

Lose everything. My inheritance. Shame. My stomach became an open pit. I heard another mumbling, indistinguishable response. Then there was a slam, as of a book hitting wood, and I jumped.

"Damn it!" came Grandpapa's voice. "I'll not have you ruining my good name yet again!"

I heard movement and, just in time, I slipped behind the hall-closet door, peering through the crack to see my grandfather storm from Papa's studio, flinging the door open against the wall in his wake.

I trembled as I stepped out of the closet into the hallway and looked into the studio.

Papa sat behind his desk, his head in his hands. His work, half packed, lay strewn about the room: blueprints, books, letters, and contracts. I rested my hand on the doorframe. "Why is Grandpapa so angry with you?" I said it so soft that my voice floated.

Papa lifted his head and looked at me.

I took a step into the room. "I can help you straighten things out. Get things ready to go." I bent and picked up a stack of blueprints and placed them in the trunk waiting to be packed.

Papa cleared his throat. "Thank you, Margaret."

"What did Grandpapa mean, we'd lose everything?" My voice trembled.

"He doesn't understand. We're going to have a whole new life." His voice was light, as though he was trying hard to be cheerful.

"When we bring her home, you mean. Then we'll have a whole new life." It was meant as a question, but he didn't answer as he crossed the room to select a stack of books from the case. I bent for another pile of papers and smoothed them on the table with both hands. The room was a mess. "I should have helped you before."

"No, no."

"When it first happened. I'm sorry I didn't help you then."

He stopped and stared at me again. All I could do was remember the months when he'd sat alone in his studio after Mama had disappeared. The months when he hadn't worked at all. That was what Grandpapa must have meant; Papa had brought us, brought Grandpapa's firm, to the edge of ruin. Without Mama, Papa had retreated into a dark place, and it hadn't been until the letters came from Uncle John that he finally woke up.

Yet clearly Grandpapa did not believe Papa had changed, and I wanted to know why. "Why does he think Mama's disappearance is your fault?"

"What?" Papa's voice was a whisper.

"I heard him. He blames you."

Papa cleared his throat. "In point of fact, Maggie, your mother disappeared a long time ago."

I didn't understand what he meant, but I felt sorry for him; Papa couldn't help Mama's behavior. But what of the rest of Grandpapa's accusations? I picked up pile after pile of Papa's papers. Papa and I worked together in silence for a few minutes, my mind racing, until I found the courage to ask my recurring question.

"Papa, this trip won't ruin my chances at finding a suitable husband, will it?" *A suitable husband like Edward* was my unexpressed thought, someone both suitable and who fulfilled my deepest desire for love. "You promised we would be back in time for my debut, since we're only going in order to bring Mama home. So it can't possibly ruin my chances, can it."

He had his back to me and I watched him square his shoulders. "I'll do whatever I can to avoid that outcome, Margaret."

"We'll find her, and then all this will be over, like a bad dream." I wanted that more than anything.

"Yes." Papa's voice rasped, soft.

"I should go speak to them," I said, meaning my grandparents. "Tell them I want to go, so they stop worrying."

"Yes." He looked at me. "That would help."

As I left his studio, he reached for me. "Remember. Say nothing to them of your mother."

"All right." I hastened back to the parlor, where the furniture was half draped, and my grandparents were conferring.

Apparently my grandfather had chased the men out with his rage.

"Grandpapa! Grandmama!" I rushed forward and kissed each of them. "Isn't it exciting? This tour of Papa's is an excellent way for me to start my season!" I smiled broadly, inwardly praying that they would see the trip in this light.

"I'm glad you think so, dear," said Grandmama, laying a hand on Grandpapa's arm. "But we don't agree. We think you should come and stay with us. We can help you plan for your debut properly."

Yes, they could. I knew they could, just as I'd known they could when Kitty had suggested that very thing. But it was impossible. While a proper introduction into society was essential to secure my future, I had to go with Papa to find Mama. Not only because he demanded it, but also because he needed me. This tore me in two, my grandparents on one side offering me the life I wanted, but making their own demands; my papa and, I hoped, Mama on the other side offering the possibility of a complete life. I knew what I had to do. I locked my fingers behind my back, as if trying to shore up my soul.

"Papa's promised we'd be gone only until the middle of July. We'd be back in time for my debut. He's made it sound like such fun." I felt the twinge of misery as I spoke, and I tightened my fingers.

"That man cannot keep his word!" Grandpapa blurted. Grandmama laid her hand gently on his arm again, but her hand trembled.

"I'm sure he will," I said in a small voice. I was afraid of that very thing, but forced myself to keep strong.

Grandmama moved across the room and slipped off the white sheet covering my mother's portrait. The frame around the enormous oil painting was still banded in black crepe. Mama's eyes stared out over the three of us, her lip curled up at one corner; the painter had managed to capture her inner light, that hint of the rebel that just could not be suppressed.

"She was the loveliest girl in her year," Grandmama said. "She had scores of suitors."

"And she chose the worst!" my grandfather bellowed like a bull.

I bit my lip until it hurt.

"It wasn't her fault," Grandmama said. "It wasn't her fault." She sank onto a chair. She looked at me, her eyes dim. "History is repeating itself."

I looked at Grandmama. With a chilling shock, I realized she meant me. She thought that I was repeating history, Mama's history. The words tumbled out of me before I could even think: "Please. Let me take this little trip with Papa. I'll find a suitable husband. It will all work out."

My grandfather regarded me with narrowed eyes.

Something snapped inside me, as I looked at my grandparents' pinched faces. I really had no choice. I had to go with Papa. I couldn't stay with them. I'd be back—we'd be back—and I'd have the life I'd always dreamed. "Let me take this trip with Papa. And when we're back I'll have a lovely debut and make you proud, and things will be better than ever."

My grandparents exchanged a look, Grandpapa's lips set grim.

I'd promised Papa. I could not tell them the real reason for this trip. But I had to go with him and find Mama, and we'd try and cure her madness. That would drive out all this shame and disapproval and then I would have the life of my dreams.

Chapter
FIVE ❖❖❖❖❖❖❖❖❖❖

June 3–17, 1904

> *A company of homeless children from the East will arrive at Troy, MO, on Friday ... These children are of various ages and of both sexes, having been thrown friendless upon the world ... The citizens of this community are asked to assist the agent in finding good homes for them.*

—advertisement in the Troy, Missouri, *Free Press,*
February 11, 1910

THE DAY OF DEPARTURE WAS A FLURRY OF CONFUSION. Papa had sent trunks on ahead to Uncle John's, including two of my own that I would not need on the train. Mina bustled about, readying me for the ride to Philadelphia, our first stop two days hence. I would wear my blue wool traveling suit. Mina tugged at the laces of my corset while I clutched at the bedpost as a drowning man would a spar. I wanted my waist to look long and sparrow-thin, the ideal Gibson Girl figure.

"Tighter, Mina!"

"*Liebchen,*" Mina muttered, "you'll never have a waist like Miss Kitty's. Your fine figure is made for the *kinder,* not for the fashion." She was right; I'd never have a waist as small as a handspan like Kitty did. Mina went on, "You should not try to be something you are not."

As I watched in the mirror, I reflected on that thought. For the second time in two days, I wondered who I was. Who I was not.

At the moment, I was a proper society girl taking a western

37

tour with her father, but without her nursemaid.

"You're right." I sighed. "I probably won't have any help along the way. Go ahead and lace it so that I can hook the busk in front by myself."

Mina finished the lacing and I tested the hooks on the busk to be certain I could manage alone, then Mina held out the petticoat and I stepped into it. She gathered the skirt and slipped it over my head.

I had barely buttoned my gloves and pinned on my hat when I heard Papa shouting for me. The coach waited, the remaining trunks piled onto a wagon behind. Papa handed Jonas papers and gave him instructions. When Jonas turned to look at me, his expression was grim and set.

"Jonas! Why so somber?" I teased. He glanced at Papa and nodded to me.

I hugged Mina, and then we were off down the drive. I turned to look back at our house and saw Jonas speak to Mina. Her hands flew to her cheeks and her eyes flew to me.

Mina looked horrified; I was startled. "Papa—look. Is something wrong? Should we go back?"

"Eh? Nothing wrong." He fingered his mustache as he looked out at the landscape of our drive. An empty lorry rumbled past us, pulled by two drays, heading in the opposite direction toward the house.

I craned back again but we'd rounded the curve and the house and lorry were out of sight. What could have made Mina so upset? A tiny spark of fear ignited in me, and I pushed Papa harder. "Papa, something is not right."

"No, no. Nothing's wrong, except that we're running behind. Driver," Papa called up, "we must be at the station within the half hour."

The flail of the station, the bustle and noise, finding our coach and settling into our Pullman compartments all took my mind away from the disturbing departure; but a niggling worry lodged deep within me and refused to budge.

⁂ ⁂ ⁂

In the first days of travel we passed through the familiar terrain of New England. From Providence we made for Philadelphia, our first stop. Papa had decided we'd spend a few days there. We took in the sights of the grand old city, although I'd seen them before. The Liberty Bell was gone—removed only days earlier to appear at the Exposition in St. Louis—but there was plenty to do. Papa exchanged more correspondence with Uncle John, though he didn't reveal the contents to me, and slipped away on numerous secretive errands.

The worry born in our driveway did not abate.

Many of the great houses on Society Hill were occupied by people we knew. We had tea one afternoon in a fine old mansion, the home of old Mrs. Delaney's married daughter, and I was uneasy. Perhaps it was the stultifying air of the first hot day of the summer and how badly my collar itched. Perhaps it was the fact that I sat across the room from Mrs. Delaney, whose glances in my direction were piercing. I hadn't seen her since the previous August, when Mama and I had visited with her in Newport.

I had thought my normal mama was finally returned to me, as there'd been no more of the awful paintings or the melancholy. We'd walked together, shopped together, even paid calls together, and all was well. While at times I thought Mama seemed distant, she was so much recovered that I'd begun to feel she was back to normal. That is, until we had tea in Mrs. Delaney's parlor on a hot August afternoon.

"Mrs. Bennet." Mrs. Delaney handed the teacup across the table. She lifted her wrinkled face to gaze at Mama. "Will you be spending any time this summer in Saratoga? My husband and I will take our usual trip to Philadelphia a bit late this year. Or perhaps you'll travel to California? That's the new frontier, so I'm told."

Mama blanched and set down her cup. I was surprised to see her eyes grow wide and hear the tremor in her voice. "No. No. We . . . I . . . no, we have no plans."

"Didn't you and your husband once travel to someplace or other out west? You were gone some time, I think?" pressed Mrs. Delaney. Her pouchy pale eyes swept ceilingward. "My memory isn't what it was, but I do seem to remember something." Mrs. Delaney tapped her cheek with her forefinger.

"I . . . don't . . . ." Mama's hands were trembling, and I grew alarmed. She lowered her gaze to her lap.

Mrs. Delaney frowned. "I'm sure I recall it. It was shortly after you were born, Margaret. Let's see. A monumental experience, I believe." Mrs. Delaney's eyes focused sharply on Mama.

Mama closed her eyes, began to sway ever so slightly. I was frightened; I feared she was returning to her place of madness.

"Why, Mrs. Delaney," I blurted. "It's so hot, don't you think? I think Mama's having a difficult time with the heat. I know I am. When you go to Philadelphia, I should hope you'll have cooler weather."

Mrs. Delaney's gaze swept to me, and I smiled as brilliantly as possible. After an instant's hesitation she smiled back. And I placed my hand on Mama's so that she would remain quiet.

I'd nearly forgotten the incident altogether, and I'd not connected it with Papa's comment about Mama's having once been west until this moment. Mrs. Delaney stared at me from across her daughter's Philadelphia parlor. I excused myself and left the room.

I wandered through the hallway. Massive oil paintings hung ceiling to floor. Stately women, regal men, dogs with bared teeth rolling about on the floor, frightened-looking children in starched collars, rotting fruits tumbling from bowls, haunches of venison dripping fat. The more I looked, the worse I felt.

⁂

That night at dinner, I asked Papa about Mama's trip west.

He pushed his plate away. "There's really nothing to tell."

I tried to hide that I was fishing for information by acting like a simple child. "Did you two go to California?"

"No. Never been there, I'm afraid. Though I hear San Francisco is quite a city now." He placed his napkin on the table.

"Montana, then? You mentioned Montana. Isn't that where we're going now?"

He placed his hands flat on the table, examining his fingers. "It's all a surprise for you, Margaret. You'll see."

I buried my frustration beneath a calm veneer. "I'd really like to hear the story of her earlier trip. Mrs. Delaney mentioned it."

He started, seeming surprised, and looked at me, his eyes narrowing. "What did she say?" His voice was harsh.

"Nothing. Not much. She really didn't recall." Papa's look frightened and confused me. "She couldn't recall any details."

He relaxed a little. "That's because there's nothing to recall." He paused. "We'll be on the noon train tomorrow. I have business in St. Louis, so I've decided we should see the Exposition. We don't have these opportunities every day. That should be fun, eh? Shall we?" He stood and held my chair for me. I had no choice except to retire.

On my way to my room the bellboy approached me with a letter from Kitty.

> Isabel's family has temporarily relocated from Charleston to New York. She's written that she's seen quite a bit of Edward, as their mothers are old friends. They'll be coming to Newport together next week.
>
> But don't fret, dear Mags. I'm certain he'll only have eyes for you. Although you should consider living in New York next winter. My parents are taking an apartment on Gramercy, for in their view, Newport is no place for a true season.

But fret I did. The uneasiness I'd been feeling for the last week since we'd left welled to a peak. Something was not right. I felt certain it had to do with Mama's earlier trip out west, and Papa's reluctance to discuss anything with me. I could sense it.

Frustrated, I threw myself into the wing chair that sat before my small fireplace. Now, thanks to Kitty, I had to endure the thought that Edward was receiving the unhindered attentions of Isabel. I wasn't sure he'd remember enough about me to resist her persistent charms.

I wrote back to Kitty.

> Please tell me all the news. Have you found the perfect gown? I saw one in a shop here in Philadelphia that I think I'll copy. I will ask Papa to turn back no later than July 1st. That should have me home in plenty of time.

I hate the close and oppressive homes of Philadelphia.
Remind me never to hang antique oils as decoration.
They reek of death and dying. Ugh.

⁂

From Philadelphia we traveled to Chicago and then to St. Louis. I'd never been farther west. The miles seemed endless, although when I counted carefully, I marked that a straight train trip from St. Louis back to Newport would only take five days. I relaxed a little then, knowing that we still had time to get to our yet-unnamed destination, find Mama, and return home before mid-July. I distracted myself at the Louisiana Purchase Exposition and tried to enjoy the marvel of its classical architecture, gardens and fountains, the astonishing array of innovations, and the exotic displays from the world over.

We left St. Louis on June 15. As we changed trains in Omaha, my foreboding returned with greater intensity as I watched the children waiting for the orphan train.

Hundreds of children, from babes in arms to girls not much younger than me, gathered in a group waiting for their ride to their new homes. Taken from New York by charitable souls, these children were supposed to be on their way to a better life on a farm or homestead. I paused on the step up into our Pullman, watching a group of giggling girls making bubbles from soap. They'd lost everything, yet they could laugh and play. I clutched at the handrail as Papa held my elbow, helping me into the car, and I felt my stomach twisting into knots.

I sank back against the plush seat and closed my eyes. Mama had left me half an orphan. I wanted her back, and that was why we were here. We were going west to find Mama and bring her home. I said it over and over to the rhythm of the iron wheels that picked up speed and ran beneath me. Find Mama and bring her home. I had to hang on to this despite my ever-deepening suspicions that Papa was hiding something from me.

Find Mama and bring her home.

The train wheels ran, sounding like muffled shots, and the light from the sun flashed through the window in dagger points. I kept my eyes closed and let my head rock back against the headrest.

Find Mama and bring her home.

⁂

From Omaha, the Great Plains swept before us as we went north and west.

"Where are we going now, Papa? And how much longer until we're there?"

"We'll be in Livingston, Montana, tomorrow." Montana. Papa didn't speak much now. He left our compartment at intervals. He seemed anxious and restless; he spoke with the conductor at length in the corridor; he peered out the windows in all directions.

All I saw were flat, barren grasslands, desolate and endless, not a tree or mountain in sight. The plains reminded me of the ocean, gently rolling and swelling. The train lurched and bucked and ran with me toward Montana. Papa paced and grew more and more distant. I thought about the rolling, grassy dunes and gray sea that we'd left behind. My home. I missed it as it slipped away behind us on thin parallel rails.

Chapter SIX ❧ ❧ ❧ ❧ ❧ ❧ ❧ ❧ ❧ ❧

June 17, 1904

*Suddenly, shaken with weeping, she bowed her face
upon the hands that held her own . . . The outward signs
of life's most poignant and most beautiful moments are
generally very simple and austere.*

—*Lady Rose's Daughter*, a novel by Mrs. Humphry Ward, 1903

WE EMERGED FROM THE FLATLANDS AND ROLLED INTO
Livingston in the afternoon. I hadn't time to appreciate the
landscape that rose so abruptly from the plains. The Rocky
Mountains, capped with snow, were bathed in slanting light that
was cut and crossed by clouds that brought on an early dusk. It was
too cold, with a brisk breeze, to spend time outside in any case, so
we hastened inside to have an early dinner at the Murray, a new and
gracious hotel just across the road from the depot.

My uncle John was there waiting for us, and Papa sequestered
himself at once with him before I was able to ask him anything about
Mama. When they emerged, Uncle John avoided my eyes. Over
dinner, my uncle talked up a storm on every subject except Mama.
My father had done well for himself, rising up from his common
beginnings to be an admired architect, but my uncle was still a
laborer—skilled, yes, but only a carpenter. He talked of his work on
the fine hotels, and waxed especially poetical about Yellowstone.

"You're sure to have a fine time. It's filled with wonders, Margaret! That's what it's called—'Wonderland'! Of course, the Indians had a different view of it—they said it was like white man's descriptions of hell, all boiling and steaming and bubbling . . ."

"John." My father nodded in my direction.

"Oh. Well, Charlie." He waved his hand over Papa's plate of trout and his own venison stew. "Maggie's a big girl now." Uncle John glanced at me, then down. "Well, anyhow. You'll see, Margaret."

"Yes." Papa smiled. "We'll be on the train into Yellowstone in the morning."

"So we're going into Yellowstone?" I asked, tentative. I looked at my uncle, busy with his stew. "And then?"

"And then everything will fall into place." Papa drank his claret.

I reached my hand to Papa's arm. "Doesn't Uncle John have . . ."

Papa shot me a harsh look and I withdrew my hand. Here we were, so close, and yet Papa was still keeping me in the dark.

"We'll retire early. The train leaves at nine sharp." He gave me no opening for further questions, and Uncle John still wouldn't meet my eyes.

❧ ❧ ❧

My room in the hotel looked out over the town of Livingston to the mountains that sat now in shadow. I closed my curtains and drew a hot bath.

I settled into the steaming water. When I lifted my arm the water ran down in thin ribbons. We'd arrived in Montana and Uncle John had news. But the news clearly wasn't for my ears, at least not yet. The nagging suspicions that had been troubling me since we departed home came to a point: it was clear Papa was hiding something from me. Maybe he now knew that Mama was dead and he hadn't had the courage to tell me. Or maybe he knew that Mama was alive but in such an awful state . . .

After her tea with Mrs. Delaney, Mama had reverted into a deep depression. She withdrew from me and Papa and took again to walking along the Newport cliffs alone. Her depression was worse than before, although how much worse hadn't been clear to me until later.

I slipped deeper into the bathwater, trying to clear my mind of terrible thoughts. Edward. I'd think about Edward.

I'd think about that night last summer when he filled my dance card. When he kissed me. The night of Mary's ball and the dress with the red sash. I closed my eyes and let my mind drift back to the happier moments of that evening.

The intense heat of that late August afternoon had been building toward a storm. Low, rolling breakers swelled to foam-topped monsters crashing on the shore. As the festive mood at the ball grew the wind picked up and rain spattered fat drops until the wind swelled to a howl. Servants ran from room to room until all the doors were closed and all but a few windows shuttered.

We gathered at the last unshuttered window to watch. The fairy lights hanging from trees and bushes swung, trembling, then were stripped from the branches and shattered by a gust. Rain came in sheets. The wind shrieked like a phantom and Mary's father sternly ordered us away from the glass. Just afterward, the great oak at the bottom of the garden swayed and toppled with a thunderous crash.

The electric lights flickered and went out. The ball was illumined only by candles, but the revelry was undimmed. Edward held me close as we danced, and then, during a fevered waltz, pulled me behind the stairs.

"Now I have you," he whispered.

"Do you? Are you sure?"

He tightened his arms around me and pressed his body against mine. "You are so beautiful," he breathed into my ear. His hand pressed the red sash at the small of my back.

I felt weak, and my hands gripped his jacket as if it were a life vest. I was in grave danger of floating away.

He lifted my chin, and I let him kiss me, my lips burning and my breath stopped. The layers of fabric that separated us crushed and melted and the laces of my corset strained.

I sighed in my bath. Such a brief, sweet moment, that time with Edward. If only I could have all of that happiness again. I lifted my arm again out of the bath and stared at it, at the tiny hairs and the streaming water. My mind drifted to the possibility of Uncle John's news, and then there was no helping where my memories went next. For just at the moment Edward had been kissing me under the stairs, Mama had turned my life upside down.

Mama had gone to Mary's ball, too, despite her sunken looks and silence. Papa had insisted. He thought she needed the social interaction. He was wrong.

Edward and I were still locked in our embrace when we heard a scream. There was a commotion at the door to a small sitting room, and I realized what was happening. The storm: I had seen Mama retreat to the safety of the sitting room when the storm hit. Mama hated thunder and lightning; she had a deep-seated fear of it. I could remember the feeling of bile rising in my throat, even now, nearly a year later.

At the time, I prayed that she had just been hiding from the noise, that something worse hadn't happened. Edward's arm circled my waist until we pushed through the crowd into the room. But once we could see her there, his arm dropped, and he slid back, abandoning me.

I was alone, as if on a cliff edge; I was alone facing my worst nightmare.

My mother, sat on the floor. Her hair hung loose past her waist, and she'd removed her gloves, which lay on the floor next to her, white and long like a shed skin. She held her diamond hairpin in her right hand and her arms were slashed, blood dripping in red splotches on her white silk gown.

My legs went rubbery; I couldn't move.

The sitting room was a gallery filled with ugly oil paintings. Bulging eyes in fat, powerful men. Narrow eyes in lean, overdressed matrons. They stuck in my mind like glue and formed a hideous backdrop to my nightmares, to my mother's breakdown. The other guests around me stared at my mother with mingled horror and fascination. One woman leaned heavily on her companion. "She cut herself! Right in front of me! I was trying to rest when she began ranting about terrible things and then she stabbed herself! I think I shall faint!"

Papa pushed through the crowd that was now growing at the door. "Anna! Anna, for God's sake!" He reached her side and bent to her; she stared at him in horror. I was rooted to the spot, my limbs numb.

"No!" Mama screamed, thrashing against his grasp. "Not you! Don't take me away! Not again!" Mama twisted away from Papa, her dress falling from her shoulder. She held her hairpin up like a weapon against him. Gasps came from every corner. "Keep away from me! I want to stay!"

I could not watch her, lost as she was in that dark nightmare. My eyes drifted up away from Mama, anything to get away, to look away.

My gaze locked on a painting of a doe, wide-eyed and openmouthed, caught in the strangled moment of death from a hunter's bow.

With a soft cry, a woman to my right fainted against her companion and I felt the world shrink to a pinpoint, the far end of a telescope. A semicircle of space opened around me, and I knew I could not escape. I was involved; it was my mama there on the floor. I saw those around me stare, at me, at Mama. Eyes widened in horror, gloved hands covered mouths, someone whispered, "Scandalous." Another, "Unacceptable." Edward stepped farther away from me and I could feel the distance between us gape.

I was ashamed of myself and of her. I was at the very edge; she had toppled over, too far for me to reach. I couldn't help her; I could only watch her fall away.

Dr. Fortner stepped into the room. His familiar physician's voice broke through the gasps and whispers like a balm. "Excuse me. Let me through." He knelt next to Mama. "Now, Mrs. Bennet. Let's not have any more of this, shall we?"

For an instant I feared she would repel him, too, like she had rejected Papa. But she looked at him, stunned, then she slumped and he took her gently, easing the sharp pin from her hand. He lifted her to her feet, bracing her body against his. The throng made a passage for them as he took her from the room.

Eyes in the portraits lining the walls, eyes of long-dead children, of decrepit old men, of sharp-as-pin women, eyes of dying animals, eyes of the living people in the room, all of them watched me.

Papa bent like a tired old man, picked up Mama's gloves, and followed her out. The crowd finally dispersed, whispering, brushing past me, casting sidelong glances but never looking me in the eye.

When the room had nearly cleared, Edward returned to my side and I felt his embarrassment even more keenly than my own.

"Maggie?"

My throat burned, my legs shook, my gloved hands clutched at the red sash tied around me, constricting my breath. "I suspect I should go," I said, and left him there in the sitting room.

The walk to the front hall felt miles long. Hundreds of eyes followed my back and I heard their whispers following me. Those whispers followed me still.

I'd heard from Edward again after Mama disappeared, and he seemed to show genuine concern. But I couldn't be sure. I couldn't know for sure. He didn't stand next to me on that knife edge in Mary's parlor when I needed him most. He slipped away that evening, slipped home to New York. I waited the year to finally put everything behind me and start fresh. I waited for my season that had now arrived to make myself new. I waited for Edward to come back so that we could start over.

And now I lay in a bath of rapidly cooling water in a primitive western town, risking my clean start with Edward, unsure of Papa's truthfulness.

I could have been in Newport with Edward and Kitty preparing for my debut, starting my life over, a life without Mama. I had been so sure of Papa only a few weeks ago. Hadn't I told Grandpapa as much? I lifted my arm out of the water, all goose bumps now.

I hardly knew what to think in this moment. The mix of emotions and memories was overwhelming. How could I doubt Papa when he was all I had left until we found Mama? My confusion must have been a result of the exhaustion of this cross-country train trip.

I rose and dried myself and slipped on my nightgown. My inlaid jewelry box nested among my linens, and I opened it and lifted the handkerchief so carefully tucked at the bottom. The lavender of Mama's perfume was preserved in the close dark of the box, and I leaned over to breathe it in. Beneath the handkerchief was the cameo, which I had not yet worn on this trip; my mama's cameo, sacred to me. Beneath the cameo was a square of folded paper that I left untouched.

My fingers traced the cameo's face. Crafted of rose-and-cream shell and encased in a circlet of gold, it was the profile of a woman with a dreamy look. Though I'd often looked at Mama's cameo, I'd never realized the meaning of the image. The woman was a maenad, crowned with grape leaves, a wild woman. I remembered my Greek myths and saw the cameo anew. A bacchante. The bacchantes tore men apart; they killed for pleasure; they killed in an ecstasy of desire. They were wild.

I closed the box and placed it on the dresser next to the pitcher with its tiny blue flowers. Forget-me-nots.

I whispered prayers for Mina and Mama, for Papa and Uncle John. I thought of Edward, and felt my stomach tighten. Edward. I imagined him with Isabel. Worse yet, a sudden impression of Edward with Kitty sprang unbidden to my mind and my eyes filled with tears.

I dimmed the light and pulled aside the curtain, stepping away from the window, afraid to look to the street below. The farther streetlamps of Livingston shed a yellow glow and here and there light shone from windows.

I was lost and on the edge again. After I'd been so sure of things, the ground underneath my feet quavered. I had had enough of Papa's surprises. If Mama was here, he should tell me. And if Mama was not here, there was still a chance that she would return home to Newport and be waiting for me. Waiting to help me start the rest of my life.

I pictured her dripping with seawater, wrapping herself in a great warm blanket the color of seaweed, her wet hair in a long plait. I'd see her first, from my shingled tower with its long view, for I would steel myself to look. I'd stand there on watch even if it made my stomach clench and my legs go numb. And when I saw her, I'd run down the broad stairs and take her hand and not let go. Never let her go again. No matter what anyone said about her or about me. Together we'd prove that they all had small pinched minds and we'd rise above them and I would marry a great love and Mama and I would stand together at the edge of things and it would be all right.

I stood in the dark room shivering. I could dream.

But I wasn't sure I had that kind of courage, and proper young society women were not rebels. Proper young women did what was right and obeyed their fathers. Proper young women had seasons and debuts and were carefully courted. Proper young women held everything deep inside and smiled politely all the while. Proper young women weren't bohemian. They didn't wear red silk sashes and gallop about on horseback.

The mountains beyond the glass were invisible but they loomed high in my imagination and I felt the terror of the unknown, of edges over emptiness. I yanked the curtains shut, threw myself under the quilts, and lay in the shadowy darkness until the night chill and exhaustion stilled my mind and forced my eyes shut.

Chapter SEVEN

June 18, 1904

*But hush! What are our poor words
in the presence of these nobler secrets
of the wrestling and mounting spirit!*

—*Lady Rose's Daughter*, a novel by
Mrs. Humphry Ward, 1903

IN MY DREAMS, I REMEMBERED THAT DAY. MAMA HAD asked me to promise.

You have to promise me that you will not talk about this with your father.

Why not, Mama? You haven't yet kept your own promise and come back to me. Why should I keep mine to you?

But something—her disappearance, my sense of duty, my love for her, something—made me feel that this promise was sacred. I held that sacred trust for my mama. As the red light of dawn pushed fingers through my drapes and the forget-me-not pitcher reflected pink, I shivered in the bed under the mountainous quilt, waking in slow dream-time.

"This way!" blustered my uncle hours later "Train's due shortly!"

We left the comfort of the balcony over the Murray lobby, where upper-class passengers waited for the train to Gardiner, and made

our way across the dusty road, followed by the porters. A fresh
wind snapped the flags on the pole, and I snatched my hat before
it took flight. My other hand gripped my wool cape against the
bitter chill. I was grateful for the shelter when Uncle John ushered
us into the depot.

Two dozen tourists were already gathered inside. We settled on
oak benches; the windows rattled against the gusts. I tucked stray
strands of hair back up under my hat and fixed the pins. I'd rarely
felt such biting wind, even on the Atlantic cliffs in spring.

Papa sat on the bench opposite me, gazing up at the high ceiling
and stroking his mustache with two fingers. His wedding band
glinted on his left hand. He caught me watching him and gestured
at the book I held. "Are you enjoying it?"

"It's lovely. I'm on page ten." I picked up the book and pretended
to read.

Over the top of my book, I glanced around the waiting room.
On the streets outside I'd seen plains-dusted cowboys. But in the
depot we might as well have been at home in Newport.

Traveling couples were attired in fine worsted and cheviot,
in excursion suits and tweed coats. Ladies' maids and butlers
attended their patrons. Small children milled about, restrained by
nannies; the few older children were composed and prim. These
were certainly not the orphans of Omaha.

Papa's voice intruded. "It's a fine day, don't you think, Margaret?
Wonderful day."

I rested the book in my lap. I wanted to ask Papa right
now—I wanted to stand up and shake him and make him
tell me the truth, tell me what he knew about Mama—but I
restrained myself, biting my lip. Proper young women. "It's

fine. Splendid." I folded my hands. "I love the breeze."

He smiled, recognizing my sarcasm, lifting one corner of his mouth. "True, the wind is a bit brisk."

Uncle John laughed. "That's Montana. You have to put up with gales! Blue northers in the fall and chinooks in the winter—it doesn't matter, from north or south, the wind here'll take your hat to the poles!"

"Charming!" I smiled at my uncle. He smiled back at me, but his cheer faded fast, and he looked away. Whatever he knew about our trip, he was not about to reveal it to me.

"The sun is bright in this clear air." My father shielded his eyes against a beam of light.

I shifted impatiently. Small talk about the weather, my book, anything except the one subject I wished to discuss. I leaned against the hard oak bench, my back stiff with frustration. "Papa—"

He interrupted me. "Not now, Margaret."

"Maggie, we'll be in Yellowstone soon enough," said my uncle. He managed an awkward smile at me before he stood and walked away.

Papa gazed after him and would not meet my eyes. I shut my book and attempted to divert myself by watching the other arriving passengers.

A boisterous and jovial crowd of middle-class travelers bustled into the depot. After another minute the door slammed open again and two men pressed inside. The wind behind them ripped through the waiting room, kicking up bits of paper and dust and forcing those nearest the door to hang on to hats and coattails. The second man—young, maybe a little older than me—shoved the door closed.

The older man wore a rough wool coat and carried a canvas pack;

the younger man—the son, I decided, since they looked alike—a plaid wool shirt. I watched the younger man. My eyes were drawn to him.

He was tall enough to look over his father's shoulder. He had a kind of presence; he looked amused by something, like he was on the verge of a smile. His hair looked like it had been cut with a razor, but he had a strong jaw and broad shoulders. I squared my own, feeling a little blush creep up my neck. He was nice looking, or would have been if he'd been properly dressed. Put him in a suit, or even pressed trousers, and he would have made even self-possessed Kitty swoon.

"Jim!" Uncle John waved like a madman. People turned and stared. I shrank in my seat.

Uncle John grabbed Papa's arm. "Jim's with the Survey, he works in the Park. You've got to meet him. He'll be a great help. Jim!" Uncle John strode through the depot, heading straight for the son and his father, extending his hand, waving like crazy, and bellowing like a bull, to my utter humiliation. "Great to see you! Come meet my brother and niece!"

I couldn't believe it. Uncle John was making a scene. I shifted and turned away; my cheeks were on fire, although I wasn't sure if that was because of my uncle's behavior or the fact that he was dragging this particular young man in my direction. I buried my face in my book, wishing I could disappear behind the cover. I pretended to be lost in reading.

"Charlie Bennet, this is Jim Rowland. Good man! And young Tom here, his son." Uncle John clapped young Tom on the back. "Tom's got a bit of a reputation in Yellowstone as something of a rebel, though the park superintendent likes him just fine. He's got a natural love of animals, don't you, Tom?" Peeking over the

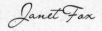

top of my book, I watched Tom's expression, the slight smile and sparkling eyes. He shot them right at me and I felt my heart give a quick jump as I ducked my chin.

His eyes were the color of the sea when it's stormy, that peculiar changeable gray with a hint of green.

"Margaret?" Papa's voice startled me. "Please say hello."

I lifted my eyes again slowly, avoiding Tom's direct gaze, and shook hands with his father before turning to him. I peered up from under my hat brim and saw that he was smiling at me. Those eyes. When he shook my hand with his firm grip, I felt the warmth even through my glove.

The three men settled into a discussion and I was left gawking up at Tom as the blood settled in my cheeks. One blonde lock fell across his forehead and he brushed it back with his hand without taking his eyes off mine. I'd never been the flirt that Kitty was, but I certainly never had a problem talking to boys. Until now. My tongue was tied in knots.

Tom, however, had no such problem. "I see you're reading Ward's latest." He pointed at my book. "What do you think?"

I didn't know what to think, since I hadn't made it past page ten. My mind was a muddle with him standing there. "It's very popular."

"That's important?"

I opened my mouth and closed it again; I thought I must have looked like a fish. The color rose high into my cheeks. I didn't know whether to resent his implication, or to feel like an idiot for not thinking it myself.

"Been to the Park before?" His tone was easy and friendly, and I relaxed a little.

"This is my first trip west of Philadelphia." I wanted to impress

Tom, Lord knows why. I sat up straight and adjusted my cuffs. Maybe if I let him know where I hailed from; maybe if I tried Kitty's approach. I knew my eyes were my best asset, so I tilted my head and met his gaze, full and frank. "We live in Newport. That's in Rhode Island; I'm sure you've heard of it? On the Atlantic coast. Though, naturally, we've done lots of traveling, just not out west. Several summers ago we were in Europe. And Saratoga—that's been a favorite getaway. So we do get around." I meant to sound like I was a sophisticated world traveler; I smiled at him.

I knew at once he was far from impressed. He raised his eyebrows. "Haven't been to Europe, myself. Or Saratoga either. Or for that matter, Rhode Island." He hesitated, his eyes bright. "Though I can read a map."

Tom was making fun of me in a quiet way, and I feared I came across as false and hollow. I squirmed. *Think of something*, I told myself. *Say something*. "Do you live here, in Livingston?"

"In Montana, but Bozeman is home."

"Bozeman." Now I really felt foolish; my ignorance was glaring. I had no idea where that was.

He changed the subject for me. "You're in for a treat."

The thought of finding Mama flashed through my mind and I spoke without thinking. "It might not be that simple," I said softly, half to myself. My face was on fire now. I looked up at him from under my hat brim. I really couldn't help it.

Tom seemed puzzled. "You're not going into Yellowstone?"

"Oh! That!" Of course Tom knew nothing about the reason for our trip. Had I ever been so hopeless? Edward was easy to impress; I'd never even had to try. With Tom I felt ridiculous. I'd completely lost my senses and yet I didn't even know him. My thoughts were random; my words tripped over themselves. "Yellowstone! Of course we are. Yes."

But then he smiled and I melted. My flustered worries floated away. He had a wonderful smile. "It's the most fantastic place on earth."

"My uncle said it's nicknamed 'Wonderland.'"

He grew almost animated. "Exactly! You'll see when you get there. The animals, the hot springs . . ." Finally I'd said something right. He was still standing and he was so tall I had to crane my neck to look up at him. That one lock of hair fell across his forehead. Under his measured gaze I felt like a little girl.

I searched for something else to say, anything that would make me sound knowledgeable and like less of an idiot. I thought about what I'd heard about animals in the west, since Uncle John said Tom liked them. "At least there aren't any wolves. They were so destructive, I've read. A problem for everyone. At least the government put that right."

A shadow crossed Tom's face. I knew right away I'd said some other stupid thing. My heart sank. All I wanted now was to impress Tom, and I didn't even truly understand why.

I tried a stupid question. "Are grizzly bears dangerous?"

Tom grinned, and my heart flipped. "You'll want to avoid them."

"Yes. Of course. I shall. I should hope I'm not that foolish." Just this foolish. Utterly unable to say the right thing to Tom. Since now it seemed he took my last words the wrong way.

"Sorry. I didn't mean an insult." He flushed a deep scarlet, and shifted his weight. "Yellowstone isn't a city park, that's all."

I was angry at myself now. I'd become a graceless bumbler. "I can take care of myself."

"I'm sure."

"I've done lots of touring. And I'm very strong. I play tennis all the time. And I ride. Horses, of course." Good heavens, what was wrong with me? My mouth was running like a leaky faucet. I looked up at Tom. His lips were curling into a smile he seemed to be trying to suppress. I was trying not to melt into the floor.

Uncle John's voice checked my further humiliation. "Great to see you!" The men were moving apart. Mr. Rowland, a pleasant-looking man with Tom's wonderful smile, tipped his hat to me.

Tom nodded to me, his own ready smile lighting up his face. "Nice meeting you, Margaret Bennet of Newport, Rhode Island, world traveler. Maybe we'll cross paths again in the Park." He started to turn away, then turned back to me, and my heart did a little flip again as his eyes met mine. "Just a thought—watch out for highway robbers when you take the Tour." And with that, he broke into an outright grin.

I stared as he and his father moved away through the milling crowd. "What did he mean, Uncle John?"

My uncle gave me a startled glance. "What? Robbers? Not to worry. It's rare." My uncle and Papa exchanged a dark look. "There are soldiers all through the Park. Why, the fort's right at Mammoth!" He leaned toward me with an amiable wink. "Young Tom was pulling your leg."

But I felt his and Papa's uneasiness and filed that away. Taking the Tour—whatever that was—was not likely. We had other plans, and not much time. I squared my shoulders. In that moment of feeling bewitched by Tom I hadn't forgotten why we were here—to find Mama and bring her back to Newport.

My eyes went back to the Rowlands. Tom was one of the tallest people in the room. He was surely taller than Edward. I watched him brush away that lock of hair, the way he moved, athletic yet graceful. He looked up, and our eyes met over the crowd. I dropped my head in a flash, my cheeks on fire.

I gripped my book, staring blankly at the page for a few minutes, then I reread the same sentence on page ten at least a hundred times.

Chapter EIGHT ※ ※ ※ ※ ※ ※ ※ ※ ※ ※

June 18, 1904

> *I went to the woods because I wished to live deliberately,*
> *to front only the essential facts of life, and see if*
> *I could not learn what it had to teach, and not,*
> *when I came to die, discover that I had not lived.*

—*Walden; or, Life in the Woods,*
Henry David Thoreau, 1854

THE TRAIN LUMBERED SOUTH TO GARDINER, THROUGH what Uncle John said was called "The Gate of the Mountains."

"Paradise Valley," he continued, his hands opening to the landscape. "That's how it looks, doesn't it? Like paradise?"

I admitted nothing, swaying with the rhythm of the train. But my eyes were drawn to the view. A blanket of clouds hovered over the summits, jagged crests spearing the sky. Mist hung like pale smoke over the deep blue-green forests. The lower slopes were the iridescent green of spring grass, laced with yellow flowers; rolling foothills were dotted with boulders like figs in a pudding. Bald eagles perched in the cottonwoods along the river. My book lay open, unread, in my lap.

Then my mind wandered from the landscape to the realization that a few rows behind me sat Tom Rowland. I'd watched carefully where he sat as we boarded the train, though I'd tried my best not to let on that I was looking at him.

My stomach fluttered. This was unexpected. Except for Edward, no other boy had impressed me. And Edward—he suddenly seemed to pale now. He was like a little boy, whereas Tom seemed so much older. My stomach fluttered again as I thought of Tom's clear eyes, of his easy smile. I searched for any loose curls to tuck up under my hat. Not that he'd be looking. My sparkling conversation could hardly have left a favorable impression.

". . . open less than a month!" I heard my uncle say. "You'll be amazed, Charlie, at the genius of this fellow. What a privilege to work at his side. Even for me, with my humble skills."

"Nonsense, John. There's no finer finish carpenter. I'm eager to call on you myself." Papa twisted the wedding band on his finger, around and around, his eyes glittering with excitement, more excitement and happiness than he'd shown in many months. My stomach fluttered again, but this time with renewed hope.

I was sure that Papa's happiness was evidence that we were near to finding Mama. We were close now, close to realizing my dream. Soon we'd be a family again. This was the last stage of a journey that had begun almost a year ago, begun with anguish and grief, and might end—today even!—with reunion.

I put my hand to my throat. Today, on my way into Paradise, I wore Mama's cameo. Somehow it seemed right.

I enjoyed the first half hour of the journey, thinking about Mama and watching the landscape roll past. Then Paradise folded in on itself. The valley narrowed, the clouds lowered, and the train climbed up along the edge of the cliff face. I glanced out the window just as we started to climb. The Yellowstone River lay right below us, dropping into a deep gorge, foaming and churning. My breath caught at the sight and my head spun. Between the drifting clouds and wild water, the train hung as if suspended. I shrank back into the train seat and my legs went limp with fear.

I tried to look at Papa but he was staring out the window. I couldn't even form words. My mouth was sandpaper. I shrank farther into the upholstery, trying to melt into the leather and find some purchase, clutching the armrests. From deep in my gut a hole formed. It was as if there were no train and it was me, alone, hanging over the void. Then I felt the train buck and sway over the nothingness, and I shut my eyes fast against what I knew was certain death.

I clamped my eyes shut, and didn't dare open them again until Uncle John tapped my shoulder. "Margaret? We're here!"

I sucked in a breath. The train car was empty except for the three of us. I felt a moment's disappointment that Tom was gone, and then Papa took my hand and helped me off the train and onto the platform. We walked, me in my woozy state, at the end of the crowd of tourists, followed by porters hauling our trunks, and made our way to the line of stagecoaches standing ready against the long curve of the Gardiner platform to take us under the great stone arch and into Yellowstone.

FOR THE BENEFIT AND ENJOYMENT OF THE PEOPLE. I read the words carved into the stone from where we stood, waiting to board our coach. I also saw Tom and his father in a private wagon already on their way through the arch. I sighed. Maybe Tom and I would cross paths again before Papa and I left for home. Before we left for home with Mama, I reminded myself, and felt a rush that overwhelmed all other thoughts.

Papa helped me into our Tally-ho coach. Our coach held eighteen passengers plus our driver, who wore a rough, gray duster. Many of the passengers sat on the roof. I was grateful Papa secured a spot for us inside as I rubbed my gloved hands together. Small pockets of snow nestled in the hollows of the rolling hills that hunched against the sky.

The coach was drawn by six matched white horses, and I thought with a pang about Ghost. I missed our rides, the freedom I felt on his back.

"Isn't it amazing?" said Uncle John as the coach made its way through the arch.

"Amazing. So this is Yellowstone?"

"Almost! Through the arch and up the road!"

In truth, I thought it was a little overbearing, that arch, looming over us. We were at our destination and yet Papa still hadn't revealed anything to me. I would still have to be properly obedient to his whims. Now that we were on our way up the winding road into the Park, I was ready for this journey to end, ready to bring Mama home to Newport. As we drew away, I looked back. Paradise Valley, wrapped in clouds, pinched shut like a vise. The arch itself reminded me of a medieval gate—I could almost hear the doors clang shut and the key turn, with a *snick*, in the lock.

"The president himself dedicated it last year. He was very enthusiastic about his visit to Yellowstone." Uncle John leaned toward me. "He shook my hand."

I raised my eyebrows.

"I was repairing some of the trim in the lobby of the National Hotel in Mammoth—that's how Mr. Reamer found me—and when President Roosevelt came through, he stopped and admired my work. And he shook my hand." Uncle John beamed.

"How exciting." I felt sorry for my uncle, so awestruck by a handshake. Isabel had a stuffed "Teddy" bear that was a gift from Roosevelt himself. I would see Isabel, if not her bear, again soon. With our family together again, I'd show her that I was worthy of respect and not her snobbish disdain. I sank back against the leather bench of the coach and smiled.

The rhythm of the coach's movements lulled me and I closed my eyes. My other senses sharpened: the smell of horses, of leather, of dust; the creak and groan of the carriage; the murmur of voices; the rock and sway.

The carriage shuddered violently, jolting me from sleep. The horses at the front of the team reared and neighed as the driver pulled up. I opened my eyes wide now and grasped the edge of the open window. A woman screamed and the men shouted exclamations.

"Bear!" someone yelled.

A bear! My eyes searched the landscape; my body tensed. I tightened my hold, fingers curled over the wood. The driver cursed as he strained to control the horses. For one awful moment, I thought the entire coach would tip sideways, top-heavy as it was with passengers. A swift and gripping fear coursed through my every muscle. The coach righted at last. Yet something else ran through me: not relief, but a longing so primitive that it worked against common sense. It pulled me out, calling to me, drawing me from the safe confines of the coach.

I had to see the bear.

I thrust my head out the window, defying rational thought. There. Just off the road, no more than twenty feet away, staring at the coach with leaden eyes. Its head was massive—too massive for its tiny, round ears. Its sand-colored coat ruffled in the wind, and it sprouted an enormous hump on its shoulders, like a growth.

"Grizzly," said the man sitting opposite me, in a quiet undertone.

Grizzly! I might have been at the edge of a cliff, my legs were so wobbly, yet I did not feel paralyzed, as I did when encountering a precipice. The bear and I locked eyes. I shrank back. It sat up, lifting its nose into the air in tiny, quick jerks. Its eyes were surprisingly small, and flat brown. We stared at each other for a long moment. I searched its eyes, but they were a void.

The animal was not like Ghost, whose thoughts I could read. There was nothing behind the bear's gaze but raw instinct. It had no soul. It watched me with those tiny, flat, animal eyes, with a deep malice that I could feel in my gut. The bear waited for me and me alone. I knew that it was chasing the air for my scent.

"Ah!" The sound escaped me almost involuntarily, and as if in response to my cry, the bear grunted. It swung its massive head back and forth and took a step forward. Its eyes met mine; sure as sure, it read my thoughts. I knew I was reading the bear as well—torn between fear and a desire to know more, to probe deep into its psyche.

The driver strained to control the terrified horses and he urged them forward. They pulled off at last and the carriage started with a jolt. We moved away, leaving the bear behind as it followed us— me—with its eyes.

I craned out the window, looking back.

"What you do," said the man opposite, "is lie down and remain still."

The bear stood on its hind legs. I felt its call as if I were a wild thing. The taste of fear rose into my mouth but I still wanted to see the bear.

The man repeated himself, leaning toward me and blocking the window to catch my attention. "Did you hear? Completely still."

"Excuse me?" What did this irritating man want? I tried to look past him but it was too late. I leaned back in frustration, breathing as if I'd been running.

"If you are out in the bush and come upon a bear," he said, flicking his hand, impatient. "You lie still and play dead. The bear sees you as a threat, but if you play dead, it will merely sniff at you and move on." His cultivated English accent matched his bearing.

I goggled at him, wondering why I would need this piece of trivia.

He smiled, revealing a gap between his front teeth, beneath the curve of his mustache. "Unless, of course, it's hungry." He extended his hand. "George Graybull." I shook it and then withdrew, gazing out the window.

The bear's eyes burned in my memory; something about it had imprinted my soul. I tried to slow my breathing. I spoke in a whisper, to myself. "It looked right at me."

"What? The bear?" He had heard me, that Graybull. "Nonsense. Bears have dreadful eyesight. Couldn't have seen you at that distance. Just sniffing the air." He caught my skeptical glance. "Been on a number of safaris. Hunted throughout the west. I know animals."

I smiled politely. Uncle John leaned over. "Exciting to see a bear this early in Yellowstone, eh, Margaret? Unusual!"

The coach climbed higher, and then the landscape opened into a series of rolling hills, until the road wound in tight spirals. I leaned with the coach as it swayed, and thought about the bear.

I knew animals. I knew animals well. I closed my eyes and remembered the feel of Ghost's shoulder beneath my hand, the ripple of his muscle when I pressed my cheek against his neck. The bond I shared with him, the way he knew me. I thought again about the bear reading my thoughts and knew there was a difference.

I opened my eyes again and looked out over the high mountains into which we climbed with a steady pace. Soon I'd be back with Ghost; soon I'd be back with Mama.

My thoughts were interrupted again when I realized that George Graybull's eyes were fixed on me. I squirmed, uncomfortable under his gaze, and color crept into my cheeks. I twisted in my seat, trying to avoid his piercing eyes, and leaned against the wood windowsill.

Neat, ordered, frame buildings capped with red roofs signaled our arrival at Fort Yellowstone. The coach drew past the fort and I looked up the hill.

"Is that smoke?"

"Steam, Margaret! You're in Mammoth Hot Springs."

"Hot springs." Saratoga's springs were mineral, not steaming. I gawked, amazed.

The National Hotel, a grand wood structure, loomed on our right. Clouds of steam rose beyond it. Elk grazed on the lawn only yards away from us and I couldn't help feeling transported into another world. Our coach stopped before the National and, following the other jabbering tourists, I turned to enter the lobby.

Papa put his hand on my arm, held me back. "Not here, Margaret." Uncle John collected our belongings on the covered porch, off to one side of the other passengers' things.

"Not here?" I stopped, confused. "But, where . . ."

"I've booked rooms for you in the Cottage Hotel." Uncle John nodded in the direction of a ramshackle log building. "It's very quaint." His smile was uneasy.

"Quaint?" It looked like a thin-walled box compared with the imposing beauty of the National. "What's going on, Papa?"

"The National is more than we need right now."

The other tourists had already gone inside the hotel. George Graybull glanced our way as he entered, clearly taking in my look of horror, and watched my uncle, who moved our belongings on a trolley toward the Cottage. Graybull tipped his hat to me, but his eyes betrayed his surprise. We looked like first-class travelers, but I could see his doubt now as we headed toward the Cottage Hotel.

We *were* first-class travelers. I straightened my back and turned to my father.

"Papa, I don't understand. Why are we not staying here?"

He cleared his throat. His eyes met mine, and what I saw made my stomach clench. His eyes were like the bear's, flat and unreadable. "Margaret. The National is more than we can afford. Let's go inside. I need to tell you something."

The air left my lungs and the ground shifted beneath my feet. I followed my father into the Cottage Hotel as if I were in a dream. No, not a dream, a nightmare. I knew, knew from his eyes, from his rigid shoulders, that something was very wrong. We couldn't afford the National. That's what he'd just said. How was that possible? Things were clearly not as he had led me to believe. And what of Mama?

My feet took step after step after my father, but they moved by something other than my own will. And I willed my heart somewhere else—over the gorge of Paradise, perhaps in the thicket with the grizzly, or in the station with Tom—because if my heart was in my chest at that moment, I felt sure it was about to break.

Chapter NINE ❈ ❈ ❈ ❈ ❈ ❈ ❈ ❈ ❈ ❈

June 18, 1904

There reigned for her, absolutely, during these vertiginous moments, that fascination of the monstrous, that temptation of the horribly possible, which we so often trace by its breaking out suddenly, lest it should go further, in unexplained retreats and reactions.

—*The Golden Bowl*, Henry James, 1904

"THERE'S NOTHING FOR US TO RETURN TO," PAPA SAID. I could not see his face. His voice spoke of finality. "It's gone."

My free hand tightened on the plain, wood bedpost. I stared at him, at his profile framed against the light from the window of my room, taking in his words. I was stunned to silence.

"I let you think this trip was about finding your mother. I had to, or you might have resisted."

"Mama isn't here? There's . . . nothing?" My throat was so tight I couldn't swallow.

"I couldn't let your grandparents take you away from me, Margaret." His voice was soft. I knew he meant that he needed me, but he had betrayed me completely. I only felt my own pain.

"You lied. You lied to me. All this time, you let me believe . . ." I choked, trying to control my voice. "You lied to me about Mama."

He didn't answer. "I've had to sell everything. We are bankrupt, Maggie. We could no longer make it in Newport. This isn't a sightseeing trip. We're going to make a new home, here, in Yellowstone."

Bankrupt. Penniless. Like a hot poker spearing me right through the middle. My guts contracted. The strange room around me spun and I held the bedpost tighter, leaning hard against it so I wouldn't faint. "We're not going back to Newport? We're supposed to stay . . . here?" I was sure I had misheard him. Misunderstood what he was saying. Newport was our home . . . my home.

"We're not going back. I've sold it, everything."

"Our house, the furniture?" My voice rose as I became hysterical. "Papa! It was my house. It was my home. It was Mama's home. How could you . . . What have you done?"

"I did what I had to, Maggie." He turned slightly but still did not meet my eyes. "Your grandparents would have taken you away from me."

"And you should have let them! Why didn't you let them?" I threw my hands up over my face, trying to keep myself from screaming. The image of Kitty came into my mind, her words about my grandparents. "Do you understand what you've done? I have to go back for my debut. It's all planned. Kitty's planned it. I can't back out. It's my only chance!" He would have to see reason, simply have to.

"I've canceled your debut, Maggie."

"You—what?" My body shook as I grasped the full meaning of Papa's actions.

"Canceled. We couldn't afford it."

"What about my future? What about me, my prospects? Without a debut, I can't find a husband, I can't build a life! Did you think to ask me what I wanted? What I had to say about this?" With one sweeping gesture, my father had destroyed my dreams, my hopes, and my future. "What about my life? No one will marry me! No one will even *look* at me unless I'm properly introduced into society. Did you think about that? Did you?"

"It all fell apart. You must have known, you must have seen it coming. I didn't hold together after your mother . . ." He paused and his voice grew softer still. My fingers gripped the bedpost so hard I could have crushed the wood to pulp. "Your grandfather was right. I didn't take care of things after your mother died."

"She's not dead!" I shouted. I didn't care who heard me, I didn't care about acting like a proper lady—there was no one here who mattered. "You let me think she was here. You let me think that that was what this trip was about. You told me you had a surprise for me, that Uncle John had news."

"He does." Papa's face was invisible. "Just not the news you imagined."

Imagined? I hadn't imagined Papa's lies, his betrayal . . . I leaned against the bedpost, clutching it with both hands. "How could you?" Fat tears welled in my eyes. He'd not only destroyed my future; he'd taken my mother away again. "I want Mama! I want to go home! I want my things, my life, my home!" Anger pushed through my misery and I dropped my voice. "You lied to me."

"Maggie." He spoke in a whisper.

Anger gave me strength. I paced the floor of the small room, my hands balled into fists. "You lied." What would become of me now? I had been preparing my entire life for a future that no longer existed, a future that Papa had stolen from me. "And what about school? I have another year of school left. Where will I attend school?" I threw my arm out. "Way out here in the middle of *nowhere*?" I shouted the last word.

He sighed. "Lifting your voice is not only inappropriate, Margaret, it is unladylike." As if he had the nerve to speak to me of what was appropriate. I seethed, but he had silenced me for the moment. "I've arranged for you to attend private school in Helena come fall. I need to make a fresh start. This is an opportunity—a change!" He turned to face me. He had the audacity to smile. Why, he looked downright thrilled. Now I could see where his earlier happiness had its roots. "There are things waiting for us here."

I trembled with furious, barely contained rage. I'd lost everything, all the things I'd been dreaming about. My home, my mother, my future, my friends . . . I grew rigid. "I won't. I will not stay. Send me home to Grandpapa and Grandmama. Tomorrow. On the first train east."

He shook his head. "No."

"Grandpapa and Grandmama will take me in." They would— they had said they would.

"I will not send you, and you have no means by which to leave." He stared at me, dispassionate.

My stomach lurched. He was right. I had no money, and even if I did, I could not board a train alone, as an unaccompanied woman. It would be impossible, improper. I was trapped here, completely at his mercy. I hated him for what he had done. I narrowed my eyes at him, but he'd turned his back on me again.

"I've taken a new job here." His voice lifted with enthusiasm. "I'll be working with Robert Reamer, the architect, on his projects in Yellowstone. This will be our new home." He emphasized *our*; it would never be my home.

"I hate Yellowstone." I said it in a quiet voice, so thick with anger the words fell like bricks. Yellowstone. An unholy place, the Indians had said. It was hell to me. "You've deceived me."

He seemed not to hear me. "The rest of your things are here already. I shipped them here, Maggie."

I had been trying to hold together the pieces of my world for months, since Mama left, and now they scattered like dust. I sank onto the bed. No matter how much I protested his actions, I had no options, no choice in the matter. I'd supported him, only to have him betray me. I'd lost everything.

Ah—everything? A thought crossed my mind, and I couldn't control the waver in my voice. "Papa. What about Ghost?" Oh, please, not Ghost.

"You did a fine job with him, Margaret. He'll fetch a high price at auction."

Now tears spilled unchecked onto the navy wool of my skirt, leaving dark, swelling blots. "You're selling my Ghost? *My* Ghost." I'd never again ride Ghost, bury my face in his mane, or feel his soft breath on my hand. Just like that, my Ghost, my truest friend, gone from my life. I sucked in a sob and bit my lip hard, my shoulders shaking. My father had taken my entire life from me. "You've . . ." I couldn't talk, I could scarcely breathe.

"I'll need your help with my papers. The way you offered. The way your mother helped me."

He wanted my help after what he'd done? He had to be joking, but looking at him, I realized he was serious. His insensitivity knew no bounds. Mama helped him all those years. Did he treat her with as much disdain, as much contempt for her feelings, as he did me? Perhaps that's why she behaved as she did. Perhaps that's why she left us.

In my mind, I saw the table in his studio in those early years, spread with papers. The straight-backed oak chairs, soft light filtering through the buttery leaded-glass skylight. Mama, bent over the table, gazing up at Papa with a look I couldn't fathom, while I stood hovering in the doorway, Mina clucking behind.

Then the next awful realization hit me. I couldn't even phrase the full question. "Mina?"

He sighed and his shoulders sagged. "I had to let her go. I had to let them all go. Mina, Jonas. All of them."

I shut my eyes. I clutched at the bedpost and leaned my forehead on my hand. I couldn't breathe. Jonas. And Mina. She had been the closest thing to a mother since Mama left. Now I understood the strange events surrounding our departure, Mina's expression, Jonas's behavior when we left home. I felt both stupid and lost. I was all alone now. More alone than ever in my life. Oh, Mina . . .

"And what if she comes back?" My voice came out a croak. I did not mean Mina.

"Maggie, please. Let's put it behind us." Papa walked to the door and paused. "It's a special place, Maggie, this Yellowstone. You'll like it. This will be a good change for us. Some wonderful things may come of it." His eyes glittered again with an excitement I didn't share. "You'll see." He left my room, closing the door with a soft click.

My room. A dreary, threadbare, green coverlet draped the bed. A small oak table served as both dresser and writing desk. It was clean, but spare.

The pitcher and washbasin were plain porcelain; if I'd been less restrained, they would already be smashed to pieces, smashed a thousand times against these flimsy lath-and-plaster walls. But a proper lady didn't throw things, didn't display such emotion. Wasn't that what he had said? And I was a proper young lady, was I not?

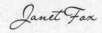

In two steps I'd reached the dresser. I picked up the pitcher and dashed it to the floor. The sound surely carried to every room in the hotel.

I stared at the mess I'd made, the scattered shards, my one moment of defiance oozing away. I sank to the floor.

I took a deep breath, and held it, and when I let it out I let my tears fall. My father's cruelty was too awful to be true. I wept until I ran out of tears. I rubbed my face with my palms until it was dry and pulled my hair down, yanking out the pins and letting my hair fall over my shoulders, clutching the pins in my fist.

I sat motionless, working to still the writhing in my stomach. My father had taken away everything I cared about in this world. I didn't think it was possible for me to hate anyone more than I hated him in that moment. My throat jammed with grief; my eyes squeezed tight. How could I put this behind me? Ghost, Mina, my home, they were gone . . . But Mama? I would never give up. Never. She was alive, I knew it. And if she wasn't here in Yellowstone, as Papa had led me to believe, then I was sure she'd return to Newport. I would find her even if I had to cross the continent to Newport on foot.

I sat for a long quiet time before I could determine my next move.

I decided I had to take care of things in proper fashion. Maybe I'd done something the wrong way, and I was being punished. Like a child's game, I reasoned. I'd jinxed myself. I would take even greater care now to mind the rules. It seemed important to tend to ordinary things; the ordinary seemed to now possess uncommon power.

There would be no more red-as-blood sashes in my future.

I unpacked my traveling trunk, and placed my hairbrush and jewelry box carefully on the table. I tidied the broken pitcher, sweeping the pieces into a neat pile. I brushed the dust from my hat. I removed Mama's cameo from my throat and set it carefully on the dresser. Each thing I did, I murmured a prayer that this was all a dreadful mistake; each movement I made I whispered a hateful curse at Papa.

Then I sat down at the table to begin a letter.

My dearest Kit. You won't believe what has happened.

I stopped and looked at the rugged hillside framed by my window. I put aside the letter to Kitty and took out another sheet of paper. I had to act, had to set wheels in motion to undo Papa's mistakes. This called for drastic action. I had no idea what the outcome might be, but I began to write again.

Dearest Grandpapa. I am in urgent need of your help.

I glanced up, searching the air for the words that might compel my rescue. I was treading a fine line, both disobeying my father and seeking help from those who might confine me even further. But it was my only option. Once again, the question sprang to my mind: What did I want? Freedom? Respect from society? A future?

My grandparents would secure my social standing, my inheritance, and give me a lovely debut into Newport society and all that entailed, but certainly not my freedom. They would dictate everything, from what I wore to whom I married.

I was trapped. I gazed through tears around the stark foreign room that contained me. If I had seen that the windows sported bars, I would not have been surprised.

Chapter TEN

June 19, 1904

Treacherous in calm, and terrible in storm,
Who shall put forth on thee,
Unfathomable Sea?

—"Time," *Posthumous Poems,*
Percy Bysshe Shelley, 1821

I WOKE WITH A START IN THE MIDDLE OF THE NIGHT AND
had no idea where I was. For a moment my terror was so deep that
I stopped breathing.

Then I heard the sound that must have awakened me, coming
in through the open window. It was a cough, throaty and animal.
Deer coughed like that, I knew, although this was a more full-bodied
sound. Elk, maybe? I closed my eyes. I'd been carted off to this
alien place where everything seemed huge and overbearing; even the
animals were larger and more frightening.

Carted off . . . I knew. I had to stop blaming Papa. I knew whose
fault it was. Mine.

I squeezed my eyes tight against the memory that came unbidden
and would not be suppressed. I lay in this strange bed, worlds away
from everything I cared about, and remembered it all. Mama's
breakdown at Mary's ball. The blood that stained her white gown;
the stares that followed me from Mary's house.

But worse, I remembered how I behaved the morning after Mama's breakdown. The dreadful morning last August when I saw my mother for the last time.

I'd huddled in bed that morning until the sun had slipped past noon. Crash and boom, crash and boom. I'd heard the noise throughout my nightmares. As I lay drowsy in the midday heat, I recognized the sound of storm-raised surf and thought of the water that battered the cliffs, and the steep descent into darkness that would greet a misplaced foot on those treacherous paths, and I shuddered fully awake.

Another sound intruded: the soft sweep of the door to my room. Mama.

She moved across the room to sit in a chair opposite me. Her arms were wrapped in linen bandages. On one I saw the brown stain of dried blood. I was surprised to see that she looked quite herself. Anger and humiliation filled me for what she did the night before, the scene she made at Mary's ball. Any sympathy I might have felt left me, and what I felt then was anger and shame.

I slipped out of bed and pulled on my dressing gown. My voice trembled. "Mama. How could you act like that? In front of everyone."

She folded her arms and tugged at the bandages with her fingers, but her eyes were unguarded and calm. "Maggie, I've come to a realization. It's time I went to take care of something. I should have done it long ago."

The rumble and crash of waves filled the room. I hugged myself hard. I wanted to hug her, but she'd made that impossible. I wrestled with my surging emotions: confusion, anger, shame. Love.

Her restless fingers worked the bandages. "Many years ago I made a mistake. I've been paying for it ever since."

I interrupted. "Was I the mistake?" My heart felt like it would crack in two.

She hung her head and her loose hair swung past her shoulders. "No, Maggie. You've been the one right thing in my life."

Crash and boom, the ocean pounded the shore. The smell of seaweed, raw and salt rank, filled the air. As she tugged at the bandages that wrapped her arms, I saw again the scene in Mary's parlor, Mama's crazed expression and the bloodstains on her white gown. She would be completely rejected by society now, and so would I. Tears filled my eyes. "Why did you do this to me?"

"I can't explain everything. Maggie, understand. Too often I've done what was expected of me instead of following my heart. In one important way I did only what was expected of me, and that was a huge mistake." She looked up at me, her cheeks hollow and dark. "Don't make this mistake, Maggie. Don't make my mistakes. Follow your heart."

My heart could not be followed; it was broken. Didn't she know? My life was unraveling before my very eyes because of her madness. My pent-up misery exploded. "Is your heart telling you to act as if you don't care about me or Papa, to act insane? Fine. Have your mad fits! Pay no attention to what people think. Go ahead, ruin any chance I might have for happiness. You don't think about anyone but yourself. You certainly don't think about me." The last words came out in a strangled sob.

Mama's face shut and she stared at the floor. "I love you, Maggie." She said it in a whisper. Her hands opened as if she would reach for me; her hands, like birds, fluttered and then dropped and landed in her lap. "In time, you'll understand." It was as if she aged a thousand years in that single heartbeat. She struggled out of the chair, pushing herself up with terrible effort, holding on to the arms of the chair for support. Her robe fell open and I saw the bathing costume underneath.

"Mama! Where are you going dressed like that?"

"I'm taking a walk. Maybe a swim."

"On a day like this? After the storm last night, the breakers will be over the seawall! You can't swim in that ocean. Are you insane?" I stood, facing her and shaking. "Well? Are you?" She must be. I was shocked and terrified—on a clear day, swimming in the ocean could be risky. After a storm, on a day like this, it was true madness.

She turned her head away from me.

"Fine. Go on, then. I don't care. I don't care if I never see you again." It was a lie. I threw myself on my bed, my stomach clenching with smothered sobs.

I didn't mean it. I wanted her to stay. I hoped she would gentle me with her touch as she had only a few months earlier. I hoped that my agony would keep her from leaving, would bring her back to me. I needed Mama so much, I needed her love.

Her voice wobbled from swallowing her own tears. "Next to my cameo, on my dresser, there's a note for you, Maggie. For *you*. Not for your father. You must promise you won't tell him about this. Once you've read what I have to say, maybe you'll hear me out. I will be back. That's my promise."

I pulled my pillow over my head and heard her leave the room.

I didn't try to stop her. Maybe if I'd thrown myself at her feet and begged her to stay with me, she would have. But I didn't. And she left.

It was my fault, then. I'd told her to go. I'd driven her out. She left my room last August and never returned, despite her promise. The consequence of my actions was that now I lay in a cold, dark room a million, million miles away from my home and my dreams. That I'd become my father's prisoner was my own fault, my own burden.

I had so few choices now, in that room in Yellowstone. Mama had told me to follow my heart, so I didn't make her same mistakes. I didn't know what my heart said, or what she'd meant by her mistakes. All I knew was that everything I cared about was gone and I saw no options before me. I couldn't leave Yellowstone of my own accord, but I couldn't stay here, either. And if my grandparents took me in, I would regain social standing, but I'd marry the man they chose and never find the love I longed for, the love I described to Kitty.

The room darkened and the night grew silent and colder, as if the sharp edges of the high peaks drew around me like living walls.

Chapter ELEVEN ❧ ❧ ❧ ❧ ❧ ❧ ❧ ❧ ❧

[He] ascended a low mountain in the neighborhood of his camp—and behold! The whole country beyond was smoking with the vapor from boiling springs, and burning with gases, issuing from small craters, each of which was emitting a sharp whistling sound.

—*The River of the West,* by Mrs. Francis Fuller Victor, 1870, describing the 1829 experience of trapper Joe Meek

I HUNG ON TO THE BRIM OF MY STRAW CLOCHE FOR DEAR life as we trailed up the path. Even with the ribbon tied firmly under my chin, it threatened to sprout wings. The sun shot, then faded, then glinted through streaming clouds. At least the air was warmer now, after another cold night.

I'd refused to leave my room for an entire day. I'd slept . . . paced . . . and slept again. That second morning, nothing had changed, but I'd grown weary of my dreadful room and was tired of staring at four pale walls. When Papa knocked on my door and offered a stroll through the hot springs, I assented.

"Time to get to know Yellowstone, Mags."

I bristled, but held my tongue. He was uncomfortable with me. Fine. I avoided him. But otherwise he seemed excited, asking Uncle John questions about everything around us. My anger at him had dissipated a little until I thought again about Ghost and Mina, and

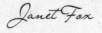

my abandoned season. How he'd lured me here with expectations and promises.

"Don't breathe in the fumes!" Uncle John seemed cheerful, and I was sure he was oblivious to my situation. "Toxic, you know." He pointed out the various rocks, naming them for us, giving us a brief history of the geology. The white, limy stuff was sinter, deposited from the springs. The colors of the pools came from bacteria. The entire park was a huge volcano, and the hot springs were water that boiled like a kettle at the surface above the magma. "Imagine!"

I did. My imagination told me that everything here was deadly. Toxic fumes, hidden magma. It was so apt to my life that this Yellowstone was a place of death. A damp vapor curled in my direction and I put my handkerchief to my mouth. It smelled noxious, like rotten eggs.

I walked rapidly away from the smell—and from my father and uncle—and turned to climb the broad and gentle path to the next terraces, my head down.

"Hello, again."

I looked up, squinting. Tom. Tom Rowland, who made me feel like an embarrassed dolt. Whose eyes I could not forget. I hadn't expected to see him again, much less so soon after our meeting. Much less right after I'd lost everything important in my life. The pleasure that I felt on coming upon him was welcome and it surprised me that I felt happiness. My heart beat faster. I looked up at him, standing above me on the slope, and wondered what he thought about me. Could he see the shadow of destruction that I trailed now?

He stepped down to stand next to me. I tried to pull myself together. I felt foolish and fluttery in his presence—more than I'd ever been with Edward. In comparison, Edward seemed pale and bland, my feelings about him almost childish. I smiled like an idiot at Tom until I thought he would see me as the very picture of silliness.

He gave me a swift grin and asked, "Finish your book?"

"Yes," I lied. I stuffed the handkerchief into my sleeve and hoped my hat would please, please stay put. "No. Actually, the book was boring."

He raised his eyebrows. "How do you like it here?"

"It's smelly." He laughed, and I smiled. "But . . ." I looked around. For all of the hellish aspects, there was an unearthly beauty. Streaks of bright green and yellow painted the white sinter rims of steaming pools, whose centers were a clear pale blue. "All right. It's beautiful. Terrifying, but beautiful."

"This is nothing. Just wait! You and your pa heading out on the Tour today?"

"No." I stared over the milky-white terraces, avoiding his eyes, plucking at my gloves. Whatever the Tour was, it would cost money. Which apparently we had none of. I sighed. "What is the Tour, anyway?"

"It's a tour through the entire Park. You'll see it all, all the geysers, hot springs—with any luck, animals, too."

"Ah." I recalled the bear, and my odd attraction and fear. I adjusted my hat, avoiding Tom's eyes. My new status as poverty-stricken non-tourist embarrassed me. Though I knew I'd have time to see this place, I wanted Tom to think otherwise.

"How's the National?" he asked. "It's new. I've only been in the lobby."

"Lovely." I wished he would leave off his questions. I didn't want to tell him we were staying at the Cottage. It was humiliating. Only two days ago I'd thought myself above him, in his humble clothing, above so many of the others in the Livingston Depot. And now . . .

It was bad enough when people of my own class rejected me because of my mother. But now I didn't belong to any class. I fidgeted with my gloves again and bit my lip.

"Tom!" A voice rang out across the springs.

"Coming!" he shouted back. "My pa. I'm giving him a hand."

"Oh!" I followed Tom's gaze up the path. "What's he doing?" Tom's father leaned over a terrace edge, chipping away at the rock. "Ah! Does he sell souvenirs, then? That must be a good way to make a living. I wondered how someone might make a living here. That's very clever, selling bits of rock." I thought I was being clever myself, until I met Tom's eyes.

He looked at me as if I'd grown scales. "Are you really as stuck-up as you sound?"

My insides froze solid. I wished I could teach my tongue to do the same.

"My father's with the Geological Survey." Tom's words were clipped. "It's his job to collect samples. And, no, you can't just whack away at the rocks collecting souvenirs. This is a protected park."

Now I saw the soldier who stood near Tom's father. "Right. I see. I'm sorry." My words tripped out of my mouth. "I'm an idiot. A complete and utter idiot." Which was true. I was acting like a full-blown fool. I had no business assuming anything about anyone's social status, considering what had recently become of mine. His words stung. I cupped my hand beneath my hat brim to hide the shame written on my face.

I dropped my hand and blurted, "But I'm not stuck-up. You don't need to say that, because I'm not." And I met his eyes with a level gaze.

That errant lock of hair fell across his forehead. "You're right.

I'm sorry." He looked at his hands that worked the canvas bag he held, kneading it like dough. "I think we got off on the wrong foot here. Can I make it up to you? Maybe we can start over." He pointed down the hill to the hotel. His clear sea-gray eyes met mine and my stomach flipped. "So, Miss Bennet, could I buy you an ice cream this evening after supper?"

I'm sure my face had gone deep scarlet because it felt like it was on fire. Tom kept me off balance, dancing on a keen edge, speaking without thinking. I'd never met anyone who made me feel this way. Certainly not Edward. I managed an awkward, "All right," wishing I could pour my heart into his hand.

It was odd. I could hardly look at him; I could hardly keep my eyes off him. To avoid meeting his gaze, I looked down the hill. That horrible little man from the coach—George Graybull— climbed the trail toward us. I moaned.

"Hello again, Miss Bennet." Graybull tipped his hat, and I inclined my head to him.

As Tom and Graybull exchanged nods, I couldn't help but see, with secret delight, that Tom towered over Graybull. I straightened my back so that my eyes were level with Graybull's. Even *I* was taller than this irritating man.

"Seen any more bears?" Graybull asked me. There was a lilt in his voice. He had a peculiar way of sticking his tongue between the gap in his teeth, like he was getting ready to taste something. "Lovely griz the other day," he said to Tom. "Unusual sighting. Frightened Miss Bennet, I'm afraid."

I felt Tom's eyes on me and my face went hot all over again; but I wanted him to look at me forever. I stood even straighter. "We're only touring Mammoth today," I said.

"Ah! I'll be out with a hunting party west of the Park in ten days or so. Hope to bag a bear." I sensed Tom stiffen. "Do you hunt?" he asked Tom.

"No, sir." Tom's words were sharp. Then he said, his voice soft, "I'd give anything to spend time really watching a griz."

"Pity. Was hoping you could spare some tips." Graybull cocked his head at the sky. "Clearing weather, looks like. Warmer." He turned to me. "Understand your father is an architect. Noble profession. And you're here for a while. Going to work in the Park with Reamer, is he? Reamer's a good man. Friend of mine. The right sort, of course." Graybull cast a sideways glance at Tom.

I fumed. Judgmental little man. Graybull was a pompous boor who had just revealed to Tom the extent of my humiliating situation and newly humbled status. My cheeks grew dark. I could feel Tom's eyes on me again and wished he'd look away. I feared that now that I was exposed as a fraud, he'd think even worse of me.

Graybull nattered on. "I've asked, Miss Bennet, if you and your father would join me for dinner this evening in the National dining room. My treat. Decent food, somewhat. Your father's agreed. At about eight."

I felt a shock of anger ripple through me. *My father* had agreed; *I* had not. But I had no choice. I was still subject to my father's rule. I smiled coldly, trying to mask my irritation with false charm. "Then I'll look forward to it."

"Right." Graybull looked from me to Tom with a rival's appraising stare. I thought he seemed to be sizing things up. Tom met Graybull's eyes without hesitation.

I wanted Graybull to be on his way. "Then I'll see you this evening."

He tipped his hat. "Cheerio." He nodded curtly to Tom and sauntered on up the hill.

"Do you know him well?" Tom asked, when Graybull was out of earshot.

"We met on the coach."

"I don't like him."

"Oh?"

"I don't like the way he talked about 'bagging' a bear."

I bit my lip to keep from smiling. I didn't like Graybull either, but Tom's comment hinted of jealousy. Perhaps he did like me, after all. I wanted him to feel that jealousy. "He's a sportsman. He said he'd been on many safaris."

"Now I really don't like him." Tom looked at me, his face dark. "The Lakota view the grizzly as a sacred totem. Grizzlies are the biggest predator in North America. We assume we're better just because we have guns."

The bear rug that graced the floor in Grandpapa's smoking room came to mind, something I decided I would not wish Tom to discover. I asked, uncertain, "It's not illegal to hunt them. Is it?"

I barely had the words out before he responded. "Does it have to be illegal to be bad?"

I had done it again—I came across as an idiot. "No. Of course not." I only wanted him to like me. I reached. "They are fascinating. The bears."

I glanced at his profile; a small smile curled his lips. "They are," he said without looking at me. I took a breath. He twisted the sample bag in his hands. "I guess we have to postpone that ice cream."

Now my disappointment was deep. I'd rather be with Tom than that awful Graybull. I resented the missed opportunity. "Maybe tomorrow? Tomorrow at noon?" I spoke so quickly I didn't grasp how desperate I sounded. I bit my lip to keep from saying yet another stupid thing.

"That's great with me." His smile made me feel light-headed. And did I detect a mirror to my eagerness? A thrill crept through me at the thought. "Shall I pick you up at the National?"

The drop back into reality was swift and hard. I looked at the white sinter at my feet. I had to tell him. "We're not at the National. Things have . . . changed. We're at the Cottage." I glanced up. I saw no judgment in his eyes, just kindness. I sighed. "It's quaint. Kind of rustic." I shrugged.

"Tom, I need that sample bag," his father called, impatient.

"Got to go. I'll find you tomorrow at the Cottage, then, around noon." He turned and walked off, his long arms swinging, the sample bag a pendulum.

"Bye!" I called. As I watched him move away I realized that for these few minutes, I'd forgotten about Mama. I'd been transported in the company of this Tom Rowland and, for that short interval, forgotten my situation. I stood on the path in the midst of Mammoth Hot Springs, a landscape as desolate as my soul, and I was enraptured.

Papa and Uncle John had disappeared; George Graybull had vanished; Tom and his father hiked away into the upper reaches of the springs. I was alone with my thoughts.

The steaming pool to my right bubbled and hissed. It looked clean and pure; the snow-white sinter invited a touch. But I could tell that the water was ferociously hot and would burn flesh to the bone. A thin crust of silica, not strong enough to hold my weight, bordered the edge of the pool.

As if to confirm this, the stark white ribs of some unfortunate animal thrust from the pool. I pressed my fingers to my eyes.

As appealing as I found Tom and the raw beauty around me, they only served to remind me of what I missed. Now that I was alone again, it all came tumbling back into my mind. I was caught here, when what I wanted was my home, my Ghost, my Mina, my comforts. My mama.

Mama. I'd thought we were here to find her. I thought I'd be on my way home now with Mama, going home to Kitty and Edward and Ghost and my season and all the things I'd planned for my life. I pressed my fingers harder against my eyes, trying not to cry, biting down the tears. Mama. Why did you leave me? Why didn't you keep your promise? My tears tasted bitter when I swallowed them, and my throat felt thick and raw.

I knew the answer. It was my fault. I'd sent her away without my love. I told her I didn't want to see her again. What I would give now to take those moments back and rearrange them as if they were pawns on a chessboard.

I took my hands from my eyes. Below me, the buildings with red roofs stretched in a thin row.

There was a girl walking between the buildings, and she had a long plait of dark hair so like Mama's it stopped my breath. I watched the girl unhitch a horse and lift herself into the saddle. I watched that thick braid as it swung over her shoulder and she nudged the horse and moved off at a trot, heading down the road toward Gardiner.

Heavy misery descended on my heart. The thought of Mama, the reminder of her, the thought that I might never see her again all weighed on me. Either my legs would collapse beneath me or I would run. I'd run away. I'd run until I could not move again. I gathered my skirts. I'd run all the way back to Newport if need be. I'd run toward the sunrise, leaving Papa, leaving this godforsaken place, even Tom.

And I did run. I set off down the slope, picking up speed. The turns of the winding paths slowed me, and I was tempted to fly right across the sinter, heedless. I lifted my skirts higher, my stockinged legs visible to the knees, so I could run faster.

And still I couldn't move fast enough, skittering along, winding and turning, and then . . . An arm stretched before me as a soldier, with two smart paces, stepped in front of me and we nearly collided.

"Miss! No running permitted on the trails." I tried to sidestep him. "Miss, I'll have to escort you back to your hotel meself." He took my arm, his grip unyielding.

People were watching us. I dropped my skirts, smoothing the fabric, and straightened my side-slipped hat. "I'm fine, officer. I'm sorry."

"Let's go. We'll just take you to your folks, right?" He tugged my arm, dragging me downhill toward the hotels.

"I'm fine! Please let me go!" He was treating me like a common criminal.

"Here, Caleb, I'm certain the young lady will be all right," a voice rang out from behind us.

I turned, and faced a genial woman coming down the path and carrying a camera case and tripod. Our eyes met and she smiled at me.

Chapter TWELVE

June 21, 1904

I have lately taken up photography & work at it
occasionally after the household has retired to rest.
It is very fascinating work but requires a lot of practice.

—letter from Evelyn Cameron to her mother-in-law,
May 15, 1895

THE OFFICER TIPPED HIS HAT. "MRS. GALE. YOU KNOW this young lady?"

I panted as I tried to catch my breath.

"You have a fine sense of duty, Caleb." Mrs. Gale rested her tripod on the ground and handed me the large, leather camera case, as if we were the best of friends instead of perfect strangers. The case was heavier than I expected; Caleb narrowed his eyes as he watched my clumsiness with it.

"Thank you, ma'am." Caleb shifted, uneasy. I was sure he sensed her ruse. "I must escort this young lady off the hill. Running ain't permitted."

"Ain't permitted" rang throughout my life. I looked down the slope, wondering if I'd see the girl whose long braid like Mama's had started my little rebellion. She was gone but no matter, it was fruitless. I was running away from a prison that I couldn't escape.

My limbs went heavy and tears filled my eyes and I set the leather box on the ground at my feet.

"Yes, but I needed something and asked her to make haste. Caleb, let me handle this, if you will." Mrs. Gale turned toward me, meeting my eyes with a quick, private look that let me know I should play along. "My dear, haste doesn't mean running."

"Yes, ma'am," I whispered.

Caleb grunted, but trailed off, tipping his hat again with a wary glance at me.

"You were in quite a hurry," Mrs. Gale said, her voice soft.

"There was a girl down below. She looked familiar. She reminded me of someone I miss."

"Missing is hard, isn't it?" She knew what I meant; she understood. I liked her immediately.

"Yes." I looked away. "Why did you help me?"

"Oh, you remind *me* of someone." I looked at her, her eyes sparkling with humor. She bent and began to unpack her equipment. She opened the tripod and took a camera carefully from the leather box. She opened the bellows and positioned the camera on the tripod, locking it in place.

I'd seen cameras before, of course, but something about Mrs. Gale—her strong, set face, the way she deftly maneuvered the equipment—was impressive. She was so independent. Here she was, alone, I realized suddenly, looking around for a companion and seeing no one. She carried heavy equipment with an assured air; yet she dressed well and wore several large pieces of jewelry. She had the refinement of a lady. I wasn't sure what to think of her, except to be grateful that she'd come to my aid.

"It is dangerous to run near the springs," Mrs. Gale said without pausing in her work. "The rules are there for a purpose."

Rules. Her words brought me back to my miserable situation. "I'm tired of being told what to do."

Mrs. Gale laughed. "Aren't we all? So many things that aren't permitted! Especially for a well-brought-up young lady."

The camera was set, and after peering through it, she stepped back and looked squarely at me. "Have a look."

I took the smooth leather gently between my gloved fingers and bent, covering my head with the hood, and gazed through the lens. I caught my breath.

I saw the world anew, upside down, reduced to a single sight line, bereft of a periphery. Time slowed. Then stood still entirely. I was suspended in the exact moment of the image in the viewfinder. I heard the hiss of steam, the soft bubble of water, the call of a crow; I smelled the sulphur. But these senses were disconnected from my vision. I experienced only the otherworldly image framed in microcosm through the lens.

I straightened. "I had no idea." It was the first moment of pure pleasure I'd had in a long time. This unexpected swing of emotion was heady. I smiled at Mrs. Gale, grateful.

"The camera focuses the eye so that the details stand out. Go ahead, have another look. Tell me what you see."

I bent to look again. The pools were edged in lace. Steam curled toward the sky in soft wisps. The cliffs were stacked in layers like a parfait, and the rocks beneath the water were banded like hard candy. These details had been lost to my naked eye.

"I see . . . stripes. Lines, curves. I see what's there under the water. Things I didn't see before, like the way the edges seem ruffled." I stepped back again. "It's magic."

Mrs. Gale turned the camera in another direction, facing down the springs toward the cottages. "Now what do you see?"

The cottages stood crisp and sharp. The road was empty of movement. It was what I didn't see that struck me. "I don't see her."

"Who, dear?"

"That girl, the one who reminded me of . . . of someone I miss very much." As much as I liked the magic of the camera, I knew that moment had passed, and it alone couldn't make wishes come true. A ripple of sadness ran through me. The world righted itself and broadened around me as I stepped back. "But I love it, looking through it."

Mrs. Gale smiled. "I do, too."

The Cottage Hotel was below us on the other side; Papa and Uncle John were now standing on the front porch, watching me. It must be close to noon and I would be expected for lunch. I sighed. "I must go."

"Please come and find me again, dear, if you're here for a while. I'll be out every morning. I can always use the company." I nodded to Mrs. Gale and watched as she got to work, setting the camera to take pictures of the terraces above us.

I walked slowly down the path toward the hotel. I had made a friend. I had found something remarkable. For the first time in a long time I felt . . . hopeful. Art was a pleasure that I'd forgotten.

Mama was an artist. When I was very little, she'd take me to the cove, a smaller, protected beach, where I would wallow in the sand and she would set up her easel and paint her watercolors. She gave me my own paints and let me make paintings with my fingers. She taught me to look with an artist's eye, to see the tiny ribbings of a shell or the partings in a gull feather. It made me sad, remembering these happier moments; but Mama had given me a way to see. She had given me art.

But later, art became an expression of her inner torture. I swallowed hard. Those strange oils, the demonic ones that were driven by her madness. Her paintings of hell, of her personal torment. Those close, tight portraits of peculiar forms, of dreamlike landscapes filled with vapors and steams, hideous . . .

I stopped in my tracks, staring at the hot springs. The thrill of recognition that shot through me nearly made me cry aloud, and I had to stifle my voice with my gloved hand. I whirled around, staring up the hill, then down; my knees grew weak as I recalled the details of her paintings, those hellish landscapes. I shut my eyes, remembering; and when I opened my eyes, there they were, all around me.

She was painting this. She'd been here. These were her landscapes. They had not been portraits of some inner hell, but memories of this place. I turned. The bubbling springs were just as she'd depicted them. The vapors. The striking colors, the white that I'd thought was ash. One view after the other, I recognized them all. Mama had been here.

She hadn't been insane, seeing vast hells of her own making. I laughed out loud, then caught myself, trying to keep the bubbling thrill of this discovery from making me appear to be on the verge of madness myself. For that was the thing: if Mama was not insane, I did not have to fear becoming insane like her.

Her paintings were not tortured expressions from her soul. Her paintings were memories.

Her paintings were clues.

But clues to what? Mama was sending me a message across time and space, but what could it mean? She'd been here, yes, of course; but that experience clearly pricked at her. Why could she not leave it behind?

And Papa—Papa had brought us here, not to find her after all. He must have known what she was painting. Hadn't they been west together? Then why did he not think he could find her here again? I stared across the hot springs and narrowed my eyes. The pieces of a puzzle lay scattered across this vast and peculiar landscape. I had to know why we were truly here, why Mama could not leave Yellowstone behind. Why Papa had lied to me again about our reasons for coming. Yellowstone was still my prison, but it was a prison that contained a great secret I had to uncover.

Chapter THIRTEEN

June 21, 1904

*The woman ran and ran, and she heard him
pounding behind her. Once she turned her head and
looked back. There was a great grizzly bear chasing her,
not a man at all.*

—"The Bear Butte," story as told by
Jessie American Horse, a Northern Cheyenne

"I FEAR WE'VE LOST THE ATTENTION OF YOUR CHARMING daughter," I heard Graybull say.

"Not at all." I yanked myself back to the moment. I was lying, of course. My mind had not been on Graybull's dull conversation but had been wandering all over the terraces outside, drifting from Tom, to Mrs. Gale, to Mama and the mystery of her obsession with Yellowstone.

We dined in the National Hotel. It was surprisingly elegant: the pianist played Strauss waltzes, the crystal was faceted lead. The menu sported baron of beef, planked whitefish, and Nesselrode pudding. I wore the green silk, for its magic properties and to celebrate my discovery—it was my link to Mama, the charm that might bring her back.

I had to admit, I did enjoy the pampering. But Graybull was dull and my entertaining uncle had unfortunately left to complete work somewhere else in the Park. Papa was distracted. I was even angrier

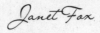

with him now, since he had imposed this dinner on me. I tried to be pleasant, but it was hard.

Graybull leaned toward me, determined to hold my wandering attention. "Do you shoot?"

"Shoot? You mean, a gun? No. I've never held a gun."

"Ah! Those slender arms of yours could use some practice. Would you allow me to lead you in a session? Take you shooting?" He smiled. He seemed thrilled to become my tutor, pushing his tongue into that little gap in his teeth. His tic reminded me of Toby, Cook's cat, when he cornered a mouse. "If your father will permit me, of course."

The last thing I wanted was a shooting lesson, especially from Graybull. I had many more things on my mind. I looked at Papa through veiled lids. In earlier times I might have been able to signal him to say no. Now our disconnect was so great that I clenched my fists beneath the table, as if to bring him around by sheer will.

Papa's face betrayed little emotion. I forced a winning smile onto mine but my eyes betrayed my thoughts and bored into his.

My attempts at telepathy were fruitless. "I think that's an excellent idea," Papa said. "We're here in the wilderness and Margaret should have some knowledge of guns." Papa smiled at Graybull. "Thank you, George. I'll only need her help for a few hours a day, and she should explore Yellowstone. Yes. That would be excellent."

My smile grew icier as Papa warmed to this awful man. "I don't want to learn to shoot. Guns rather frighten me." I didn't want to spend five minutes alone with Graybull, either. Graybull was smooth and slick, with a neat mustache and attire chosen to compliment his powerful, short frame. His accent was charming and his eyes were sharp; like a badger, he had keen, narrow eyes.

And he had the self-assurance of someone who was used to getting his way.

"But, my dear, I should like the pleasure of your company." Graybull leaned toward me, laying his hand on my arm, his fingers wrapping around my bare wrist. "I can allay your concerns about bears. Be my treat."

I watched him, and Papa's deferential behavior toward him, and a hole opened in my stomach. Here was the ideal husband. He was rich and single. Never mind his age; younger girls than I had married older men than Graybull. I sucked in air. Oh, I might find a suitable husband after all, despite our drop in fortune. A husband who could take me back to Newport in style. Was I prepared to make that sacrifice to secure my future? I would not find the love I'd hoped for with this horrid man. Far from it. But it was clear that what I wanted or hoped for was irrelevant in current circumstances.

"Shooting, then. Why not?" I flipped my hand gaily and withdrew my arm from Graybull's clammy touch in the process.

"Splendid!" Graybull leaned back in his chair, signaling the waiter for more claret. "I'll make arrangements, shall I? Perhaps day after tomorrow, before I head out on my little expedition."

I attempted to be cordial. "Tell me about your expedition. I'd like to hear more about hunting bears. Do you have trophies?" Maybe a head or two? I tried to keep the sniffy tone out of my voice. But I was picturing my own head, stuffed and mounted, upon his wall. The waiters were deferential toward Graybull, and he was clearly a man of power.

My grandfather would have approved of Graybull. He was just the sort of man my grandparents would choose for me. And if Papa

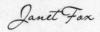

decided that Graybull was my suitor, I'd have no recourse. I had to play things very carefully.

Graybull launched into a story and I listened with half a mind. I thought of Tom and how he felt about hunting bears. He would have hated this conversation far more than I did. And once Tom slipped into my mind, he wouldn't leave.

Tom's father was a scientist, a fine profession, but it was clear he didn't have much money. My heart might skip a beat when I thought of Tom, but as I watched my father's eyes watching Graybull, I knew he'd never approve of someone like Tom. And what of Edward? Edward had made it clear the night of Mary's ball that he could not or would not stand beside me. And, in any case Edward would look down on me now, in my base situation.

I felt like a caged animal with nowhere to turn. Like the mountain lion Graybull was presently describing, caught high in the tree, trapped by dogs, waiting for the hunter to kill her, a cold, dispassionate, merciless death.

It was still dusky when dinner ended around ten; a late sunset in summer due to the high latitude, Graybull reminded me. I left Papa and Graybull to enjoy cigars on the veranda while I wrapped my wool stole over my shoulders so that I could take some air. The hot springs beckoned, the steam rising into the air in soft clouds. I began to walk up the slope.

"Sorry, miss." A soldier, coming up behind me, tapped me on the shoulder. "Not allowed to go up there at night." He thumbed at the springs. "Too dangerous."

I turned away, anger churning in my gut. I'd had enough of men ordering me about for one day. "Not allowed" defined my life, as a woman, as a lady of class. "Not allowed" to run, "not allowed" to walk alone, "not allowed" to marry for love. At home in Newport, surrounded by comfort, I hadn't appreciated how the life I led was governed by rules. I'd been oblivious; the shackles were soft. Now my eyes were opened by a father who'd betrayed my trust and by the rigid confines of this new raw life.

I flipped the stole over my shoulder and marched down the road away from the springs without giving the soldier the courtesy of a response.

Electric streetlamps glowed above my head as the last pink traces of light in the sky dimmed and streaked to red and violet and then to blue-black. I passed the clapboard curiosity shop fenced with elk antlers and the red-roofed barracks and staff houses of the fort. When I reached the last house in Officers' Row, I stopped and stared through the trees into the vast wilderness.

The green dress was too thin as the cold night air settled over Mammoth. I pulled the stole tighter around my shoulders.

Mama was tied to this place. Despite what Papa believed, I still nurtured the hope that she was alive. She'd promised me she'd come back; and the things she'd said in her letter kept me holding on to that promise. Her letter. I would not break my own pledge to her, and so I still couldn't say anything about it to Papa, but now its contents held deeper meaning. I'd reread it so often over the past year that I could recite it from memory, the creases in the paper soft with wear. It had not made sense before, but now I understood that this place was special to her and I felt my hope growing again. I'd find her.

I stared into the dark woods as if I were staring out over the gray ocean.

And Papa. He'd brought us here, and regardless of what he had told me, I didn't think it was out of coincidence. I couldn't read Papa's motives at all. It was as if I were in the center of a great wheel spinning around me, with Mama on one side and Papa on the other. It was yet another thing that was out of my control.

I turned back toward the hotels as the cold and silence of the night settled on me and made me shiver.

Snap. I jerked my head at the sound. Some forty feet away, strolling through the encampment of buildings in determined indifference, was an enormous bear. I could make out its shape as it shuffled under the streetlamps that cast pools of yellow. It had a mountainous lump on its shoulders. Grizzly.

Graybull had told me what to do back in the coach: "You lie still and play dead." I stood as still as stone, ready to drop to the ground. My shaking legs would be only too happy to oblige.

The bear stopped and swung its great head from side to side. The air was so still I could hear it grunt as if it were right next to me. I held my breath when every nerve in my body told me to run.

The bear hesitated. Could it smell me? There was no wind. The blood pounded in my ears. The massive head hovered. I remembered how I felt in the coach when those eyes, flat and driven by instinct, had met mine. Raw animal emotion—mine and the bear's—could not be contained. A void opened before me, yawning at my feet, no different than if I'd been standing at the edge of the cliff. I feared I'd be sick or make some sound. It was all out of my control.

I watched the bear for what seemed an eternity.

Finally it moved on, with slow purpose, toward the back of the last house on the road.

I watched until it disappeared entirely behind the house. I waited a few more seconds before walking as fast as possible up the road in the opposite direction, thankful for the streetlights, thankful for the hotels, my breath quick and hard as the adrenaline coursed through me. As I grew closer to the Cottage Hotel I broke out in a run, my combs falling forgotten from my hair, the exhilaration of my close brush flooding me like joy.

I went straight to my room and locked the door. I collapsed on the bed, panting, my brown hair loose and tangled, my green silk gown soaked with sweat.

Chapter FOURTEEN

June 22, 1904

"It isn't a question of any beauty," said Maggie;
"it's only a question of the quantity of truth ...
That's a thing by itself, yes. But there are also such
things, all the same, as questions of good faith."

—*The Golden Bowl*, Henry James, 1904

"IT WASN'T VERY CLOSE. I DON'T THINK IT KNEW I WAS there." I could feel Tom's eyes on me. I tried to be dismissive, even a little flippant, so he wouldn't see my nervousness. I couldn't meet his eyes because each time I did, my heart skipped a beat. My anxiety was not all about the bear.

"It wasn't hungry, that's all. Besides, you're too skinny. Not much more than a mouthful. All bony legs and arms." I did look at him then. I could have sworn he was trying not to laugh. There it was— that irreverence that kept me off balance. I wasn't used to having someone needle me. And I was in a cranky mood.

I hadn't slept, throwing my covers off in a sweat then yanking them back on in a chill, and I'd awakened late. It was noon now, and I had not set foot outside until an hour earlier. His teasing tipped me over the edge, even if I did like him. I spoke through clenched teeth. "And how many bear episodes have you survived?"

"You win." He was grinning. "I've only watched bears from a

safe distance." He was trying to make me feel better. It worked. I relaxed and met his smile. "You were wise not to run. A griz can move at about thirty-five miles an hour."

My smile faded. "Do you know anyone who's been attacked by a bear?"

"It doesn't happen often. Bears want to keep to themselves. Except around garbage, which isn't fair to bears. We shouldn't be feeding them. It's the people who have a problem there."

"So the bears have rights? More rights than the people?"

"They were here first."

Tom was serious. I was still trying to shake off my exhaustion and the memory of that great hulking beast. I shook my head. "Still."

"Still, he wouldn't even be around here, looking for a handout, if we kept the garbage locked up." I looked into Tom's eyes. When he was solemn, they were stormy gray like the Atlantic. I could have looked into his eyes forever. It didn't matter whether I agreed with him or not.

Our ice cream arrived. It was in the popular new cornucopia, which I'd first sampled when Papa and I'd stopped at the Exposition. Ice cream in a turned waffle with delicate tissue wrapped around the cone. We ate in silence.

Nothing about Tom felt familiar. He was hard to measure against the other men I knew. His opinions were confusing, and his teasing—I didn't know where I stood. I hadn't found a way to speak to him without feeling like a fool.

And he looked like he'd just stepped out of the backwoods. His shirt was clean, but plaid. I'd wager Edward thought plaid belonged in Scotland, not on his back in a dining room. And hiking boots in the National! Really, Tom was ridiculous.

Yet I wanted to reach across the table—right then, reach my arm over both our ice creams—and lift that lock of hair off his forehead, and then see him smile for me. Only for me. I would have followed his sea eyes into the bear's teeth.

He glanced up. "Good?" His index finger pointed at my ice cream, now dripping down my fingers while I mooned.

I flushed right to my toes. "Thanks. It's delicious." I licked my fingers and I grasped for the sparkling wit that seemed to elude me in his presence. "Are you in Yellowstone for a while?"

"The whole summer."

"You help your father?"

"Yes. I love this place." He put his ice cream down and leaned across the table, as if to share a secret with me. "I wish I could just stay right here forever."

I took a breath. Only six inches spanned the distance between our faces. "Why?" I whispered.

He leaned back. "For one thing, I want to be a wildlife biologist. Of course, for that I'll have to attend university." He grinned. "But, say! You could help me locate bears—you seem to have a knack for finding them."

I laughed. I surprised myself, and actually laughed, open-mouthed, in a way I hadn't done in years. I threw my hand over my mouth. I'm sure I looked like a ninny. But for once, I didn't care, because it felt wonderful.

And Tom didn't seem to mind. "What about you? What would you like to do?"

His question sobered me right up. "I haven't thought much about it." I hadn't done anything but think about it, but not in the way he meant. I hadn't thought about what I'd like to *do* at all, just what was expected of me. My future in Newport had been forecast: marry well, entertain well. University? School was not for learning a trade, but was a way to put a proper finish on things, like polishing the silver. Now, of course, my avenues had narrowed. Marriage seemed my only hope. The thought of Graybull crossed my mind and I shut my eyes. When I opened them, I looked at my lap. "I've never thought about it. All I've done is help Papa with his papers."

"He's an architect, right? So maybe you could study architecture."

"No! Don't be ridiculous!" I met his startled glance. "Women don't do that sort of thing."

"Why not?" I could see he was serious. How could I explain?

"First of all, I've never met anyone who . . ." I paused. "My mother was an artist. *Is* an artist. And she taught me how to draw."

"There you go. Art is a profession."

I started to laugh again, not meeting his eyes. "You don't understand. It's just not done." I could feel him looking at me, his entire attention fixed on me. His sincere expression pierced my soul. I liked the feeling. My cheeks flamed and I folded my hands. "I wish things were different. But where I come from, that's the way it is. Ladies don't have professions." And a sadness came over me that threatened to sweep me away. I looked out the window at the curling steam.

"Would you like to go for a walk?" he asked.

I looked up at him with an enormous, grateful smile. I nodded, unable to speak. We left the dining room and walked down the road toward the barracks. Tom talked, leaving me free to listen to his warm voice.

"The Army has an outpost here. The soldiers protect the hot springs and wildlife from vandals and poachers. And people selling chunks of the rock formations." I blushed at his tease, thinking back to my silly assumption about his father. He sensed my embarrassment. "Hey. You didn't know. It's just that people looking for souvenirs have done a lot of damage around here. Even Old Faithful has lost some of its cap."

"Old Faithful?"

He paused, watching me. The sun sparked off the snowy peak behind him. "You don't know a thing about Yellowstone, do you? Come on. I want to show you something."

We picked up the pace now, walking down the road past the barracks. Swallows winged overhead, garrulous, dipping and turning. The breeze kicked up without warning, and I reached for my hat and realized that I'd left it and my gloves in my room. I tugged at the loose wisps of hair that swept my cheeks.

I watched Tom out of the corner of my eye. His head was up. He reminded me of a colt, enjoying the breeze, living for the moment. My stomach tightened into little knots. I wished he would reach out one long arm and take my hand, and then look at me with those eyes. I could almost match his long-legged stride, and that felt nice, too, this swinging movement next to Tom—both of which made me giddy.

"It's not too far. Just over there."

"Oh, I don't mind. I like the walk."

Our eyes met, and we exchanged a smile, and in that instant I thought my heart might melt.

"There!" Tom pointed. I shaded my eyes. Just below us was a large corral. Inside I could make out a dozen animals grazing. They were huge and shaggy. "Buffalo."

"Buffalo!" Tom was right, I knew nothing of Yellowstone, but I knew enough to know that bison were nearly extinct.

"Only forty years ago, they were here, tens of thousands of them. One old-timer told me he saw a herd so large the plains were black as far as he could see. Black with buffalo. They went on forever." Tom was quiet a moment. "There are about thirty left. That's it. Most are there, the rest on an island in the lake. And these aren't really wild. They had to bring domesticated bison up from Texas."

I felt the need to impress Tom, somehow, and dragged up something I'd heard my grandfather go on about. "Killing the buffalo did help subdue the Indians, though. And so we could settle the west."

Tom wheeled on me, his face alive with emotion. "Is that what's important? White man's way? Conquer and destroy?"

I took a step back, surprised by his outburst, my mouth agape.

Tom looked at me as though seeing me new. "Do you mean all of what you say, Maggie? I know, it's just the way you were brought up. You can't help it, can you." He shook his head. "You're a snob."

I felt as if he'd slapped me, and the tears came to my eyes. "I'm . . . I'm only telling you what I know."

"And what you know is what you've been told. And it's wrong." He was looking at the buffalo now, not at me. His voice was bitter. I wanted to say to him, "Then tell me something I don't know. Tell me what's right. I can learn."

"Have you ever even seen a live buffalo before?"

I whispered a tiny, "No."

"Look. Just look at them. Big, old, mean-tempered . . . they're built to survive the cold winters and dry summers." He turned to me, his eyes shining. "For the Lakota, a buffalo was a spirit guide. Their life support. The bison gave them everything they needed— clothes, food, shelter. Then here we come, big white man with big gun, and we took the animals down for sport, just shot them down. They're big targets. Even a fool with a peashooter could hit a buffalo."

"I didn't know," I whispered. Please, oh, please, don't be mad. How was I supposed to know, when everything around me, everyone around me, for all my life so far focused on parties and balls and weddings and clothes?

He backed off a little, but only a little. "While you're here on your little working holiday you'll learn a lot."

"We're not on holiday." I regretted the words the minute they left my lips. But I was exhausted and miserable, and all the confused feelings I'd harbored for weeks bubbled up. In my misery, I forgot that I was talking to Tom, forgot that I liked him and wanted to impress him with my so-called worldly ways. I only knew my life was upside down. "We're moving here. We're moving here, all right? My father lied to me, sold our home. My mother left us. And my grandparents want to own me. I've been betrayed, and I have nowhere to turn." I burned with pent-up emotion now, and it steamed out of me, directed at him. "You think you know so much. You may be smart about animals and Yellowstone and nature, but you're not so smart when it comes to a girl's feelings. So, I'm a snob? Well, fine. At least I was brought up to behave properly and not call people names, thank you very much. You've never even faced a bear! Maybe when you face something really fearful, maybe when your life turns upside down, maybe when you confront something so awful you can't imagine the world ever being right again, well, sir, maybe then . . ." I sputtered out like a dying candle.

Tom stared as if I'd struck him in the chest. I stood shaking, with my anger and loss all exposed and raw.

I couldn't stand it. I whirled and strode up the road toward the hotel, taking brisk strides that caused my skirt to flap and flutter.

"I'm sorry." I heard his voice from behind me. "I didn't mean to . . ."

I stopped and faced him. "I need to write some letters, if you'll excuse me. Then I'm going to dress for dinner. Me and my snobbish clothes." I turned and continued my march back to town.

He caught up with me, but his face was averted. "Of course." His long legs matched my hurried pace.

I stopped again, my hands on my hips, and I glared at him. "And you could do with a cleaning up, you know. Looking decent won't kill you."

"Okay," he said, drawing the word out. I watched as color rose into his cheeks.

I turned and continued stomping up the path, Tom matching me step for step while I tried to tuck my loose curls behind my ears, irritated that I'd forgotten my hat. It was a useless gesture.

And as we kept walking, the soft afternoon air swelled around us, and my temper ebbed. Tom was right there with me. What he'd said was so hurtful that I wanted to drop down into the grass and weep. But I had stood my ground, and he was still there, matching me stride for stride, when everyone else in my life had either abandoned me or wanted to control me. Mama, Papa, my grandparents, Graybull, even Edward and Kitty—they'd never matched me stride for stride like this lanky man whom I hardly knew, but whose eyes penetrated my very soul.

I marched on up the road, tortured, having no idea how to undo the pain that circled my heart.

Chapter FIFTEEN

June 22, 1904

Any schoolboy or girl can make good pictures with one of Eastman Kodak Co's Brownie Cameras. $1.00

—newspaper advertisement, 1900

At last I am sending you the photographic proofs, they are untoned therefore will darken by degrees in the light.

—letter from Evelyn Cameron to Kathleen Lindsay, a client, 1897

WE WALKED, NOT SPEAKING. THE PATH TO THE HOTELS felt longer on the return than it had when we set out. The swallows chittered above, and the breeze stirred the tall grasses, *swish, swish.* The sun washed the hills with a languid light. Tom and I shared a rhythmic cadence, our arms and legs moving together as if synchronized. It only made me feel worse, to think that we had some link yet we were so far apart. I glanced at him sidelong. He chewed his lip. I looked at my feet and chewed my own.

I had to break the silence.

"It's light around here until late, isn't it." I pulled at a stalk of grass, tugged it loose and twisted it in my fingers. "Why, last night, I thought I could have read my book until well after supper. I guess that's because we're so far north?"

Tom took a deep breath, as if relieved. "That's right. And the solstice was yesterday, too."

"I'm sorry?"

"Midsummer. Longest day of the year."

"Oh, of course. Midsummer." I remembered my Shakespeare, thankful for a neutral subject. "Midsummer's the time when wishes come true, right?" I sighed. "I could use a time like that."

"Be careful what you wish for."

I glanced at him. "That sounds sad."

He didn't look at me. "Sometimes you think you want something, only to get it and find out it's all wrong."

"That *is* sad." I glanced at him again, wondering what wish had gone wrong for him, but I couldn't ask. A breeze lifted my hair and I looked past Tom to the mountain that seemed gilded in the late afternoon light, dusted with fairy magic. "Midsummer's a magic time, too."

"Do you believe in magic?" Tom met my eyes; he was smiling now.

"I did when I was little." I smiled back, then looked at my feet. "I used to think there were mermaids. In the ocean by our house. Once I saw a seal, or that's what Mama said later, but I insisted it was a mermaid. She laughed at me." But she'd liked it, my story. She told me that she believed in mermaids, too. I hoped she did. "Sailors have sworn up and down that they were rescued by a mermaid. Saved from drowning. By magic." Saved by magic, pulled from the sea by a mermaid—I hoped Mama had believed that. I had to believe that.

"I believe in things that I can see and touch." Tom's voice was clear and firm.

I put Mama out of my mind. "Oh, so, what about those spirit guides you mentioned? The bear and the buffalo?"

He laughed and stopped walking. I felt a wash of relief and faced him and smiled. I liked the way he threw his head back and how his laugh sounded deep and genuine. Our eyes met and I could scarcely breathe from the joy of it.

"Margaret Bennet, you have a way of turning my words inside out. You're right. Animals can be magical, or at least spiritual." He cocked his head. "In fact, I'd wager the bear you've seen is trying to tell you something."

I looked at the grass in my hand. I'd unconsciously twisted it into a bowline. The knot was one of several good knots Mama had taught me one warm summer afternoon as we lay stretched and lazy on the deck of our little sailboat, listening to the slap of waves on her wood hull. She was laughing, and I told her that the slapping waves might be the hands of merpeople saying hello.

Tom and I stood on the walk in front of the Cottage Hotel. Steam from the springs trailed up into the air and disappeared. I wished for a way to make the moment with him last.

As if rising up out of the ground, Mrs. Gale appeared through the steam, walking down the path, carrying her equipment.

"There!" I cried. "There's magic right there. Pictures that come from a box."

Tom grinned, and I felt giddy as I smiled back. "Photography's not magic," he said. "It's science. It's a way to use light, the same way the eye makes a picture in your brain."

"Yes, but with a camera you see differently. You see things as they were meant to be seen. One at a time, without all the extras added. That's a kind of magic." I was so sure of what I was saying that my fists were clenched into tight balls.

He looked surprised and—to my delight—impressed. "So, you win. Maybe there is a bit of magic there."

Mrs. Gale joined us and set her equipment down with a sigh. "Hello, Tom."

"Ma'am." Tom glanced at me. "Mrs. Gale works on commission for the Haynes Studios here in the Park." He thumbed toward the rustic building fenced by antlers—the Haynes building. "My friend Margaret thinks your camera is magic." His voice lifted as if he was trying not to laugh.

"Oh, but it is, my young friend, it is." Mrs. Gale smiled at me. "Hello again, dear. Your friend Margaret and I met yesterday, when she was in a terrible hurry."

I blushed, but my mind was already churning with something new, something surprising. Mrs. Gale wasn't a tourist taking pictures for her own pleasure. The camera in the box at my feet was not for her entertainment. She worked. She, a woman who seemed of means and social standing, was employed.

I'd said it to Tom earlier: women of my class in Newport were not employed; it simply wasn't an option. The only path for an upper-class woman was marriage and family, not working a trade. Girls like me did not chase after dreams, like men did. I stared at Mrs. Gale. She wore the right clothes, had the right bearing, was clearly a lady of proper upbringing. I didn't know what to think. Kitty would have been horrified; my grandparents, scandalized.

But I was neither, I came to realize. I was impressed. I liked the fact that she did what she loved and made money doing it. I stared at her with newfound respect.

"Hello?" Tom laughed and waved his hand in front of my eyes and jolted me out of my mind-wandering. "Margaret?"

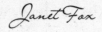

"Right!" I blushed as red as the petunias on the porch behind me. "At home my friends call me Maggie."

"Maggie." I liked the way Tom said it, and I felt my blush deepen. "So, Mrs. G, what do you think? Is it science or magic?"

Mrs. Gale squared her broad shoulders. "There are mysteries in life, Tom, and I think the most mysterious is art. Inspiration. Sometimes when I watch a picture grow on the white paper in my darkroom, I can't even tell you where it came from. It's not always what was in my mind. But there it is, pale and evolving, blooming like a flower." Mrs. Gale smiled, and I did, too, at her eloquence. And I thought about Mama and her paintings and how she must have felt watching an image evolve beneath her fingers.

How she must have felt when I asked, demanded, that she destroy such a precious thing. I felt a sudden, stabbing guilt. I wished I could take it back.

Tom's laughter brought me back to the moment. "You've got me there."

"Well now, Tom, your father contacted me. He'd like me to photograph some outcrop or other," said Mrs. Gale. She bent and wrestled her equipment up into her arms. "It's a pleasure to see you again, Maggie."

"You know where to find us?" Tom said as he helped her adjust her burden.

"Indeed. Good-bye, then." Mrs. Gale smiled at me and I smiled back like an awestruck child, and I watched her make her way down the road toward the National.

Tom stood so close to me that I could have touched his hand with mine if I'd only lifted my fingers. He shuffled his feet. "See you around?"

I tucked wisps of hair behind my ears, wishing the afternoon would not end. "Thanks again for the ice cream. And the buffalo." I smiled up at him.

He looked back at me, his eyes warm. "I'll be here in the Mammoth area a bit longer. My dad has work around the Park, but we're here for now."

I laced my fingers behind my back. I didn't know what was in store for me now. "I'm not sure where I'll be. I haven't asked my father about it." I hadn't talked to Papa since that first night. I didn't want to talk to him.

"The Tour through the Park is worth taking, if you can get away."

"Then I'll think about going. Since you recommend it." I hesitated. "But didn't you say something about highway robbers?"

He laughed, just as I'd hoped he would. "You're an easy girl to tease."

I blushed. I liked being easy to tease. I liked Tom's laugh and the way his eyes met mine.

"Maybe I'll see you around tomorrow." He waved his hand at the springs.

I tossed the knotted grass as I remembered what I had to do tomorrow. Annoyance pricked me. "Probably not. Tomorrow I have to learn the art of shooting a gun from that dreadful Englishman."

Tom's face darkened. "I see."

"I don't want to go. I'd much rather . . ."

"Rather see a live bear than a dead one?"

Not exactly, but I kept that thought to myself. I smiled. "Rather be somewhere else." With Tom. I looked at my feet.

"Well. Enjoy." He swung away, lifting his hand. "Look out for magic, Maggie."

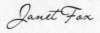

I stood in the shadow of the Cottage Hotel watching Tom as he walked down the road past the National. I wondered if he felt my eyes on his back, and if it pleased him. I watched him until he was out of sight behind the other tourists who wandered between the buildings and up into the springs.

I liked Tom. Really liked him in a way that felt so different from Edward. Edward. He now seemed so far away. Was it only last summer that I had kissed him? I walked along the front of the hotel until I found a rustic bench and sat down, gripping my knees in a hug. A coach passed by—the well-dressed woman inside turned a quick eye at me and then away. I knew I looked a fright with my hair loose and my boots dusty, no hat or gloves. I didn't look like a proper young lady. Edward, if he was here, wouldn't even notice my existence.

All the familiar trappings of my world had turned topsy-turvy. For most of my life I'd pictured myself in a privileged, if sheltered, marriage with a wealthy husband like Edward. For almost a year I'd clung to the promise of my season as my saving grace. I'd blamed Mama for her behavior, for her madness. And for abandoning me. Now it was clear, I'd have no season and no Mama. And in my current situation, what respectable man would marry me? Perhaps that repulsive George Graybull, desperate for who-knew-what. Yet here I'd met Mrs. Gale, who worked. And Tom Rowland, who was nothing like Edward Tyson—or George Graybull. It was all so confusing.

I sat on the bench and watched steam from deep in the earth curl into the sky like a question mark. My heart seemed to be moving, but in what direction I was not at all sure.

Chapter SIXTEEN ❧❧❧❧❧❧❧❧

June 23, 1904

> *The rooms are canvas, formed with a flap for a door.*
> *A deal bed, a small table, and a washbowl, with a*
> *four-by-six looking glass furnish the accommodations.*
> *Scrupulous cleanliness prevails . . .*

> —*A Western Trip*, a memoir by Carl E. Schmide, 1910

DINNER THAT NIGHT WITH PAPA WAS A STIFF AFFAIR. The only dining was in the National, which was fortunate because the orchestra filled the silence. And I slept restlessly yet again; buffalo and bears crowded my imaginings.

Papa came to my room before breakfast the next morning. He stood in the doorframe, hat in hand. "I've got some good news."

I said nothing; the thought that floated through my mind was, *What now?* I distrusted my father after his lies. But then there was still the matter of the yet-undisclosed news from Uncle John; I wasn't ready to give up on finding Mama alive. I sat in the one chair in the room and folded my hands in my lap and stared at Papa.

"Mr. Reamer is leaving the Park soon, but the superintendent likes my work. I've been asked if I would supervise some projects here. That means I have a permanent position, Maggie." He squared his shoulders, as if lifting off a burden.

I leaned forward. "Does that mean I can afford to return to Newport?" Perhaps we could get our things back, our home. My Ghost. Had Mina found other employment already? Mama had promised she'd return to me, to Newport. If she wasn't here, then perhaps she was there. I felt a spark of hope that my world might soon be righted and my confusion banished.

Papa smoothed his mustache. "The salary is not enormous, Maggie. It will allow us to live satisfactorily here, for now. And I'll need your help until I'm settled. My papers are . . . disorganized."

I felt as though a rock had dropped into my stomach. "Fine." He'd made a mess and wanted me to help him clean it up.

"Now that we have some income, perhaps you can take the Tour. Explore the rest of the Park."

I said nothing. Even if the Tour was something I wanted, I knew he was only trying to buy my forgiveness.

"The other news is that we now have lodging elsewhere. It's one-half of one of the officers' cottages, but it will give us privacy and more room and we'll be settled."

A tiny frame cottage. *Half* of a tiny frame cottage. Compared with our Newport home—I tried not to roll my eyes.

"George Graybull is taking you shooting today, yes? I've arranged for our things to be brought over to the cottage while you're out." He paused. "Maggie, I hope you'll be polite with George. He's a man of considerable wealth and influence. In fact, it's his influence that secured the cottage for us."

"I'm always polite." My voice was like cut crystal.

Papa didn't miss my insolent tone, but looked surprised. He sighed. "He could offer you opportunities, Mags. George Graybull may be the answer to your prayers."

I sat up. I had been expecting this, and still the hollow in the pit of my stomach opened wide. George Graybull was repulsive; regardless of what he could give me, I could not bear him. I pretended not to understand. "How so?"

"He can offer you what I can't at the moment. Money. Social standing. A return to Newport, or New York, or wherever else you'd like to be."

A chill settled over me. "George Graybull."

Papa examined his hat, flicking off pieces of lint.

I rose out of the chair. "He's . . . he's . . ." I clenched my hands into fists.

"He's a respectable single man with a great deal of money. I know that he's a bit older, but given a long engagement . . ."

"Engagement!" I clenched my hands tight, my arms rigid against my sides. "I haven't even made my debut! How can I have an engagement?"

Papa held his hand in the air. "A debut would not be necessary, under these circumstances. Your grandfather would approve this match. You would have your inheritance as a dowry. And George—he is influential. You would have a place in society. He can help me get back on my feet."

I was speechless, in shock. What about what I wanted?

Papa's eyes met mine straight on. "Ultimately, Margaret, you must do as I ask. And I ask you to be polite to George Graybull. He is important to your future as well as to mine."

I had no choice. He was leaving me no choice, no say in my own future. I turned my back on my father and walked to the small window. "I need to change for my outing, Papa."

"Yes. Of course."

I waited until I heard the door close, and then I sank back into the chair and rested my forehead on my palm.

I should be at home in Newport riding my horse and preparing for my debut. I should be attending parties and flirting with men—with Edward—and dancing and being wooed by potential husbands of my own age. I should have fine clothes, made for me. And Mama should be there, instructing me and guiding me through all of it. Instead I had no mother and my father was trying to recover from financial ruin. I had a suitor who repulsed me. I could return to my life back east with him, but at what cost? I was trapped in Yellowstone by bad fortune and by my position as a woman.

The only thing here that made me happy was Tom Rowland, and that was . . . impossible.

I tried not to think about the impossible as I changed into my gray excursion suit, the closest I had to hunting attire. I waited for George Graybull in the lobby of our hotel. The men who passed barely tipped their hats; there were no ladies of my class in this hotel. I was out of place everywhere.

"Here we are." Graybull arrived. "Shall we?" He took my elbow in his viselike grip and steered me out the door to a small waiting carriage. His voice dropped. "Will be nice to get you into decent accommodations, eh?" I looked at him as he grinned. "I've arranged with the park superintendent—he's a friend of mine, you know—to allow you into the military target range. Just a little practice today, get you started."

I tried not to shy away from him, but I couldn't manage a smile.

To my relief, once we set off I didn't need to talk. Graybull drove the carriage and rattled on and on about his hunting exploits and his travels. He bragged about his connections, his possessions, his homes in London and New York, his "cottage" in Newport. He was dull as dry toast. I could let my mind wander over the landscape of tall pines and banded-rock outcrops, and watch an eagle soar high above, and follow the *swish-swish* of the horse's tail in front. I could at least admire my velvet prison.

We passed a broad semicircle of tents spread across a meadow. Children ran laughing through the camp; women hung wet clothes from lines strung between trees; men stacked firewood next to low campfire rings.

"What is this place?" I asked.

"One of the Wylie tent camps." Graybull leaned toward me as if to share a secret; I suppressed a shudder. "How the other half experiences the Park. Much less expensive. Mostly teachers, young families, single men, that sort. The hotel staff calls them 'sagebrushers,' I presume because they tumble about the landscape." He winked at me.

I peered around Graybull. At first, I felt guilty for having complained about the Cottage Hotel. I could hardly imagine sleeping in a tent, out of doors. But I could see that the encampment was tidy; the tents were gaily striped; the women wore dark skirts and white shirtwaists, looking perfectly decent. There was a rugged charm about it.

"I believe your young friend is staying here." Graybull's voice lifted slightly and I detected a dismissive tone.

"My young friend?"

"That boy. With his geologist father." Graybull clicked his teeth with his tongue. Tom. He meant Tom! Graybull turned to look at me, and I avoided his eyes, sneaking another look at the camp. I had to be careful not to let him know how much I'd rather be in this carriage with Tom.

As we passed the tents, something caught my eye: it was the same girl, the girl with the long dark braid I'd seen from the hot springs. I was certain it was her. I watched her stride through the encampment, a sack in her arms. Her long braid swung from side to side. Why I was drawn to her so, I couldn't say. There was something compelling about her, almost magnetic. It was something that pricked at me . . .

Graybull snapped the reins and brought me out of my reverie. "Not too far now to the range." The horse picked up its pace.

The range was primitive and barren. While I had a good eye for the target, I found the rifle heavy and tiring to hold. But Graybull grew increasingly animated as I grew more restless and exhausted. He especially enjoyed steadying my arm. At one point, I couldn't help thinking about Tom standing that close to me and the warmth that flooded me caused me to miss the target altogether.

After a while, clouds masked the sun and the temperature dropped. Rain threatened as a low rumble of thunder echoed through the mountains. I protested that I was growing bruised from the rifle butt in my shoulder and was relieved when Graybull finally took the hint. On the way back to the hotel, he waxed enthusiastic about my "native ability with the gun."

I tried not to laugh. It wasn't as if I'd ever shoot anything.

"You enjoy the out-of-doors? Of course you must. Why we get along so famously, I expect. We shall have to explore more together. Skeet shooting is a fine sport. Have you any favorite activities?"

I thought about Ghost. I sighed, missing him. "I love to ride."

"Riding. Very civilized. How many horses do you have?"

"None, at the moment." I didn't try to hide my bitterness, and loss filled me as I looked over this landscape. Ghost would like this place. It would be beautiful to ride here, beneath those dark blue mountains with their snowcaps, to weave among the pines, the forest silent and expectant.

"Perhaps that will change. In the west and all that." He glanced at me sideways, but I turned my head away from him.

Graybull insisted upon buying lunch. Papa joined us, much to my relief, and was talkative, having moved our belongings into our permanent lodgings. It was the perfect excuse to leave Graybull at last—to go unpack my things.

The little frame house we'd moved into was solid and plain. Behind the small parlor to the left of the door Papa had commandeered the dining room. His papers were spread over the table, a crate of books lay in the middle of the floor, and rolled blueprints were stacked in the corners.

I recalled the golden light that played across his drafting table at home in Newport, the papers strewn across the two broad, oak assistants' desks, the bustle that attended important projects. The parlor there was large enough for our fancy-dress party at Christmas, and for my sixteenth birthday party only last year. I could still see the Tiffany lamps, Stickley chairs, and the cozy niche near the fireplace where I'd lie on green velvet while Mama read to me.

All of that was gone—the velvet, the oak, the bustle, Mama. Replaced by bare walls and tiny rooms and the absence that was the largest hole in my life and my greatest longing. Sometimes this past year, back in Newport, I'd wake up in the earliest dawn and in my half sleep I had forgotten that she was gone; my eyes would catch the familiar room, my wardrobe, my window, and I'd think she was still there with me. Here in this stick house in the wilderness, there would be no dreaming.

These small dreary rooms were outfitted with dark mahogany. My bedroom, upstairs, was tiny, with one window looking out at the parade grounds. And with Papa's work spread out through the dining room, we'd have to eat in the kitchen. At least with no servants or cook, no one would be in our way.

I stood in the doorway and sighed, leaning my head against the frame, sagging against it. We were setting roots in Yellowstone.

Oh, Mama. I miss you so. If you hadn't left me, we'd be in the midst of planning the second-biggest event of my life. I wouldn't be tolerating a George Graybull or a tacky house. I wouldn't be subject to a father who'd lied to me. I wouldn't be stranded out here, friendless . . .

I stopped myself. Not friendless. I had Tom. My heart skipped a little beat. Yes, there was Tom.

Chapter SEVENTEEN

Can I say of her face—altered as I have reason to remember it, perished as I know it is—that it is gone, when here it comes before me at this instant as distinct as any face that I may choose to look on in a crowded street?

—*David Copperfield*, Charles Dickens, 1850

"THERE'RE TO BE FIREWORKS, AND A DINNER, AND A BALL with an orchestra from Bozeman!" Gretchen Mills was breathless after her recitation.

Ten days had passed since we'd moved into the cottage. I unpacked trunks and set about placing our tiny house in order, and got to know Gretchen, who lived with her officer husband and their girls in the adjoining apartments. Now Gretchen and I sat in the Millses' parlor, watching her daughters play with their dolls and discussing plans for the next evening, the fourth of July.

There was a sense of camaraderie among these inmates on Officers' Row. They packed a busy social life into the short summer. I liked Gretchen. She was sweet, if a little sheltered, wrapped up in the life she made for her family, and she was the first woman other than Mrs. Gale to really befriend me here.

Gretchen chattered on. "I ordered a new dress from the Elite catalogue. It arrived the other day. Would you like to see it?"

I smiled and nodded. It was nice to talk of fashion and put aside my worries for the moment. Left alone with the two children while Gretchen fetched the dress, I watched as they buttoned tiny waists and laced miniature shoes, pretending to be little mothers. I had a doll—Sara Jane—with a bisque head and auburn hair and a wardrobe full of handmade clothes. She had her own bentwood cradle, painted black, all curls and arches, and a place of honor in my room.

I swallowed hard. She was gone with all the rest of my things. I felt weary with loss.

Gretchen returned with a summery, embroidered, white lawn dress with a pale blue satin girdle at the waist.

I fingered the satin. "It's lovely." I sighed. I would have liked something new. We'd packed so quickly for this trip. Many of my gowns were—where? Had Papa sold my clothes with everything else? By all rights, I should have an entire new wardrobe, ordered especially for my season; instead I had things that were beginning to show wear. I wasn't very handy with needle and thread. I'd never had to master those skills. I wondered what I would wear to the ball the next evening. I supposed I could wear the green silk again. Especially since Graybull, who had already seen me in it, was off on his hunting trip, to my immense pleasure.

"All the young officers will be at the ball tomorrow," Gretchen said. "Including several unmarried men." She giggled. "I met my husband at a ball in Washington."

Oh, heavens. I smiled at her expense; the last thing I wanted to do was marry an officer. The thought was appalling. There were no military families in our crowd at home. I hoped she took my smile for encouragement.

She did, nattering on about possible suitors for me. None of which were realistic, of course. I allowed myself to daydream about what I thought of my prospects. I'd only just begun to realize the great divide between wealth and passion. I could marry for one or marry for the other, but I realized it was rare to marry for both. That love who stood next to me on a high cliff, he was what I wanted, wasn't he? Practical Kitty might have said, fine, but money is an excellent cushion if you should fall.

Edward? I'd written him twice during the journey out here, before Papa revealed that we were staying here permanently. He hadn't responded. I suspected he had heard news of my situation from Kitty by now. The kiss last summer seemed like a distant dream.

Graybull. As Papa said, he had the status and money. He could return me to the proper circles. I watched Gretchen as she talked; watched her girls. I saw in my mind's eye Graybull and the way his tongue pushed into the gap in his teeth, the steely way he held his shoulders, the way his hand grasped my arm as if I were something to be steered and controlled, like an unruly horse. I shuddered and rubbed my forearms.

Tom. He couldn't possibly be a suitor. He didn't have two nickels to rub together. He teased me incessantly and thought me a snob. There was no future there for me. But still. Tom. I could not avoid thinking of him. His eyes, like the sea. When he looked at me, I felt as if our souls met. That funny lock of hair that wouldn't stay put, that I kept wanting to touch, to brush aside. That lanky stride, and his hands that could cup both of mine . . .

"Oh, Maggie, how you blush!" Gretchen giggled. "I assure you, these officers are gentlemen, though they do love to dance."

I smiled back. I wasn't thinking about dancing.

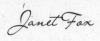
The nanny bustled in to fetch the girls for a nap and I felt a twinge of jealousy. The senior officers were provided with help. Papa and I were managing alone, and I'd never been in a home without servants, let alone managed one. Cook would have laughed herself silly at some of my dreadful attempts in the kitchen. And cleaning . . . Gretchen was only an officer's wife and she had a nanny and a maid.

Gretchen leaned over and patted my hand. "I'm so happy you're here. Most of the wives are older—it's exciting to have someone new and almost my age. You'll have coffee, won't you? My maid's just come back from one of her protracted vacations—honestly, you'd think she'd appreciate the position, and not dash off at a moment's notice! Kula!" Gretchen called. "Where is that girl? She's always disappearing when I need her. Kula!"

Someone stirred at the door, and I met the eyes of a girl only a little younger than me. I knew her at once, though I'd only seen her at a distance. Both the coal-black braid and her bearing were unmistakable. She was the girl from Mammoth, that first day, and then again from the Wylie tent camps. Her skin was the color of tea-stained cloth and her eyes were dark, almost black. Clearly, Gretchen was right; she had no thought for her station and wore her pride, which bordered on insolence, like a badge.

"Fetch the coffee, girl, for pity's sake!" said Gretchen, and the girl swept from the room. "I don't know what to do with her. Her manners are appalling. She takes off for days at a time, never mind her responsibilities. I'm going to ask Timothy if he can find her other employment in the Park."

The girl came back with the coffee and dropped the tray on the

table so that the cream slopped and the cups clattered. I leaned
back quickly as the cream splashed across the table.

"Careful, Kula!" Gretchen chided. "Honestly!"

The girl stood erect and stared boldly at Gretchen. She was
haughty; it was obvious she resented her position. I tried to catch
her eye, but she glared at me and flipped her long braid over her
shoulder and left. There was something about her movements that
joggled my memory.

"Who is she?"

"Kula? Just some girl who works for people here. Indian." I heard
my grandmother's voice in Gretchen's comment and the disdain
that she, too, would have expressed. I shifted, uncomfortable. Tom's
words echoed through me: "white man's way."

Kula. "She seems young."

"Perhaps. I really have no idea. It would explain her careless
ways. Still, she'd better learn to mind her business."

For the rest of the visit, my mind drifted to Kula. I no longer
listened to Gretchen; but she didn't seem to mind, wanting nothing
more than an audience.

I compared myself with Kula, imagining myself in her shoes.
Kula would have no season; it never would have been a possibility.
Her clothes were handmade, but not by a dressmaker. Her finest
fabrics were calicos, not silks. She wouldn't live in a grand house
unless she served there. She had no expectation of privilege. And
when she married, she'd marry for love alone.

I looked down at my crisp, taffeta skirt, touched Mama's cameo,
pushed my fingers up into my hair that was tucked into fat, ivory
combs. Why was I needled by guilt? Or for that matter, checked by

fear? I could avoid the hard landing if I fell. I had options—Kula did not.

I twisted my hands in my lap and looked at the white dress on the chair next to Gretchen, and leaned over to fondle the blue silk ribbon. I'd always expected to have beautiful things in my life. I'd been brought up expecting to be surrounded by expensive things. I'd never thought of myself as a beautiful and expensive thing, but seeing Kula had cast a distorted reflection my way. I was like Ghost, pampered and spoiled and able to be bought and sold to the highest bidder. In Newport, I thought I knew my track, that I had a say in how my life would be, but I was deceiving myself. I never had a choice. Here, all was laid bare. Marry well and live as expected or . . . Or what?

For the remainder of the afternoon I couldn't shake these troublesome thoughts.

Chapter EIGHTEEN ❦ ❦ ❦ ❦ ❦ ❦

July 4, 1904

> *Our music was the finest . . . On one occasion*
> *we had the ladies' orchestra from Butte, Mont. . . .*
> *Our officers at different times added to the*
> *enjoyment of the occasion by appearing*
> *with their wives.*
>
> —"Bath's Soldier Boy," W. H. Walsh,
> in Bath (ME) *Independent*, 1895

THE INDEPENDENCE DAY DINNER AND DANCE WAS HELD in the National Hotel. The event was open to anyone with a dollar fifty to spend, and I could tell by the number of carriages out front that it was popular with the Wylie sagebrushers.

I looked for Tom but was disappointed not to see him in the crowd. Despite that, I felt lighthearted for the first time in Yellowstone. With Graybull off on his trip, at least I wouldn't feel like his personal trophy, bought and paid for.

The cooks had prepared "a traditional American picnic," with barbecued chicken and pork ribs, potato salad and biscuits, and apple cobbler for desert. Red, white, and blue bunting was strung through the chandeliers and along the front porch and the tables were set with red carnations. It might not have been the extravaganza of Mary's ball with its millions of tiny electrics and handsome favors, but it was most festive and happy.

After dinner, the tables were removed as the orchestra set up at one end of the dining room. The weather was perfect and the windows were thrown open so that those on the porch could hear the music. There were enough giggly young women to capture the officers' attentions. I danced, but could also sit out and watch. After one strenuous waltz, I retreated to the porch with my shawl loose about my shoulders.

"Evening, miss." The voice I heard from behind slipped up my spine in the nicest possible way.

"Tom!" I spun around. I was so pleased to see him that I almost became a giggly young woman myself. "Have you been here all evening?"

"We've been working up near Gardiner the past week. Just got back." He was dressed in clean, pressed pants, a starched shirt, and polished boots. Even his hair was slicked back from his face, the cowlick held firmly in place. I smiled and bit the inside of my lip to keep from grinning outright. He'd dressed up. I wondered if it was because of what I'd said. He looked handsome and dashing. "Have you been on the Tour yet?"

"Not yet." I couldn't stop looking at him.

"You'll be astounded." His smile was dazzling.

We stood on the porch together and I found it hard to believe that anything could be nicer than this moment. I had to turn away and look into the distance to keep from sinking into his eyes.

The last light of the day graced the peaks, on fire with red sunset. The sky above the mountains melted upward into deeper blue, like velvet. Steam from the springs curled up and vanished into the night air. A small herd of elk emerged from the hills behind the hotel and took up position for the night on the parade ground opposite.

I watched the sky darken above the hot springs and the stately elk grazing and thought about Mama's paintings. Being here, seeing this, I saw the paintings differently now, in my mind's eye. I recalled them as being close and accurate, not hellish. The amount of detail she had included—the color and texture of every rock, every leaf—I could feel her longing for this place. I understood why she was captivated by Yellowstone. It had a magic beauty.

Tom's arm brushed my shoulder and my stomach turned somersaults and all those other thoughts vanished. Only inches between us, charged with energy, and I let my shawl slip a little so that I might feel that electricity through the silk of my sleeve.

The orchestra played a slow waltz and the laughter of revelers washed out through the windows and into the night. I wondered whether Tom would ask me to dance. I wished he would. I glanced at him and caught him watching me. We both blushed and looked away.

"They'll have fireworks soon," Tom said.

"I guess that'll send the elk flying." I laughed.

Tom stepped away, feigning shock. "She laughs!"

I couldn't erase the silly grin from my face.

"You have a nice laugh. You should try it more often."

"I haven't had much reason to laugh lately." I looked at him. Tom made me feel like laughing; Tom made me happy.

"I'm glad to see that's changing." He looked at me, serious, with those sea-gray eyes. I felt the warmth in my cheeks rise and turned to watch the soldiers begin to set up the fireworks display.

"There won't be any bears at the backdoor tonight," Tom said.

"No matter what scraps they've tossed, the fireworks will scare all the wildlife away."

No bears. Good. I drew my shawl up over my shoulders. "I wish people wouldn't do that. Feed the bears." I shuddered as I recalled the grizzly's flat but mesmerizing eyes.

Tom turned and faced me, his eyebrows raised. "You listened to me. I appreciate that."

I wasn't motivated by the naturalist instinct, as he imagined, but by my fear. I wouldn't let him know that. It felt wonderful to have his approval. "You're a good teacher." We exchanged a long look in which time seemed to stop before I had to drop my gaze. He did not look away, but lifted his hand toward mine.

"Would you like to dance?"

At last! I raised my head to agree just as the music stopped. Disappointment flooded me as he dropped his hand. I gave a small shrug. "Next time, I guess." Next time, if we danced, I feared I'd become lost in his arms.

Revelers poured out onto the veranda, surrounding us, and the spell broke. Soldiers on horseback herded the elk off the parade ground. Suddenly, rockets roared into the night sky, whistling and screaming, fire in the blackness. The hills reflected the light, scattershot. People laughed and cheered and there were huzzahs and toasts to our nation's birthday. I stood inches away from Tom and felt as though the fireworks came from inside me.

At one giant blast, I took Tom's arm without thinking and felt his fingers fold over mine, warm and strong. Finally, when the last blast crescendoed and the night grew still, the crowd roared its approval and then began to disperse, drifting into carriages and hotels. The fireworks inside me had not quieted as Tom and I stood together, touching, not moving.

Behind us waiters and busboys cleared the hall. Outside, the evening faded into quiet with only a small number of laughing couples left around us. The stars reappeared in the black sky above. My hand still rested on Tom's arm, his fingers still covering mine; the current between us was electric. I could not speak.

He broke the silence, his voice soft. "Can I walk you back to the hotel?"

I took a breath. "We moved. We're in a house on Officers' Row. That's home, for now."

"Good!" He pulled away a little, but he was smiling. "That means you're staying." I wanted to ask if that made him happy, but my tongue was in a knot. I was off balance once again with him, this time from shyness and longing. All I could do was smile.

We walked down the road in silence and I left my arm linked with his. We reached the cottage and he turned to face me.

As I looked at him something moved in the shadows behind. I stifled a yell, throwing my hand up over my mouth, and I backed away as Tom spun around. Fear gripped my heart. *Bear.*

But it wasn't a grizzly. Kula stepped into the circle of light cast by the streetlamp.

"You!" I said, relief flooding me.

Kula glared and said nothing but turned on her heel and marched up the steps and in through the Millses' door.

Tom started after her. "Kula!"

"You know her?" I had regained my bearings and was annoyed with her, both from the fright she'd given me, and also at what

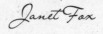

she'd interrupted. And there was still that haunting feeling she raised in me each time I saw her.

"I've met her a few times. She does washing. Comes around to the camp to take things up or drop them off every week or so." He stared at the house where she had disappeared, and not at me. "Does she live here, then? I never knew."

"She's a maid. She works for the Millses." I remembered the jealousy I'd felt when I heard that Isabel and Edward knew each other. This was far worse. I folded my arms over my chest.

"She does good work. She's nice. I've thought maybe she was part Crow, with those cheekbones. Do you know anything else about her?" Tom still looked at the house, and not at me.

"I wouldn't know a thing. She's just a maid." Jealousy made me speak without thinking. "She's rude, as you can see. She doesn't know her station."

He turned and looked at me then, but his eyes were ice. "So?"

"She's a maid." I wanted to kick myself, watching his reaction.

He stepped away from me. All I could see was the reflection of light in his eyes, like two sharp pins. "You know, Maggie, just when I think you're all right, you come up with these obnoxious comments."

I struggled to keep the tears in. I wanted to say something, anything, to win him back, but words melted away like butter.

"Who are you, Maggie? A spoiled, rich debutante or a decent girl?"

I couldn't answer. My throat was thick with stopped tears.

"I'd like to think you're decent and you just don't know any better."

I could think of nothing to say. Nothing.

He took another step away and I wished I had the courage to reach my arm out to him. "See you around." He moved off, and I felt the world collapse inside me.

He was yards away when I whispered, "Good night," and dragged myself inside the house.

Instead of lighting the parlor lamp, I stood in the window and watched Tom as he walked beneath the streetlamps lining the row. He appeared, vanished and reappeared, as he drifted from one to the next pool of golden light until he vanished completely, swallowed into the inky dark.

Chapter NINETEEN

"We Never Sleep"

—motto of Pinkerton's National Detective Agency,
founded 1850

"ISN'T THERE ANYTHING?" I ASKED THE CLERK AT THE mail depot. "Not a single letter?"

"Nothing," he said, and turned away.

"Can you check on telegrams? Maybe a telegram has come and been misplaced."

The clerk turned back, leveling his eyes at me. "Miss, we deliver telegrams immediately."

I could tell I'd insulted him. "Of course you do." I turned to leave, then turned back. "If anything comes . . ."

"I'll let you know right away, miss." He was most annoyed with me now. It was all over his face.

"Right. Thanks." I made my way back to our lodgings through the clear morning light. I'd written the letter to Grandpapa two weeks earlier; I thought I would have heard from him by now. Since my awful parting from Tom last night, I knew I had to escape from Papa's prison, no matter the cost.

There had been a few days when Yellowstone hadn't seemed so bad. When despite the misery of Papa's lies and Mama's absence, despite Graybull's obnoxious attentions, despite the low conditions in which we lived, despite the loss of my Ghost, my season, my things, when Tom had made this place appealing. But I could not rely on small moments that could be banished by Tom's cold shoulder and Kula's interference.

It was just a little spark of jealousy on my part, for pity's sake. I spoke stupidly; but Tom's response had been so harsh. Kula *was* a servant, after all. I kicked at a stone in the road. Ugly thoughts circled me like buzzards. Without Tom I had no reason to like Yellowstone, no reason to stay here. I wished for the hundredth time that I had held my tongue. I wished for the thousandth time that he hadn't been so curt. He was probably gone from my life forever.

So I looked back to my grandfather to come to my rescue. To come and take me home to Newport, where at least my prison would be comfortable, and my future secured. Edward might like me again, and I could pick up the pieces of my life. Mama would come home as she'd promised. I kicked another stone in the road. I'd get over Tom, surely.

This waiting for my grandfather was frustrating. This mooning over Tom more frustrating still.

I arrived at our little house. Papa was off somewhere—he seemed to have endless appointments since we'd moved into our cottage. I hung my hat by its ribbons on the hall hat stand. The dining-room door was open and Papa's papers were scattered across the broad table.

I drifted in. I'd never pried through his things, just helped him as he directed. Now my disappointments enclosing me, and my renewed desire to have my old Newport life back, sparked my curiosity. Perhaps Papa had some information here that I could use. I felt a sneaky guilt, sifting through his secrets, but also a reckless misery.

I lifted blueprints: They were additions to various hotels in the Park and sketches for buildings in the rustic style so popular here. Other papers were scattered in untidy piles. I picked up one stack and leafed through it.

A letter caught my eye. Attached were several copies of a photograph of Ghost.

I ran my fingers over the picture, feeling the tears well up. Ghost. It was high time I got Grandpapa to take me home. Beneath the photograph was a notice for a princely price on Ghost: $400.

I gripped the letter, wanting to rip it to shreds. Papa had no right to have done this to me. Ghost wasn't property; Ghost was my friend, my only friend, it felt like now. I pocketed one copy of Ghost's picture in a tiny theft. Hah! My jaw was tight, my lips were pressed together. Once I returned to Newport, leaving Papa alone, maybe then he'd suffer the way he made me suffer now. Maybe then he'd understand what it meant to lose everything you loved. I rubbed my eyes hard with my palm and went at my task anew.

There were dry business letters regarding Papa's employment in the Park. There were bills and receipts; the numbers on these were shocking. I had not known much about our finances in Newport, but I could see here that Papa had not been lying: He had lost everything. Our debts were enormous. Some of the letters from creditors were threatening. If he had not sold our things, he'd be in prison.

I spent what felt like hours looking through these papers.

They made me feel sick. I hadn't seen how far he'd fallen after Mama left, how his work had suffered, all as a consequence of her disappearance.

I touched Ghost's picture in my pocket, feeling painfully aware of my selfishness. Papa *did* know, after all, what it was like to lose what you loved. He and I both knew. I wondered what I would have done had he taken me into his confidence and let me know of our situation earlier. Would I have let go of Ghost on my own?

I rifled deeper. I uncovered a telegram, dated March 20, 1904.

CERTAIN COMPLICATIONS STOP UNABLE TO
FIND TRAIL STOP MAY BE DEAD AFTER ALL
STOP GOOD NEWS JOB WAITING GET HERE
SOON AS POSSIBLE STOP JOHN

I dropped the papers and placed my hands on the table, trying to still the room from spinning me straight off the face of the earth. I backed away from the table.

Complications. Dead.

My mind circled the words around and around. Mama. Papa had been searching for her and Uncle John had been helping him. But it didn't make sense. Papa had been so happy that day he heard from John—there had to be more. I had to understand. I grabbed the entire stack of papers—letters, telegrams, documents—and ran upstairs to my bedroom. I locked the door and then spread all the papers out on my bed in a broad fan.

I prayed I could resolve the mystery, find the answers at last. The stories of Mama and my future were written in these papers. I could feel it.

Here: a long letter from Uncle John dated April 6. It was full of John's ebullient descriptions of Yellowstone, his work, his companions, and on and on, of little interest to me, until

> I've engaged some Pinkerton men, and they report that they have found evidence of a trail. But, Charlie, this may not lead in the direction you think. Are you sure you want me to pursue this? Think of Maggie—is this fair to her? I don't mean to intrude, but perhaps your fixation is unhealthy.

I reread the paragraph over and over. Of course Papa's fixation was unhealthy, anyone could have seen that. But what direction, what evidence, what trail . . . ? My hands shook and I leaned over the papers and rested my fists on my bed and let my hair fall out of its pins and over my shoulders. I had to do this, I had to know.

I resumed my search, flipping page after page. Finally, this, from John on May 23:

> Success! But the trail goes hot and cold. Suggest you come out at once to assess. And other good news regarding employment.

It was dated after the telegram. After the "may be dead." Mama could indeed be alive.

I sat down in the chair across the room, holding this letter in my trembling hand. "Success!" I read again and again. Mama could be alive. Papa was keeping all of this from me.

I grabbed another stack of papers, dropping the ones not of

interest to me on the floor, careless now, desperate for news. Here was one, very early, addressed to Mama before her disappearance.

15 August 1903

Mrs. C. Bennet: We regret to report we have been unsuccessful in our attempts to locate your subject. All avenues have proven fruitless. Should you wish to continue your search, the fee will double and must be remitted in advance.

H.K. Wilkinson, &c., Private Investigative Specialists

It was baffling. Mama had been searching for someone? But who? I was missing something, I had to be. I pawed fruitlessly through the remaining papers, tossing them aside in a general mess. Nothing. I sat on the floor, my head swimming, trying to pull myself together, trying to make sense of everything I knew.

It didn't make sense. Both Mama and Papa had hidden things from me; and from one another, I suspected.

I got up on wobbly legs and took from the box on my dresser the folded letter that Mama had left for me that I'd kept these many months and buried it in the pocket of my skirt.

I threw my shawl about my shoulders and went outside. I needed air. I needed to clear my head, to think. I crossed the parade ground, making a wide arc around the four elk grazing languidly in front of a knot of tourists. Holding my skirts, I started up the hill to the springs and then veered off on the path that led into the woods.

"Miss!" The voice from behind me was unmistakable. I stopped and turned.

"Why, Caleb. I'm correct, am I not? It's Caleb?" I smoothed

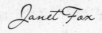

my skirt and gave the familiar soldier my prettiest smile. "What can I do for you today?"

"Can't go alone into the woods, missy." He marched up and planted himself between me and the woods above.

My smile became fixed. "Why not?"

Caleb drew himself up. He was a self-important little man. I'd had enough of self-important little men. "It's very dangerous to be on your own in the woods."

"Is it a rule?" I asked, all sweetness.

"Hey?" He seemed surprised.

"A rule. You know, like running near the springs."

He seemed put out. "Not precisely."

"Well, then." I tugged the shawl tight about my shoulders and pushed past him and continued up the path. My words came out staccato. "I'll go where I please." Fearful woods and wildlife or not, I was sick and tired of being ordered about. Papa, Graybull, Grandpapa—they kept secrets from me, treated me like property, made all the decisions in my life, and I'd had enough.

His call from behind me reeked of frustration. "Missy, I cain't be responsible."

I kept walking. "Then don't be," I stopped and looked back at him. "Oh!" I pointed over his shoulder at a group of tourists. "Are they defacing the rocks?" They weren't, of course, but I suspected he would follow me and I wanted rid of him.

He turned, confused. "Hey!" he called down to them. Defacing rocks needed his attention more than the prospect of a girl walking alone. He twisted back to me, "Don't you go off, missy!" he yelled, then he turned and ran down the hill shouting after the tourists, "Hey! Hey!"

I swept on, more determined to assert my independence than to avoid an unnamed threat.

The day was clear following a cool night. I climbed higher up the hill, into the trees. The path skirted the edges of the springs and I glimpsed the hot-spring terraces through the pines as I walked. Even in the trees the ground was white with sinter; there were abandoned and lesser springs everywhere. The smell of pine mingled with the smell of sulphur and the whole of it was quiet.

I came out on an overlook suddenly, and immediately stepped back, my stomach lurching with the vertigo. I touched the trunk of a nearby pine to steady myself as I looked across the view and not down. Anything but down. I kept a safe distance from the edge and kept my hand on the tree, my fingers on the rough, solid bark.

The sky went on forever, over the peaks, over the distant snowcaps, and it rolled up and over me into a sharp robin's-egg blue hung with clouds like piled foam. I'd been so tied up in the cottage that this was the first expedition walk I'd taken in Yellowstone alone in the two weeks we'd been here. I took a deep breath and it was like inhaling that blue, the air was so clean, the pine smell pungent and tarry.

I took Mama's letter from my pocket. I didn't need to open it. I knew it by heart.

> . . . There is something I must do. There is someone
> I left years ago to whom I must return. You must
> promise—swear on your love for me—not to tell your
> father. He will not understand, and knowing that I've
> made this choice will only serve to bring him pain. I
> will be going away, now, and may not see you for a long
> time. But I've neglected a trust.

Sometimes we do things because we've been told that society holds them to be important. Don't believe that, Maggie. Believe in yourself. Take chances. Find true love, no matter where, and hold on to it. Don't let go. Don't ever let go. Remember, dear heart—nothing is more powerful than love.

I stuffed the letter back into my pocket, buried it deep. I believed Mama was alive. She'd been searching for someone, and when she came up empty in Newport, she had set off to find them. Papa had known of her search; he had this information about Mama, and had lied to me. Papa had lied to me so many times in the past year that his lies were a web of confusion.

"Don't let go . . . nothing is more powerful than love." Tom roared back into my mind and I gripped the trunk of the pine tighter. Thank you, Mama, for that sage advice. I'd try to follow it the next time I met someone I liked, since I'd so utterly mucked up this one.

A twig snapped and I heard something grunt behind me. I froze. Fear sucked the strength from me. All other thoughts vanished and were replaced by the memory of the bear swinging its head back and forth, back and forth. I turned in barely perceptible movements, my throat tight, not daring to breathe. I was ready to fall to the ground and lie there as still as death.

It was a doe, a tiny fawn at her side, two sets of brown eyes huge with fear, mirroring mine.

Eyes of a doe, in the strangled moment of death, in a painting hanging on the wall of a house on the other side of the continent, a painting that hung above my desperate mother while she bled onto white silk.

I cried out, and at the sound of my cry the doe coughed, then turned and leapt across the clearing behind, to the edge of a small hot spring that bubbled a sickly yellow, the sinter around it fragile like ice in a melting pond. And before I could breathe, the doe stumbled onto the sinter, which cracked and gaped, and she dropped into the boiling water like a rock, dying before she could finish her scream of pain.

Both the fawn and I watched this happen, frozen, panting. The fawn bleated once, then turned and leapt into the woods.

I turned and vomited into the leaves.

My fault. All my fault.

I vomited again, trying not to look at what remained of the doe. I heard the fawn bleating from somewhere in the woods. Both of us were lost, alone and bewildered.

Chapter TWENTY

So I lost her. So I saw her afterwards, in my
sleep at school—a silent presence near my bed
—looking at me with the same intent face—holding
up her baby in her arms.

—*David Copperfield*, Charles Dickens, 1850

"MARGARET?"

My heart was cracked open as I entered the hall, the horror of the doe and the memory of Mama looming fresh in my mind. Papa was standing by the dining table.

"Come in here, please." His voice was tense and tight, his eyes hard.

The papers. I'd left them scattered all over my room.

"Have you been . . ." He stopped and peered at me, concern crossing his face. "What happened? You look terrible."

He seemed to care. I couldn't remember when Papa had last seemed to care about me. But the impact of his concern faded against my fevered misery and guilt. I'd killed the doe as surely as if I'd shot it. I waved my hand. "I'm feeling ill. May I be excused?" I swayed.

His face softened. "Of course. We'll talk later." I climbed the stairs with lead feet and I could hear him shuffling the papers, no doubt looking for something that was in fact on my bedroom floor.

I locked my door and collapsed onto the floor, dragging the

154

papers toward me. I tidied them as best I could; I lifted my mattress and slid the stack underneath. I'd have to sneak them back downstairs later.

I rinsed my face in the washbowl and lay across my bed, trying to keep the nausea from rising up again, trying to gather my thoughts. They spun in dizzying circles like a game's teetotum, pointing this way and then that.

My mind turned from the doe's eyes to Mama's eyes, and at last to my memory of her on the last day I saw her, after she'd left my bedroom. After my last words to her: "I don't care if I never see you again." It was my fault, as surely as if I'd pushed the doe into the hot spring. It was my fault, as surely as if I'd pushed Mama off the Cliff Walk and into the raging sea.

I had wanted to stop her from leaving, but I didn't. She left my room that last day and I lay in my bed in misery, hoping she'd come back. Finally, I threw off the pillow and crept as close as I dared to my tower window. Beyond the sea grass and rocks, the waves frothed high, as high as I'd ever seen them. I looked out for her, and there she was—walking away from me. She walked away from the house, robe billowing, her black hair streaming. As she reached the edge of the cliff, that fearful cliff of my nightmares, where the walk passed through the hedgerow, she turned. Even from the distance safe away from my window's edge, I could see her expression, the slight parting of her lips.

I reached my arm toward the window. I tried to edge closer but couldn't. The fall was too great, the edge, the empty space. My stomach dropped and then my arm. I called out to her, but it was too far. She could not hear me over the thunderous sea. She turned away and disappeared over the rocky ledge and I drew back deep

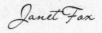

inside my room. I didn't run to her; I didn't stop her; I sent her away with a curse. It was my fault.

Now, nearly a year later, I lay on a different bed in a far different room with the turmoil of guilt raging through me, struggling with my spinning thoughts. Mama had been in Yellowstone. She'd been obsessed with Yellowstone, in fact, abandoning her tranquil landscapes as her pain grew, choosing to paint the most tormented views of Yellowstone hour upon hour. The letters said that she'd left someone behind, tried to find them. Could it have been a lover? Sadness shot through me as I thought how Papa might feel if that were true. Did she not love him? Did he not love her?

I stared at the ceiling and my thoughts spun faster. Tom. I'd disappointed him. I felt my cheeks flush with shame. I wanted to see him again and explain myself. I wanted to touch him, to brush back that silly lock of hair that fell across his forehead, I wanted him to touch me. I clutched the coverlet in both fists, holding tight.

I could not escape the question of what would become of me.

In one direction my future was wide open. A great gaping hole waited there with nothing to hold me up. I imagined I was standing at my window at home, right at the sill, or on the cliff facing the sea. What would it be like to leap, to let go and fall?

In the other direction, everything was predictable and I wouldn't need to worry, to be in control. My mind drifted to George Graybull, whose attentions were unpleasantly focused on me. Papa envisioned our salvation through Graybull. Me marrying Graybull. That was a sickening thought. I could see it rationally: my prospects would be settled, in a manner appropriate to our station. To our former station. And wasn't that what I had wanted, even demanded? To return to Newport, to pick up my former life, to be accepted in society and take my place beside Kitty and the others? But Graybull . . . oh, heavens. His face appeared in my mind's eye, his leering smile and that dreadful gesture with his tongue. The way he looked at me as if I were his prey . . .

I shifted onto my side and tried to focus on something else, anything else.

A photograph hung on the wall above the bed, a picture of a spray of water arcing into the air. OLD FAITHFUL GEYSER was inscribed across the bottom. I pulled myself up onto my elbows and stared at it, shoving Graybull firmly out of my mind.

I imagined seeing the image of the geyser through the lens of a camera. I focused my eyes on the photograph, almost able to see every droplet of water, looking at line and shape and not at water as substance. Art as movement; art as expression. Art the way Mama had taught me to see it. The art of making pictures.

Making art and real, solid, concrete magic. Mrs. Gale did that, here in Yellowstone. Every day she made her own magic in her art and in her life. She was not subject to the rules of men. She was not beholden to Newport society. In my experience only girls like Kula worked, not girls like Kitty—or me. But Mrs. Gale dressed well and lived well, working at something she was passionate about. I had not ever considered this as an option for me. It had never been one before. Could it be now? I stared at the photograph thinking about how, if I held a camera, I might frame that same shot and feel that same passion.

And as I lay on the bed and wrapped my thoughts in and out and around the twining vines of my future and Papa's secrets and

Mama's secrets and Uncle John's letters, the answer came to me. I sat up and tossed my hair back over my shoulders. It was so obvious, so easy. I had to speak to Uncle John.

My uncle would have the answers I sought; he could help me fit the pieces of the puzzle into place. He'd returned to his work at the Lake Hotel on the other side of the Park. I could try to send him a telegram; but it would be tricky to manage Papa, and I couldn't expect a clear answer. Or any answer, if my experience with my grandfather was any indication. I could telephone if I could find one—they were rare enough in Newport, never mind Yellowstone. Trickier still. I needed to see Uncle John face-to-face. I had to convince Papa to send me to the Lake Hotel.

I stood up and paced, gathering my hair into a single braid as I wrestled with this idea.

The Tour.

Of course. Tom had mentioned it, and then Papa had said something about sending me to see the rest of the Park. Tom had said that I should go, and now I had a reason to. Papa would never suspect my reason.

I stayed in my room for the rest of the day, weaving my plan together and firming my resolve, avoiding memories of the doe and her orphaned fawn and of my mama's eyes the last time I saw her.

Chapter TWENTY-ONE

*Hurry you hounds of hell to the
mountains where
The daughters of
Cadmus hold their wild séance.*

—*The Bacchae,* Euripides, c. 408 BCE

THE FOLLOWING MORNING THE SAME SURLY CLERK I'D encountered at the telegram office delivered a telegram and a letter addressed only to me. I was glad Papa wasn't at home to question their contents. First was this telegram:

YOU HAVE BEEN TAKEN WRONGLY STOP WILL
SUE TO BECOME LEGAL GUARDIAN BRING
YOU HOME STOP YOUR INHERITANCE AT
STAKE STOP WAIT FOR FURTHER NEWS STOP
GRANDFATHER

And then this letter from Kitty:

Maggie! This is dreadful! But I have stunning news—
Edward was shocked when I confided your condition to
him and he has offered to come to your aid. A knight

riding to your rescue—isn't he sweet? He's so adorable I
could just steal him from you. I shall send you some new
gloves, as your old ones must be getting terribly frayed.
And there are some lovely new hats in fashion—quite large
but I shall try and ship. I have a perfectly darling little
tricorn with a veil.

I stared at the papers in my hand. Grandpapa was suing to
become my guardian. And Edward was ready to ride to my rescue.
It was everything I wanted, everything I'd hoped for—a return
to Newport, to my friends, to wealth and position, to a young man
who cared enough to rescue me. I'd have money and a home, and
would not have to endure Graybull for it. I could have my Ghost
back, maybe even Mina. I sank onto the stairs and stared through
the glass panes of the front window, absorbing this news.

I should be rejoicing and yet I was not. According to Grandpapa,
Papa had all but kidnapped me. Should Grandpapa win, my father
would become a pariah. His lies would cost him whatever he had
left in this world, including me. I felt ill at this thought. Though
he had lied to me, and I wanted him to know the hurt he had caused
me, he was my father; I didn't want him to suffer that horror.

And there was my newly devised quest to uncover the truth.
The timing of the letter, the telegram, so soon after I had resolved
to find Uncle John and perhaps even find Mama, the timing was
all wrong. I couldn't abandon my search, not now. Not yet. Not
when I could be so close to learning the truth. Even returning to
Newport and to Edward's arms was not tempting enough to lure
me away from possibly returning to Newport with Mama and Papa
together, as a family.

Edward. The perfect husband, perfect for a life of balls and society. But Edward didn't send fireworks through me with a touch of his hand. I tried to remember what Edward looked like, and . . . nothing came to mind. Oh, I remembered our moment behind the stairs; a blush crept down my throat at that. But . . . Tom.

I couldn't get Tom out of my thoughts. He both infuriated and thrilled me. I couldn't leave Yellowstone without apologizing to Tom. I wouldn't leave without seeing him again. I sat on the stairs and stared into the bright morning light, and had an idea. I went to find Mrs. Gale.

She was working in the Haynes Studios, examining prints. I burst in without even a hello. "Do you know where I might find Tom Rowland?"

She looked up at me with a bemused smile. "Even here in the wilderness, we try to maintain a sense of decorum. I trust you are well?"

I took a deep breath, ashamed. "Of course. I'm sorry, Mrs. Gale. I have to speak to him. It's important." I tried to stand still.

"Yes, I know just where the Rowlands are. I also happen to know that they are soon off to work in another part of the Park and are busy with preparations." She paused as she took in my nervous anticipation. "Young Tom is out at the Wylie camp."

My shoulders slumped as I realized that the distance to the tent camp was a buggy ride and not a walk.

Mrs. Gale pursed her lips. "I happen to be going in that direction, if you'd like to come along. In, say, an hour?"

I couldn't help myself; I hugged her with a spontaneity that made her laugh. I would see Tom again, thanks to her, and delight made me want to dance.

When we drove into the tent camp, the sun was slipping through the trees like slender fingers. The camp was cheerful and welcoming, and was spotlessly clean. Mrs. Gale stopped her buggy near a large, fixed tent on a wood platform. She pointed down the path. "That's the one, about halfway down."

My heart pounded hard as I hurried along, trying to come up with the right words.

Tom was there in front of a tent, loading a wagon with dry goods. He hoisted barrels and boxes into the wagon and swung his long body up to sort and stack and lash them down. I watched him move. I missed him already, even if it had only been two days. I missed him, and I longed to jump right up next to him and tell him so, straight out.

He caught sight of me and straightened. "Hello." His voice was cool.

"Hello." My thoughts were a jumble and my tongue a lead weight. I looked at my feet and took a deep breath and plunged. "I just wanted to tell you that I'm sorry." He was silent. I glanced at him, worried that he hated me. "Mrs. Gale said you're off somewhere?"

"That's right."

"I'm hoping to take the Tour. As soon as Papa will let me go." I was sure now that he hated me, and I wanted to melt away in misery.

"You won't be disappointed."

He was so quiet, so remote. And still, I rushed in, foolishly. "Tom, I'm sorry. I'm sorry that I offended you. I'm sorry for what I said about Kula. I . . . Can we still be friends? Please?"

A smile crept over his face. He leapt off the wagon and walked over to me. My misery vanished at the sight of his grin.

"Margaret Bennet of Newport, Rhode Island, I can't help liking you. I accept your apology."

The smile on my face now must have shone like the sun. "So, maybe we'll meet on the road."

"We very well might." He stood so close now. My throat tightened; he was so close I thought he might kiss me.

But instead he stretched out his hand. "Friends."

"Friends." When he took my hand he held it and he didn't let go, and my heart lifted and my eyes lifted to meet his.

And then, as if from thin air, Kula appeared behind Tom. She came walking around from the other side of the wagon, her arms burdened with a sack.

"Ah!" The sound escaped my lips. I had to admit, she had a sense of timing that was most annoying.

Tom dropped my hand. I bit my lip hard, afraid I'd say something to Kula that I'd regret later. Tom looked from me to Kula. "Kula. This is Maggie. She's living here with her pa."

"I know who she is." Kula put the sack into Tom's wagon, not taking her eyes off of me. "These are done."

"Thanks. Nice to have clean things," Tom said. I watched the flush creep up his neck. He was not looking at me, but at least he wasn't looking at Kula, either. He seemed to be studying something by his right foot.

I fumbled for the right words. "I'm sure you do excellent work." There. That was neutral enough not to insult her, not to put something new and bad between me and Tom.

Kula narrowed her eyes—what was it about her that troubled me so?—and turned away. "I'll see you later, Tom."

"Good-bye," he said. Kula moved off and Tom and I remained

silent. "I don't know her well." Tom looked at Kula's retreating back. "Anyhow. I need to finish loading this wagon. So, see you around?" He pulled away, looking at me only briefly, those gray eyes connecting and then retreating.

"Yes." Oh, I hope so. I only had so much time left here, and I wanted to see him as much as I could. I lifted my fingers as he pulled away, going back to his work. "See you." I sighed. He was busy. Maybe he was embarrassed. I couldn't tell. But I knew my own feelings: I would have stayed and watched him all afternoon if I thought he wanted me to.

I found Mrs. Gale. On the way back to Mammoth we were both quiet, lost in thought, but when we arrived I gave her a quick hug. She said, "My dear, I was young once. Happily married, too."

I smiled. "I'm going to ask Papa if I can take the Tour."

"Ah! Do! I'll be heading out myself in a couple of days. I need some photographs in the geyser basins. Perhaps we could travel together."

I held her hand warmly and thanked her again. Then I made my way back to the cottage, thinking, making plans.

Seeing Tom had clarified things for me. Though I wanted a return to normalcy, I couldn't leave Yellowstone yet. I couldn't let my grandfather deter me from my quest to find Uncle John. I couldn't let Edward come for me, come rescue me, when all I could think about was Tom. It was odd; only a few days ago, I'd wanted to be rescued and to be free of this place more than anything, and now . . . Now I needed time here to resolve these matters. Time in Yellowstone.

I sent my grandfather a telegram telling him that I might have important news about Mama and that I required time to investigate.

I sent Kitty a letter in which I gushed about gloves and hats, and, yes, wasn't Edward a gem?

At dinner I pressed Papa about the Tour. He'd said I could go once we were settled and he had an income now, didn't he? I told him that Mrs. Gale, the Haynes photographer, would be taking the Tour and that she could chaperone me. He stared at his plate of burned potatoes and overcooked steak, at my feeble attempts at cooking. When our eyes met, I could see his guilt and his sadness, and for the first time in a while, I was sad for him. But I used that guilt to my advantage, and he agreed to let me go.

Chapter TWENTY-TWO

July 8, 1904

The roads were good, they are government roads. It was uphill all the way and we went very slowly, trotting gently most of the time until we reached a spring where passengers always alight to get a drink . . .

—testimony of Mrs. Jenny V. Cowdry to Yellowstone Park Transportation Company, 1908

ON THE MORNING OF THE EIGHTH, I STOOD IN FRONT OF the National Hotel, ready to board my bright yellow Yellowstone Wagon with the rest of the "dudes."

"Dudes." That's what the coachman called the passengers. All of us were offered linen dusters, but I had my own, which I'd pulled, still pressed, from my wardrobe.

The other "dudes" in my coach included the Hodges family from Philadelphia: a man, his wife, and their young girls, Emmy and Eliza. There were two older ladies—schoolteachers, I wagered—Miss Braggs and Miss Pym, both bony and wiry, stretched thin. A single man with a nervous demeanor, Mr. Connoly, settled on the seat in front of me. A young couple snuggled beside him, the Monroes; they were clearly on their honeymoon.

And, of course, a joy to my heart, Mrs. Gale. She sat down next to me, her camera box in her lap.

Papa stood at the coach door and cleared his throat. "Enjoy

the Tour, Margaret. You deserve this. Maybe when you get back we'll . . ." He paused as if uncertain what to say next. I felt a tug of sorrow for him. I knew what it was like to lose someone you loved. Hopefully my trip would be a success, but I wasn't ready yet to forgive him for the lies. I looked away.

The coach started with a jolt. Papa lifted his hand. I lifted mine and thought about finding Mama and bringing her back to him and making us a family, the three of us.

Our driver was a thin man with a handlebar mustache that almost reached his throat. He called out the sights in a shout. "At any moment, ladies and gents, prepare to see wild beasts— elk, bears, maybe even a moose! The flowers are all wild, too, but they're harmless, leastwise we think so. We'll stop to feed critters we meet along the way.

"If you want to see a mountain lion, just look off over to your right and you can see a mountain lyin' in the distance, hah! Ah, there's steam rising from springs on your left! Yellowstone is a natural thermal wonderland!"

I had to laugh. My spirits rose as Mrs. Gale and I exchanged glances, shook our heads, and smiled. When the Hodges girls giggled helplessly, the rest of us pitched into fits of laughter.

The road wound through stretches of tall, lodgepole pine and open rolling hills covered in groves of aspen and wildflowers. We stopped at the Apollinaris Spring to sample the sweet water there and to stretch our legs. We passed the Obsidian Cliff— "Arrowheads! The Indians carved their sharpest points from those rocks!"—and Roaring Mountain.

At the Devil's Frying Pan, a hot spring, the driver regaled us: "the birds round about drink that water and they get so hot they

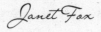

lay hard-boiled eggs! Yessir, you just check out them nests and see for yourself!"

His banter and the jollity that rocked the coach put me at ease, and provided a respite from my painful memories and lingering sadness. I almost forgot the reason I was taking the Tour. And the landscape took my breath away.

Mrs. Gale, beside me, swayed as I did with the rocking motion of the carriage. The camera box rested on her lap. There, in that black box, was a mystery and a promise. What if I didn't go back east? What if? I saw blooming, line by line, shadow by shadow, a future of my design, one that I might focus on right here and now.

We began climbing the steep mountainsides along roaring rivers. I could not bear the sway of the carriage as we negotiated the steep hills, so I leaned toward Mrs. Gale. "Tell me about your camera, please. How does it work?" Mrs. Gale was happy to oblige. She distracted me from the sheer drops by explaining the camera's workings. She opened the bellows and instructed me on the focus; she showed me how the plates were mounted. As we rode mile after mile, I grew increasingly fascinated with this otherworldly instrument and grateful to Mrs. Gale for her kindness to me.

A few hours later, we smelled Norris Geyser Basin, though we were still miles away from it.

"Hottest place in the Park!" said the driver as we drew nearer. "Scores of hot springs, including the second-largest geyser in the world! Why, just two years ago when Steamboat blew its top, yours truly was one of the lucky witnesses!"

The carriage crested a hill and I spied a bleak landscape from the window. It was gray, barren, with steam from fumaroles spiraling into the sky. The sulphur smell here was almost overpowering. Norris was ugly and I wasn't alone in thinking so.

"Good heavens," exclaimed Miss Pym. "A frightful place!" She turned to the other ladies in the coach as we pulled up to the carriage dock. "I've brought my own water," she said conspiratorially, holding up a flask. "I'm sure there's none fit to drink here."

A genial gentleman waiting to help us out of the coach said stiffly, "I beg to differ, madame! Here you will find the finest foods in the Rockies and your thirst will be slaked by the most magnificent vintages of imported ales!"

Mrs. Gale and I sat together at the long table under the tent's shelter. Our luncheon was simple—tinned biscuits and slices of ham—but served as if it were a rare feast.

"Your father and I had a nice chat while we were waiting to board. He told me about his plans to stay in Yellowstone," said Mrs. Gale.

I looked at my plate. They were *his* plans, I wanted to say. They might not be mine. But I changed the subject. "Do you live here year-round?"

She laughed. "I can see that you are not kindly disposed to your father. That's all right. It's quite natural at your age." She paused. "I began to take photographs some years ago, when my husband and I had a ranch and ranching wasn't profitable. By the time Harold died, I'd made a career of photography. Haynes has hired me for the season." She smiled. "People like having their picture taken. I prefer the landscapes."

This was a mystery to me: How could a woman manage without

a husband? She was so strong and sure, but most of all, she was comfortable. I found the idea frightening but thrilling, too. "You must miss your husband."

"Of course. But we had an excellent life, and I have my memories. Harold gave me permission to do what I wished. Not to worry. He was good and kind, and he brought me to Yellowstone. I would live nowhere else."

"Why?" I looked down to the end of the tent and out the door to the white wasteland that lay beyond. Why would she want to live here?

"It's beyond the confines of society." Mrs. Gale sat up, spreading her broad hands, the rings on her fingers catching the light. "Here I've been able to do all the things I was never allowed to do as a girl back home. I ride, I wear comfortable clothes, and I don't have to attend social engagements that don't suit me."

I knit my hands together. While I couldn't say I liked being under the control of my papa, or, potentially, my grandfather, social engagements had suited me just fine back home. I missed Newport's swirl: the gay music, the whispered gossip, my silk dresses, Kitty. I missed having my debut. I even liked my corset, on occasion. At least, I had liked the way it made me look—not as wasp-waisted as Kitty, but still fashionable. I tugged on the whalebone pressing on my ribs, as if that might settle the matter.

But what I missed most was what I'd dreamed about since I was little: Mama helping me through my season, with my wardrobe, with my debut, laughing with me over boys, gossiping with me about girls. I didn't have that. I might never have it. My throat constricted.

It was as though Mrs. Gale read my mind. "Your father told me about your mother," she said. "I'm so sorry, dear."

I placed my fork, then my hand, on the table.

"It must be difficult for you, her passing," said Mrs. Gale.

My emotions welled, all the sorrow, all the hope, tears in my throat. "I think Mama left us. I think she ran off. Maybe she had someone else. I don't know. But I don't think she's dead." I met Mrs. Gale's eyes and leaned forward and whispered. "In fact, I think she may be here. In Yellowstone." I sat up then, straight as a stick. I put my hand on Mama's cameo, pinned at my collar. "That's why I'm going to find her. And then I'm going to get my life back."

Mrs. Gale said nothing; she pursed her lips, her eyes flicking between mine and the cameo.

Mrs. Gale spoke in a gentle voice. "It isn't easy being a young woman without a mother." She patted my arm. "Margaret, I hope you find what you're looking for."

I whispered again, pleading almost. "She might not be dead."

"Ah." She sighed. "I suppose it is . . ."

"Possible." It was. The letters from Uncle John. Papa dragging us out here. It had to be possible. I needed it to be possible. I stared at the table. "I'm not crazy." Hoping that something was true didn't make one crazy. Having a dream didn't make one crazy. The image of Mama at her easel, unseeing, flashed through my mind. I clenched my fists as I recalled the old whispers: mad; eccentric; the apple doesn't fall far from the tree. "I'm not crazy."

"No, dear. Of course you're not." Mrs. Gale was silent. I wove my fingers together carefully, making a nest. "Would you care to help me with my photographic work? I could use a hand now and then."

I looked up at once. "I . . ." I felt a swing of emotion, from sharp sadness to quiet joy. I was being offered a gift. I composed myself, watching Mrs. Gale. "I'd like that very much."

"After all," said Mrs. Gale, "while you're waiting, you might as well keep busy."

I smiled at this wonderful new friend, grateful for her. Images, appearing like magic, from a box. Something I might hold on to. Something I might have forever. I was scared and thrilled all at once.

We heard exclamations from up the path. "Come," said Mrs. Gale. "You haven't even begun to see the beauty here. Come see what waits for you in Yellowstone." We stood and left the tent, carrying Mrs. Gale's equipment. When we rounded the bend of the trail, my mouth fell open in the astonishment of seeing something I'd never imagined.

A fountain played straight from the ground, alternately bubbling and roaring, every few minutes sending up a jet of water forty feet into the air.

It was my first encounter with a geyser.

"Steamboat," shouted the driver, who'd come along as a guide. "This is just a little play, not the real thing."

"How high is the real thing?" I asked, thinking that this little play was high enough.

"Oh, hundreds of feet! Taller than these tallest trees!" The driver threw his arm wide to take in the pines, which topped out at several hundred feet.

I stepped back in terror. "Could it erupt now?" Oh, please, no.

"Why, any minute now!" exclaimed the driver. "You can't predict this one!"

Unpredictable, uncontrollable, and only a few feet away: scalding hot water that might sweep us into a deadly pool like the one that had swallowed the doe. I stepped farther away.

At that moment the geyser sent up a great spray, the earth rumbled, and sulphurous droplets of wind-borne water splashed my cheek. I gathered my skirts and ran back up the path, my hat flapping about my neck, fear driving me like hounds at my heels.

"Maggie! My dear!" called Mrs. Gale.

I ran until I reached the lunch tent. Panting, sweating, I collapsed at the long table, empty now except for the linen tablecloth. I rested my head on the table. What was I doing here, so far away from home? I couldn't erase from my mind the vision of the seething hot spring that had trapped the doe, and the terror in her eyes as it swallowed her alive.

Chapter

TWENTY-THREE

July 8, 1904

> *Now, of course, I might have jumped on him ... but he*
> *might have gotten me ... generally the man who blows the*
> *loudest gets his hands up the highest when the time comes ...*
> *We think we got off cheap and would not sell our experience,*
> *if we could, for what it cost us.*

—"Echoes on Frontier Days—Holdups," quoted from Hiram M. Chittenden (1858–1917), describing a 1908 holdup

MRS. GALE ENTERED THE TENT CARRYING HER equipment. I sat alone at the far end of the table staring at my fingers. Waiters padded in and out clearing the remaining lunch dishes.

My hair tumbled about my shoulders, my combs lost; I didn't care. This was an alien and inhospitable place, and like a whiny child, I wanted to go home. Mrs. Gale came up behind me. I mumbled, "I'm sorry. I guess I won't be much help to you."

"I've managed alone for some time, dear." Mrs. Gale's hand rested gently on my back. "But I do enjoy your company." A waiter passed by. "Water, please."

"Doesn't it frighten you?" Fear like a thousand writhing snakes stirred in me.

The waiter came back with bottles of water and glasses. The water was icy and refreshing.

"What, the geysers? Not at all. Occasionally a foolish tourist has fallen into a hot spring. But you don't strike me as foolish."

Not foolish, maybe; but filled with enough guilt to feel that this indeed was my boiling, steaming, personal hell. The doe's eyes loomed; Mama's eyes pricked.

"I understand your caution, my dear. Nature is a powerful force."

A powerful force. Nature's raw power threatened to send me spinning out of control. Which might send me spinning right into madness. Mama's paintings drifted into my mind's eye. I didn't want to be like her. I could hear the rush and rumble of the geyser and feel the tremor in my feet through the soles of my boots.

Mrs. Gale sat with me until our party regrouped to head farther south. The others bubbled with enthusiasm; I felt exhaustion steal over me. Once we were in the carriage and under way, I shut my eyes, leaned back against the seat, and listened to the excited chatter of the Hodges girls and the soft laughter of the other passengers. The carriage swayed over the dusty road and I dozed in fitful spurts.

We stopped once to allow a view of Gibbon Falls. I took one look out the window without thinking and yanked myself back inside, plastering my back against the seat and shutting my eyes. "Does he have to have us so close to the edge?"

I heard Mr. Connoly's voice. "Come out on this side." I opened my eyes and saw that he'd extended his hand, and I slid out if only to put my feet on solid ground and to place the coach between me and the gaping gorge. While the other passengers scrambled down the steep trail, Mrs. Gale took photographs from the road's edge. I kept as far from the edge as possible and sat on a rock playing simple guessing games with Emmy and Eliza Hodges, who were too young to risk the trail.

The falls roared; the sun warmed my shoulders. Emmy climbed

into my lap and touched Mama's cameo. Eliza picked up small rocks to show me tiny, glistening minerals. I tried to forget that behind the coach was a sheer drop; I swallowed my fear by burying it deeper within.

Finally we got back on the dusty road, away from the falls, from the gorge. We passed one narrow meadow where the driver stopped the coach and pointed out a bull elk lounging in the tall grass. The elk's massive antlers showed above the grass, moving as his head drifted in our direction.

"Can be mean, those bulls. That one, he's got a mighty big rack," said the driver.

A powerful force—a huge force. Steep cliffs, unpredictable geysers, terrible animals. It was a raw place, Yellowstone. It had more power and unpredictability than even the ocean. The coach swayed and rocked through dark pine forests that blossomed into broad meadows strewn with wildflowers like stars in the heavens; we jostled past vistas of high peaks laced with snow. I felt alone and insignificant, a tiny bug easily crushed. I'd come on the Tour to question my uncle, to find my mother, and that thought alone kept me from succumbing to fear. As the coach jiggled and bumped over the road, I closed my eyes again, putting the geyser and the cliffs out of my mind.

The muffled scream jolted me out of sleep, and the terror rose from deep in my dreams. Dazed, I thought I'd entered a nightmare.

"Whoa, there; hey, there!" the driver called to the horses, reining them in.

I remembered the bear and peered out the window.

But it wasn't a bear. Four men straddled the road, barring our way. They wore scarves that covered their faces except for their eyes;

they carried what looked like long sticks. I shook, trying to clear my head of confusion. Four horses, tied to a nearby tree, whinnied anxiously. Then I realized that the men were carrying rifles, not sticks, and the rifles were pointed at the carriage. I leaned back hard against the seat, trying to breathe.

"It's a robbery!" said the young groom, Mr. Monroe, in a coarse whisper. "Highway robbers! I've heard about this!" I remembered what Tom said when we'd met: "Watch out for highway robbers." He'd been grinning, joking. Mr. Monroe was not.

"Oh!" Miss Pym leaned back in a faint, her eyes closed. Her companion fanned her face with her hat. I barely moved a muscle.

"Get down from there, and be quick about it," one of the robbers called to the driver. The driver leapt from the coach and moved to hold his stamping, nervous horses.

"Ladies and gentlemen, your valuables please!" called another of the men as he waved his Winchester at the coach. He mounted his horse and rode up to the window across from me. "You there," he said to Mr. Hodges, "use this and take up a collection!" He tossed Mr. Hodges a bag. "Alms for the needy!"

Another of the men snickered. No one in the coach laughed; fear circled us; Emmy whimpered quietly in her mother's arms.

Mr. Hodges stared at the bag, and then looked at his wife and two young daughters, who watched him with wide eyes. "Let's do as he says," Mr. Hodges said, his voice soft and calm. "I'm sure they don't mean to hurt us." He smiled at his daughters to reassure them. Then he gazed around him, and his fear was obvious to the rest of us. "It's best if we do as we're told."

He held out the bag as the passengers emptied purses and pockets. I emptied my purse, thankful that my small roll of bills was buried deep in my traveling bag, stowed away out of their sight.

"What's that?" The robber pointed the end of his rifle at Mrs. Gale's camera box.

"My camera," she said. She stared straight into his eyes, calm and sure. "Not easily sold." Her hands gripped the box, and I glanced at her sidelong in admiration.

"Too big," he muttered.

"Exactly so. Too big," Mrs. Gale added.

"The rings, then," he said, pointing at her hands.

Mrs. Gale's wedding band! I felt anger begin to boil in me and I almost spoke out. But the older woman tugged the rings from her fingers without a word and dropped them into the bag. Her eyes were cold steel.

"Watches, gentlemen!" called the robber. He rode quickly around to the other side of the coach. My back was to him now. "Let's get a move on!"

"Oh, Jeremy, not your watch. My gift!" whispered Mrs. Monroe. Tears began to stream down her face. Now my anger really was peaking. I didn't care whether he had a gun or not. I hated this man. He was stealing more than things; he was stealing memories.

Mr. Monroe held the watch in his fingers, turning it to read the inscription, his face white.

"Move it!" the robber called.

Mrs. Monroe let out a sob and her husband dropped the watch into the bag and took his wife's hand. "Though dear to me, you are dearer still. We'll find another watch."

Mr. Connoly, trembling, dropped the bag as it was handed to him. It landed on the floor of the carriage with a heavy *thunk*, the jewelry clinking like chains.

"Careful!" yelled the robber.

Mr. Connoly retrieved the bag and tossed it to Mr. Hodges.

I covered my mother's cameo with my hand. He might have taken the others' memories but he would not steal mine.

"Let's go!" shouted the robber. "Everything!"

Mr. Hodges's eyes met mine. I held his gaze fixed, but I kept my fingers over the cameo. Then I shook my head, ever so slightly. I would not give up the cameo; I would not give up Mama. Mr. Hodges's eyebrows arched; his lips were thin, but he said nothing.

Mr. Hodges closed the sack and swung it out over the side of the coach.

My back was still to the robber, but I sensed that he took the bag, and I felt a sweep of relief.

The cold steel on the back of my neck was like an electric shock.

"Give it over," came the voice.

My eyes again met Mr. Hodges's, and then Mrs. Gale's. I dropped my hand to my lap and twisted to face the robber, looking down the barrel of his gun.

He stared over the mask that covered his nose and mouth. To my surprise, he looked startled. Perhaps he'd not expected to meet the eyes of a girl who would not yield.

"Let's go!" he said, motioning at my throat with the rifle.

Then, so unexpected: "No," I said. I heard the others' reaction to my defiance. Mrs. Monroe gasped. Miss Pym moaned. My back stiffened with resolve. I felt a shock of joy as I refused to yield to the orders of this man. "No."

Mrs. Gale's voice was a whisper. "Margaret."

"You will not take my mother's brooch." My voice was so clear and loud that the driver arched around the nervous horses to stare.

I met the robber's eyes. They were a bright blue, like the sea on a summer day. Thin lines etched outward from their corners as if he smiled a great deal. He had beautiful eyes. Not eyes like the bear. His were warm, thoughtful. And from another part of me: what a peculiar comparison, a man to a bear.

For one long moment we stared at one another.

His expression was odd—I thought I caught a glint of recognition in those blue eyes. His brows furrowed; he looked at the cameo, then back at me. It was as if he were seeing a ghost. His eyes widened. Was he afraid of me? I couldn't imagine why, and yet there was something in his look. He reined back; his horse took one, two steps away.

He turned and tossed the bag to one of his companions. The man caught the sack and twitched his rifle in my direction. "What about that pin? Looks valuable."

"Save it. We've got plenty. Let's go."

The remaining men lifted into their saddles and rode off over the hill in a trail of dust and pounding hooves. Our driver shushed the whinnying coach horses and cursed and spat. Inside the coach we all sat frozen until the robbers were out of sight.

Then everyone began talking at once.

"Unbelievable—"

"Oh, Jeremy, your watch—"

"It's the Old West! Just like the stories!—"

"Mama, that was exciting! Were you scared? I wasn't scared!—"

I said nothing. I felt as calm as though I were sitting in a parlor in Newport having tea.

"That was not wise, my dear," said Mrs. Gale in an undertone meant just for me. "You might have been killed." She paused. "But it was exceedingly brave at the same time. You might make a western girl yet." She smiled. "I'm glad you still have your mother's brooch."

"I'm sorry about your rings."

"Yes." Mrs. Gale sighed. "You see? You were braver even than I was."

Yes, and where did that bravery come from? Not from a part of me I recognized, that was certain. It was only a cameo. No, it was my mother's cameo. It was the one thing I had left of her. My hand went back to my throat, where I stroked the cameo, feeling its familiar texture, the delicate carved face, the grape leaves, the maenad. I was not going to let him rob me of my memories, of my mama.

I left my fingers on the cameo for the rest of the drive.

Chapter
TWENTY-FOUR

July 8–9, 1904

The structure is built of logs, peeled but otherwise in their natural state. In the lobby there is an immense fire place with eight openings ... The lobby is open from floor to roof except for beams and girders ... the distance from floor to ceiling is 160 feet. The hotel will be lighted by electricity and heated with steam ...

—"Local Layout," *Livingston Enterprise*, January 2, 1904

ELIZA HODGES DANCED ON TIPTOES IN FRONT OF ME. "WERE YOU very scared? Did you think he would shoot you? I wasn't scared, but Emmy was. Didn't he have lovely eyes, for a robber? They were blue like the sea. I love the holidays at the seaside, don't you? You were so brave."

We'd arrived at the Fountain Hotel. The news of the robbery had spread like sparks from a wildfire, and we were surrounded by an excited crowd. Most people called me foolhardy—a silly girl—but a few called me brave.

"I expect it was not a wise thing to do," I said to Eliza. While the other passengers displayed varying degrees of nervous energy—the Hodges girls practically bubbled up and over like the geysers—I was entirely calm. I'd discovered something hidden in my core, something steely and pure. Something I'd never expected of myself. Miss Pym sat on a rough log bench fanning herself with eyes closed. The men gathered in a tight clutch.

"Then why did you do it?" Eliza asked, gazing up at me.

I pondered this. I'd looked into his eyes. When I looked at him I saw something—recognition. It was as if he knew me. As if he were seeing a ghost. I knew he wouldn't shoot me because he was uncertain about me. "I didn't think he'd make me hand it over if I refused. I didn't think he'd shoot me, either. I can't explain it, Eliza. I only know what I saw in his eyes." I knelt down to her. "You were a very brave girl."

She touched the cameo. "Is it special?" She stared at it. "It is, isn't it. I can tell."

"It's old. I suppose he wanted it because it's nicely made. But I kept it because it was my mother's pin." I kept it because it was my mama.

Eliza nodded. "He was clever not to take it."

"Clever? Why?"

"Because it's magic."

"Ah!" Magic, like the camera. Or, more like the bear. I touched the cameo, tracing the face with my fingers. Yes, that kind of magic.

"It's like my dolly, the one Grammy gave me. Dolly keeps me safe at night. But Emmy can't have her. She wouldn't work for Emmy." Eliza stroked the doll in her arms. "Unless I said so."

I watched her, thinking, *Yes, that's exactly how it works.* It's the kind of magic that faith is made of, the kind of magic that powers dreams. That powered my dream of finding Mama. That core of steel in me, newly forged, made me smile.

"Eliza!" Mrs. Hodges called to her daughter.

"Well, bye!" Eliza turned and ran off.

The hotel desk clerk eyed me. "Is that the pin?" He pointed at the cameo with his pencil.

I touched it, saying nothing.

"Nice," he said, but he seemed to be thinking, *sheer madness*. "If you want to see Great Fountain Geyser, it should be active within the hour. Head out that way. After what you did, you might as well jump in for a swim." Then he laughed, thinking himself a great wit.

And I smiled. The fear I'd felt at Steamboat had been swallowed up, the way a small ripple can be scattered and absorbed by a larger wake. My brave show before the robber had changed everything for me.

Though the rest of the passengers from our coach stayed behind, Mrs. Gale and I decided to go watch the geyser. I followed her out to the trail. White sinter coated the ground; we passed smaller geysers, all quiet. Pools of hot water steamed in the afternoon air.

I helped Mrs. Gale set up the camera to one side of the viewing area, a low bench of grass that bordered the sinter. Then we waited, the crowd quiet. A Steller's jay cackled in the pine trees behind us, and from deep in the woods came the chittering of a squirrel. I held my breath, not knowing what to expect. Would I run again? I felt changed, but was the fear truly gone?

The water in the pool began to boil in violent bursts and the tourists around us erupted into applause. I stood up and took a step backward. Fear rose like bile in my throat, the same horror I'd felt back at Norris, and for a moment I thought I might lose my wits yet again. The bubbling pool, the fragile sinter . . . but it had changed for me. I had changed.

The geyser threw skyward into a broad fountain, receded, then roared upward again. I was so close that I felt the spray and I stepped backward, moving fast. My foot caught and I fell smack on my bottom in the rough grass, skirts flying, my petticoat a white flag.

"About a hundred and fifty feet," shouted one man. In the

afternoon air, the steam billowed and puffed in great, roiling, white clouds, almost masking the hot water itself.

The noise! I covered my ears as the ground trembled under me. This was nothing like the geyser at Norris—this was a spectacle. Steam shrieked from a vent like a train whistle.

Mrs. Gale disappeared beneath the black hood of her camera.

The geyser lowered a little and then sprayed again, even higher than before. I couldn't breathe. And yet . . . and yet it was seductive, that raw power. A thrill rose in me. A longing for more. I sat before the geyser and let my conscious self vanish.

Beneath my fingers, the ground was alive. It rumbled, creaked, and groaned—with each spray, the earth heaved. And as I sat there helpless and trembling myself, I began to sense the rhythm of it, just as the sea had a rhythm that I knew. The geyser roared and ebbed and roared again, like the ebb and flow of tides. I pressed my hand onto the ground and felt it shudder.

I cringed as another jet of water shot skyward, but the water caught the sun. It glittered and sparkled like a million diamonds, while the air roared and the ground trembled, and then the magic of Yellowstone caught me, and I was lost to it forever.

The geyser display lasted nearly an hour. I didn't tire of watching it even after the other tourists trickled away and left Mrs. Gale and me alone.

Finally, I turned to Mrs. Gale. "There are others?" I asked.

"Oh, my dear." Mrs. Gale laughed, pleased with my reincarnation. "We've only just begun."

With the childlike delight of anticipation, I clapped my hands.

In my room that night, I placed Mama's cameo on the dresser. I'd witnessed such changes in myself in one tumultuous day. I looked into the eyes of a man who held my life in his hands; I saw the earth disgorge its raw power and welcomed it.

I carried the geyser inside, the rumble and surge, pressing on me like the sound of the ocean beating on the beach. Like the storm-driven waves that I heard at night in a howling nor'easter. Like a shell pressed to my ear, echoing with the wash of the surf. Like hearing my mother's voice calling from far off, crying, sighing.

I dreamed of a sea that surrounded me as I stood on an island where geysers played and steam billowed from the ground. I was with Mama, and we were fearless. The mermaids sang to us and our hair was laced with grapevines. We needed nothing else—nothing—for I'd found her and we were home.

When I awoke in my bed the next morning in the Fountain Hotel, I let that dream float through my mind. I felt that I was closer to Mama than ever.

Our coach made the short trip to the new Old Faithful Inn, arriving in time for lunch. There were no untoward events. Misses Pym and Braggs nattered in endless exchanges about the dangers of wilderness travel, to the amusement of the rest of us.

I felt a tug of excitement when I saw the clouds and towers of steam that signaled new geysers and hot springs. I strained to look out the carriage window, and from there had my first look at Old Faithful Inn.

The inn was a huge log structure with a dozen dormers jutting from the steeply sloping roof. We left our coach and stood under the porte cochere, awestruck by the massive, twisting trunks that formed the columns.

Mr. Hodges opened the enormous wood doors of the inn, and I gasped. My eyes were drawn up, and up, through a maze of twisted tree trunks and branches that formed balconies, stairways, pillars, and beams. Fires crackled in two hearths of the gigantic stone fireplace facing the door.

"My!" exclaimed Miss Pym, having a new diversion. "How magnificent!"

For the first time I understood my father's excitement at coming to work here. Robert Reamer had designed something unique and beautiful. It was like standing in a fairyland forest.

In the crow's nest above the lobby, a string quartet played gentle ragtime. The light from the sun filtered through diamond windowpanes that marched to the top of the great hall. Small desks nestled in corners on the balconies that wound around the four walls. Candles, wired for electricity, cradled against posts, glimmering. The wood floors creaked and groaned as visitors milled about, their eyes raised to the rafters.

We went back outside along with a crowd of tourists to watch Old Faithful erupt. A gentle mound of white sinter belched steam, and occasionally water splashed and bubbled, then subsided. We stood a short distance from the geyser.

"Old Faithful is dependable," said Mrs. Gale. "We shouldn't have to wait long."

She'd barely finished speaking when the geyser exploded in a tall, thin tower of water shooting a comb of spray to the lee.

I thrilled again at the magnificence of it all, the fear I'd felt at Norris completely vanished. "Impressive, isn't it," Mrs. Gale shouted. "And some geysers in this basin are even taller, although not quite as regular."

I'd fallen in love and I could scarcely contain my desire. "I want to see them. I need to see them all."

"I have to stay in this area a few days photographing the geysers," said Mrs. Gale. "I'd enjoy having you stay with me to assist me, if that's possible. We can remain at the inn rather than moving on with our tour group."

I hesitated, thinking about what Papa might say, and about my goal, the reason I came on the Tour—my desire to find Mama. I was pulled in two directions; but somehow it felt they were both tugging me toward the same end.

"I'll stay," I said at last. I couldn't shake the feeling that I was meant to be here. I thought about Mama's paintings, how they had once frightened me so. Her paintings were of all these features: the steaming amethyst springs, the swirls of amber bacteria, the mounds of white silica. She could not forget this place, nor would I, ever. And with the information I'd gleaned from Papa's correspondence . . . If I were to find her anywhere on earth, it would be here.

"I'm glad you've lost your fear of the geysers," said Mrs. Gale. "Two brave moves in two days. Not only a western girl but a thoroughly modern one."

I touched the cameo at my throat and felt my newly born strength. "Yellowstone isn't what I expected."

"I'm always disappointed when things turn out as I expect them to," said Mrs. Gale. "Shall we go in to our rooms? We can explore the rest of the inn."

Before dinner Mrs. Gale suggested that we observe the Old Faithful eruption from another vantage point: from the widow's walk on the roof. On the roof! I'd managed one great fear, but this was different.

She said I'd see the entire geyser basin, and only because of that did I go. I asked her to take the outside while I clung to the inner wall, trying not to look through the open log railings to the lobby below. I remembered how Mama protected me when we walked on the Cliff Walk, how I had to hug the inside wall of the path.

We wove up the steps, past the musicians, now playing the popular "Meet Me in St. Louis." I had to move slowly and stop from time to time to shut my eyes. But I made it through the crow's nest and out onto the broad widow's walk that crowned the hotel.

An electric searchlight on the roof of the inn probed the dusk. We joined thirty or so tourists on the rooftop. I stepped out from the stairs, not certain what to expect, clutching Mrs. Gale's hand. The air was cooling now that the sun had set. The widow's walk was so large that I could stand where I had no sensation of the edge. I could breathe again.

I stared out across the landscape at the steam that rose from across the basin, from multiple hot springs and geysers. The Indians had been right: Hell would look like this. I once thought Mama's landscapes were demonic. I was wrong. If you liked the geysers, it was heaven. And the fumes and vapors would become warm mists, the haunts of angels.

After the eruption, when we had to go back down the stairs, I clung to Mrs. Gale like a limpet and tried to stay tucked against the wall and within the descending crowd. The mass of people tempered the view downward, but still my palms grew slick with sweat and my knees wobbled. I peppered Mrs. Gale with questions to keep my mind busy. At one turn I made the mistake of looking over the rail. Mrs. Gale had to hold my arm against her side and soothe me like a baby. When we reached the lobby I fell, exhausted,

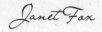

into a chair and mopped my damp forehead with the sleeve of my shirtwaist. Though I was glad to have gone to see the view, I was relieved to be on solid ground again.

The company of passengers from our coach gathered before the great stone fireplace. As recompense for our having suffered the robbery, the management of the Yellowstone Park Association offered us a free dinner. Before we went in to eat, a young Army lieutenant questioned us about the experience. The thing that everyone recalled most clearly was the color of the ringleader's eyes.

"Baker," said the lieutenant, nodding in recognition and tapping his pencil. "Nathaniel Baker and his gang. They've been around the Park for years but we can't find them. He has a canny way in the woods."

Eliza looked up at the lieutenant. "Did they ever kill anybody?" she asked, her eyes wide.

"No," the lieutenant replied, smiling. "Baker's a thief, not a murderer."

"See?" Eliza said, turning to me. "You knew." She pointed at the cameo. "It was the magic," she whispered, eyes round, solemn. I smiled; but I thought she was right.

We ate as a group at one of the long tables in the dining room. The wine, following our excitement, had given everyone a tipsy air. Toward the end of the meal, thin, timid Mr. Connoly raised a glass.

"I'd like to salute young Miss Bennet, who bravely held on to her jewelry under terrifying circumstances."

I felt my cheeks color. I wanted to tell them that it wasn't bravery. I wasn't brave. I couldn't stand at the edge of a window, never mind the edge of a cliff. I'd only begun to recognize the beauty of the geysers, as opposed to their terrifying unpredictability and threat.

"I've done nothing," I murmured. I touched the cameo. I wouldn't give up Mama, that was all.

I was just a foolish girl, not brave at all. I followed all the conventions, obeyed the rules. Not like Mama, who obeyed no conventions except her own.

But there my thoughts troubled me. Was my unconventional Mama brave, or merely foolish—or worse, mad? No one swam in the Atlantic the day after a hurricane passed, and there she had been in her bathing costume. Ladies hardly swam at all. I touched the cameo again.

Unless her disappearance was an unexpected outcome. Her note said it: "someone I left years ago to whom I must return." Someone she had left behind. In which case she was never mad or foolish or unconventional. Perhaps it was as simple as this: she rejected society as a place where love grew stagnant and false and she went in search of her love.

And what if Mama were here in my place, in this dining room? I knew that she would have accepted the toast, laughing and enjoying the attention and the loose and undignified camaraderie of the evening. I'd never enjoyed anything so unfashionable in my life. It was not proper. And so I did something I might not have done only a few weeks ago: I took a small sip of wine and, ever so slightly, raised my glass.

It was a rare moment of bringing my mother back, through me; of standing fearless on a peak. I couldn't know what I'd find on the other side of this high point.

Chapter
TWENTY-FIVE

July 12, 1904

I again visited the mud vulcano [sic] today. I especially desired to see it again for the one especial purpose . . . of assuring myself that the notes made in my diary a few days ago are not exaggerated. No! they are not! The sensations inspired in me to-day . . . were those of mingled dread and wonder.

—Diary of the Washburn Expedition to the Yellowstone and Firehole Rivers
in the Year 1870, Nathaniel P. Langford, 1905

"LET'S SET THE TRIPOD HERE. I THINK THERE'S ENOUGH contrast in these algae to capture on film."

After only three days assisting Mrs. Gale, I was becoming familiar with the language of photography. I positioned the tripod and stepped back. Mrs. Gale locked the camera in place, and when she focused the lens, I leaned to look.

All of my experience shrank to what I saw through the lens. My fears, my losses, Mama's disappearance, and Papa's lies all left me. The patterns made by the ribbons of algae-rich water running by my feet were complex whorls of texture—only a moment earlier these details had been lost within the huge landscape.

"You take the photo," said Mrs. Gale. "Think about what I've said about exposure, now. This is not like the larger landscape. This is a miniature."

I focused the lens and held the exposure. I removed the

celluloid sheet and labeled it, sliding it with care into one of the slots in the leather box.

Everything about photography appealed to me—the soft leather, the polished brass hardware, the smooth mahogany, the sure click as the shutter locked—but most of all the feeling of being in a place so special, so pristine, that only I could see it.

Over several hours we worked our way from one geyser to another. At one point a young man ran up shouting, "Beehive's a-goin' off! Beehive's a-goin' off!" We followed, and were treated to an eruption that shot off at a rakish angle, and another almost as tall as Old Faithful. The excitement of the unexpected was contagious, and I found myself searching for more eruptions.

We walked through the basin, stopping at intervals. I stared for a long time into the steaming Beauty Pool watching bubbles slowly emerge from its depths.

"Inviting, isn't it. It looks like a lovely place to swim," said Mrs. Gale.

I knew full well—as did Mrs. Gale—that it was not, and again, the image of the doe rose up in my mind.

"Do you swim, dear?" asked Mrs. Gale.

"My mother was a great swimmer." I saw Mama on that last day in her swimming costume, another dark thought to tamp down.

"Quite a woman. She was ahead of her time. Did she teach you?"

"She tried, but I was a poor student." I stared into the inky depths of the pool. From the orange and yellow bacteria at the water's edge, the pool graded to turquoise, then to deep blue, then to blue-black. "I had to stay in the shallows. I don't like floating or being over deep water. I could never get used to the idea that there was nothing

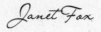

beneath my feet." Mama wasn't afraid. Perhaps she should have been.

I turned my back on that inviting but deadly pool and looked out over the hot, white landscape into the cool woods beyond. Steam from Daisy Geyser spiraled into the pure blue sky.

Satanic. That's what I'd called her paintings. Now I thought her paintings were beautiful and wished I had one. Mama had been here and seen this. I could almost feel her presence. Since the moment we'd left Mammoth, and especially since I'd realized my love for Yellowstone, I felt that I was drawing closer to Mama with every passing day.

We were returning to the inn for a late lunch when I caught sight of a familiar, lanky figure striding in our direction. My heart leapt. Tom! I felt so many changes in me in only these few days and I wondered if he would notice them as well.

He laughed out loud when Mrs. Gale and I reached him. "Miss Margaret Bennet, are you following me?" He gestured a salute, acknowledging Mrs. Gale.

"Would it offend you if I am?" I asked, giving him a warm smile and knowing that I would follow him just about anywhere if I could.

"So, now that you've taken the Tour, what do you think of Yellowstone?" he asked, throwing out his arm to encompass the geyser basin.

"I think it's the most fantastic place on earth." I meant it, and knew that he was part of the reason why.

His smile broadened to a grin. "Then we share a great love," he said. We walked together now, our strides matching but slow, Mrs. Gale having moved ahead of us on the trail. "I heard you had quite a time the other day on your way down here."

"You warned me, back in the Livingston Depot." I remembered

the first day we met, and felt myself blush, partly from the memory of our meeting.

"I did. But I never thought it would happen. I've heard some wild tales about that robbery. One tourist said that bandits should be paid to hold up the coaches, it was so exciting. And then there's the story of a young woman who faced down the robbers." We stopped walking and our eyes met. He wore an impish grin. I stood straighter. I hoped he wasn't mocking me.

"And?" I asked with trepidation.

"I wouldn't want you to face me down, that's for sure." His smile grew, but he seemed sincere.

I smiled back. He wasn't mocking me. I shrugged a little. "I suppose it was stupid."

He reached out and took my hand and a thrill ran right up my arm. "It would only have been stupid if you'd been hurt. That would have made me miserable."

My voice came out in a squeak. "Really?" He cared about me. I could have floated right away. I touched the cameo with my free hand. "Would it have been worth it for this?"

He held my hand in both of his and examined my fingers. "Some things are worth fighting for." Our eyes met again and I tried to swallow but couldn't. He still held my hand. After the longest moment—the earth must have turned on its axis at least once—he gently let my hand drop. We walked on then; or, at least, I put one foot in front of the other, since in reality I floated.

I scrabbled around in my jumbled brain for something to say. "What are you up to now?"

"We're sampling here, and in a couple of days we'll move on to the next site."

"Which is where?"

"Well, where will you be in a couple of days?"

My heart took a leap; he wanted to be where I was, too. I answered honestly. "I'm on my way to Lake Hotel to find my uncle."

"Then maybe we'll head in that direction next."

"That would be wonderful." A second after I spoke, I hesitated. I liked him so much. Much more than I'd ever liked anyone. But I could not forget my mission here, in Yellowstone. What if I discovered something at Lake—what if I discovered Mama? I wasn't sure I could share this with him. I would have to tell him about her. Her painting, her fits, her madness . . . It would mean sharing her and everything about her, about me, and about how we might be alike, her madness . . .

"Are you okay?" he asked.

"I'm fine." I looked back at him and smiled. I kept my thoughts tucked inside and I could feel the little space that grew between us.

We arrived at the inn. I wished he'd take my hand again, but he didn't. He said, "I probably ought to go find my dad."

"I have to go have lunch."

"Maybe I'll see you later?"

I looked up at him again, at his clear and searching eyes, and I felt a great yearning. "I hope so." I watched him, wistful, as he walked away from me, his long arms swinging.

After our lunch, Mrs. Gale and I sat in the lobby of the inn enjoying a few quiet moments. I stared into the fire, which crackled in the great stone fireplace more for show than need, and I let my mind drift. Tom liked me; I liked him. But there was still Mama, ever present. I began to grow anxious now, ready to move south to

Lake and discover what I could. I was wrestling with these thoughts when I heard my name.

"Margaret!"

I started. It was Papa, his face distorted with concern.

"Mags, are you all right?"

I sat up, too stunned by Papa's sudden appearance to form words. Behind my father was the hulking figure of George Graybull. Instinctively I felt the prickle of every hair on the back of my neck. It was as if I were being stalked.

"We heard about the robbery." Papa was so agitated his mustache practically vibrated. I stood smoothing my skirt. My world closed in; I felt like a trapped animal as Graybull circled behind Papa and examined me, his eyes searching me up and down. "We came down right away."

"Papa, I'm fine. Please. You didn't need to come." I wanted them both to go away. Their very presence was stifling.

"Fine? What were you thinking? You might have been killed." Papa held me at arm's length, appraising my rolled-up sleeves and dusty skirt.

"Papa, really. I'm just fine." I needed him to leave me be; he would only hinder my attempts to find out anything about Mama. To find out anything about myself. I forced a smile on my face as I pushed loose tendrils of hair behind my ears and tucked in my shirtwaist.

"When they said a young woman refused to give up a pin, I feared they were talking about you. And it turns out they were. This is not like you! What were you thinking?"

He was right about one thing—it hadn't been like me. Before. "I saved Mama's cameo," I said, touching it.

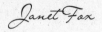

"Margaret. Is that worth your life?" He sounded irritated. "And you don't look fine. You look a mess."

I stiffened. Maybe I didn't care so much about looking like the perfect lady every minute anymore. Maybe I wanted to look a mess now and then.

He cleared his throat. "At any rate, you've got a guardian now." He gestured behind him at Graybull. "I'm making sure you're taken care of from now on."

George Graybull smiled, his tongue pushing through the gap in his teeth. Horror filled me. How could I possibly search for Mama now? He was to be my guardian—or my prison guard. I felt my face flush as my anger grew. "Papa, Mrs. Gale and I are managing quite well."

"Clearly not," said Graybull, his cheerful tone contrasting the substance of his words. "Charles and I believe that you require a masculine presence." Graybull tipped his hat toward Mrs. Gale, who gave him a cool smile but said nothing.

"I can't stay, Margaret," said Papa. "I can't accompany you, I won't be here. I have business elsewhere." He paused. "It's my wish that you allow George to accompany you from this point."

I moved away from Papa and Graybull, putting a chair between us. My new taste for freedom had grown strong in a short time. I understood for the first time how Mama must have felt, why she rebelled. My hands gripped the chair back as I stood rigid behind it. "I'm helping Mrs. Gale. I do not need another guardian."

"Indeed she is." Mrs. Gale faced Papa. "She's been quite a help to me with my photography."

"Ah, wonderful occupation, photography," Graybull said, addressing Mrs. Gale directly. "Particularly for a single lady. But I'm sure you'll allow Margaret to finish her tour of the Park with me."

Mrs. Gale drew herself up. "Miss Bennet is free to do as she pleases." I stood straighter, moving closer to Mrs. Gale.

Graybull laughed. "Within reason. So long as her father approves."

Yes, I thought. *Of course.* Because I'm still young. Because I'm a woman. Because I have no say, no control. A bitter taste rose in my mouth. I had no choice in this.

I knew what I should say, what I wished to say. I looked from Papa to Graybull, and then to Mrs. Gale, whose sympathy was obvious. But Mrs. Gale couldn't help me now. I knew my place and my limitations.

"Of course," I said, my back as stiff as a board. "As you wish."

"Understand that tomorrow is your birthday," Graybull said. He moved closer, until his arm touched mine. "We'll have to celebrate in style."

I arched away from him. My seventeenth. I was so caught up with my quest to find Mama, I'd nearly forgotten. Tomorrow should have been the true start of my season, culminating with my debut in August. I should be at a ball, with Kitty, dancing with Edward. I felt a pang at the loss of my dreams. "I'll keep my own celebration, thank you."

Graybull laughed as if I'd made a joke.

Mrs. Gale moved toward Papa. "Perhaps, Mr. Bennet, you would allow Maggie to continue to assist me in my work. We could travel together with Mr. Graybull. I need photographs from other areas of the Park."

I could feel the blood course to my face as gratitude toward my mentor flooded me. Mama might not be here, but at least I had one ally in Mrs. Gale.

"Charles, think I can manage the two ladies," said Graybull. He pushed his tongue between his teeth.

"Manage?" I said, my lips tight. Stable hands "managed" horses.

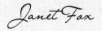

He bowed. "Shall be sure you are well taken care of."

"I think that that will be a fine solution," said Papa.

I looked away. "I'm returning to my room for a rest."

"Then we shall see you for dinner," said Graybull.

I'd already turned to leave, when Papa touched my arm. "I'm relieved that you're all right, Mags. I must leave straight after dinner. I'm sorry I have to miss your birthday." He lowered his voice. "George Graybull is a powerful man, Margaret. He can make or break people." Papa was trying to make me understand, almost pleading with me. "He has an interest in you. It means everything to me that you return that interest, at least a little." Tears welled in his eyes. I could see genuine sadness there.

For a moment I remembered how he felt about Mama, and I understood his loss and his tenuous position. But he'd committed me to a prison. My anger at him returned and I wasn't ready to forgive him for it.

But I was still a dutiful daughter. Proper. I still understood the rules and I still obeyed. I might smash a porcelain pitcher or two but only in the privacy of my room. I nodded a single, tense nod; then I turned my back.

Chapter TWENTY-SIX

July 13, 1904

She was so evidently the victim of the civilization which had produced her, that the links of her bracelet seemed like manacles chaining her to her fate.

—*The House of Mirth,* Edith Wharton, 1905

THE NEXT MORNING, THE MORNING OF MY SEVENTEENTH birthday, I sat at my dressing table. I stared at a dress that Mama and I had chosen together, and that was now hanging on a wood hanger from a nail driven into the log-paneled wall: a dress of the deepest blue velvet trimmed with ecru lace, with folds and gathers cascading into a train. The velvet reflected the light in the folds, and I touched it, feeling its weight and nap. I'd brought it west with me because my father had insisted. When Mina had been packing, I couldn't fathom why he'd been so adamant about bringing this dress. Now I knew why; it was made for me, and far too expensive to be left behind.

It was really much too fancy for the Old Faithful Inn, even if it was my birthday.

On this birthday I had imagined I'd be back in Newport, with Kitty, maybe even with Mama, and enjoying the life I was born into, the life of an upper-class girl.

I sighed and returned to my morning toilet and began the now unpleasant task of hooking the busk of my corset. Only a few weeks ago, I'd asked Mina to tighten the laces. While it helped my posture once I had it on, I hated having to inhale as I stretched the bones over my ribs and compressed my stomach. I'd hooked it halfway up when I stopped.

I'd spent my life being ordered about, following the rules, doing all that was expected. And where had that taken me? My future was unsure, my old life was in tatters, my family lay in ruins. Yesterday I acquiesced to Papa, and that awful Graybull would now follow my every motion with his penetrating stare. But here was one thing no one could order me to do. A new freedom, like an open door, blew in and I unhooked the corset and threw it on the bed. I buttoned my white shirtwaist over a simple, and much more comfortable, lace chemisette. I'd never have a waist as small as Kitty's, anyway. At least it was my waist to do with as I wished.

If I looked like I slouched, fine. I decided that I no longer cared what the others thought of me.

"I believe the fresh air of Yellowstone agrees with you, my dear," Graybull remarked at breakfast. "You look as though you've gained a few pounds. It's quite charming."

I stifled a laugh. If he only knew!

Later that morning George Graybull, Mrs. Gale, and I set off to explore the geyser basins and take photographs. Mrs. Gale engaged Graybull in polite conversation, mercifully giving me a ready excuse to avoid being close to him. He kept trying to slip to my side, and I'd stop and gaze into a spring or stare through the lens at the low play of water in a geyser until he moved off. I felt we played a cat-and-mouse game, and I was happy each time I gave him the slip.

"You have a wonderful eye, Maggie," said Mrs. Gale as we worked. Her tone was pleased, even respectful. I felt joy blossom at her praise. "You're a natural artist. Look at the way you've captured the texture of that outcrop, and the tree branch in this one."

I could not suppress my huge smile.

"How nice that you have this little hobby, my dear," said Graybull. He examined his Park guidebook, carelessly turning the pages.

I stared straight at him, my smile turning to ice. He was just self-absorbed enough not to feel the chill in my look.

We watched Grand Geyser for much of the morning. It was a large and long-lived event—and to my immense pleasure Graybull could not be heard over the roar of the water. Mrs. Gale arranged for a surrey so we could visit the Handkerchief Pool in the mid-afternoon and witness for ourselves its well-earned name. Mrs. Gale had told me that visitors would toss dirty handkerchiefs into the pool, only to have them sucked into the depths and return to the surface moments later cleaned.

We were to leave the next morning for Lake Hotel. Lake! In the excitement of the geyser basins and photography, and with Graybull hovering over my shoulder, I'd buried the urgency of my plan to visit Uncle John. But the prospect of being there so soon brought it all back—my uncle's letters. My father's lies. I knew Mama had loved Yellowstone; I was sure of that now, for I loved it and I recognized what she'd been trying to convey in her paintings. It was as if Mama were calling me and I could hear her with increasing clarity.

I hugged myself as we stood in the soaring lobby of the inn. It was late afternoon, and the fire snapped in the massive stone fireplace, and we were heading toward our rooms to dress for dinner. Graybull

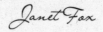

pulled me aside. He waited until Mrs. Gale retired to her room.

"I have a gift for your birthday," he said, leaning close to my ear.

I felt surprised and embarrassed. And more than a little horrified.

He took my hand in his, handing me a flat envelope tied with ribbon. I opened it, slid out the paper, and stared in disbelief at the photo inside.

"You should recognize him," Graybull said, a hint of triumph in his voice. "Fine animal. My stable master telegraphed me that he has a perfect gait."

Tears clouded my sight. Ghost. Papa's photograph of Ghost. "How . . . ?"

"I've acquired him and had him transferred to my stables in upstate New York," Graybull said. "He's yours." He laughed. "Again."

Acquired. Bought. "But, how did you know . . ."

"Margaret, your father and I have had some conversations about your future." I stared at Graybull. His tongue slid into the gap in his teeth. "I have asked his permission to court you, Margaret. He's consented."

Graybull placed his hand beneath my elbow. I froze, feeling my skin prickle through the thin cotton of my sleeve. Acquired. Ghost had been acquired. *I'd* been acquired.

I took a step backward, lifting my arm away from his touch. "I'm seventeen. Just barely seventeen." I'd wanted a husband, a rescue, but at the hands of someone like Edward. Not like this. Not from George Graybull. I hadn't had a chance to have a life. No season, no debut, no romance. Tom's face flitted through my mind and yawning regret chased it. I'd follow Tom anywhere, wasn't that what I had thought?

"I'm prepared to wait," Graybull said with a smile. "My sister can take you in as her ward until you are of age. She lives in Newport. You'll be home. You'll have everything you want, everything you need. I have an excellent income." What perfect irony. My only option upon confronting my father had been calling on my grandfather. My grandfather who I knew would approve this match with Graybull with great enthusiasm. I was trapped in a tight net. There was still Edward, but did I even want that? Graybull touched me again; I flinched. "And your father, Margaret. Why, he, too, will have everything he wants. This job in Yellowstone, for instance. I'm an influential man, Margaret."

I understood just what he meant. Papa had said as much. My father's future depended upon me. I stood in the lobby of the Old Faithful Inn, disembodied, holding the picture of Ghost in my right hand, diminished by the position that I held as a girl, as a daughter, helpless and unable to do as I pleased. I'd been sold, and bought. Like an animal. Like Ghost.

"Of course." It was the only thing I could say. I stared at the picture. Graybull was giving me what I'd thought I wanted. Papa was instructing me on what to do. I had to obey. "Thank you," I added, my voice flat.

He moved closer, so that we were face-to-face. I sensed his desire and felt my visceral response. Husband? To share . . . everything with him? He smiled again, but it was a smile of triumph, of conquest, not of love.

Tom.

"My pleasure, my dear Margaret." Graybull reached out and took my left hand, then brought my fingers to his lips.

His kiss sent me reeling, the pressure of his lips on my bare

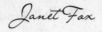

fingers. "Please excuse me for a few minutes," I said, and pulled back, withdrawing my hand from his. "I'm . . . overwhelmed."

"We shall meet right here." It was not a question. "Say, in an hour?" Graybull said with a smile.

I didn't plan to run to my room, but my feet moved faster the farther I was from the lobby. Tears streamed down my face and blinded me. When I reached the door I didn't notice that it was ajar. I stumbled inside and felt a rude shock.

A girl stood in the middle of my room with my blue velvet dress draped loosely over her own rough clothes, turning back and forth, gazing at herself in the mirror.

Chapter TWENTY-SEVEN

July 13, 1904

> *Today, if you go to Bear Butte, you can still see*
> *the claw marks the bear made when he tried to climb it,*
> *and if the light is right, you can see the moccasin*
> *tracks of the woman and the little boy at the bottom.*
> *It is one place in the old Cheyenne country where*
> *women can go to look for power.*
>
> —"The Bear Butte," story as told by Jessie American Horse,
> a Northern Cheyenne

"WHAT—?" NOW EVEN MY CLOTHES WERE SUBJECT TO manhandling. I was living a perfect nightmare.

It was Kula. Kula who kept showing up around Tom; Kula who reminded me of something, something I couldn't put my finger on. I'd seen her at the tent camp; I supposed Gretchen Mills had let her go, and now she worked here.

Kula whirled, dropping the dress to the floor. Her dark eyes were wide with a combination of fear and defiance.

Tears streaked down my face. "What are you doing?" Was she stealing, or just pawing through my things?

Kula bent and gathered the dress in her arms, her long black braid swinging forward of her shoulder, her eyes never leaving mine. Her cheeks flushed and, as she regarded my tear-streaked face, her expression changed to one of puzzlement. "I didn't mean harm," she said, sounding perplexed. "I just wanted to try it."

I sank onto the bed. "Please leave," I said, my voice breaking. I wanted to be alone with my misery.

Kula hung the dress back on the hanger, her eyes still on me. "I'm here to do your room," she said. She gestured at the bed, not yet made up, though it was late in the afternoon.

"Not now." I lay back on the bed and closed my eyes. Thoughts crowded my head. Mama wouldn't have let this happen to me, a forced marriage, and to such a disagreeable man. Mama would have fought them all—Papa, Grandpapa—for me.

Kula busied herself, straightening the room, picking up the towels that I'd tossed in the corner. "If I don't make it right the management will have my job."

I sat bolt upright, my frustration spilling into pointless rage, which I unleashed at Kula. "If you don't leave, I'll make sure the management removes you!"

Kula dropped the towels in the middle of the room. Her dark eyes shone with tears, yet she looked more angry than fearful. "Sorry, miss," she said in a near whisper, and made for the door.

I remembered Tom and how he hated the way I'd treated her; and, after all, my unhappy state wasn't her fault. "Stop!" I said. "I'm sorry." She couldn't be blamed for Mama's disappearance or for Graybull. "Go ahead and finish. You must have had a long day." I slid off the bed and sat at the dressing table, putting my head in my hands and letting the tears fall onto the tabletop.

Kula worked quickly and silently tidying the room and making up the bed. I could feel her looking at me. I knew I looked a mess but I didn't care.

She came and stood by the table. "I'm sorry for mishandling

your dress. I didn't know it was so precious." She didn't spend an ounce on humility; but she did sound genuinely sorry.

"You think . . . ?" I began to laugh, and Kula's eyes narrowed. "It isn't about you. It isn't about the dress." Seeing Kula with my dress was the excuse I needed to let my wretched feelings flow.

"Can I help, then?" I could sense her confusion at what must have seemed bizarre behavior. I felt as though I understood my mother more with every passing day.

"No one can help me." I dropped my head back into my hands. Kula didn't move. For a long moment I sat, head bowed, feeling her eyes on me. I felt a shift inside; I was grateful for Kula's presence. It felt like having Mina back, someone who didn't care about how proper I was, someone who didn't try to control me.

"Is it for something special?" Kula asked, twisting toward the wall, toward the gown. "That dress?"

I lifted my head and stretched out my fingers and rubbed the thick, soft velvet. "It's my birthday. I should be wearing it tonight." I didn't say that I should also be preparing for my debut with my mother by my side. That I should be escorted to parties and balls by Edward—charming Edward—or any of the other eligible young men of Newport. That I should be giggling with my best friend, Kitty, at our joint ball at the end of August. Or . . . that I could be walking with Tom through the forests of Yellowstone. Instead I was half an orphan and a prisoner of circumstance and the trophy of a man twice my age. The velvet nap shone, and I let my hand fall against it, caressing it, before I looked up at Kula. "I'm seventeen today."

She smiled. "Happy birthday," she said. She stood straight, and pressed the front of her linsey-woolsey skirt with the flat of her palms. "I'll be sixteen soon."

I wiped the tears from my face with the back of my hand. "You worked for the Millses."

"Yes," Kula said. Her face darkened.

"Is this a better situation?"

She shrugged, looking away. Gretchen had been rough; but Kula was hardly a model servant.

I shifted subjects, sensing her discomfort. "Kula's a pretty name," I said. "I've never heard it before." I wanted to get on a better footing with her. We were so close in age. And Tom would appreciate my generosity. And there was that pricking feeling I had each time I looked at her.

"My father's choice," she said. "He's white but his ma was half native." Tom had been right. Kula's olive skin and high cheekbones spoke to her ancestry. "I expect you think your birthday should be special. Me, too." She looked away. "Mothers know how to do things right, like birthdays." She looked at me. "Mine's gone."

I felt my throat close with grief. "Mine, too." We had much in common, then. Our stations divided us, but still.

"Ah," Kula said, her eyes keen now, sharp like a dagger.

We remained silent for a moment.

"But that's not the worst," I said. No, not the worst. The one had led to the other. The loss of my mother had led to my imprisonment.

Kula waited, regarding me.

"I mean, that's not what's wrong now. Now my father is arranging my marriage to someone I don't like." Kula was a good listener. I thought about how much I'd missed having Mina, especially after Mama left.

Kula looked at her hands, lacing her fingers together. "Is it that Tom, the geologist's son? The one who stays at Wylie?"

I sagged. "No." Oh, how I wish.

"Oh." A flit of a smile crossed her face before she looked solemn again. "Is he rich? The husband?"

I was startled. I might open up to her with *my* woes, but this was not the kind of question I expected from a servant. "Yes."

"Then maybe you can put up with him," Kula said. "Maybe he'll give you beautiful jewels. And more clothes like that dress."

I hesitated, not certain how to respond to her plain and forward talk. She was right. Graybull would give me everything: jewels, clothes, and position. Even Ghost. "But I want something else," I said. Yes, that was right. I wanted something else. I wanted what I'd told Kitty—I wanted love.

"I'd put up with him," Kula said, and her face darkened again. Before she dropped her eyes I saw the flash of jealousy. I couldn't blame her; my life must have seemed desirable. "I'd please him well, get him to give me everything I wanted. I'd never lift a finger again." She laced and unlaced her fingers. "I'd get him to dress me fine," she said, and nodded her head at the dress. "I'd do anything for a man who'd take care of me right. Lie, steal, anything."

I stared into Kula's dark eyes. I found her statements shocking. She'd gone over the line. Had we been at home, she would have been let go on the spot. She was not my equal; she was not my friend; she presumed too much just by saying such things to me. Yet, here in Yellowstone, everything was different. And I understood what she meant. Jewelry, fine clothes, position in society—these had been everything I'd ever wanted. Graybull would give them to me, most assuredly.

Edward could give them to me, too. He was sweet, he was rich. He would dote on me, put me on a pedestal, I would be his fine object. He would have made a fine husband for me. But I knew in my heart I never loved Edward. Liked him, felt secure with him, but never truly loved him.

Tom could give me nothing. No money, no position. No Ghost, no grand house in Newport. Nothing—except the one thing I wanted most. Tom treated me as an equal. He spoke to me as if I had a brain. He would not put me on a pedestal, but stand next to me in the face of all fears so that I could meet them, with him at my side.

He would stand next to me on the edge of the cliff and make it safe. He would be with me for the person I am, not for what I had or who my grandfather was. He was gentle and kind and with his love for all things wild—I smiled to myself—would not try to control me.

Tom.

"Remember, dear heart—nothing is more powerful than love."

Suddenly I knew what Mama meant. I knew that all the things I thought I wanted, all my Newport life, was worth nothing in the face of having real love. I'd thought I understood what I was telling Kitty those many weeks ago, but now I felt it in my very core. I sat up straight and brushed the wisps of loose hair back from my face.

"I'll be going," Kula said. "You have to fight for what you want, miss. No one's going to fight for you."

I regarded this presumptuous girl, this honest and right girl. "You can come back in half an hour to finish up. I'll be at dinner."

"Yes, miss," Kula said with a slight smile. She curtsied

perfunctorily and left the room, pulling the door shut quietly behind her.

I looked in the mirror. Green-gray eyes looked back, eyes that brimmed with loss.

I let my hair down and shook it loose down my back; then I brushed it and pinned it back up. I would, somehow, fight for what I wanted. It might take time to persuade my father, time to find the right way. But I had time. I dried my eyes and pinched my cheeks. I straightened the cameo—my talisman—that hung on a black ribbon tied around my throat. Now I was girded for my next encounter.

Chapter TWENTY-EIGHT

July 14, 1904

*But her passion swept every other thought
out of its way. With dim agony and rage she began
to perceive that she had been duped.*

—*Lady Rose's Daughter*, a novel by
Mrs. Humphry Ward, 1903

THE MORNING AFTER MY BIRTHDAY, WE READIED TO LEAVE
for Lake Hotel. I began packing my clothes by heaping them in my
trunk. I stood back with my hands on my hips. Hopeless. I needed
Mina. I'd never even watched her attend to these details, and I felt
stupidly ignorant. There was a knock at the door; Kula. The girl
clicked her tongue when she looked at the mess I'd made.

"That's not the way to treat these beautiful things," she said. She
was chiding me. It was forward yet I knew she was right.

"I'm not very good at it." No, I was pathetic and dependent upon
others.

Kula bent over the trunk and began to pull things out, sorting
and folding them with care. I kept my eyes on her deft handiwork,
watching her work. She glanced sideways at me. "I heard about
that pin," Kula said. "The other girls talked about some silly
tourist trying to get herself killed because of some pin, and I
added up two plus two."

I touched the cameo.

"Did he want it that much?" Kula asked, looking at the stack of folded silk shawls and lace underclothes. "That Nat Baker."

"He wasn't going to get it even if he did want it." I watched as Kula moved between the bed and the wardrobe, her skill at folding and packing. She reminded me of Mina, she was so sure-handed. "I wish you could come with us," I said. "You could help me."

Kula looked up. "I work here now," she said.

A thought came to me. "Could you wait? Just a few minutes?" I almost tripped over an elderly couple in my haste to get to the lobby, where Graybull sat reading the newspaper and smoking a cigar. I'd used so little charm on him to this point that it didn't take any pleading to convince him of my plan. I realized how I might use this to my advantage later, should it be necessary.

"I'll arrange it immediately," he said, and raised my hand to his lips. "I have a bit of influence with the management here. It would be my pleasure to treat you to this trifling indulgence."

I tried not to wince as I slipped my hand from his. I hoped he would think that my blush was charming. How vain his boasts of influence sounded. But my deceit worked. Kula had finished the packing and was tidying the bed and table when I blustered in with the news.

"You're coming with us. You can be a help to me and Mrs. Gale. A proper lady's maid!"

"Oh?" Kula said. She seemed annoyed. I stepped back in surprise. I'd expected gratitude. "I have a job, remember?"

"My—friend—he'll arrange it with the management. He'll pay you well." I watched Kula's dark and wary eyes. "Would you come with me?" I pleaded.

She tapped her fingers on her arm. "I'm not a servant. I work hard, but I take care of myself. I won't be somebody's slave." She paused. "The Millses treated me like a slave. Then they tossed me off." She looked at me, suspicious, her anger evident. "I won't let that happen again."

"No," I said, feeling humbled. "You'd help me, that's all. Be my companion. Not a slave. A help, that's all."

She cocked her head and raised her eyebrows. "A help, huh. I expect decent wages."

"I'll make sure of it."

"I need time off to be with my pa."

"Your pa." I saw the fire in her eyes.

"My pa. He lives around here, and I like to visit him. From time to time."

"All right."

"If I don't get treated right, I leave." I would treat her right. I would not treat her the way Gretchen had.

"I promise. You'll be treated fair and square." In the back of my mind, I figured Tom would find out and be proud of me for giving her a decent job, for accepting her, even if we could never be equals.

Kula smiled, a slight smile. "All right, then."

I reached into the trunk and found a narrow, pale lemon-yellow silk shawl. "Here," I said, handing it to her. I wanted to show her I meant what I said, wanted her to know I was generous.

Kula hesitated for a moment, her dark eyes regarding me with suspicion.

"I just want you to have it, as a friend," I said. "It'll look so well on you. Please take it." *Friend* was strong; but she was only a girl, after all. I wanted her to like me.

Kula took the shawl and pressed it to her cheek, closing her eyes for a moment. "All right. I'll go get my things."

I headed out to wait in the lobby as Kula finished the packing. Graybull was busy arranging for our luggage to be put in the surrey. I had my head buried in the road map, checking the distances, when I heard Tom's voice.

"Leaving for Lake?" he asked, and my heart lifted so fast I was breathless. His face was bent close to mine, and that lock of hair had fallen across his forehead.

"Yes." Then tears filled my eyes as I thought about how I was, at least for the moment, promised to a man I couldn't stand. "Where are you off to?" I asked, looking away, trying to hide my emotions.

"My dad has a bead on some mining prospects near Red Lodge," Tom said. "After a time at Canyon, we're heading out of the Park for a bit."

Heading out of the Park, and not to Lake. My heart sank as I thought about not seeing him. "I hope you won't be gone for long." I prayed not.

He didn't have time to answer me before Graybull's firm voice penetrated the din of tourists.

"Margaret! There you are!" He marched across the lobby toward me and Tom.

"Mr. Graybull," Tom said, his voice pleasant but guarded. "Did you get your bear?"

"Regrettably, no. I'm sure to have better luck when I'm out again in a few weeks."

"Too bad," said Tom, sounding anything but sorry. "Maybe Maggie can catch one on camera for you."

I felt Graybull stiffen beside me. "Indeed." He took my elbow, his fingers clamping me hard. "We must be going, my dear Margaret."

Tom's eyebrows shot up as he recognized the familiarity of Graybull's behavior. "Well, see you around, then," he said to me. Longing flooded me as he lifted his hand in good-bye.

"Come along, Margaret," Graybull said. He nodded at Tom, positioning himself between us and placing his hand on my arm.

I turned my head aside so that Graybull would not see the frustration in my eyes. I had no say. Then I remembered Kula's words: fight for what you want. I had no say at the moment. I straightened and pulled away from Graybull and searched the lobby for Tom's tall form.

I couldn't see him until . . . "See you soon, Maggie!" Tom's voice rang out across the lobby.

Graybull stiffened. It was all I could do to suppress a delighted smile. Yes. See you soon, that was the promise.

"I should like you to avoid that young man, Margaret."

I froze. "Why?" Graybull's hand tightened on my arm, reminding me of the facts: he possessed me; he owned me. For now.

"It's unseemly," Graybull replied. His voice was cool and dispassionate. "You are now spoken for." He gazed off into the distance.

I felt frustration well up and had to close my mouth tight to keep from speaking out. I couldn't jeopardize my chances and Papa's position. It would take me time to change my life, and I had to be careful with this man.

"This photography hobby is one thing," he continued. "So long as you are taking pictures of inanimate objects while here in the Park, I'll have no objections. But conversing in an intimate fashion with strangers, particularly young men, will not be tolerated."

My arm felt bruised by his vise grip. I had disliked him before; I began to hate him now.

"There now," Graybull said, looking at me and then across the lobby, his tongue making that ghastly gesture as he smiled. "I believe your maid has your things ready."

I turned and followed his gaze. Kula was there in the lobby with my trunk. She was talking to Tom. Wearing a pale lemon-yellow silk shawl that was so becoming. They were talking, old friends, smiling, Tom talking with Kula—touching her arm—casual, intimate, more than friends.

I felt betrayed and trapped all at once. Tom and Kula were both free and I was not. Kula thought I had anything I wanted, and I did not. I didn't have what she had, right at that moment, as she reached up and touched Tom's shoulder and met his eyes.

Oh, but it looked as though it was my choice to be a caged bird, a pet, to be cared for and confined. I would have money and position and all I could ask for—I would have Ghost!—and Papa would be pleased, and I could return to Newport, to Kitty, to my grandparents, to my life. It looked as though I had it all.

All but one thing. As I watched Tom and Kula talking, laughing, free and easy, I knew I would have to fight to get it.

The bars of my pretty cage pressed on me, pressed so tightly I could scarcely breathe.

Chapter
TWENTY-NINE ❧ ❧ ❧ ❧

July 14, 1904

Just out of Steins Pass we could see a large bon-fire.
One of the trainmen remarked, 'Wonder what the big
fire is, I hope we don't run into any trouble.'.... we had to
find out why the train came to an abrupt stop ...
We found ourselves looking into the barrel of guns.

—an account of the Stein's Pass robbery of the late 1880s

IT HAD BEGUN TO RAIN AS WE LEFT THE GEYSER BASIN and now it poured, the rain hammering the roof of the surrey. Our driver called over his shoulder, "This'll keep the dust down!" It rained continually on our two-hour drive to the Lake Hotel. When we finally arrived, damp and chilled, Kula, Mrs. Gale, and I dashed into the elegant yellow frame building, while Graybull supervised unloading our trunks.

We were finally at Lake and my anxiety was acute. I felt that I was so close, now, to uncovering the truth about Mama. As soon as we were settled I went back down to the lobby. I paced before the window staring over the vast lake, trying to decide how to locate my uncle. The rain, coming down in sheets, obscured the distant shore, so all was gray water meeting gray sky. Kula lounged near me in one of the overstuffed chairs that graced the vast lobby. Graybull had not come down yet from settling our things.

"I need to find my uncle," I told her. I needed Kula's help. I couldn't risk Graybull intervening.

Kula raised her eyebrows. "And?"

"I need a diversion, so that I can speak with my uncle privately." It was, I thought, the least she could do. Though I couldn't put the image of her with Tom from my mind, I shoved my jealousy aside and sat on the chair next to her. Perhaps she'd help a friend, so I tried to act like one. I leaned over and spoke in a whisper. "I don't want Mr. Graybull to find out where I've gone and what I'm doing."

Kula regarded me with those dark, placid eyes. She shrugged. She said, her tone flippant, "You have a headache. You've gone up to your room. I'll tell him."

I squeezed her hand; she looked surprised. But this moment was so important and I wanted to be sure she understood how much I had to trust her.

I went to the reception desk, nervous. "How do I find someone who works here?"

The man's eyebrows shot up. "In what capacity?" He looked me up and down.

"As a carpenter."

Now the man stared pointedly at me. "We don't encourage the help to mingle with guests."

I felt my face go hot. "I've admired the man's work. I would like to give him a commission." I stood up straight, embarrassed but determined.

The man's lips twisted into a grimace, but my lie worked. He picked up his pen and went back to his tasks, speaking to me without looking at me. "He's probably in the carriage house across the way. That's where the workers wait out the rain." He pointed his pen outside the window to a large barn closer to the lake's edge. "Umbrellas are there, in the stand by the door. Help yourself."

I gathered my skirts in one fist and clutched the umbrella in the other as I dashed across the road, trying to stay dry. I shoved open the carriage-house door, where a cheery warmth and the sound of laughter greeted me. There were about twenty or so men gathered around a woodstove.

"Hey, miss!" A portly man stood up as I closed the umbrella and stamped my feet, shaking off the rain. "Come for a visit? You've come to the right place!"

"I'm looking for someone," I said, unsmiling. "John Bennet. A carpenter." My heart pounded. This was humiliating; what if he wasn't here?

"John, John! You've got a charming visitor! What've you been up to, man?"

My uncle rose from among them, while the others laughed and jostled, making sly, bawdy jokes.

"Margaret!" John looked at the others. "My niece, if you please, gentlemen." This silenced the group, and they watched him cross the floor toward me. He didn't look happy to see me.

"Is there somewhere we can talk?" I whispered.

He took my elbow and steered me into the tack room and shut the door. The smells of horses and leather and hay mingled. Thunder cracked, and then shuddered the walls of the carriage house. The voices of the men, their laughter, carried through the building in soft waves.

I turned and faced my uncle and plunged in. "Uncle John, it's high time you told me the truth." I felt no need to feign manners anymore. My heart pounded so hard it beat out the sound of the rain. "Why did Papa bring us here, of all places?" I wanted to ask him if it was because Mama was here, but I held my tongue.

He shifted, shrugging his shoulders. "Now, Margaret, you should ask your father these questions, not me." He gave me a nervous half smile.

I would not be put off. I'd been put off for too long. She was my mother; I had to know what he knew. "Papa hasn't told me a thing." I grew frustrated and yanked off my damp beret, twisting it around my hand. "He's trying to marry me off to someone I scarcely know and don't love because he thinks it will save us from falling into complete ruin." I caught my uncle's shocked expression. "You didn't know? That Mr. Graybull."

"Oh, Maggie." Uncle John sounded genuinely sad.

"You have to help me find her, Uncle John." I touched his arm. "You can see how grave this is. When she left, Papa fell apart. Grandpapa blames him for everything that's gone wrong. He says that Papa ruined her, that she married . . . beneath her. And the only solution is for me to marry someone who is rich and of the right class and awful . . ." I choked with a sob. "I need Mama. She can straighten out everything with Papa. She can help me. I know she was unhappy, Uncle John. I think she probably left him. Am I right? Did she come out here?"

My uncle looked at the floor, slowly shaking his head back and forth.

I began to tremble. "Uncle John?" Fear and frustration mingled in me as I watched him shake his head. My voice rose with my denial as I said, "I don't believe she's dead. I read your letters.

She's got to be alive and I want her back." It was what I had believed, oh so passionately, all these months. I couldn't have been wrong. She must be alive. I bit my lip so hard I tasted blood. "I want her back, Uncle John!"

Uncle John raised his eyes and put his hand to his lips, trying to quiet me.

"Don't shush me!" I shouted. The pent-up frustration of the past weeks burst from me like the storm that raged outside. "I've had enough of men ordering me around!" I heard silence from the men in the other room. I lowered my voice, barely in control. "Don't tell me what to do; tell me the truth. Why did we come here? Why did she leave us? I need to know." I shook as hard as if the room were filled with ice, so hard my teeth knocked together. I wrapped my arms around myself and leaned on a barrel for support. I was afraid of what my uncle was about to tell me, but I was done with hiding.

Uncle John's face fell. He rubbed his eyes hard and took a gasping breath. "Oh, Margaret. This is hard, girl. This is hard." He sat down on a stool and dropped his head into his hands.

My stomach dropped, too, and my anger left me in the face of what I feared he must be about to tell me. "It's all right, Uncle John. I need to know. That way I can . . ." I didn't know what to say. I was already choking with sobs.

"All right. All right. Here it is, then."

Chapter THIRTY ❧ ❧ ❧ ❧ ❧ ❧ ❧ ❧ ❧

*Then she shrank from her own wavering. Look where
she would into her life, it seemed to her that all was
monstrous and out of joint.*

—*Lady Rose's Daughter*, a novel by
Mrs. Humphry Ward, 1903

IT IS A CURIOUS THING HOW A REVELATION CAN SPLIT
experience, so that there is a "before" and an "after." In that
defining moment, everything is stilled and details become precise,
clear. Time is stretched thin and transparent.

It had happened to me once before, the moment it became certain
that Mama had not returned from her walk and that she likely
would not return. It was a night and a day after she'd left. Papa had
searched and the hapless police had searched—"the waves, sir . . .
the riptides, sir . . ."—and all had given up on her, except me. But
I felt that turning moment nonetheless because it surrounded me,
the stench of grief. I froze my memories of that moment like living
pictures in a scrapbook: the smell of salt water blowing through
an open door; the cry of a lone seagull; a corner of the wide front
hallway of our house washed in low, late afternoon sunlight; the
reflection off the polished wood floor broken by the shadows of
scurrying servants; the soft weeping of Cook, muffling the sound

in her apron; the low voices of the men from behind the parlor doors; Papa's one anguished shout, quickly quelled.

I hadn't given her up then; I held to my faith that she was alive. But I knew that was a defining moment. And I knew what waited on the other side of it. And now, here in the carriage house, I knew that this was another such moment. Everything I'd held on to before, everything including Mama, had slipped away.

I perched on a rough barrel in a barn by Lake Hotel in Yellowstone, watching motes of hay dust twist and fall behind my uncle. I heard the rain on the roof, pattering the shingles with fat rapid drops. I smelled the leather and oil; I picked at the splinters that stuck out from the barrel with the thumb and index finger of my right hand.

"It was a long time ago. Right after you were born, in fact," said Uncle John. "Oh, and you were such a bonny baby, Maggie! Very lively. I think your father didn't know what to make of you. Anyway, you were still an infant when Charles took your mother on a holiday. He was anxious to see this wild place that he'd heard talk about, the west." John coughed. "And to fix his marriage."

"Mama was unhappy with Papa." This was a statement, not a question. It confirmed what I'd known, what I'd seen but denied.

"You have to understand, Maggie. Some women have an easy time of childbearing. Some women"—John paused—"struggle." He glanced at me and added, "Your mama was prone to fits of melancholy, Margaret. Long before you came along. I think when she married your father . . . Well, anyway . . ."

"Go on with the story." I plucked hard at a long, fibrous splinter. I knew this about my parents; it made me feel sad and small but I'd known it all along.

"So they took the trip; I guess he thought it would cure her. You were left at home with Mina. You were too little to travel. Otherwise maybe it would have changed things. Who can say? It was in eastern Montana. Their train was stopped by bandits. A gang, and a famous one at that. They laid logs across the tracks."

"Bandits!" I exclaimed. That explained my father's anxiety on the train when we passed through eastern Montana. And his reaction to the news of the coach robbery.

"It wasn't uncommon in those days. These gangs, it was still the Wild West. The men boarded the train, made the passengers disembark, stripped them of jewelry, watches, money. They blew the safes and took the gold. Then came the bad part."

I waited, not moving.

"The men plucked several of the women from the crowd of passengers and made off. Your mama was one of the women taken by the robbers." John paused here, his face ashen with his own memories. "She was so pretty. Just so pretty."

Dust rose behind Uncle John, turned, and fell like mist. The rain washed the roof in soft pats. The men in the next room laughed, then resumed a low murmur.

"It nearly killed your father. For a month he scoured the countryside looking for her, but he had to return to Newport. To you. You were just a baby, after all. He hired Pinkerton men to continue the search. The trail grew hot and cold by intervals. We all thought she was dead. Or as good as dead." His face grew red. I felt sick. Mrs. Delaney, Mrs. Proctor—they'd all judged her a ruined woman. "All except your father. He wanted her back no matter what." Uncle John paused. "He was desperate. It nearly drove him insane. I came out west to help with the search. I couldn't stand to see him grieve so.

"It was almost a year, and we caught a break. The gang had split, it seemed, and one set had made for Wyoming. There were reports of a woman among them who fit your mother's description. There was only one issue: that woman was traveling with a baby."

A baby. Slow swirls of dust. The smell of leather oil.

"When the Pinkerton men found the gang, there was a brief firefight. Two gang members were killed outright. Some escaped, but the detectives managed to catch a few—and find your mama. Indeed, it was her."

John looked at me again. "It wasn't ever about you, Maggie. She was desperate about the child. She was crazed. The detectives had failed to take the child. It was lost in the confusion. I had to calm her before returning her to Charles. The doctors prescribed laudanum. It was two more weeks before she was fit to travel. By then, she'd gone silent as a stick, wouldn't discuss a thing, only asked about you, over and over. When we arrived back in Newport, your mama devoted herself to you. We all thought that was that. It was bad, but nobody talked about it—nobody. At least not in the open. Your grandfather saw to that." Uncle John spat on the floor.

Oh, I knew better. They talked, all right. I sat very still, seeing, as if anew, in my mind's eye, Mama painting in a half-dark room, in her loose dressing gown, her hair wild about her. I saw her dressed for some society event, and the barely masked chill of the other women toward her. And how something in her changed as I grew older, as if seeing me grow up, but not the other child, made her miserable with longing. I thought she was insane. In fact, she had been, in a way. Insane with a grief of her own, one she couldn't share. I leaned my forehead against my palm.

"We all thought she was over it," Uncle John said. "Until last summer. Your father told me she had been getting worse. Her breakdown at that party. When she had herself that great public display. The way he described it, it was pretty bad, I guess." Uncle John shook his head.

Mama at Mary's ball, her arms dripping blood on her white gown, one white glove splayed across the floor. I remembered how humiliated I felt; now I felt shame and remorse. I had not understood. My finger and thumb pinched the splinter. If she had told me, if Mama had told me . . . ah, but I was involved with myself, wasn't I.

"That's when Charles found your mother's journal. And some other things. Letters, business things." John paused. "I almost wish he hadn't," he said as his voice dropped in misery. "Then maybe he'd have picked himself up back there in Newport and you wouldn't be here right now, chasing phantoms and such . . ."

"Go on," I whispered. I was close now . . . close to the whole truth.

"It was clear your mother had, while she was captured—and you can imagine how hard it must have been for her—she had"—he paused and cleared his throat—"grown fond of her captor. Even loved him. But it wasn't clear about the child. The age of the child, things your mother said, it wasn't clear who'd fathered it. Your father came to believe the child was his. He hoped the child was his. Isn't that what any man would hope for? That his wife wouldn't have a child by another man? That he'd fathered the baby before she was carried off?" Uncle John lowered his head. "Bad enough your pa discovered that your mama didn't love him. Not in the same way he loved her, leastways. At least, he hoped, he prayed, he had another child with her.

"Your pa went back to the Pinkertons. They showed him everything, all their notes. Things they said made him believe he could be the father. They told him the baby was a boy."

It was as I'd suspected, and still so different. It wasn't Mama Papa was looking for; it wasn't revenge, either. He was looking for his child. He had me right there and I wasn't enough; he had to find this child, too.

Motes of dust. Fat drops of rain. A boy. Of course I wasn't enough.

"Your mam's dead, Maggie. That seems pretty clear. Whether accident, or not, whether she meant it or not, that Cliff Walk took her. Maybe she wanted to come back here, but she didn't. She didn't come back here, by all the evidence those detectives could muster." Yes. Mama was dead.

I knew then what it meant, a broken heart. I could feel it deep inside, a great, sharp pain, like someone had cut my heart out and snapped it in two and shoved it back into my chest.

"The Pinkertons found the trail of the man your mama fell in with. He's got the child. So, your father is hoping he has a son, somewhere out here. A son only a year younger than you are, Maggie. In Montana, Wyoming, Yellowstone, even. Still with the man who stole your mother. Your papa wants his son, wants to take him away from that man, wants to bring that part of her back, and wants to see that contemptible thief empty and alone."

I did not feel the way I'd imagined, knowing the truth. The truth was a bare plain, drained and dry, like the desiccated sinter of an abandoned spring; though a terrible pain dwelt far below, ready to erupt. But not in this moment. I held it in. "So, I have a brother," I said. "And Mama's dead."

My uncle looked so miserable that right then I felt more sorry for him than for myself.

Before, and after.

Chapter
THIRTY-ONE

July 14–15, 1904

Nestled among the forest-crowned hills which bounded our vision, lay this inland sea, its crystal waves dancing and sparkling in the sunlight as if laughing with joy for their wild freedom.

—*The Valley of the Upper Yellowstone*, the explorations
of Charles W. Cook, David E. Folsom,
and William Peterson, 1869

"WHERE IS HE NOW?"

Uncle John looked startled. "That's why you and your father came to Yellowstone. To find him."

I waved my hand, impatient. I hadn't meant the boy. My brother. I had a brother. I shook my head, trying to shake out the confusion. "Not him. I mean Papa. Where is he right now?"

Uncle John sighed. "He told me he was off to the Canyon area. That's where the detectives said they had the latest bit of news. He was to meet them at the hotel there."

The splinter, worked free at last, stabbed my finger. I looked down at the fat drop of blood, detached from the pain.

"Sometimes, when your father looks at you, it reminds him . . . you're so stubborn . . ." His voice trailed off. "He wants to keep you from making your mama's mistakes. He wants you to marry right and be well protected. He wants you to be a proper young woman, not like your mam." Uncle John looked at me from beneath his brows, his head bent. "Your pa's afraid of that impulsive streak in you. He's afraid you'll do what she did. Everything she did."

I started. Impulsive? No. I followed the rules, didn't I? I was not like Mama; I'd rejected her and all her bohemian behavior. Oh, at times, once or twice, that dress with the red sash, the photography, the porcelain pitcher . . . but impulsive? I shook my head. "He doesn't know me, then," I said. "He'd like a son," I went on. "It's perfectly natural. A daughter is . . . incomplete. Inadequate. Not what a father wants." I wrapped one end of the yellow sash of my dress over my finger and watched the blood darken the silk. What I saw was memories: a red silk sash; blood on white silk.

"He feels like he's had no control over things," Uncle John said. "Over your mama, over the robbery, over you . . ."

I snorted. "He has no control? I'm the one with no choices. And I'm nothing like her." I looked at the spreading stain. Impulsive? "I wish I was impulsive, and could do as I pleased." I'd get away from that dreadful Graybull. I'd stay by Mrs. Gale and learn the ways of photography and I'd ride like a man and I'd throw away all my corsets . . . I'd run straight to Tom and throw my arms around him, shamelessly.

My uncle looked at me, so miserable that I felt sorry for him again. He wasn't to blame.

I stood on shaky legs. "I've got to go back." My throat was tight now and I couldn't say any more. Uncle John walked me to the door of the carriage house; the men fell silent as we passed as if they knew what we'd been discussing.

I didn't bother to open the umbrella on the way back and I walked directly through the puddles without seeing them.

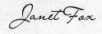

Kula had unpacked my things and, back in the safety of my room, I changed out of my damp clothes and pulled on my dressing gown. Watered silk, pale ivory, so soft. It had once belonged to Mama and I'd borrowed it. I'd thought to return it to her, but now it was a token that I'd stepped into her place. Become a prisoner like she was. Silk made such soft shackles.

I had a brother. I had no mother. No Mama. I had been an only child; now I was half an orphan with a brother. Life was thrown far out of balance.

At dinner, I was quiet, thinking about what Uncle John had said: that I was like Mama. I did my level best not to pull away when George Graybull touched my arm or smiled at me, his tongue flickering between his teeth. I thought about Mama, about her longing, and I knew that I was lucky to be under the protection of a respectable man. I wasn't impulsive. If I were, I'd be running out of this dining room as fast as my legs could carry me. I'd be on my way to Tom. Instead, I stared quietly out the great glass windows at the darkening lake.

Gray water meeting dark gray sky, drifting into distant black mountains. I threw my mind back: the day after Mama disappeared, the sun over Narragansett Bay sank into a scarlet ribbon that rimmed the water, the sky above it a purple bruise that smeared to black.

After dinner, Graybull retired to smoke on the porch. Mrs. Gale went up to her room, and I found Kula still lounging in one of the chairs in the lobby.

"You've had dinner?" I asked. I thought for a moment; I'd entirely forgotten about Kula. I sank into the chair next to her. "Where were you all afternoon?" I asked it out of kindness.

Kula regarded me with disdain. "I know how to manage. Thanks for asking."

The windows were black, now, the lake invisible. But I felt it. The water drew me, like a deep longing, like the ocean as restless as Mama's soul. For all this time, a year almost, I'd clung to the belief that she was out there. I'd tucked that belief into my pocket like the picture of Ghost and carried it everywhere. Her cameo was my talisman; the green dress was a magic garment meant to draw her to me; she was alive, she would keep her promise and return, she'd be there for me in the season of my womanhood. That's what I'd believed.

No. She would not. Water, deep and wild and uncontrollable, had taken my mother from me. I wanted to conquer that water, those black and bottomless depths. I wanted to take my mother back.

I'd closed my eyes for some minutes; now I opened them and looked across the lobby. There was a sign on a stand by the door. It advertised boat trips on a steamboat, the *Zillah*, out to Dot Island in the lake so that tourists could see the buffalo and elk that were kept in pens there up close. I remembered Tom talking about the animals, the bison on the island. An island. I could perhaps find privacy. Make my peace. I rose and went to the desk. "I'd like to book a boat trip," I said, pointing at the sign.

The man at the desk looked at me with a faint smile. "Alone?" I knew what he was thinking: I was not a respectable young woman.

"No," said a voice beside me. It was Kula. "I'll go, too." Kula stared at the clerk, daring him to question her as well.

The clerk looked at us, eyebrows raised. First I consorted with employees; now with an Indian, and a servant at that. I didn't care what he thought, what anyone thought anymore.

I narrowed my eyes at the man, feeling a quiet fury. Who was he to judge me? "Two tickets, please. For me and my friend," I said, emphasizing *friend*. I paid for the tickets for early the next morning, and then turned away from the desk. I could feel the change in myself already.

"Why do you want to go out there?" Kula asked, gesturing toward the lake.

"I'm looking for something." I'd called her a friend; but she wasn't, and I couldn't tell her my heart. I stared out the window into the blackness. Kula had been right about one thing. I had to fight for what I wanted. Mama was gone. I was alone. And now I needed to find out who I was by myself.

⁂ ⁂ ⁂

The next morning dawned clear and windy. The still-wet trees glittered in the early light. I'd asked Mrs. Gale if I could borrow the camera, and Kula and I avoided Graybull, sneaking off to the docks without breakfast. I didn't let Kula in on my plan; I wasn't sure of my plan. All I knew was that I needed to find my way to the water.

We boarded the boat and I stood in the bow, clutching the camera to my chest. The steamboat chugged away from shore, turned, and plowed through the rough water toward the island. Kula stood silent, her black braid snaking down her back, so like Mama's, wisps of hair lashing her strong cheeks.

I took off my hat and, as the boat gathered speed, pulled the pins from my hair and stuffed them into my jacket pocket. I gripped the rail, letting the breeze whip my hair loose. It was risky, leaving without word. The water gave up no secrets: It was opaque, inky, racing beneath the boat. I held the rail so tightly my knuckles were white.

We docked, the bright sunshine throwing sparks off the water. The wind whipped the women's scarves into banners. Men pressed their fedoras to their heads.

I touched Kula's arm. "I'll be along in a minute. I want to get a picture of the lake." It was a lie meant to protect us both. I wasn't really sure what I was going to do, but I had to do it alone.

Kula looked at me curiously. "I'll come."

"No. I need to go alone."

Kula's dark eyes met mine, and she regarded me, suspicious. "What are you planning?"

"Did I ask for your help?" I was abrupt. She would only get in the way.

Kula's gaze grew sharp. "Mr. Graybull told me to keep an eye out. Not to let you go off wandering."

"Mr. Graybull is not my master." My throat was tight. Then I looked away from her. "Anyway, it's only for a picture."

"Whatever you say." Kula shrugged and turned away.

I picked my way along the shore away from the steamer. I needed to find a place out of sight of the tourists, the steamer, the buffalo pens. It wasn't easy going, as the underbrush grew thick and tangled right to the edge, and there was only a rocky shelf. Several times I slipped into the water, soaking my feet. My stockings were heavy cotton, but my shoes were thin, and the cold penetrated to my bones.

I found my way to a small inlet that faced the vast expanse of the lake. The blue sky was reflected in the water that rippled in the strong breeze. Mountains ringed the lake; snow glowed white in the morning sun. I set up the camera. The image, upside down, made me dizzy: water at the top. I glanced back toward the boat,

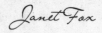

just out of sight around the spit of land, and made up my mind.

Until that moment I'd thought I was only here for a picture, as I told Kula. I thought that might answer the questions inside me, but it was inadequate. Now I knew why I was here and what I had to do.

I had to see how much I was like my mother. I had to have her experience. I had to try to bring her back. I had to bring her to me.

It was risky, but no one could see.

I pulled off my jacket and stepped out of my shoes and skirt. I slipped off my shirtwaist, camisette, petticoat, stockings, bloomers. Naked, I waded, fast, into the lake, picking my way through the rocks, and then let myself fall.

The cold water hit me like a wall and I gasped. Instinct took over and I drew up and began to swim hard as Mama had taught me, knowing that working would warm my limbs. At first my arms and legs wouldn't respond, but after a few poorly made strokes, I began to move and pulled myself out to deeper water. My feet left the bottom and my gut clenched.

But it was the cold that was more terrifying than the depth. This water was much more frigid than I'd expected, and that made it much more difficult to swim. My legs felt heavy, and dragged me down. I turned back toward the shore. It wasn't far, but I had to fight for every inch, and I grew colder and colder, made dreamy and stupid by my icy limbs.

I wasn't afraid of drowning, or of the deep, deep void beneath me. Not anymore. Even in my increasingly dreamy state, I knew what I feared most: I feared living a life without love. A shallow life. A life where I could always touch the bottom, where impulse was a curse and everything I had was given to me by someone else. I feared living a life like Mama's, where I yearned for what I could not have.

Had the Atlantic felt like this when Mama had vanished over the cliff? I began to grasp the reality of drowning. Was this what it felt like, Mama? A serene calm . . . I stopped moving. I thought about slipping under the water, about the cold green water that would fill my lungs, about the sense of peace that must be my last thought.

It was so cold, so cold in this lake, like liquid glacier. I felt so tired. Heavy. These heavy legs and arms pulled me down. Weights. The shore. So far, like the wrong end of the camera lens.

Slipping beneath the water, drifting like seaweed—there was no void here; cold sapped me of fear. That's what it felt like. Peaceful, blissful. Why not? It would be easy to do what she did. To escape.

From beneath me, I felt a hand pushing, pushing.

First I thought, magic! A mermaid. Then, Mama. Mama's arms wrapped around me and pushed me out of the water. Her long black hair streamed through the water, her hands pushing; I was dimly aware, my eyes were so hard to focus. I was sure I was being carried toward shore. Mama was there, carrying me back. I turned my head, and met her eyes, and she looked at me, so sad. So sad, like the doe, before her face disappeared into the green light of the water.

"Mama!" It wasn't even a whisper because my throat was frozen tight. Her impulse had been to move toward love, to find her child. She'd slipped on that rocky cliff—she must have. I was sure that she hadn't chosen to die. All her decisions had been made for her; but I could follow a different path. I could make my own choices. Live fully, impulsively, live on the edge if need be, or die by bits and pieces as my soul was swallowed by the shallow things in life.

At this instant I had to choose whether to quit and succumb, or to face life and all its pain.

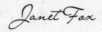

My foot scraped something hard, and I shoved against it. I nudged at the rock and it nudged back, sending me toward the shore. I lifted out of the water, head back, like a newborn infant, and the shock of air bit into my skin. I gasped and, in a fog, knew that I was crawling onto the rocky edge; and as I pulled out of the water into the wind, I felt a deep ache.

I'd been in the water for less than a minute, but it felt like a lifetime. I lay on the rocks, shivering uncontrollably. I knew that if I didn't get dry I'd freeze to death right there. I crawled hand over hand to a sheltered spot on the rocks, my body shaking in violent shudders.

The sun was out, and I leaned back against the rocks, seeking their warmth. It seemed to take forever to seep into me. My long hair was matted; I had a splitting headache. The more I warmed up, the more I shook. I fought with my clothes, tugging as my hands trembled. My cotton underclothes, even my stockings, seemed pathetic. I was grateful that I'd worn the tweed suit. When I was dressed, I sat in the sun, willing my body to recover. The pain in my head was excruciating.

I looked at the dark lake. Mama was not there. No one was there. Had I imagined it? No. I believed in magic. I stood, shaking, and went to the camera, still waiting for me where I left it.

Staring down the viewfinder, I framed the picture. I focused into the water where it was shallow enough to show the rocky bottom, the rocks forming a soft pattern of light and dark. In that narrow world, there was only shape and form. Everything in the picture was finite, in the moment. My stiff fingers worked the lens with difficulty, but I managed.

The steamer blew its horn, and I knew they were missing me. I packed up and worked my way back along the shore, my wet hair pinned up but still dripping icy streams down my neck. I thought about what I would say to Kula to explain myself. I rounded the cove and saw the *Zillah* and a number of tourists, including Kula, watching my return. I knew how odd I looked with my soaking hair and full-body shivers. The tourists gathered on the dock stared at me and whispered. Kula grabbed my arm and pulled me along.

"I slipped," I lied.

"You'd better get inside." I was grateful that she didn't scold me, that she didn't ask me what I'd really done. She found a blanket and draped it over my shaking shoulders as the steamer made passage back over the lake. I watched Dot Island grow small.

Graybull paced the dock; I could see him from a distance as the *Zillah* approached the landing. The desk clerk had evidently informed him of our unauthorized excursion. He was furious, and hissed at me through clenched teeth when we docked. "Where have you been?"

"I wanted some photographs."

"No business going without me! Such a state. Your hair. Disgraceful!"

"There was spray. Waves. And some spitting rain on the island."

He turned toward Kula. "I gave you a task. You failed."

Kula drew herself up, straight and proud, her lips a tight line. She walked two paces behind us on the way back to the hotel.

"It was my idea to go out there. Kula tried to stop me. When she couldn't, she decided she'd better go with me." I was getting good at lies. They were a useful weapon.

Graybull turned on Kula. "Is this true?"

Kula didn't answer. She remained mute and defiant, her dark eyes seeming even blacker as she looked at him.

"Of course it is," I said. "I wanted to get some photographs."

"You are not to leave without my permission again, Margaret. Kula, see to it."

"I'm going to my room," I said. "I have a headache." I'd taken one step, only one, a big step but yet . . . I discovered what I wanted but not how to get it. I found something of Mama but couldn't complete the circle. I would not live a life without love, but I wasn't sure how to create that life. I made only one choice out of a vast ocean of possibilities.

I could feel the walls of my prison pressing in on me.

In my room, I stared out the window. Kula drew me a bath, then left me. After soaking for an hour, I pulled on my silk robe and sat down at the desk. I wrote to Kitty for the first time in days.

> Dearest Kit,
> I hope your debut will be beautiful. And that you are enjoying your season. I have no need of either, now, for I am engaged to a very wealthy man. Isn't that exciting? Oh, and I've discovered that my mother is indeed dead. And that scandal had surrounded her, including some astonishing surprises, so her disappearance did in fact

A huge round splotch marred the words as one of my tears fell on the paper.

It was a beautiful afternoon, the wind had kicked up even more, and little whitecaps foamed on the lake. I sat and watched the water sparkle in the sunlight, and cried for everything I had lost.

Chapter THIRTY-TWO

July 17, 1904

The black and brown bears are becoming so numerous as to be an actual nuisance if not dangerous. All hotels are nightly invaded by from six to eight of them. The slop bones and waste materials furnish all the food they need. They have become too indolent to hunt for themselves.

—"Uncle Sam's Big Menagerie," *Sundance (WY) Gazette,* November 25, 1898

"THEY FEED THE BEARS EVERY EVENING," SAID GRAYBULL.

It was two days since, as Graybull put it, I'd made a spectacle of myself on my Dot Island excursion. Papa had just returned from Canyon, and Mrs. Gale, Papa, Graybull, and I walked out behind the Lake Hotel before dinner. We hadn't yet experienced the bear feedings and Graybull had finally insisted on it.

I'd kept to myself these past two days, feigning illness and taking meals in my room. Kula had disappeared without informing me; but I owed her a debt. She'd disobeyed Graybull for my sake. So I'd been alone, not even seeking out Mrs. Gale's company. I needed to think, sort things through.

Mama was gone. Truly gone. And I missed her. I spent hours sitting at the window of my room overlooking the lake. Each afternoon, the clouds gathered into great lenticular stacks, then settled into the red dusk. I let myself think about Mama as I watched the lake spark diamonds, but I knew I had to let Mama go.

I had a brother. Would I like him? A year younger than me—we might be friends. He held a piece of Mama.

I was still trapped—Graybull had a hold over me through his hold over Papa. I couldn't spurn Graybull; Papa, Grandpapa—both either needed or wanted this attachment. This part of my life was a house of sticks: pull one out and the rest fell down.

First, I had to try to determine what Papa knew about my brother. I hadn't told him that I spoke to Uncle John, nor that I knew about Mama. I couldn't talk about Mama yet. As we gathered in the lobby to walk out for the bear viewing, I set in: "How was your trip? Was it productive?" I almost never expressed an interest in his affairs; I could sense his surprise at my questions.

"It was fine," he said.

"Is the hotel there attractive?"

"Not really. A new one is to be built." He pulled on his mustache.

"Any other interesting news?"

"No." I waited; he pressed his lips together, the discussion closed. I would learn no more from him.

There was plenty of afternoon light as Papa, Mrs. Gale, and I followed Graybull to the stands set up to overlook a grassy clearing where they fed the bears. A soldier kept us from walking farther, and we settled onto the benches. Then I saw why we were held back. Four black bears scavenged at a pile of rotting food. From time to time they stopped and sat on their haunches, or stood up sniffing the air. We were close to them, but it wasn't like seeing the grizzly.

"Isn't this marvelous?" Graybull asked. "At Canyon there's even a captive bear on a chain for our entertainment." Our entertainment. I thought about Tom and what he'd think about a captive bear. Just the passing thought of Tom sent my stomach into somersaults.

I watched a cub scampering around its mother, bleating. The sow turned over a large log and stuffed her nose into the scraps. Then she looked up, staring into the crowd.

"I don't like it," I said. I remembered the doe and her bleating fawn.

"What?" said Graybull. "Why ever not?"

"They shouldn't eat our food," I said. They were Tom's words, and I was proud to use them.

"Oh, come now, Maggie," said Papa. "They're animals. It can't hurt them. Aren't they scavengers, at any rate?"

"Quite," said Graybull. "This helps to keep them happy and well fed. And, it's a park attraction."

"And why do we have to interfere with nature?" Interfering men were wearing a groove on my nerves.

"My dear Margaret," said Graybull, as if he were speaking to a small child, "it is up to the superior human race to control nature."

"Control?" My voice was sharp. "Why do men always want to control everything around them? In fact, why do they think they are *able* to control everything around them?" I had to be careful; I was stepping over the bounds. I still had no place to turn. I bit my lip and looked at my hands before looking back up.

Graybull gazed at me, frowning. "Believe that splash of cold water the other day has made you a bit snappish, my dear."

Papa gave an embarrassed laugh. "Maggie's mother had some radical ideas. I'm sure she didn't introduce them to Maggie." He looked at me and ran his fingers over his mustache. Yes, she did, Papa. More than you know. I grew impatient again.

"Ah," said Graybull. "Can't have that, now, can we?" He smiled, his tongue dashing through the gap. I felt my face burn.

I opened my mouth to speak, but Mrs. Gale placed her hand on my arm. "Margaret, please come with me," she murmured. "I'd like your help with a photo."

I turned away from the men, my skirts swirling in a frustrated flounce.

Mrs. Gale set up the camera and asked me to shoot the picture. I waited until one bear turned its head toward me, then captured it. Its animal eyes were right on me. Those flat animal eyes meeting mine. Then I felt the weight of my own captivity. I was alien to the bear; I was akin to the bear. As much as I feared the bear, we weren't so very different.

"The right time will come," Mrs. Gale said as she put away the film, "for you to stand up for yourself."

"Why not now?" I knew why not now. But I wanted to hear her thoughts.

"You are very young. Your father will come around. Remember, he's still grieving."

"So am I," I whispered, furious. In fact, I was grieving now in a way I'd never admitted before.

"Of course you are. But he doesn't know how to handle it, nor how to handle you."

"He can't wait to be rid of me." I fought for words. "He wants me out of the way." Now that he'd found a son, I was only a burden. Marry me off to someone rich—that solved every problem.

"All your father hopes is that you will be cared for. Give him time."

I felt anger rising unchecked. I was seeing things around me with a different eye. I was alone, and feeling more betrayed with every moment. I watched the bears as they foraged, and then, one by one, they drifted like ghosts into the woods. The tourists began their return to the hotel, and the men rejoined us on the path back to our own dinner.

We walked in silence until Mrs. Gale spoke. "Margaret may have a point. It is a new century, after all. Maybe it's time for some new ideas." I glanced at her quickly, grateful.

"Possibly," said Papa. He looked at me, and I saw in that look something of the way he had sometimes looked at Mama. Uncle John was right: Papa feared I was like Mama. Maybe I was. Maybe each day I grew more like Mama. And now that I knew she was gone—maybe I had to acknowledge Mama in me.

"I think it's high time. High time for new ideas." I said it loud, and tore off my hat to punctuate the comment, so that the breeze caught loose tendrils of hair and chucked them about my face.

Graybull took my arm. "Dangerous," he said, dismissive. Then, abruptly, he leaned over and kissed my cheek, his coarse whiskers scratching my face.

I recoiled, appalled, feeling branded. I was nothing more to him than a possession. Like Ghost. Acquired.

He took my gesture the wrong way. "Such an impulsive thing." He sounded pleased with himself.

"I think you mistake me," I said through gritted teeth. I could barely control myself. This man repulsed me.

He raised his eyebrows, his smile now frozen.

"Maggie, dear . . ." Mrs. Gale began.

"I'm not impulsive," I said, for the second time in a few days. But now I meant it in a different way. "I know exactly what I want."

Graybull's eyes darkened. "I'm all for spirit. So long as a woman knows her place."

My feelings welled up. "Spirit is one thing I have in spades." Inside me, rising from a hidden part of me, kept under wraps for far too long, grew the spirit of my mother. Not the madness, but her strength, her fortitude. I'd unleashed it in the water. I unleashed it now, when I admitted to myself that she was gone from me forever. I held my hat in one hand; I reached up with the other and pulled out first one of my hairpins, then another, until my hair flew loose in the evening breeze; as my hand worked I never took my eyes off Graybull's face.

Graybull regarded me for a moment, uncertain, then turned away. Papa stared and I couldn't read his expression, and he, too, turned away. Mrs. Gale gave me a wry smile and followed the men.

I waited for a few minutes as they went on ahead. I turned and looked after the bears. They had all disappeared into the darkening woods.

I would discover the answer to who I was, who I wanted to be, on my own. The deep blue of Yellowstone dusk hung over me like an arch.

Chapter THIRTY-THREE

I walked out on a rock & made two steps at the same time,
one forward, the other backward, for I had . . . looked
into the depth or bowels of the earth, into which the
Yellow[stone] plunged . . .

—"Narrative of a Prospecting Trip in the Summer of 1867,"
diary of A. Bart Henderson

THE NEXT AFTERNOON, GRAYBULL, MRS. GALE, AND I SET off to travel to Canyon. Papa was to remain at the Lake Hotel. Kula arrived back in my room just as we were preparing for departure; I was proud of my newly acquired packing skills until I saw how quickly she stepped in and, with her deft hands, finished the job. I asked for no explanation of her absence and she offered none.

We arrived at Canyon Hotel in the early evening. At dinner I looked furtively around the dining room. My brother might be among the waiters, or perhaps he was a diner at one of the other tables. There—that dark-haired boy who looked like Papa; no, he was too young. Or there—he had a mouth like Mama's, a little . . .

It was like searching for a needle in a haystack; and it hurt like a needle driven into my palm, thinking of what Mama had suffered in never knowing what had become of her own child.

I retired to my room after dinner. When I opened the door,

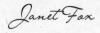

Kula was standing at my dresser. She whirled around and I spied something clutched in her hand.

I put my hand to my throat; for once I was not wearing the cameo, and now it was not on the dresser where I usually placed it. "Kula?" I was puzzled. "What's that?" I pointed to her hand.

Kula's eyes narrowed, but she didn't open her fist. She acted like a cornered animal, angry and defensive.

"What are you doing?" I whispered. Hurt rose in me, the pain of betrayal. I trusted her; I didn't understand.

Kula's mouth curled in a sneer. She squared her shoulders. "I was going to take it to someone. For a gift." She turned and dropped the cameo, with a hollow rattle, onto the dresser, where it caught the light. She walked to the other side of the room. "It wasn't for me. I don't even like it."

I went and picked up the pin, still warm from her hand. I was bewildered. My voice came out in a whisper. "How could you do this to me, Kula?"

Her eyes narrowed. "Wouldn't you like to know." She shook her head. "You are thick."

"What are you talking about?" My throat swelled. She had turned on me with no explanation. She'd been my ally, my . . . not friend. No, she was only a servant.

"I think I'll let you figure it out on your own."

Kula pushed past me out the door and slammed it shut. Jealous— was she jealous? All the things I had—all the things she wanted. I could only think she must hate me out of jealousy.

❧❧❧

The next morning I tried to act as though nothing had happened.

I sneaked glances at Kula, who ignored me. But I wore the cameo all the time now. I could not risk losing it—it was all I had left of Mama. Everything had changed between Kula and me, and I could only guess as to why.

"Shall we have a look at the canyon now?" Mrs. Gale asked after breakfast. "I'd like to try for a photo or two in the early light." I moaned. I'd seen the paintings; the canyon was deep and sheer. The very thought of it made my head spin and my stomach drop. I trailed along at the tail end of the group, following Mrs. Gale, Kula, and Graybull. I decided I would only walk so far and wait for them well back from the edge.

From far up the trail I heard the thunder of the falls. The trees opened to the view, and I stopped at once. I could only look between the pines, and even that was terrifying.

We were at a point where the river ran slow, upstream of the canyon itself. The canyon walls were yellow and white, glowing in the early sun. The river plunged over the edge into the depths below. Deep in the gorge, the river rushed away, a narrow ribbon. The falls themselves were not so broad as Niagara, but almost as high. The cliffs rose straight up, a series of steep edges and angles and points of rock.

"Ah!" The air escaped my lungs.

Mrs. Gale turned to me. "Perhaps this is not for you, dear."

"Nonsense!" Graybull took my arm. "Best thing to do is buck up. Tackle your fears head-on."

Tears started to my eyes at his cruelty. Kula turned and looked at me, and a mean little smile began at the corner of her mouth.

"We'll cross the bridge. It's brand-new and built to the highest standards. Surely you can manage, Margaret." Graybull steered me in his firm grip toward the bridge that crossed the river above the falls. Mrs. Gale came round to my other side. Walking between the two of them in this fashion, I could keep my eyes closed for most of the crossing, could keep the idea of walking over nothing out of my mind. But the worst was yet to come.

From the other side of the bridge we walked through a pretty sylvan setting, but all the while, the roar of the falls formed an ominous background. The trail wound closer and closer to the cliff's edge—I could feel it—until we emerged at the head of a gully. There, tourists were descending into the gorge by a length of heavy rope that draped out of my sight over the edge. I sat down at once on a fallen log, feeling weak-kneed.

"I want to climb down for some photographs," said Mrs. Gale. She tucked her camera inside a shoulder bag and prepared to lower herself. As she disappeared over the edge, I thought I might pass out.

"Lovely idea!" said Graybull. He turned to me. "Come, now."

I shook my head, unable to form words.

"Margaret, Mrs. Gale requires your assistance," Graybull said. His eyes showed no sympathy at all. I hated him.

"I'll help Mrs. Gale," said Kula with an exaggerated sigh. She moved to the edge and lowered herself over, following Mrs. Gale. Both of them had now vanished from my sight.

Something stirred in me—anger at Graybull and annoyance at Kula, mixed with a bit of my mother's bravery, too—and I stood up.

"There," Graybull said. "More to you than you thought."

Yes, there was, and my desire to best him in every way spurred me to move right to the rope. I thought about Mama; I could almost feel her holding my hand. From the edge I could see that the gully down which the rope threaded was not so steep—as long as I didn't look at the view farther out, I would be all right. If I held the rope and faced in to the rock . . . my stomach roiled. I gripped the rope in my gloved hands and followed Kula and Mrs. Gale over the edge and into the rushing void.

I did not look down. I stared straight into the rock wall, or up at the soles of Graybull's shoes. The rocks were stable and rough enough for good footholds, and the slope was gentle, but I felt as if all my insides had dropped as far as the canyon floor. Small scrub trees hung on in notches and there were sheer drops of several hundred feet to either side. I could hear only the roar of the falls. As we neared the bottom of the climb, about halfway down to the canyon floor, there was a ledge on which tourists could stand and stare up and down the river and at the falls. I risked a single peek, and then turned my back, examining every crystal in that rock face from an inch away. I clutched the rock as if I would melt into it.

Mrs. Gale took photographs. I was no help at all—my hands gripped the rope and I never moved that inch away from the rock wall. At last we began the slow climb back up. I pulled myself hand over hand, bracing my entire body against the cliff. Graybull was ahead of me, Kula behind, and Mrs. Gale last. I'd been useless, but Mrs. Gale didn't seem to mind. I started to feel as though it was going to be all right, and I would show Graybull that I could hold my own.

We were about twenty feet below the top of the cliff. So close now. Mrs. Gale called up, but I couldn't make out the words over the roar of the falls. Anxious, I turned to look at her and felt the sick weakness of fear as I saw her take the camera from her shoulder bag and open the bellows. She held the rope with one hand. I shut my eyes fast, and when I opened them again, I saw that Mrs. Gale had moved away from the climbing route. She stood on a point of rock that thrust out over the sheer cliff edge. I felt the bile rise in my throat.

Mrs. Gale looped her arm over the rope so that she could adjust the focus. She leaned far out, propping the camera on her arm. The world slowed to a crawl and all my senses narrowed to the roar of the falls, thundering in my ears. I registered the surprise on Mrs. Gale's face as she fell away and the camera arced lazily through the air, both of them seeming to disappear into the vast and rushing void of the canyon.

Chapter THIRTY-FOUR ❦ ❦ ❦ ❦ ❦ ❦ ❦

> *The Indians who were with me, were quite appalled . . . They believed them to be supernatural, and supposed them to be productions of the Evil Spirit.*
>
> —Life in the Rocky Mountains, 1830–1835,
> Warren A. Ferris, 1842

I GRIPPED THE ROPE HARD AND LEANED INTO THE CLIFF, panting. Kula, just a few feet below me, shouted in surprise. I couldn't see Mrs. Gale or the camera. I could only take in the fact that she'd fallen and I had no idea how far.

Kula grabbed my foot and shook it. Our eyes met. "Come on!" she yelled. "Get down here! Help me!"

But I froze. I couldn't move; I could barely breathe. I pushed my cheek against the rock, pressed my entire body into the rock, hanging on to the rope with all my strength.

"Come on!" Kula shouted again. I looked down. She stared at me and then retreated out of sight. I was still as a statue, while she moved faster than I would have thought possible, scrambling back down the cliff after Mrs. Gale.

I heard Graybull clambering up the rope to the top. I could think of nothing but hanging on to the rope, leaning into the cold rock wall. Time ceased to move; the stars wheeled overhead and fell as the centuries passed, while I clung to the cliff like lichen. The void yawned at my feet and I felt drunk with the stench of death, the widening fear.

It was half an hour before the soldiers reached me and dragged me up the rope hand over hand, then swung down past me to search for Mrs. Gale. I sat, rocking back and forth, wrapped in a blanket, listening to Graybull bark useless orders into the void. I stared at the dust at my feet and recalled my last image of Mama, her face as she turned, searching the windows of the house for me. Mama's expression, the slight parting of her lips, her look of surprise—it was Mrs. Gale's expression as she fell backward, away from me, into the roaring yellow chasm.

My heart clutched when an hour later they pulled the sling with Mrs. Gale up over the edge of the cliff. I threw off the blanket and bent over her, searching her face. With a flood of relief, I could see that she was breathing.

"She was lucky," a solider said. "Trees broke her fall. Fell right into a scraggly old pine. Just a busted arm, near as we can tell. And this here girl got to her before she could go down any farther. Held on to her."

Kula hoisted herself wearily over the cliff edge. Her face was scratched and covered with dirt, her skirt tucked up into her belt, freeing her legs, her white stockings, ripped and dirty, showing. She glared at me, her hatred evident.

"Guess you didn't want to dirty your pretty things," Kula hissed after the soldiers moved off with Mrs. Gale. "Didn't want to lose your precious pin."

I touched the cameo. "I couldn't. I couldn't." She didn't

understand; no one could. I'd failed Mrs. Gale; I'd failed Mama. I'd failed myself.

Kula turned away.

⁂

Mrs. Gale was attended by the doctor from Mammoth, and rested in the Canyon Hotel. She had a broken arm, but by the second day she was sitting up and eating and laughing in her usual hearty way. I stood outside in the hall, feeling useless, while the hotel staff brought her blankets and tea and freshly baked pie. So many people surrounded her that she didn't see I was there. That was for the best. I was ashamed. I was invisible even to myself. All the brave thoughts I'd had at the lake were gone.

Kula was given a heroic welcome at dinner by staff and guests, which she dismissed with a toss of her head, although she ate a splendid meal with the doctor from Mammoth and several other park employees. After that I saw very little of her. She came to my room to tend to my clothes when I was not there, but was gone, missing, for hours at a time. That was for the best, too, for her antipathy for me had grown sharp as a dagger point.

I tried to clear my head but my guilt was crippling. The weather over the next two days grew cold and gray with light rain. I took walks in the damp woods, always aware of the noise of the rushing river and falls nearby. I trod the paths, crushing the pungent pine needles, avoiding the chasm. I saw Mama's face, Mrs. Gale's face. I felt my own helplessness and failure. I could have stopped Mama. I should have tried to stop Mrs. Gale. If I'd carried the camera for her, or held her arm . . .

On the third day after her fall, I sat in Mrs. Gale's room, having crept in while she slept. I must have dozed off in my chair; when I awoke, she was watching me.

I looked at my hands. "I'm sorry."

"Oh, my dear. I must have been down that cliff a half-dozen times. I know I should always keep two hands on the rope."

"I didn't come after you." I didn't go after Mama, either.

"But Kula did. So there's nothing to worry about."

"I couldn't. It was so high. So steep." My throat filled with tears that I couldn't swallow.

"Maggie," said Mrs. Gale, reaching over with her good arm to pat my hands, "I'm fine."

"You might have died. I couldn't help you." I looked at her, so much guilt boiling in me that the tears streamed despite my every effort to hold them back.

"It was my own foolishness. Margaret, stop punishing yourself."

I rubbed my cheeks, brushing away the tears. Mrs. Gale sighed. "I lost my camera. I'll have to order another."

"Maybe I can pick one up for you," I offered. I wanted to do something, anything. I leaned in and clasped her good hand. "I can take the carriage to Mammoth and bring one back."

Mrs. Gale laughed. "Oh, my dear, they can send a camera." She paused, and sighed again. "But I have a commission to travel to Tower Falls. I doubt very much that I'll be able to complete the work with this useless arm. It's disappointing."

"Then let me go." I could help. I had to. If I'd known about Mama, why she really grieved—if I'd asked instead of condemning her—I would have helped her, too. She never would have walked on the cliff that day, and she'd still be here, with me. "Oh, please let me help."

Mrs. Gale regarded me. "You could, you know. Your eye has become exceptionally good."

"Please. I have to do something for you."

"You'll have to convince your guardian, I think," Mrs. Gale said, with a touch of sarcasm. "But, yes, I would be delighted if you would take my commission."

When I found Graybull, he was in the lobby of the Canyon Hotel. Papa was there, too, having made the trip up from the Lake Hotel as soon as he'd heard about the accident. I didn't bother with greetings. "You can see that even in the company of Mr. Graybull, accidents do happen." I hated him with every bone in my body. But I tried hard not to show it, plastering a false smile on my face.

Graybull drew himself up. "Well!"

"That's disrespectful, Margaret," Papa whispered.

I bit my lip, not wanting to jeopardize my chance at a trip to Tower Falls. We were still beholden to Graybull. "I'm sorry," I said, not meaning it but sounding as ingratiating as possible. "Of course, I had no intention of suggesting that you were responsible. I only meant—"

"Mrs. Gale is not a seasoned outdoorswoman," Graybull said, staring into the air above my head. "Hardly a proper companion and mentor, Margaret."

"She's teaching me photography," I began. "In fact, I have an opportunity—"

"Fine hobby, my dear. Delightful. But time to move on." Graybull turned to Papa. "I leave for Mammoth in two days' time. Joining a hunting party north of the Park. Would like Margaret to accompany me. Obvious she could use more experience in the woods herself."

"No!" The protest slipped out before I could stop myself. I was desperate. "I don't want to go hunting. Mrs. Gale has asked me to work for her. She wants me to take photographs at Tower Falls. Please, can't I go?"

"Margaret, really," said Graybull, narrowing his eyes. "Charles. You'll speak with your daughter." He nodded good-bye to Papa and left us in the lobby alone.

We stood in silence. Papa stroked his mustache and stared into the distance. I felt his sorrow; we were both trapped. He looked at me and sighed. He handed me a telegram addressed to me, the envelope opened. "I intercepted this last week. I didn't tell you, because it's no longer relevant." It was from Edward.

Though it had been only weeks, it seemed like years since I'd heard from Kitty about Edward's vain desire to rescue me.

LEAVING TOMORROW TO BRING YOU HOME
STOP WILL FIND YOU MAMMOTH ON 20
JULY STOP BE READY TO LEAVE AT ONCE
STOP LOVE EDWARD

"I wrote him back at once," Papa said. "I told him you are now spoken for, and that he must not come here for you." He sighed again. "Your grandfather has contacted me. He favors George over this young man, at any rate, however worthy he might be."

"I know." My old life was fading behind me. "It doesn't matter." I meant Edward. He no longer mattered. I could not go back to him, not when I knew he wasn't what I wanted. But what if I wanted Tom? My heart fluttered at the thought. I began to realize that I faced another choice, that I stood close to another edge. "What if I don't want to be spoken for?"

"That's impossible, Maggie. Your grandfather will only drop his claim against me in favor of your marriage to Graybull. He feels Graybull's a man of impeccable standing. Your grandfather has made it clear: your entire inheritance from your mother's side depends upon your marriage to Graybull." He paused and continued more quietly. "My entire career depends upon it. It's our future. It's the only way." I felt that Papa was pleading with me.

Tears welled in my eyes and I sank into a chair. I couldn't hold back my bitter words from Papa any longer. "So, that's it then? My life is spoken for? A life with a man I can't stand, because he can bail us out?"

"George Graybull can give you the life you want. The life you had before. The life I can't give you now. It's what you want."

He was partly right: It was what I had wanted, but so much had changed since we arrived in Yellowstone. I had changed. I'd wanted love but I hadn't known what that meant. Now I was beginning to understand. It wasn't Graybull, and it wasn't even Edward. I didn't know yet if it was Tom, but I wanted to find out. I took Papa's hand.

"What if that's not what I want anymore? What if there are some things he can never give me, Papa?" I bent my head and bit my lip to hold back the full weight of my feelings. "He can't give me love."

Papa cleared his throat. "Maggie."

I looked up at him, thinking he'd lost patience with me. He shifted his feet and clenched and unclenched his fists. But when he turned his face, he had tears in his eyes, and he looked desolate.

"I'm sorry, Maggie." His sadness was so deep; it brought back those months after Mama died.

I held my breath. He was beginning to understand my loss, just as I was beginning to understand his. "Must I go with George Graybull?"

He looked away, his jaw working with emotion. Then he cleared his throat. "The park superintendent wants to look at the idea of improving accommodations at Tower Falls, near Yancey's camp. At some point I must make a trip there." He was not looking directly at me, but I watched him closely. "I require your presence to help me document my observations with photographs." My heart leapt. Papa had given me this. "We could leave in a few days, if we can gather the provisions and equipment by then."

I threw my arms around him, hugging him hard.

He held me for a moment, then pushed me away. "But, Margaret. When we return from this trip, you must make amends with George. You must settle with George Graybull. He's your future, the only future I can give you now."

"But . . ." My mood changed from elation back to misery. Papa had only gone partway.

Papa held up his hand. "George is a powerful and wealthy man who wishes to make you his wife. It's not impossible to fall in love after knowing someone for a time. He'll take you back to Newport. He'll give you what I can't. You may come to love him, in time. Graybull is your intended. Your grandfather will insist. And I must insist."

"But . . ." I no longer dreamed of returning to Newport. I dreamed of something bigger, and I was only beginning to discover it.

"I'm taking you to Tower to give you a final chance to do—" he hesitated—"something you enjoy."

I stepped back, holding my tongue. At least for the moment, I had what I wanted. I didn't have to accompany Graybull. I could take photographs at Tower for Mrs. Gale. Papa gave me that. And without knowing it, he'd given me something else. He'd made me aware of the scope of my dreams.

I dreamed of a life I'd never known was even possible. I was drawn to the fearful beauty of Yellowstone. I desired not a marriage of convenience, not an easy life, but something impulsive, unexpected. I wanted to do something extraordinary, not watch and wait. Mama had tried to escape, but she came back for me. I had failed her, but now I understood that I couldn't fail myself. I did have choices, and in choosing I would be forced to face things that terrified me.

The window of my tower was open, and my unchained soul flew out and away, high over the vast pine forests and broad meadows, high over the precipitous yellow cliffs and billowing plumes of steaming water, high over the narrow ribbons of rushing rivers; fearless, and far, far from the sea.

Chapter THIRTY-FIVE

July 21, 1904

*I saw an old Indian go up a hill and pray to the
sun . . . he held up his arms, and oh, God, but did
he talk to the Great Spirit about the wrongs the white
man had done to his people.*

—We Pointed Them North: Recollections of a Cowpuncher,
E. C. "Teddy Blue" Abbott, 1884

"TRY TO TAKE PHOTOGRAPHS OF THE PEAKS," MRS. GALE
instructed. She and I were going over the last preparations before
my trip with Papa. "Panoramic shots are tricky. You must have
something that puts the distance into perspective." She knew that
I preferred close-ups and the pattern of detail. "And the sky—the
exposure—you must account for it."

I handled the new equipment with trembling fingers. The camera,
which arrived within two days from Bozeman, was less bulky than
the one Mrs. Gale had lost. It folded more compactly and used only
celluloid film. "I'll do my best," I said.

"And please, watch for grizzlies," Mrs. Gale said. "They're
rumored to be abundant in that part of the Park." We would be
camping on this trip, as the roads were not yet improved and there
were no hotels north of Canyon.

Grizzlies. I recalled those flat, black eyes. "I think bears are my
talisman. So maybe they like me." I smiled, trying to be brave.

Mrs. Gale raised her eyebrows. "In that case, definitely watch out. You usually attract your talisman to you, you know."

I didn't know. I tapped my fingertips together and pursed my lips. My brave front slipped away.

⁂

Kula still avoided me. I wanted her to understand why I hadn't helped at the accident, to tell her why I'd acted so badly. And I wanted to ask her why she tried to take my cameo.

On the morning before Papa and I left for Tower, I found her walking. I followed her out from the hotel into the woods, to the edge of the canyon. She moved like a dancer, weaving through the woods. She was too fast, far too fast for me to catch up. As I chased after her, I was reminded once again of something about her that troubled me, some niggling memory.

The roar of the falls grew, and I fell back, cursing my fear.

Kula slowed as she reached the edge of the canyon, stopping at an overlook. She was alone for a moment when, coming up the path from the opposite direction, Tom Rowland walked toward her, a broad smile on his face, his lanky arms swinging.

I hadn't even known Tom was here in Canyon. He hadn't come to see me.

I couldn't breathe. He put his hand on her shoulder, and spoke to her, but between the roar of the falls and the thick woods and my distance from them, I heard nothing. I watched his expression of pleasure, saw her tilt her head, her long thick braid hanging behind her like black rope. I turned away, unable to watch more, stumbling through the woods away from the ravine. I was so jealous that I hated myself; I was so jealous that I hated Kula and Tom, both.

I went back to the hotel and sat alone on my bed, my legs bent at the knees, hugging myself and rocking.

About an hour later, Kula came to pack my things. "Don't fold it like that!" I snapped.

"Don't shout at me," she said in an undertone. "You, who can't even get your precious things dirty to save a life."

"I didn't help with Mrs. Gale because I couldn't." I didn't care anymore what she thought of me. I wanted a reason to argue with her.

Her back was to me as she moved from the wardrobe to the canvas packs. "Of course not." Her tone was smug.

"I was frightened."

Kula gave a snort. "You're frightened of everything."

She was right about that. I held myself back. But I was changing. I fought on. "That's not true. I went into the lake."

"Well, there, you were being stupid. Lord knows why."

I snatched the skirt Kula was folding from her hands, trying to grab her attention. "The only one who's stupid is you." I could no longer control my jealousy, my rage.

She turned on me. "What's wrong with you?"

"Me! What's wrong with you? You've been acting snippy for the past week!"

She stared straight at me with those dark eyes, her expression filled with hate. "You're rich. You have a good life. You have that rich man. You have all these beautiful things, and still you're not happy."

"Take them!" I lifted a handful of clothes out of my trunk and thrust them at Kula. "Take them! I don't want them!"

Kula paused, staring at me with a half smile. "You said you'd treat me fair and square."

"And I have." Tears filled my eyes. I'd begun to try and think of her as a friend and not just a servant. She was my age, my contemporary. But she repudiated me, slapped that attempt back in my face. She'd tried to steal Mama's cameo. She'd stolen Tom. "You're nothing but a thief, anyway."

She was quiet. Then, "I'll leave now." She headed for the door.

"Kula." I reached for her arm, stopping her. We looked at one another for a long moment. I released her arm. I was wrong; she could never be my friend.

She turned away. "I know you were looking for her."

My blood turned to ice. "What do you mean?"

"I've known for a while," Kula said, looking back at me, her lips curling in a thin smile. "I figured it all out. Your mama's gone."

"I told you that when we first talked."

Her smile grew. "Yes. But you didn't tell me you were *looking* for her."

I took a step back. I couldn't imagine how she knew this. I hadn't even told Tom.

"She's gone but there's someone else to find, isn't there? Someone your daddy wants to find? Maybe someone who could really shake up your life."

I was breathless. "What do you know?" Maybe she knew Uncle John. Maybe he talked openly among his friends. Maybe there were rumors.

"As if I would tell you now," Kula said. "As if I would tell you that I've got some answers for you." She relished this position of power. She picked up the blue velvet gown, my birthday gown, examining it, holding it up from the shoulders as if trying to decide whether or not to wear it.

"Take it," I whispered. "It's yours."

Kula looked at me. "Why, thank you, miss. I surely can use it."

I snatched at a small beaded purse, a pair of white leather opera-length gloves. "Here. These, too." I went to the dresser and took a pearl necklace from my box. "And this." I tossed it onto the bed with the other things. I'd give her anything. Everything she wanted if she would only tell me what she knew.

"How kind."

"Please, Kula." I moved toward her. "Please tell me what you know."

Kula held her head up, triumphant. "I'll tell you this. Your uncle talks a lot. He says things he shouldn't. He makes assumptions about people. So do you." She regarded me with dark eyes. "Lots of folks think they know things, by the way someone looks, or by their position. They don't know anything." She gathered the dress and other things in her arms. "I can sell these. Make a pretty penny."

"Please, tell me," I pleaded.

"You have everything," Kula said, low. "Money, a rich fiancé, a lazy life . . ."

"My mother . . ." I began.

"My mother's gone, too, Miss Perfect," she snapped. "All I have is ghosts, and hard work—something you'll never understand—and now you, thinking you're so sad." She imitated a whimper. "Lording it over me."

I sank onto the bed. I had no idea she hated me so much. I hadn't treated her badly; I'd tried to be nice. I couldn't imagine . . . Tom. She wanted Tom.

I wanted Tom. I couldn't look up at her.

She moved toward the door. "You were right. I was stealing your pin," she said. "But it wasn't for me." The velvet dress rustled softly in her arms as she gathered it up. "It was for someone I love."

I sat on the bed for a long time after Kula shut the door. I couldn't cry, couldn't move. One soft leather glove lay on the floor where she dropped it, like a disembodied hand.

Chapter
THIRTY-SIX

July 22–23, 1904

This flight lasted only 12 seconds, but it was
nevertheless the first in the history of the world in which
a machine carrying a man had raised itself by its own
power into the air in full flight . . .

—"How We Made the First Flight," Orville Wright, 1903

THE NEXT MORNING, PAPA AND I SET OUT ON A DAY THAT promised to be warm and clear. Our driver, Bill, was a pleasant, older man who'd worked in the Park for years. He drove a small wagon, pulled by two sorrels, a mare and a gelding, all our goods loaded carefully in the bed.

"This is the route we'll take," Papa said as we ate breakfast. He pointed to a thin line on the map, and I saw the names Dunraven and Mount Washburn. There were no true roads.

"I'll see you in a week." Mrs. Gale smiled. "Your first commission." She patted me on the cheek. I hugged her tight.

I did not see Kula; no one in the hotel knew where she'd gone.

I was relieved when our wagon pulled away from the canyon. For days I'd felt as if the falls were sucking me into the foaming green water of the river below. Now we rode through peaceful woods, the tall pines towering above us. The track climbed into higher and higher country. Alpine buttercups nodded yellow, mountain gentian, its bells the deepest blue, popped from stone outcrops, and tiny, pink elephant flower, on its dense spike, waved in the slightest breeze.

"The pass 'n the mountain are up ahead," said Bill.

We rounded a bend and I gripped the side of the wagon. To our right, the meadow slipped away to a deep ravine. Above us rose Mount Washburn, its upper slopes rocky and open. The wind whipped through the wagon now that we were out of the woods, and Bill pulled the horses in to steady them. We climbed higher against the edge of the mountain. When we stopped for lunch, Papa and I rested in the sun, sheltering from the wind against the wheel.

By mid-afternoon, we'd circled the mountain to its north, and Bill suggested that we make camp. While the men set up the tents, I found a stream, and washed myself as best I could in the icy water. Then I sat on the edge of the meadow above the camp and watched the meadowlarks swoop and swing overhead. At dinner, the beans and salt pork tasted better than anything I'd eaten in the finest hotels.

"It's the fresh air 'n exercise," said Bill. "Make you hungrier 'n a one-eyed polecat."

I lay in the dark in my tent and listened to the night sounds: the distant cry of a coyote, the screech of an owl, a high piercing woman-wail of what must be a mountain lion. Despite the rocks that drove points into my back, I slept, and when I woke in the morning, stiff, I heard the men stirring. I lay for a while with a smile on my face, wondering what Kitty would think of me now. I imagined Kitty sitting in this tent and laughed out loud at what I was sure would be vigorous complaining. I'd have to write to her and describe my privations.

I wondered whether Mama had spent many nights sleeping

in such a primitive fashion. I suspected she had, and I felt both sympathy and admiration.

I wouldn't have a proper bath in hot water for at least another seven days, but I didn't care. The air smelled like frost, and there was a stiff breeze, so I pulled my hair back into a long braid rather than pin it up. We set out again, stopping along the way to take pictures. I tried to frame the shots, but began to have an understanding of the difficulty of depth perception. It was such a huge country.

Huge and extraordinary, and it filled me up with a raw longing, the kind I'd felt on rare evenings in Newport when I looked out across the ocean and watched the seals in joyful play.

We stopped at one vista when the bounce and creak of a wagon came floating up from the rutted road ahead. As the wagon emerged from the trees, my heart did a bounce of its own. Tom Rowland and his father drove toward us from the direction of Yancey's camp. It seemed that no matter where I went in Yellowstone, there was Tom.

The men greeted one another. Tom strode over to where I stood with the camera. He stood so close that our arms brushed; my stomach fluttered. "Taking pictures on your own?" he asked.

"Yes." I straightened. I kept seeing him with Kula. I looked up at him, wishing he'd put his hand on my shoulder as he had with her. "I have a job. Mrs. Gale had an accident. She asked me to fulfill her commission." At least he seemed to show the same pleasure in seeing me as he had with her.

He raised his eyebrows in that familiar, quizzical way. "I heard about that." From Kula, I was sure.

I stiffened and looked away lest my eyes betray my jealousy. "Oh! I guess the word got around."

"I guess." I didn't want to think about Tom and Kula together anymore.

We stood in awkward silence. I looked at my hands, and quickly thrust them behind my back; my nails had dirt beneath them, and the backs of my hands were beginning to darken from the sun. And then I realized Tom wouldn't care. Which I liked, enormously. Graybull would care. Edward would have. I needed to stop worrying about what Tom would think and be myself.

"Maggie's having a last adventure before she returns to Newport to announce her engagement," said Papa.

Tom turned to look at me with surprise. My heart turned to stone. I cringed that Papa had to plunge me right back into a reality I hated. "Really?" Tom asked. "Who's the lucky fellow?"

"George Graybull," Papa said.

Tom started, then looked away, chewing his lower lip. Was that disappointment I saw in his eyes? My heart melted, stone no more, then the blood pounded in my ears. "So, congratulations," he said.

"Thanks." I wanted to scream, "It's not my choice!" I looked at the ground and scuffed my toe in the dirt. I heard Papa talking to Tom's pa; then I heard Tom whisper to me.

"Are you happy?"

I looked up at him. He leaned toward me and I swam in his gray eyes. I shook my head, no. His smile grew like the sunrise over the Atlantic on a summer dawn.

"Good," he said softly. "Good."

I glanced at Papa. He was watching me carefully, no longer in conversation.

Tom said loudly, "Keep that camera handy. You'll have tons of chances now to see animals in a new light."

I returned, "You never know what can happen on a last adventure."

"Ah! The unknown. Yellowstone is famous for its surprises." His eyes met mine, and he was smiling, and I just about burst out laughing.

I tamped down the laugh. "I'm learning all about surprises. I'm learning that I want them in my life."

"Really?" His eyes were shining now.

"I think the unexpected should be welcomed. Some people are beginning to think I've become almost impulsive."

Tom grinned. Papa coughed.

I went on. "I think . . . I think it's fine not to have everything you want and expect. Maybe life is richer when things don't turn out as planned." I folded my arms across my chest and stood up straight. The wind kicked up my skirt and strands of loose hair fluttered around my face, and I brushed the hair back with my fingers, letting Tom see my grimy hands. I smiled at him.

Tom turned to his father. "Dad—you wanted more samples from this area, didn't you?" Tom looked at Papa. "I know the Tower region pretty well, if you need a hand."

Papa surprised me by saying "I could use the company."

"And we might see some wildlife," Tom said. "I still haven't seen a bear this season." He paused and then said, with a sly grin, "Maybe Maggie can snap a photo of one for her fiancé. Before he snaps its head off."

"Fine with me if you stay with the Bennets." Jim Rowland tossed Tom a sample sack, then handed him a rock hammer. "I'll be back in Canyon by nightfall. You can catch up with me next week."

"An extra pair of hands will be most useful," Papa said. "Tom can accompany Margaret while I'm working."

My heart jumped—no, my whole soul leapt around as if it were newly born. I felt as if Tom knew me better than anyone on earth, that he understood me, even when I couldn't fully speak my mind. We exchanged another smile, and my heart beat so hard I feared he could see it.

So much had changed in only a few days that I felt as if I were standing on the edge of a new world. And, for me, as always, the edge of anything was a terrifying place to be.

THIRTY-SEVEN

July 23–26, 1904

Had the cub thought in man-fashion, he might have epitomized life as a voracious appetite ... hunting and being hunted, eating and being eaten, all in blindness and confusion, with violence and disorder, a chaos of gluttony and slaughter, ruled over by chance, merciless, planless, endless.

But the cub did not think in man-fashion.

—*White Fang,* Jack London, 1906

FOR SEVERAL DAYS TOM AND I CLIMBED UP AND DOWN the slopes of Mount Washburn. Tom collected rock samples, storing them in canvas bags in the back of the wagon. He showed me how he plotted the sample locations on the map. I followed him as he collected, photographing the rock outcrops and observing the intricate patterns made by layers of the rock he called rhyolite.

I took to sitting and listening to him, his lectures about the region's geology; but my mind wasn't on the rocks. I watched Tom, his every gesture. It was like watching a ballet. He would get so excited about some mineral, or something he saw in a rock face. Where I saw only striations, he saw continents, universes, the infinite. I focused on his face, lit from within. I felt on fire, too.

Papa, with Bill, traveled back along the road making notes about road conditions and improvements. I often found myself alone on a slope gazing over the view. The earth and sky seemed to expand so that I felt I could see far cities, the broad sweep of the Great Plains, distant blue-green oceans. We saw mountain goats that retreated on nimble feet to tottering rocks and then peered back at us with suspicion. I watched bald eagles sweep overhead, moving to heights where they became black dashes against the sky.

Mama might have walked these very slopes. I suspected she'd loved what she saw just as I did. I missed her so, even more, now that I knew she was truly gone.

Once, my eye was pulled across a deep ravine as something moved through the pine trees on the other side: a herd of elk. Some fifty or sixty snaked through the shadows beneath the pines, making their passage in total silence. I heard not a twig snap, not a snort of breath; I watched, enchanted, as the ghostly animals rounded the curve of the hill out of sight.

Tom gave me a spare sample book and I collected flowers, pressing them in the pages and making notes. My photographs took another turn to the detail I loved so much, as I focused on the smallest of blossoms: tiny dicentras—bleeding hearts—and edelweiss on the high rugged slopes.

I watched Tom when he didn't know it, too. I admired his sure, deft manner on the slopes. I watched his long fingers, his unconscious habit of pushing his fingers through his hair. I felt as if I would lose something precious by losing him. I didn't know if I'd lost him to Kula. I didn't know if I was lost to George Graybull.

This time with Tom and his landscape was a dream-time and I wanted it to never end. But, of course, it did.

We broke camp after four days to head farther north. I packed the camera and the negatives, padding the cases between the canvas packs of food and lashing the tarp over the top.

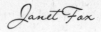

"Maggie!" Tom came running toward me. His excitement made me smile.

"You look like you've found a pot of gold."

"I have! Scat! And tracks—big ones! And a deer kill!"

"That doesn't sound good," I said, my smile fading. I did not consider this happy news.

"But it is! Big bear, from the look of it. Probably a grizzly."

My hand tightened on the strap I held. A grizzly. "Where?" I wanted to be away from it.

"Just ahead. What a treat! If we stop up there"—he gestured up the road—"we can observe him when he comes back." He looked at me. "It's perfectly safe. As long as we keep our distance."

"I have no interest in seeing a bear." I pulled on the strap, tightening and tying. These were not the black bears being fed out behind the hotels. I remembered the night I was too close to a grizzly. It drew me yet it terrified me. It held an overwhelming mindless power, attractive and deadly. Mrs. Gale had said it: "You attract your talisman to you." Well, I wanted none of that. "No, thank you."

"No interest?" He sounded puzzled.

"None. I want to stay as far away as possible." I had to pull the knot apart when I failed to do it right. My fingers fumbled and my patience was gone. It pained me that Tom didn't understand the seductive pull that the bear had on me, its tantalizing malevolence. The fear rose in me like metal filings in my mouth. "I want nothing to do with bears!"

"But . . ." Tom leaned against the wagon to try to meet my eyes, that were firmly fixed for the moment on my poor knot-tying. "It's what I want to do. I thought you understood."

I turned to stare at him. Please, no. Just because it was important to *him*. He couldn't see how I felt. My fear was that Tom was like every other man. That and my fear of the bear, my jealousy of Kula, my hateful position as Graybull's prize suddenly were all mixed up. "It may be what you want to do, Tom Rowland, but what does that matter to me?"

He looked at me as if seeing me anew. "I thought . . . I thought you cared. About what I did. About what I want to do."

"You presume too much," I said, yanking the new knot tight. My mind's eye focused on one thing, Tom with Kula, and I forgot entirely our last four days together. Some stupid irrational feeling rose in me and I spoke without thinking. "You and Kula," I said, not knowing how to finish it.

The air was thick with tension. Then he broke the silence. "I was right. From the minute I met you, I knew it. You're a snob." I whirled to face him. But he mocked me. "You have a fancy fiancé now, and you're taken with yourself." There was something else in what he was saying. His eyes were on fire. Tom was jealous of Graybull. "And don't think I don't know how you treated Kula."

"How I treated . . . !" I stuttered, reeling from one emotion to the next.

"Accusing her of stealing! Treating her like a slave!"

"But she was . . ." I began, then stopped. It was no use. There was no point.

"I thought, maybe, there was a chance for us. Maybe you'd tell me something that would make me believe in you. I wanted to, Maggie. I wanted to believe in you. To believe that maybe we could have something, together. But no. You treated Kula like dirt. You don't care about anyone else in the end. You'll marry this Graybull fellow because he can give you what you want, and I can't. Fine, Miss Margaret Bennet. You're shallow and snobbish. Yellowstone is no place for you. It's way too big for your small heart."

His words were cruel, cutting me to the core. He strode away, leaving me hanging on to the wagon, my small heart so swollen it would have filled an ocean.

Papa came up the slope from camp with Bill, equipment in hand. "Ready?" Papa asked, oblivious, as usual, to my emotional state.

I nodded, swallowing tears.

The day had dawned cloudy and now the wind was kicking up, spattering big drops of rain as clouds scudded overhead.

"Good thing we're gettin' off the top," said Bill. "Blowin' bad, now."

"There's bear sign up ahead," Tom said. He sat next to me, but he acted like I didn't exist. I felt the ache deep in my heart.

"Never mind," said Bill. "We got to get down. Bear'll move off. But this wind won't, and it'll make the horses spook." Still, the wagon swayed each time a gust of wind smacked the side, and Bill drove the horses with care as they picked their way down the steep and rutted track. I gripped the wagon rails, trying not to look as we rode past a steep slope that fell away to the river far below. It was close to midday.

"Wha' the . . ." Bill pulled hard on the horses' reins. "Griz!" he yelled.

I half stood, looking between the shoulders of Bill and Papa. I heard Tom's voice, low, "There it is."

Only twenty yards ahead, in the middle of the track, stood a bear. It was tawny yellow with shoulders sprouting a massive hump, and it rotated its great head in our direction. The horses snorted and neighed, drawing back in fear.

"Whoa!" yelled Bill. "Ho, there!"

The grizzly faced us, raising its nose into the wind to catch our scent. Its eyes were small pins of malice. One of the horses began to dance in the harness, and Tom leaned over to help Bill hold the reins.

"My God!"

The grizzly lifted its massive body off the ground, standing upright, its head more than ten feet in the air.

"We have to pull back!" Tom yelled. "Get out of its way!" He and Bill wrestled with the horses, trying to pull them back or at least turn them, but the wagon was cumbersome.

Then the bear opened its mouth and gave a roar, shaking its head from side to side. Drops of saliva sprayed the air around its terrifying mouth. The horses could stand it no longer. Both reared and bucked, and the wagon swayed wildly. Bill and Tom shouted, and I heard myself screaming as the wagon tilted, almost dreamlike, over to the right. The horses leapt in their traces, and I saw the slope below rise up toward me.

Out of instinct, I jumped, as if the ground were a pool of water. I cleared the wagon as it rolled over, and landed hard in the grass, rolling to break my fall. The back wheels of the wagon careened past my face by inches. The wheels were upside down.

I watched the wagon roll over and over down the slope, carrying the screaming horses and the shouting men, as bags of rocks littered the hill in its wake, and it left large gouges in the earth like a trail. The wagon crashed and splintered, the noises echoing in the woods, until it reached the bottom of the slope far below. Then all was silent. I lay stunned and still faceup in the grass, and heard the angry chittering of a squirrel, as a drop of wind-borne rain hit me square on the cheek.

Chapter THIRTY-EIGHT ❦ ❦ ❦ ❦ ❦

July 26, 1904

*"What does this mean?" I whispered in my dream . . .
"Listen, Plenty-Coups," said a voice . . . "Develop
your body, but do not neglect your mind, Plenty-Coups.
It is the mind that leads a man to power, not strength
of body."*

—"Vision in the Crazy Mountains," from Plenty-Coups, Chief of the Crows
(1848–1932), 1957

I SAW SCUDDING CLOUDS THROUGH A BLUE SKY, AND FELT
the prickle of grass beneath my back. I gripped a tuft of grass,
holding on tight, afraid to let go, my head spinning and my body
a mass of pain. I heard a noise and forced myself to sit up, to look
at the wreckage below.

Things were scattered across the slope—bits of clothing, paper,
tins of food. The camera box had sprung open and negatives floated
across the grass, dark squares that reflected the sky. I pulled myself to
my feet, turning to look back at the road above; the bear was gone.

Papa. Tom. Bill.

"Papa?" I stumbled down the long slope, tripping and falling
more than once, painfully aware of the bruises on my hip and back.
Halfway down to the wagon I heard a noise, a moan. Tom lay on
his stomach in the tall grass. I knelt by him. Oh, heavens. I could
not lose him.

I touched his arm. "Tom?"

283

He turned, wincing with pain, his face pale. "You all right?" he asked, hoarse.

I took a breath, thankful to hear him speak. "I'm okay. You?"

"I think my arm is broken. Can you help me up?" I took his left arm and steadied him while he got to his feet. He clutched his right arm to his chest, breathing hard. Gingerly he pushed the sleeve up to his elbow. The arm was swelling fast. "I think it's a simple break," Tom said.

I saw that he was gasping, and knew that the pain must be intense. "We need to tie it up."

We took in the scene—the wagon at the bottom of the slope; our scattered belongings, drifting across the meadow; the prone horses, one of which tried to lift its head, its body. No sign of Bill or Papa. "My God," he said, and clutching his arm, stumbled down to the wreckage.

I was right behind him. "Papa?" I called. "Papa?"

Halfway down, the body of one of the horses lay on the grass, its head pulled back at an unnatural angle, the harnesses in a tangle.

"Dead," said Tom, kneeling by the horse.

I scrambled to the wagon, nestled next to a thin pine tree. The front wheels were in the air, still turning in slow drifts; the rear axle and wheels were shattered. "Papa?" I climbed onto what had been the wagon's floor. The wagon swayed, and I saw that it sat, perched, on the edge of a steep drop of about sixty feet, to sharp rocks and the river below. I shut my eyes, freezing stone still. The void yawned, and I floated in darkness.

Mrs. Gale on the edge of the canyon; Mama on the cliff; I'd left them both because I could not master my fear. Now Papa, too, hung in that balance and I could once again choose to let it tip. I could feel my body start to go slack. I had a choice.

I dragged every ounce of courage in me into one tight bundle, the steely core of me. I held my focus there.

"Maggie?" Tom was standing by the wagon on the uphill side. I turned my head slowly, careful not to lose my balance. A leg protruded along the side of the wreckage, and I knew by the clothing that it was Bill. Tom was bent over him. "He's dead," Tom said in a flat voice.

"It's on the edge," I whispered as I thought the very sound of my voice would cause it to tip. "The wagon." I looked inside, trying to steady myself. Rock samples, clothing, cans of food, maps, cooking equipment—everything was a mess. There was no sign of Papa. "He's underneath it all. He must be." I thought I would be sick.

The other horse, the mare, lying on her side heaving and breathing heavily, let out a pained cry. Tom scrambled to her, soothing her with soft words. The mare heaved her head off the ground, then, with Tom's encouragement, stumbled to stand. Blood poured from a gash that ran across her flank, and Tom took an empty canvas bag to staunch the flow.

Tears ran down my cheeks. I could not lose Papa. Would not. I'd lost Mama, twice. No more. "Papa?" A low moan issued from beneath me. I pulled away from the swaying wagon, away from the cliff, crawling backward on hands and knees, inching back to where I could look through a gap in the broken planking. There, lying on his back at the very bottom of the pile, partially buried by the wagon, yet crushed under the wreckage, was Papa. "Papa?" I said, reaching down through the boards to touch his cheek.

He opened his eyes, and then shut them. "Mags." I could see

blood on his lips, on the ground beneath him. He closed his eyes and coughed. "Help me."

"You're at the edge of a cliff, Papa." I removed my hand and backed farther away from the wagon. It swayed again, and I caught my breath. I didn't know what to do. "It's too steep."

"I'm trapped. Can't feel my legs."

"We've got to get him out of there," Tom said, coming up behind me, clutching his arm to his chest. Then he saw how the wagon was perched, wedged against the leaning pine tree and some loose boulders. "Good God."

I stood and took two steps, backing away from the wagon. Tom looked at me, sharp.

"I can't use my arm," he said.

I touched the wagon, felt it sway again, felt my soul fall away into the void, saw the depths of the sea rise up around me, felt my arms and legs go numb with cold fear.

"Look." Tom swung around and grabbed my shoulder with his good arm, snapping me out of my nightmare. "We can tie it off to the trees. We've got to stabilize it."

"Yes." I focused on that core in me, that steel. "Yes." Crawling back up the slope, I found a stocking, and, returning, bound Tom's arm in a sling, trying to touch his arm as little as possible. Still, he sat down hard, clearly in pain and shock from even the slightest movement. I went back up the slope and cut away the traces from the dead horse, careful to leave enough leather intact to use as a harness later. I tied the long rein to the front axle, then to a stout pine, my knots good solid slipknots. I went back to loop the leather around the still-intact footboard, when the wagon began to shift.

It happened so slowly, like a dream. My stomach heaved, and then I forgot to think and moved entirely out of instinct.

There was a cry of pain from Papa and a shout of fear from Tom. The wagon slipped, inching over the edge, gaining momentum as it tilted.

I knotted the reins around the footboard, pulling the knot tight with a jerk. For one dizzying second I could look down, past Papa's crumpled form, through the splintered seat, and into the abyss below, to the rocks that stuck up like fangs, bare and monstrous. I stared right into the void and denied its power; and then it was as though I had acquired astonishing strength, even as fear tried to close in on me and its weight pushed on my limbs. I looped the reins and ran back to the tree, threw the end of the leather around, then around again, then leaned with all my weight. The wagon heaved and pulled toward the edge, then groaned to a stop, Papa's moans weakening beneath it.

Everything was still for a moment as I held my ground, my feet dancing back, then catching, the leather biting into the tree and into my raw and bleeding palms until the reins grabbed the bark, and the yawning, stretching sound of the leather snapped into place.

I tied off the reins, and then turned. Papa's legs were still pinned beneath the wood and iron. But he was more exposed now, his arms free; I could reach his face, which was twisted with pain. I knelt and touched a hand to him and brushed the blood from his lips.

"We'll get you out," I said. The blood from the gash on his arm was flowing freely, and I reached under my skirt to my petticoat, tearing a strip of cloth. I bound his arm, but it needed fastening. My hand went to my throat. The cameo was still there. I pinned the cameo to the bandage, making it fast. "I'll get you some water." His face was pale, and he could only nod. I carried one of the pots to the stream. Tom was on his feet again, leaning against the mare—she was trembling but alert. She'd been hurt, but not so badly as I'd thought.

"Think she's going to be all right," Tom said. "Don't think she broke anything. Not lame either. Miracle, really."

Given that the gelding was dead. That Bill was dead. That Papa was gravely wounded. That Tom was badly hurt. Miracle.

I took the water to Papa, who sipped what he could, his eyes closed. With the remaining traces, I harnessed the mare to the wagon. "I'm going to try using the horse to pull the wagon off you. Okay? Are you ready?"

Papa nodded, eyes shut.

The mare snorted. When I urged her forward she took tentative steps. I heard the creak as the wagon began to move.

A harsh cry echoed through the woods. "Stop!" Papa shouted. "Stop!"

I ran to him. The wagon impaled him; metal and wood ripped open his legs with every tiny movement. If we tried to save him, we risked killing him.

"Oh, God, I'm so sorry. So sorry."

"You—can't . . ." He was panting.

"All right, it's going to be all right." Tears had started down my cheeks again, and I looked at him, pale and helpless and breathing hard from the pain. I sat down, exhausted.

The wind moved the treetops; clouds scudded across the sky, with ribbons of blue alternating with gray. Sunlight exploded and then vanished. Occasional drops of rain spat and stopped. The stream rushed by as the mare breathed and snorted; Tom stood next to the horse's head, comforting her. My eyes met Tom's. I shook my head. "I don't know what to do."

"Get help," I heard Papa say. I turned and looked at him, then reached over and stroked his cheek. "You need to get help," he said, his eyes open and clear.

"All right, Papa. Tom'll stay with you."

"No!" His eyes flashed, and he made an effort to lift his hand. "You can't go alone."

"Fine. Then I'll stay here with you. Tom can go." I looked at Tom.

"Okay," he said. He began to pull the harness off the horse. "You've got to help me rig a set of reins."

I worked the remaining leather into a rough bridle, watching Tom's face. He was beginning to tremble. He didn't look right. "What's wrong?"

"Don't know. Think I might've injured something else." He was breathing hard, and his eyes were sunken and glassy.

I froze as the realization sank in. "You can't go by yourself."

Our eyes met. "No. I don't think I'd make it."

I leaned my head against the mare's shoulder. She reminded me how much I missed Ghost. Lovely Ghost. The mare turned, nudging me with her nose. I knew what I had to do, but wasn't sure I could.

I went back to the wagon and hauled two pieces of wood to lean over it as a shelter for Papa. I took crackers, jerky, and cheese from the wreckage and made two piles. I placed one pile in a canvas sample bag and took the other pile to Papa. He lay quiet, his eyes closed. I put the food and a large kettle of water where he could reach them. Then I touched his pale and sunken cheek again. "Daddy?" The name I'd called him when I was very small.

He opened his eyes. "Be all right. Get help."

I touched his cheek once more, and then touched the cameo that held the bandage tight. Mama would have to take care of him. I looked at my hands, and saw Mama's hands, her long fingers. I was Mama and she was me. *Take care of him for me, Mama. He loved you. He failed you. He didn't understand. But I do, and I beg you to help him now.*

Tom groaned. He was trying to pull Bill's body away from the wagon. He looked up. "Bears. They're carrion eaters," he said. "Might come back, find your father."

I bent and took one of Bill's arms while Tom took the other. *I'm sorry.* I tried not to look at Bill's face. *I'm sorry, I'm sorry,* over and over, as we dragged him as far away as we could. We laid him in the grass, and I could look only at Bill's feet, one leg scissored outward at the knee. I straightened it gently before leaving him.

"Can you get up?" I asked Tom, pointing to the mare. He seemed to be growing weaker. He nodded and dragged himself onto the mare's bare back. I climbed up behind him, riding astride, with my skirt hiked up, exposing torn stockings.

I wheeled the mare, urging her forward. Then I glanced over my shoulder at the wreckage, knowing what I had to do, feeling my heart break as I left Papa behind.

Chapter THIRTY-NINE

July 26, 1904

> *The wolf scents us afar and the mournful cadence of his howl adds to our sense of solitude. The roar of the mountain lion awakens the sleeping echoes of the adjacent cliffs and we hear the elk whistling in every direction.*
>
> —*The Valley of the Upper Yellowstone*, the explorations of Charles W. Cook, David E. Folsom, and William Peterson, 1869

I STEADIED TOM YET AGAIN, AS HE SWAYED IN FRONT OF ME. He was drifting in and out of consciousness, his head nodding, so I took it slow. We'd ridden for two hours. On a sound horse, under different circumstances, it might not have taken so long. But with Tom and the mare both hurt, I couldn't make better time. Though we were making steady progress, we were still miles from Canyon. It was mid-afternoon and I tried to quell my rising panic. If we couldn't move faster, I didn't see how Papa could be rescued before tomorrow.

The bear loomed in my thoughts.

Ahead through the trees I saw a plume of white; steam from a hot spring, as I made it out to be. I rode for it, thinking that the hot water might soothe the mare's weeping flank.

But when I came through the clearing I saw that it was not steam but smoke. A campfire! I urged the horse forward again, my heart pounding. Here might be the help we needed.

I saw them, six or seven men, lounging around a fire, their horses picketed nearby. I urged the mare forward, shouting as I gave her my heel.

"Help, please! There's been an accident! My father's trapped! Please!"

The men started, several of them leaping up and pulling out rifles.

"No, no! We need help!"

They leveled their guns. Why would they think I was dangerous? This was ridiculous. Weren't they just on some hunting trip or other?

Then I saw. The man at the center of the group, a slender, dark-haired man with a lean, weathered face walked toward me as I rode into the clearing, and our eyes met.

His eyes were as blue as the Morning Glory Spring.

I reined in the mare, feeling my heart catch. I knew those eyes. They made me angry. I had to put those feelings aside; in front of me, Tom swayed again, and as I clutched his waist, he moaned.

"Better get him down," the blue-eyed man said, nodding toward Tom.

"I . . ." I began, "I need your help." I didn't care that he was a robber; I didn't care that he'd once tried to take Mama's cameo. He had a camp and men and medicine.

"Nat," said another man, "you think that's a good idea? Maybe it's a trap."

Nat Baker. He looked at me, glancing at my torn and bloody clothes and taking in my desperate expression. "Not likely." He hesitated for a minute, and I could feel him weighing a decision. "Where's this accident?"

"About three miles north." I told him what had happened, describing Papa's state, making sure he understood about the grizzly. He listened carefully, never taking his blue eyes off me.

When I'd finished, Nat smiled a little. "Gus," he said over his shoulder, "get this kid off and look after him. The rest of you, saddle up." Relief flooded me, and Nat disappeared back into the camp.

Gus approached the mare and slid Tom, moaning, off her back. He half carried Tom to a blanket already spread on the ground near the fire.

I stood at the mare's head. One of the men brought a bucket of water for her and I took the opportunity to examine her wound. It was superficial and she wasn't lame. I rubbed her nose, thankful, then pulled away to find Nat. I had to urge him to hurry.

My eyes swept the camp as I looked for him. It was not a permanent encampment, but they had plenty of gear—cooking fires and pots, bedrolls, even a few makeshift chairs and tables.

I turned the other way, looking across the clearing, and my heart stood still.

Kula stepped from the large tent at the far end of the cluster. "What . . ."

If she was surprised, Kula didn't show it. She walked up to me, facing me straight on, the slightest smile on her lips. She was wearing men's clothing, borrowed from someone bigger. She went to Tom and bent over him, adjusting his blanket, brushing the hair from his forehead with a tender hand. I was so stunned to see her there that I felt no jealousy at all.

"Kula! Girl!" Nat's voice broke through my shock. "You're going with us."

When Kula glanced up at Nat, I knew. I saw the exchange as that between father and daughter and I remembered what she'd told me about needing to see her pa.

I stated the obvious. "Your pa."

Kula straightened and shrugged.

I turned to Nat Baker. He was watching me with those eyes like the sea, piercing my soul. I had the same uncanny feeling as I had the first time we met, when he robbed the coach. He looked at me with a glint of recognition; he shook his head, and his soft smile spoke of mingled joy and sadness. I asked, staring straight into those blue eyes, "Have we met somewhere before? I mean, other than the stagecoach. Do you know me from someplace else?"

He whispered, "I knew your ma."

I looked back at Kula, feeling dizzy. Nat knew Mama. Even though I'd heard my uncle and remembered the story, I was not ready to accept what Nat Baker seemed to be telling me. "What?"

"Your pa and uncle had it all wrong," said Kula. "They kept asking, searching, everyone around these parts knew. It was a joke. The Pinkertons, they aren't exactly—what's that word?" She turned to Nat.

"Subtle," he said.

"That's it. Looking for a boy." Kula narrowed her eyes. "I hate them. Those stupid detectives with their assumptions and their gall. Them and your pa. Your pa took her away from me. I never had her, like you did. Never. Never knew her, never had her with me all those times when I needed a mother. And I look like what I am. Look at me! Poor, lucky, lucky me. Little native girl. And you, with all your fine stuff, pining away, whining about how terrible it is to be engaged to a rich man. To have everything you want on a platter! Hah! I couldn't feel sorry. I wasn't about to tell you anything." She was on a tear, pacing back and forth.

"Kula," said Nat in a low voice. "No need to be unkind."

"Well?" Kula spat at him.

"I've given you the best I could, girl." He regarded her narrowly, as a father would.

She stopped pacing and frowned, dipping her head, but said nothing more.

I put my hand to my forehead, feeling the denial grow into a splitting ache. "What are you talking about?" I whispered, although I already knew exactly what they meant.

"That half brother of yours?" Kula said slowly, looking at me as if I were stupid. "He ain't a brother."

I looked at Kula, at the dark braid that snaked down her back like Mama's, at her eyes, dark like Mama's, and the full understanding of Kula's words bloomed. That niggling recognition. The next thing I knew I was sitting, inelegantly splayed in the grass, at the feet of the patient mare.

Nat bent down and gripped my arms in his hands, standing me up on my feet, though I leaned back against the mare for support.

"You," I said, and I wasn't sure whether I meant Nat, or Kula, or Mama.

Nat and Kula stood close together, regarding me as if from a great distance.

"You do favor her," Nat said. Kula tilted her head back at this, chin thrust forward.

"She . . ." I started. She'd loved him, this Nat. She'd wanted to come back to him. Back to Kula. I had to tell them.

Nat waved his hand, looking away. "Kula's sorted it all out. From all the things you said, from those Pinkerton fellows and what your uncle made known." He paused, then said, almost wistful, "We know your ma's gone."

I wanted him to stop, right there. I put my hand up, held it up, and all I heard for a long minute was the caw of crows and the scattering of songbirds in the trees. The pines sighed with a small zephyr. "But she loved you." Oh, she so loved you. Her loss made her crazy. She was on her way back here when the sea stole her from me. From them.

Nat stared at me, blue eyes like still, still water.

I went on. "She loved you more than anyone else. You and her." I nodded at Kula.

"What?" Nat's voice was low.

I dropped my head. "More than she loved me, I think." Though even as I said it I knew I was wrong. Because Mama had devoted herself to me and stayed by my side until I was old enough to understand.

"No." Kula shifted, arching her back in a prideful stance. "That's not true. She went back to you."

"Only because she was caught," I said, fast. I ran now, a deer in the woods, a doe running straight. "Let me tell you. There was never a moment when she didn't think about you. About you both. I know because Mama . . ." I hesitated, reflecting. Mama, at her oils. Mama, on the Cliff Walk, staring west, over the water. Mama, always sad about things. Mama, despised by the other people in our class and not caring a thing about it. Mama, not really looking at Papa, even when he looked at her so sadly it broke my heart. Now it all made sense. "My mama—our mama"—and here I looked squarely at Kula—"was never really happy. All that time. All that growing-up time she spent with me. And yes, she did stay in Newport for me. But her mind was here. Now I know why."

"Why?" Kula's voice was sharp, and Nat put his hand on her arm.

"Enough," he said, his voice tender.

"It's all right. I wish she'd been able to get back, I wish it for her. Because her heart was here, with you." I looked at Kula. "And you." I nodded at Nat. "Yes, she's gone. But it must have been an accident. Because she never would have given you up. She was ready to leave me because she thought I could handle life on my own now. She was ready to do whatever it took to get back here to you both."

Kula bit her lip and Nat turned away, fully away, facing the sun that split the trees with golden light.

"It's not the end," I said, insistent now, firm, even though I trembled like the shiver of water in a breeze. "She loved you." And I meant both of them. "If she wasn't dead, she'd be here looking for you. Staying with you." I was sure because I'd been right all along, even when I hadn't seen clearly. What I'd said to Kitty; what I'd known the first time I met Tom Rowland. What Mama knew. Nothing mattered more than love.

Kula rubbed her eyes hard, looking at her foot that dug in the dirt.

Nat said, "Well. Well." He dropped his head, shook it a little.

"So, please now," I begged. "Since you know, he can't harm this. He can't hurt you. It wasn't his fault. He loved her, too, and it wasn't his fault. But could you please, please help my pa?"

297

Chapter FORTY

She had expected reaction, but it did not come ... All that she was about to do seemed to her still perfectly natural and right. Petty scruples, conventional hesitations, the refusal of life's great moments—these are what are wrong, these are what disgrace!

—*Lady Rose's Daughter*, a novel by Mrs. Humphry Ward, 1903

NAT'S MEN WERE USED TO A FAST GETAWAY. AT LEAST that was my thought as I saw how quickly they were geared up and ready to go. I sat in the saddle they had fitted for me, wearing the trousers I'd borrowed, and leaned my head against the mare's neck, resting, wanting solace. I looked over at Tom. Gus was wrapping his chest in a tight bandage.

A minute later Kula trotted up bareback on a small pinto.

Nat said, "Let's go."

I turned and looked back at Tom, who raised his hand in a weary farewell.

I led Kula, Nat, and a group of Nat's men back through the woods toward Papa. The sun sank through the clouds, and low ribbons of light played in the pines. We rode in silence; I was aware of Nat's blue eyes on me and of Kula's dark eyes on him. We'd ridden two miles when Nat pulled up right alongside me.

His voice was soft. "I guess this came as something of a shock."

"Yes." I paused. "Well, no. I mean, Kula, yes." I thought about Mama. "I guess all my life I knew she was sad. Missing something. A piece of her was missing." I saw again in my mind's eye: Mama, her hair flying, eyes staring at, but not seeing, a painting that exploded with pain. All those times she went walking alone. Those times she'd looked at me as if she wanted to cry. She'd been trying to get back here, even if only in her dreams.

"It was an accident, my meeting her," Nat said. "I was part of a gang, just a party to it. Back then, we robbed trains. Easy targets. We were in eastern Montana then. When we first took her and the others, it was for hostages. One of the other guys wanted us to have what he called insurance. I was pretty young. So was your ma. We spent time together. I tried to protect her. I couldn't help it, I fell in love, and she fell in love with me. Then I couldn't let her go." He laughed in an embarrassed way. "She was the love of my life. But she was torn. I know she thought about you, all the time." He was quiet. "Thank God she left me Kula."

I kicked the mare to pick up the pace. In another mile I saw the wreckage two hundred yards below the road, at the bottom of the slope, and made to push the mare again. My papa was down there. He was all I had left. I had to help him. My hands moved up on the mare's neck to urge her forward.

"Hold up," said Nat, and he reached over and grabbed my arm. I followed his gaze up and across the meadow, to its far side. The grizzly was back, and it found the dead gelding. I closed my eyes. Then the fear in me rose up: my father.

"We're going to have to wait until he's had his fill," murmured Nat. "Back off, boys."

We pulled back into the shadows of the woods, so that we could just make out the bear in the distance.

"Why don't you shoot him?" I began to feel frantic. "My father's down there. What if he goes after him? For pity's sake, shoot the bear!"

Nat looked at me. "No."

"But, why? Just shoot the bear!" Panic filled me now, bile in my throat.

"Because it's a bad shot, too far to be sure. Because we'd spook him and he'd charge us, and then we'd have a bigger problem. Because he ain't eatin' your pa. Because once we're done here, he can have the horse. Because this is his place."

"His . . . ?" I stared at Nat. I tried to speak but couldn't find the words. I sat back, helpless. The bear's place. I thought about what Tom had said. The bears were here first. But my father lay down there waiting . . .

The sun was a thin line in the west, while the men sat on horseback around me, letting their horses graze. I felt like the bear was eating me, devouring my insides. I edged the mare around in a circle, moving, constantly moving. It was only minutes but they ticked by like hours.

Kula reclined on the pinto like she was on a chaise. "So, you want to save your pa?" She nodded at the wreckage.

"Of course!" I felt hot and wanted to scream. How could Kula not understand that—she, who wanted her mother, our mother, back. The bear had not moved off the carcass, but the carcass was only a short distance from my father.

Kula looked at me with those level, dark eyes. "I thought you wanted to be rid of him, ruling your life."

I looked past Kula, at the bear that was wrenching away pieces of raw flesh. She was right: I had wanted him to quit ruling my life.

I still wanted that. But not like this. I loved him. I kicked the mare again, making her move in a tight circle around Kula. The pinto lifted his head and snorted.

"It doesn't matter what Papa's done. Would it matter to you? He's my flesh and blood. He's all I have." My mouth felt dry, my legs tired from gripping the mare in tight fear. My back ached.

"Hold up." One of the men pointed.

The bear had caught our scent, perhaps; it lifted itself off the ground, nose in the air. For a minute it didn't move. Then it dropped to all fours and moved away from the carcass, nosing down toward the overturned wagon, down toward where Papa lay helpless underneath.

I couldn't stop myself from crying out.

There was a rifle in a holster behind my left leg. Without thinking, I reached across with my right hand and yanked the rifle from the holster. I urged the mare forward into the meadow so I could see the bear more clearly. I propped the rifle against my shoulder and squinted, taking aim at the bear, sighting over the mare's neck, my finger on the trigger, hearing George Graybull's instructions in my ear.

But before I could pull the trigger, in my narrowed vision I saw Kula, who had swept down from the pinto and run into the sun, into the meadow, arms raised up, Kula between me with a rifle and a grizzly who could be across that meadow and on top of her in seconds flat.

Kula was an offering, a sacrifice, a prayer. Time slowed to a single heartbeat.

I saw my mother in my sister, a girl with black hair and eyes like deep pools reflecting moonlight. Saw her in the rolling hills behind the girl, the hills that rimmed the horizon. In the lodgepole pines, in the sea of grass, in the small white asphodel that dotted the green.

I saw Mama in the bear, whose head snapped up at the sight of the girl with arms raised high, the girl who stood in a narrow pane of sunlight at the edge of the meadow, her fearless back to the bear.

Mama rested in the great brown eyes of a dying deer. She lay in the nascent life arrayed at the edge of a hot spring.

She blew in a breath that kissed my cheek, a breath so gentle it was easy to mistake for the wind that settles the day's end.

I sat on the mare, marking the soft working of her jaw as she pulled at the fresh grass, tears rolling down my cheeks unchecked. Mama was everywhere. *You've found me. You were right: I was here all the time.*

Nat Baker hissed, and I lowered the rifle, as if Mama's hand were on the barrel, pushing it away. *No, Maggie. Let it be. He'll be all right; the bear won't bother him.* We sat poised until the imperceptible moment when it was over.

The grizzly dropped its head and moved back to the horse's carcass to feed again, away from Papa, and Kula lowered her arms. I felt hot tears on my cheeks as Nat gently took the rifle from my hands. Kula walked back to the pinto and pulled herself up. She looked at me with something like pity; I looked at her with respect. I loved her, in that moment.

It was another quarter hour before the bear stretched, then rolled on its back and left its scent, and wandered off into the woods away from us. The men waited, listening and watching, until Nat let out a breath. "Okay."

I kicked the mare, trotted her down the slope to the wagon, jumping off the horse before she even stopped moving, grabbing the reins and tossing them over a branch as I ran to the wagon and Papa, the men and Kula behind me.

"Papa?" I reached my hand to touch his cheek, feel for breath.

He was alive but unconscious. The men worked as a team, cinching ropes around the wagon, cutting away as much of the wood as possible before they heaved the wagon's bulk up and away from him.

"Whew," whistled Nat, peering over the cliff edge. "Lucky guy. Nice work, tying it off like that, so it didn't go over the edge and take him with it." I turned my back to the cliff edge, shaking.

"His leg's broke bad," one of the men said. I could see the splintered bone in Papa's shin sticking through the torn flesh. I suppressed a gag, and Nat wrapped a cloth gingerly around the wound. Papa's arm bandage was holding, the cameo still fastened tight.

Nat touched the cameo. "Nice dressing," he said. I caught Kula's sharp look, her raised eyebrows, before she turned away. Kula and one of the men pulled apart lumber and canvas from the wagon to fashion a litter. I watched as Kula wove rope, her deft fingers flying.

"A travois," Nat explained. "We'll be able to lay him out flat this way." Kula lashed the travois to Nat's mare.

One of the men took Bill's body across his saddle. "Not going to leave this fellow to old Griz," said the man, and he spat on the ground.

I followed the travois carrying Papa, watching his face, so white, deathly white. It felt like it took forever to get back to the camp. When we arrived at last, Gus came over and lifted the blanket covering Papa's leg.

"I cain't do nuthin' with this," he said. "Got to get him to Mammoth. They got a army surgeon there."

I went to Tom. He was sitting up. Gus had done his arm in a sling that looked professional.

"Yeah, he'll be okay," Gus said from behind me. "A little coffee, some rest. Gave him something for the pain, that's what's worked good."

Tom smiled, a woozy off-smile. "I guess I got a nasty bump on the head. Gus here says I have a broken rib, too. That and the arm. I'm okay. Just tired. Go look after your dad."

Nat was working on the travois, and packing more gear. One of his men was speaking to him in a low but urgent voice.

". . . go to Mammoth and get arrested? Didn't sign up for this. Don't want no part of it."

"You don't have to come," said Nat. "I'll take my chances." He raised his voice so that everyone in the camp could hear. "I just need two to come with me. We need to get this man to Mammoth if he's going to live. We don't have to get caught doing it, but I can't go alone with the girl."

The men shuffled and muttered. Gus stepped forward. "I'll go," he said. "Me, too," said a younger man. Kula stepped forward, saying nothing. Nat gazed at her, then gave a slight nod.

"Saddle up, then," said Nat. "We got a four-hour ride cross-country, and it'll be dusk in one and a half."

Kula pulled herself up onto the pinto and I held the mare's head. Tom stood unsteady, looking between us.

"I think I need to hitch a ride," he said. He put his good hand on my arm, leaning against me.

I felt my face turn scarlet, and I grew bold. "You can ride with me." His hand on my arm felt warm, and I looked up and met his eyes, those gray eyes that I wanted to look into forever.

Kula turned the pinto's head and walked off. Gus and I helped Tom onto the mare, then I settled in front of Tom. He slipped his good arm around my waist and I felt his chest inches from my back, his fingers on my waist. We rode single file through the woods.

"I'm sorry," I whispered.

"What for?" he asked.

"For being, I don't know, not who I really am." I didn't know how to say what I meant. My tongue tied into knots. I almost smiled; Tom still made me feel foolish. I looked at Kula, riding ahead. "I'm not a snob. Maybe I was once. But I'm not now. At least, I don't want to be."

"Who do you want to be, then, Maggie Bennet?"

Who did I want to be? "I'm my mother's daughter," I said. "My sister's friend."

We rode in silence a while.

"You sure surprised me," he said. "I didn't know you had it in you."

"Didn't have what?"

"What it took to get your father help."

"I didn't know either," I said. "I couldn't have done it without you there."

Standing next to me on the edge of a cliff, I thought. Not rescuing me. I wasn't afraid, because Tom was there. I put my left hand on his arm that was looped around my waist, and squeezed it. He leaned his cheek against my head and I felt his breath in my hair. I heard him whisper my name and thought I'd never heard anything so sweet.

In the waning light I caught a glimpse of Papa. He was unconscious and his face was still, but he was breathing.

It grew darker still, and I tried to follow by shadowing Kula, the white of the pinto's rump showing even as the night fell. The moon rose—luckily, a full moon—and the landscape around us appeared foreign, huge, and ghostly. We seemed to ride forever, sticking to level ground as much as possible, but at times we had to stop and lift the travois across streams or over rocky terrain. I dismounted to help, my feet soaking in the cold water of the streams, bruising on the rocks as I stumbled in the moonlit dark. I was grateful for Tom, steadying me when I climbed back on the mare. Each time I sat back he circled his arm once more around my waist, gentle and firm. Each time he touched me I knew that, though I had much to discover, right now I had found what I'd been looking for.

"Almost there," said Nat.

We rode through a gap in the hills and I saw the lights of Mammoth below us in the darkness. Steam curled up above the hot springs into the cool night air. I wanted to urge the mare faster, but I held back and followed Nat down through the trees. As we approached the first set of buildings, Nat slowed.

"Gus, you and Johnny stay here," said Nat. He mounted the horse pulling the travois and took Bill's body from Gus.

I looked at Gus in the moonlight. "Thank you."

"Good luck, miss," Gus said, one finger to his hat brim.

Nat, Kula still by his side, led us past two frame houses and then stopped just outside the circle of light from the windows of a large building I knew to be the infirmary. "The surgeon's in this one," I said.

Tom and I slid off the mare's back, and Nat joined us. We lowered Bill's body to the ground. I bent over Papa. His breath was ragged, but he was breathing. Nat unfastened his horse from the travois and rested the litter on the ground. Tom knelt beside Papa.

The cameo caught the light, shining. I bent, and pulled the pin from the dressing on Papa's arm. I stood, and handed the cameo up to Kula. Mama would have wanted me to. Because it was all of Mama that I had left. Because I wanted Kula to know that I was her friend. I could feel Kula's eyes on me, sharp, as she took it, looked at it. From the tree behind the building I heard an owl, its hooting mournful in the still air. Then came the sound of men's voices, and I turned to go.

"I don't need it," Kula said, her voice crisp. "I have what I need." She leaned over to hand it back to me, but I stepped away, and she sat back, tightening her hand around the cameo.

I tried to see her expression in the darkness, but her face was shadowed. "I know you have a place," I said, "but if you ever, you know, want . . ." I let my voice fade. "I want you to have it. She would've wanted you to have it."

The pinto shifted his weight, but Kula didn't move. "Thanks," she said, not unkindly.

I looked at Nat. "You were the love of her life." I heard the quick intake of his breath. I turned again toward the building. I felt light, unburdened.

Nat swung into the saddle and urged his horse around to block my path. He leaned over me from the saddle, reaching down and taking my hand in his own. "Take care of your pa," he said.

I could just make out his eyes in the moonlight, and knew that shade of blue even in the dark. Then he and Kula turned and disappeared into the shadows.

"I'll see you," I called after them.

I could feel Tom's eyes on me, but I walked past him, then began to run, calling for help.

Chapter

FORTY-ONE

*. . . the impressions made upon my mind . . . one evening as the
sun was gently gliding behind the western mountain and casting
its gigantic shadows across the vale were such as time can never
efface from my memory . . . I almost wished I could spend the
remainder of my days in a place like this where happiness and
contentment seemed to reign in wild romantic splendor.*

—*Journal of a Trapper*, Osborne Russell, 1835

PAPA MADE A SLOW RECOVERY. HIS LEG WAS BROKEN IN
several places, and there was the danger of infection. It's a wonder
he'd survived at all. The surgeon thought at first that he would
have to amputate the leg at the knee, but he grew more optimistic,
due, he said, to my vigilance in changing the dressing. For the first
few days I barely slept, only dozing in the chair next to Papa's bed,
where I remained, day and night.

Tom's arm and rib were broken, and he had a slight concussion,
but I heard from the surgeon that he was improving quickly.

Graybull had not returned from his hunting trip, to my relief. I
had to think about how I would deliver the news that I would not
become his wife, and how to handle the outcome. I sighed as this
reality settled on me. I worried that Papa would lose his job here at
the Park, since Graybull was so connected. My grandfather would
be furious. We'd be penniless, Papa and I. But as I watched Papa's
face while he slept, I knew we'd also be all right.

The same young lieutenant who had questioned me one month earlier at the Old Faithful Inn after our stagecoach robbery came to question me about the accident.

"I'm sorry. I don't understand. How exactly did you make it all the way back here with an unconscious man and an injured friend on a single horse?" He looked up from his pad, pencil poised to take notes. "Not to mention the deceased," he added, meaning Bill.

I looked him straight in the eye and gave him a broad smile. "It must have been the excitement of the moment," I said. "I guess I had a superhuman strength, from being so worried."

His eyebrows lifted, but he wrote on his pad, tipped his hat, and excused himself.

Later that same day, Uncle John came by, with the news that the park superintendent had taken care of all of our expenses—and provided Papa with permanent employment, if he would accept. Papa seemed pleased, and I, well, I thought that was the best news I'd heard in a while.

Five days after the accident, there was still no sign of Graybull, but Papa was ever improving. Mrs. Gale arrived—her own arm in a sling—and, to my relief, took charge of the hospital room. She bustled me off to rest on a proper bed, and slipped a letter from Kitty into my hands as I left the room.

Dearest Mags,
Engaged! And to George Graybull. Quite a catch! He's quite rich, I'm told. I'm so thrilled for you! Now you can take your place again in society and we can be friends.
We can, can't we? Even though—and you will be happy

for me now, Maggie— Edward has become my constant
escort. He told me that your father and grandfather
closed all doors between you and him. That's why I
feel no guilt, and know that we are still friends. Why, I
believe Edward and I will announce our engagement by
Christmas! . . .

I stuffed the letter into my pocket.

I walked through the August sunshine from the infirmary to
the cottage, feeling dazed and exhausted. I hadn't had much sleep
these past five days, and relished the idea of a soft bed.

Though I saw Gretchen Mills on the walk, shaded by a parasol,
walking with a gentleman, I didn't realize until I was almost upon
them that the man with Gretchen was George Graybull.

It had only been two weeks since he'd left on his trip and I'd left
with Papa on ours, but it seemed a thousand years since I'd seen
him. When he spotted me and turned in my direction, I knew it
was time for me to do what I had to do.

He called to me from a distance. "Margaret! I've just returned
and your kind neighbor has been informing me of this accident
business. Dreadful! Knew it was a bad idea! Had I been along, I
would have taken care of the bear myself!"

I stopped dead in my tracks. He was an outrageous, arrogant
cad. I remembered Tom's words, and they bolstered my spirit: "The
bears were here first," I said, almost too soft for him to hear.

One of Gretchen's girls flew past us. "Milly! Honestly! Behave
like a lady, please! Where is that Susan?" Gretchen turned to me.
"You've been so attentive to your father, I know you haven't been
eating properly. I've had my cook make dinner for you. It's waiting

in the icebox." Before I could muster a "thanks," Gretchen darted off after her daughter, leaving me alone with Graybull.

"Now Margaret," Graybull said. "Heard some things that frankly I find difficult to believe." He drew himself up, squaring his powerful shoulders. "Is it true that a young man joined your party when you reached Mount Washburn?"

I folded my arms and stared at him, silent.

"I've been told that Tom Rowland was with you and your father as you made your way toward Yancey's."

"He joined us, yes. He was collecting rock samples. Papa thought it would be good to have his company."

"I'm shocked, to be honest, that your father would permit such a thing."

"What 'thing' do you think he permitted?" I was irked and tired, and wanted to end this conversation. *Permitted* was a word I vowed to strike from my vocabulary.

"The mere fact that a single young woman was accompanied in the woods by a young man—"

"Oh, for pity's sake! My father was there, too," I interrupted. "And poor Bill, God rest his soul. And, I might remind you, if you'd had your way, I would have been with you on your little hunting excursion, even without my father present!"

"That's quite another matter," he retorted. "We're engaged."

Not for much longer, I thought to myself. I could almost hear Mama laughing.

"Well, Margaret. There will be no more of those shenanigans. Made some plans." Graybull cleared his throat. "My sister will be here in a week. By that time your father should be well enough. You'll come back to the East Coast with us. Leonora will take you in as her ward." He looked at me, reaching for my hands, gripping them both in his. "This is one way I can keep an eye on you." His tongue slid between the gap in his teeth. I had had enough.

I yanked my hands away. The surprise on his face was gratifying. "I'm not going anywhere with your sister, or with you."

He hesitated for a moment. "If you'd rather wait until your father is back on his feet . . ."

"Not now. Not ever." I began to smile and I stood straight and put my hands on my hips, defiant.

Graybull frowned. "Obviously, you're tired. You look . . . disheveled. We shall finish this conversation tomorrow."

I almost laughed in his face. "No, we shall not. Not tomorrow. Not ever." If Kitty had been there, she would have fainted. If Mama had been there, she would have clapped.

His eyes narrowed. "Arrangements have been made, Margaret. Your father and I have an agreement. Have you forgotten your precarious situation? You are spoken for."

"I speak for myself. My wishes are . . ." I paused. "My wishes are that I'm staying here, and I won't marry you. I don't want to see you again, in fact. Moreover"—I took a step away from him—"I plan to pursue a career in photography. I plan to be an artist. I don't want to be engaged to anyone just yet. You were right. I am impulsive. And I'm going to do extraordinary things." I enjoyed his expression of shock. In fact, I laughed right out loud at the look on his face.

He looked me up and down. "I've clearly misjudged. Made a grave error. Thought you were of the right class. Can see now I was wrong." He drew himself up. "Tell your father I sever my ties, terminate the engagement."

I thought I was floating, I felt so light. "Tell him yourself. We don't need you." I turned my back on Graybull and marched into the cottage. I went straight to my room and fell onto the bed, into a dreamless sleep, without even removing my muddy shoes.

When I woke, many hours later, I felt the pleasure of knowing that I had dismissed Graybull. And then worry crept back into me: I would have to tell Papa that I'd done away with his careful plans. No more Graybull; no inheritance from Grandpapa; we'd have to make our own way, here in Yellowstone. I sat on the stairs of our cottage staring out the window at the parade ground, chewing my lip, thinking.

I'd handled bigger things than this in the past few weeks. Wealth and society hadn't saved my father—I had.

But I wasn't sure if Papa could take such a shock in his state. And so, for a time, for his health's sake, I put off having the discussion with him.

⁂ ⁂ ⁂

Two weeks passed before Papa was well enough to move about. I was relieved when the surgeon concluded, definitely, that he would not lose his leg.

I decided it was time. I sat by his bedside, took a deep breath, and began. I started with the most important thing. "I know you came to Yellowstone to find someone. And it wasn't Mama you were looking for."

Papa gazed at me, silent.

"Uncle John told me everything. About Mama, and the kidnapping, and the child. Everything." I waited again. "Papa, I found the child."

He tried to lift himself from the bed, his eyes bright, his hand grasping the quilt. "Mags . . ."

"Now, stay put and listen. It's not the news you wanted. I'm sorry, Papa. She didn't have a son. She had a daughter. Nat Baker's daughter, Papa, not yours." I watched him, anxious, as he lay back, sinking into the pillows, his eyes closed, digesting this news. "I'm sorry, Papa."

"Ah." He lay very still, tears dampening his eyelashes. Then he opened his eyes and reached for me, the tears slipping down his cheeks. "But I have you, Mags."

"Yes, Papa, you do."

"And you are so much like her. All I wanted was to have her back, in some form. All this time, I had you." He closed his eyes again. "All this time. So. You have a half sister."

"I do." I didn't need to tell him that Mama loved Nat Baker; I was sure he knew. I hesitated for a moment before continuing, "Papa, there's something else. I sent Graybull away. I ended the engagement." I leaned back in my chair. I hoped he'd understand; I hoped he knew that it was my life and he had to let me live it. I hoped he knew that I needed to live a true life with true love.

He did. His eyes were still closed, and he only nodded, but he also smiled.

❦ ❦ ❦

Not many days later, on a brilliant August afternoon, Papa lay in the hospital bed, still weak, but improving, accepting the soup that I spooned into his mouth.

Mrs. Gale bustled into the room. "My dear, it is too lovely for

you to stay inside. You go out. I have no work to do at the moment."
She shrugged. "No camera."

I felt bad even though I knew she wasn't blaming me. "I'm sorry
I lost it. And all those pictures."

"Ah, but now we have a reason to work harder," said Mrs. Gale,
perching in the chair next to the bed and helping Papa to some
soup. "That is, I was hoping you'd become my assistant until you
must return to school."

I looked at my father. His eyes met mine, and then he reached
for my hand. It was what I wanted more than anything, and my
heart beat so fast I was sure he could hear it.

"Whatever you want, Mags," he said. "It's your life."

"Yes," I said. "It is." I paused. "So, then you aren't angry with
me about Graybull, Papa?"

Papa winced. "That man. That man might have been a mistake
on my part."

"Ah, I do believe I heard a rumor about him. George Graybull
has left the Park," said Mrs. Gale, leaning past me with another
spoonful of soup. "I heard that he was caught poaching within the
park boundaries and was asked to leave."

I could not suppress a smile. Perhaps the bears would have their
justice after all. I stood to leave.

"Maggie, before you go . . . shall I write to Edward?" Papa asked.
"I owe you that much."

"And say what?" I hadn't thought about Edward for weeks.
He—and Kitty—were the furthest thing from my mind.

"That you are free to become his fiancée," Papa said. "He'd make
a fine husband, Mags. Good social standing, moneyed family." He
smiled. "Even if he is a little—"

"Young?" I interrupted. "Papa, I am, too. I want to do things. I'm not finished finding my way just yet."

"But Newport, your debut . . . What about everything I took you from, everything you wanted?"

I looked out the window of the infirmary. I could see the hot springs, the steam rising up into a crystal-blue sky. "I need to sort out what I want, Papa. But I don't think it's Newport anymore."

Papa smiled at me. "Well then, go along, get some fresh air. I'm better than I look."

"Oh, I almost forgot," said Mrs. Gale as I stood in the doorway. "You should go to the stables. Your little mare is quite well, and may need exercise."

"My little mare?"

"She belonged to Bill, God rest his soul. The park superintendent has given her to you, since there were no other claims."

I walked over to the stables and stood blinking in the warm sunshine, my mind at rest. Tourists wandered back and forth from the steaming hot springs, pointing at the elk that lay near the springs, basking in their warmth. There was a slight breeze, and the smell of sulphur hit my nose as I inhaled it deeply.

I felt a touch on my shoulder.

"Want to go for a ride?" It was Tom, leading two horses, already saddled. The familiar mare nudged me with her nose, and I leaned my cheek against her head. "Mrs. Gale said to get you out."

She'd set me up. Good for her. Good for me, too.

Tom and I rode through the hills around Mammoth, talking only a little. We didn't need words. From time to time we'd ride together, side by side, and then he'd reach for my hand, and our fingers would touch for a minute before we moved apart. I rode astride, in a split skirt that I'd made myself just the week before, with Gretchen's guidance. My mare had a smooth little trot and a beautiful canter. I decided to call her Miracle.

For the next several days, we rode together every afternoon, until one morning when Tom called early while I was helping Papa in his convalescence.

"My dad and I are going down to the inn. Dad needs to work in the geyser fields. Your father said it was all right if you came with us."

I looked at Papa, surprised. He was hobbling around the room on crutches.

"Yes! Go! I don't want to see you back here until the day after tomorrow. John will be here this afternoon, and the surgeon said perhaps in two days I can leave this place. And a man needs a little privacy now and then." He smiled at me.

I hugged him and kissed his cheek. I packed quickly, still not as neat as Kula or Mina, and met Tom and his father at the cottage door. We drove the wagon in a train of tourist coaches, reaching the inn near sunset.

Before dinner, Tom and I walked out to Old Faithful. I looked at the warm pools of algae that traced the outermost edges of the geyser runoff. I bent, touching the sinter, and looked into the water, teeming with life. Not treacherous, not lurking death, but new life, a birthplace, a beginning.

Mama had lost her heart here, and now I knew she'd lost it in all ways. She lost it to love, and to a magical place that defied description. And though I'd also lost my heart, I'd won my soul.

I framed the patterns of the algae in my mind, creating a picture. Then I looked at Tom, watching me. That shock of hair fell into his eye, and I almost reached up to brush it back.

"How much longer will you be in Yellowstone?" I asked him.

"I've got some time before school starts." His eyes were on me, not on the geyser.

I cleared my throat. "Do you care for her?"

"For who?"

"For Kula."

"She's a friend. She's a good friend."

I felt his eyes on me; I turned my own away to stare at my feet. My heart pounded. "Do you have many, um, friends?"

He started to laugh. "Maggie, what are you trying to say?"

"I want to know. Am I a friend?" I asked. I looked up at him, at that impertinent lock of hair, at his smiling eyes. "A good friend? Like Kula?"

"More than that, I hope. More than good," he said. He reached out to me and drew me to him. I looked up into his eyes, and he kissed me then, and it was like no kiss I'd ever felt. Deep and pure and filled with longing, as he pressed me to his chest.

My heart danced, like the sun on the Firehole River that ran beside us.

"Are you going back?" His voice was soft, husky.

"Where?" I asked, surprised.

"Home."

I looked at the hills framing the geyser basin. I looked at the inn, and the white sinter mound, and the steam that pulsed from the earth. I looked at Tom. "I am home."

Tom smiled. Impulsively, I took his hand, weaving his long

fingers through mine, and then it was my turn. I brushed that lock of hair up off his forehead with my fingertips, pulled up onto my toes, and kissed him, unhesitating.

Old Faithful thundered before us. I felt the tremor under my feet, and a spray of warm water dappled my face. Steam swirled in the air around us; the wind whipped my hair into a banner. I pulled away slightly from Tom so that I could watch the geyser.

I leaned my head against his shoulder as I sniffed the air, and I closed my eyes, and I could not contain the smile that bubbled up from inside.

AUTHOR'S NOTE

"My narrative is finished. In the course of events the time is not far distant when the wonders of the Yellowstone will be made accessible to all lovers of sublimity, grandeur, and novelty in natural scenery, and its majestic waters become the abode of civilization and refinement; and when that arrives, I hope . . . to enjoy . . . their power to delight, elevate, and overwhelm the mind with wondrous and majestic beauty."

—*Thirty-Seven Days of Peril: A Narrative of the Early Days of Yellowstone National Park*, Truman C. Everts, 1871

Faithful grew out of my love of and familiarity with the Greater Yellowstone. My husband and I have had property in the mountains of Montana north of Yellowstone National Park since we met thirty years ago. We fell in love with each other and with Montana, much as Maggie falls in love with Tom, and with Yellowstone, after she meets him in the Park at the turn of the twentieth century.

My research was conducted during many trips to the Park, and I was fortunate that the new Park Heritage and Research Center, located in Gardiner, Montana, opened while I was writing *Faithful*. I chose to set Maggie's story in 1904 because the world was changing so rapidly at that time (automobiles and airplanes, moving pictures and women's suffrage), and because the Old Faithful Inn, designed by Robert Reamer, who designed many of the most memorable of Yellowstone's buildings, opened in early June of that year.

My husband and I lived in Rhode Island for ten years, and I'm familiar with Newport: the mansions, the lifestyle of the Gilded Age, and the Cliff Walk. The story of Maggie's mother's kidnapping is based on a true story told to me by a friend whose great-grandmother was kidnapped off a train (and later released unharmed) by a gang at the turn of the century.

I can empathize with Maggie's desperate sense of loss over her mother and her desire to return to the life she had when her mother was alive. Maggie's rebellion against the powerlessness she feels as a woman of her class and time echoes my own rebellious streak.

My master's degree in geology allows me to write with a naturalist's perspective, but there is something truly magical about Yellowstone. Nowhere else on earth is there such a collection of spectacular thermal features. Most of North America's largest mammals, from grizzly bears to bison, roam wild in the Park. Yet what is gorgeous in Yellowstone is also frightening, from boiling hot springs lying hidden underneath tissue-thin crusts of silica, to the bears and bison that can pose a very real threat. I am drawn to the fragile balance of life and death in Yellowstone. I hope that Maggie's story in *Faithful* reminds readers of that fragile balance and of the important place that love occupies in our lives.

ACKNOWLEDGMENTS

Faithful was born as a vague idea while I was on a long hike with my husband, Jeff, whose probing questions and clear insights shaped the novel. Jeff is also the family cook, and his delicious meals sustained me though many a long working evening. And Kevin, my talented son, suggested the character of George Graybull, and thought I needed (rightly) to enhance Maggie's romance with Tom Rowland. Thank you both.

My mother and father, Barbara and Dudley Stroup, did not live to see *Faithful* come to fruition, but they are ever present in my words and thoughts, especially my mother, who gave me the gift of writing.

My early readers were my critique partners, Kathy Whitehead and Shirley Hoskins. Their suggestions over many drafts including the last were critical to the novel's growth. Thanks for being there, ladies.

Rachel Haymon and Kari Baumbach gave me careful and

enthusiastic readings, and their ability to uncover the smallest of errors is humbly acknowledged.

I have tried to present Newport and Yellowstone in 1904 with the greatest degree of accuracy possible; any errors are entirely my own. The Yellowstone National Park Heritage and Research Center in Gardiner, Montana, is a treasure, and the museum's curators, including Colleen Curry, were generous with time and energy, allowing me to view archival materials from 1904, such as the Haynes Guidebooks and the daily logs of the Park's Superintendent. Additional Park resources include Carl Schreier's field guides to the thermal features. Books by Lee Whittlesey, longtime Park historian, and especially Aubrey Haines, author of the two-volume *The Yellowstone Story*, served as the basis for much historical research.

Additional research sources were the Depot Museum in Livingston, Montana, and the Montana Historical Society in Helena. Kathleen Kaul gave me a tour of the Murray Hotel in Livingston, pointing out the original features of this 1904 structure, which gave me an even greater "you are there" appreciation for the period.

Jennifer Lancaster helped me with music selections. Sheila Ruble (also my source for things equestrian) guided me to the photography of Evelyn Cameron, who became the basis for the character of Mrs. Gale. John Fryer, of Livingston, painstakingly showed me the workings of an original long-focus bellows camera of the period.

I have many, many writing friends in SCBWI, at the Vermont College of Fine Arts, and in the debut classes of 2k9 and 2k10, whose support in countless ways makes it possible for me to do what I love.

Finally, there are two people whose contributions to *Faithful* are without measure. My agent Alyssa Eisner Henkin, who found *Faithful* and me and guided me through many revisions, and then sent the manuscript to Jennifer Bonnell, my guiding star and gifted editor; you clearly love and understand Maggie's story, and have invested your hearts in helping me bring *Faithful* to a new level. Thank you, thank you.